B O N D A G E

A N
A N T H O L O G Y
O F
P A S S I O N A T E
R E S T R A I N T

BONDAGE

AN ANTHOLOGY OF PASSIONATE RESTRAINT

Credits: The Art of Bondage" is an excerpt from *The Loving Dominant* Copyright © John Warren, 1994; "Bound by Love" is an excerpt from *Sensuous Magic* Copyright © Pat Califia, 1993;"Blue Sky Sideways" first appeared in *Blue Sky Sideways* Copyright © Alison Tyler, 1996; "Loony Ward" by Cynthia Freeley originally appeared in *Come Quickly: For Couples on the Go* Copyright © Julian Anthony Guerra, 1996; "Six-Handed Fugue" by Anonymous is an excerpt from *Love's Illusion* Copyright © Masquerade Books, 1989; "Cinderella" is an excerpt from *Cinderella* Copyright © Titian Beresford, 1992; "The Game" first appeared in *Blue Sky Sideways* Copyright © Alison Tyler, 1996; "The Initiation of Caroline" by Paul Little is an excerpt from *Sentenced to Servitude* Copyright © C. J. Scheiner, 1997; "A Woman of Passion" is an excerpt from *Point of View* Copyright © Martine Glowinski, 1996; "Desert Diary" by Alexander Trocchi is an excerpt from *Helen and Desire* Copyright © Masquerade Books, 1991; "Midwestern Holiday" is an excerpt from *Tessa's Holidays* Copyright © Lyn Davenport, 1996; "Alice" is an excerpt from *Man with a Maid* Copyright © Masquerade Books, 1997; "Richard's Correction" by Anonymous is an excerpt from *The English Governess* Copyright © Masquerade Books, 1990; "Kibbles and Bits" is an excerpt from *Carrie's Story* Copyright © Molly Weatherfield, 1995; "The Party" is an excerpt from *Compliance* Copyright © N. Whallen, 1995; "Softly, Slowly" is an excerpt from *Fantasy Impromptu* Copyright © Carole Remy, 1997; "The Movie-House" is an excerpt from *The Catalyst* Copyright © Sara Adamson, 1992; "Helga's Pleasure" is an excerpt from *The Many Pleasures of Ironwood* Copyright © Don Winslow, 1995; "The Parlor" is an excerpt from *The Parlor* Copyright © N.T. Morley, 1995; "Presented in Leather" is an excerpt from *Presented in Leather* Copyright © Claire Willows, 1997; "Kathi's First Time" is an excerpt from *Legacies* Copyright © Grant Antrews, 1997.

Cover Photograph by Peter Carter
Cover Design by Alana Lesiger

First Printing 1998

Manufactured in the United States of America
Published by Masquerade Books, Inc.
801 Second Avenue
New York, N.Y. 10017

BONDAGE
AN ANTHOLOGY OF PASSIONATE RESTRAINT

Non-Fiction

Fiction

The Art of Bondage

John Warren

Bondage—who can look at the bound and helpless submissive and not feel a stirring of excitement and pride? In a very substantial way, this is the scene made real. While not all submissives long for rope, leather, and chain, all long for the spiritual essence of these things: confinement, restriction, being controlled and held.

A man in a French maid's costume kneeling quietly at his mistress's feet can be more tightly restrained than one in a cocoon of rope and leather. Freedom through constraint is the quintessential nature of D&S.

Sadly, however, few things are done more poorly than bondage. Like Olympic-level gymnastics, to do it well is to make it look easy. Bondage is far more than simply grabbing a length of old clothesline, wrapping it around your partner, and tying a granny knot at the end.

Before we go any further, remember that bondage—unlike diamonds—is not forever. You should always have the means to release your submissive quickly and efficiently. No one should ever do any bondage without a set of EMT scissors (also called paramedic scissors). They have extremely sharp, serrated blades that can cut rope or even heavy leather. The bottom blade has a spoon-shaped end so that the scissors can be used next to a struggling person's skin without doing any damage. Of course, the scissors won't cut heavy chain. If you are doing chain bondage, keep a bolt cutter handy.

What Should *Not* Be Used for Bondage

Let's look at the actual tools for bondage. First, what should not be used? If a submissive is going to lie quietly, without any movement, almost any long, flexible material including (ouch!) barbed wire could be used. However, short of posing for a cover shot for *Hogtied Quarterly*, submissives do not lie there quietly. Many enjoy struggling, for the confirmation of constraint it gives them. Others are "stimulated" to movement by the dominant's activities.

Therefore, it is best to assume a certain degree of struggle. This eliminates many of the favorites of the bondage artist. Handcuffs, for example, are notorious for causing abrasions and can even cause nerve damage and broken bones. While this quality may be considered a plus by policemen seeking a docile prisoner, it is definitely not a plus in the scene.

At the very least, if you are going to use them for anything more than an attractive ornament on your belt, buy good-quality handcuffs. These are available to the general public in many states through police-supply stores. Avoid the cheap handcuffs sold in novelty and leather shops. The differences are twofold. First, the machining on the professional handcuffs is much better, and there is less likelihood of burrs or rough edges which can tear the skin.

The second reason is even more important. Professional handcuffs have a lock that prevents them from continuing to tighten after they have been applied. This lock is either missing or ineffective in the cheaper models. Never use a pair of handcuffs without this lock, even for the lightest play.

Regardless of the quality of the handcuffs, they should never be used for suspension or even for holding the hands above the head for a substantial period.

Police have begun to use long plastic strips with self-locking tabs as disposable handcuffs or "plasticuffs." Because they were developed by electronics companies for bundling cables, these are available through stores like Radio Shack. While they should not be used when the submissive may struggle, they are nice props for psychological scenes. Once the tab has been inserted through the lock, the plasticuffs are sealed permanently and must be cut off.

Hose clamps are another bondage item that should not be used in connection with any potential struggle. They are long strips of metal with a screw-locking mechanism designed to tighten over hoses until they are sealed to a nipple. They come in sizes big enough to hold a pair of legs. However, they have several important drawbacks. They are metal and can do damage if they are overtightened or if the submissive struggles. They are slow to take off because the tab must be unscrewed slowly. Because paramedic scissors may not be able to cut them, if you are going to use these, you should have a pair of bolt cutters handy in case something goes wrong.

Articles of clothing, like scarves and pantyhose, figure commonly in bondage fantasy; however, in the real scene, they should be used with care. Both can clump until they are very narrow and can cut deeply into the skin. Hold a silk scarf; it feels soft. However, if you pull it tightly between your hands, it forms sharply defined folds. Imagine those folds cutting into your submissive's wrists, and you can see what I am warning about.

Knots in scarves and pantyhose are also notorious for jamming. Eventually, you are going to untie your submissive. It is definitely anti-erotic to break fingernails while struggling unsuccessfully with a bulky knot. You are the dominant; you are supposed to be in control. Being bettered by a inanimate hunk of silk is not the image you are trying to project. Even more importantly, it interrupts the flow of the scene and destroys the mood for both of you.

Plastic clothesline rope is a definite no-no. Not only can its wire core cut deeply into the submissive's flesh, but it has an uncanny ability to jam almost any knot put in it.

Leather laces are definitely another no-no for immobilization. First, they are so narrow as to be almost certain to cut into the skin and stop circulation. Second, leather shrinks when it gets wet. Even if you're not into water sports and don't plan to dunk your submissive into a bathtub, he or she is going to sweat. Just a bit of sweat is enough to turn a tight—but safe—tie into a tourniquet. Worse, this same contraction will turn a relatively safe knot into a solid mass of dense leather.

Thin cord or line can be used for a decorative binding to produce interesting patterns on the submissive's body or for controlled compression of body parts, like the breasts or penis, but it should never be used for immobilization. For example, these should never be used for securing the wrists to each other or to a solid object. Keep thin cord for decoration or for secondary tying where a lot of strain will not be brought against the binding.

What Can Be Used for Bondage

What to use, then? The best bondage tools are well-made leather restraints. Although they are expensive and may be daunting to the novice, they are actually the safest way to render a submissive helpless. Their width and the nature of the material make it harder—although not impossible—to do something wrong, like cutting off the blood supply.

Of course, leather binders do cut into the dominant's creative flexibility. Wrist cuffs go on wrists. They won't go around waists or upper legs. When using them, at least part of the choreography is already laid out.

Rope is cheaper and inherently more versatile. Sisal or manila rope is rough and stiff. Some submissives like the harsh touch of these materials, and some dominants enjoy manila's ability to hold knots without jamming. Both, however, must be handled carefully because they can cause severe rope burns. Polyethylene rope—the yellow stuff that floats—is stiff and hard to handle as is mountain-climbing rope, which consists of a core of nylon lines inside a jacket of woven nylon.

Before the ghost of my father, a Merchant Marine officer, descends to crack me alongside the head and yell, "You're talking about line, son!" I'll admit that what seafarers call rope is more suitable for fastening the QE2 to a dock than a submissive to a table. However, rope is what most people call it. Sorry, dad.

Perhaps the best all-around material for bondage is plaited cotton rope. Cotton rope used to be used primarily to hold sash weights in windows and for clotheslines. With the passing of sash weights and the use of weatherproof nylon for clothesline, cotton rope largely disappeared. The modern version has a plastic stiffener inside that renders it inappropriate for use in bondage. However, some pure cotton rope is still available, and those who have been able to obtain it swear by the material and guard their supply with care. A number of these lucky individuals report buying theirs at a magicians' supply store.

If you are lucky enough to find some without the plastic stiffener, wash it first to get rid of the starch that manufacturers use to make it look pretty in the store. Follow the directions in "Scrubbing Up" in the appendixes for washing unless you want to spend the next few hours untangling a Gordian knot.

The best generally available material, in my opinion, is nylon rope. It is smooth and flexible and takes knots well without jamming. I prefer 5/16- and 3/8-inch rope for immobilization bindings, while 1/4-inch and the so-called "parachute cord" are best for decorative bindings. Ropes of 1/2-inch diameter or larger are relatively difficult to work with, but can be worked into the scene as psychological props.

Nylon rope usually comes in two surfaces: three-strand-twisted and plaited. Plaited rope slides more evenly over skin, while the three-strand can leave "interesting" patterns when it is removed and lends itself to splices. Three-strand-twisted should be cut by wrapping it with electrician's tape and cutting through the tape. This also provides a nice temporary whipping.

The ends of both kinds should be sealed with a flame so that they will not unravel. When you are melting the ends, keep away from the smoke: it is not healthy to breathe it. Work outdoors or in a well-ventilated room. The melted ends are also very hot. Use a stick or pencil end to tamp them down. Don't even consider using your finger. If you are cutting a lot of nylon rope, you might consider getting an attachment that goes on a soldering gun and turns it into an electrically heated knife.

For a really kinky look, dye the rope black or red. Cotton rope dyes easily with any commercial dye. However, nylon rope requires something stronger. I use a dye manufactured in Germany called Deka L. It is available in 1/3-ounce packages from Earthguild. A 10-gram package is enough to easily dye 50 feet or so of 5/16-inch nylon rope.

Another interesting bondage medium is mountain-climbing webbing. Available in a number of colors, this nylon webbing is fairly thick and comes in widths from one to three inches. Because it is so broad, there is less chance of cutting off circulation, but it can be tied as easily as rope and does not jam. You can cut and seal it in the same way as nylon rope.

The most common mistakes beginners make with rope are first, to buy too little of it and, second, to cut it into lengths that are too short. The shortest useful length is generally 5 to 6 feet. Anything shorter tempts the dominant to tie the submissive incompletely and too tightly.

You should have several lengths available. My kit usually contains five 5-foot lengths, five 10-foot lengths, and a 20-footer. If I am planning a webbing (see further along in this chapter), I bring two 50-foot lengths. Of course, specific plans may call for a different mix, but this combination is good for, say, a visit to a scene club like Hellfire or to a private party.

It is a good idea to code your ropes according to their lengths so you can quickly and easily select the proper one for the job. I use plastic tapes on each end of the rope. As a mnemonic aid, they are coded by the spectrum. Blue (blue has the shortest wavelength of the visible colors) is for the 6-foot length, yellow is for the 10, green is for the 20, and red for the 50.

Colored tapes are also useful for establishing ownership at the ends of group scenes. All of my ropes have a black piece of tape at one end in addition to the color code.

Of course, rope isn't the only material to use for bondage. Fiberglass-reinforced packing tape is impossible to break. I like to run a few turns of gauze bandage over the area before putting the tape in place so that the adhesive does not bond to the submissive's skin. Although it isn't necessary, if you are going to use the tape against the submissive's skin, experiment by putting a small piece on his or her skin in an earlier session and checking later for any redness or other signs of an allergic reaction. In later scenes, keep checking because a single exposure may not be enough to trigger a reaction. Also, pulling out fine hairs as the tape is being removed may not be what your submissive would call positive pain.

I've seen photographs of submissives bound in 12- or 14-gauge heavy-duty electrical extension cords. It looked attractive, and the thick plastic coating would provide more than adequate protection against cutting into the skin.

Velcro provides impressive opportunities for creative bondage. One couple I know has glued strips of hook-and-loop Velcro together to make a versatile tool. To "tie" it, all she does is gives the strip a half-turn and press it against the opposite side. I have seen Velcro replacement wristwatch bands that look as though they would be quite effective as cuffs if they were attached to wide pads so that they wouldn't cut into the skin.

Hook Velcro will also stick to nylon rope, although the bonding is not as strong as against the proper loop material. Velcro does have the tremendous advantage in that the dominant can free the submissive quickly and easily from most bonds using this material.

Knots: Knot So Mysterious

There is nothing mysterious about knots, and a dominant need not become an apprentice to a pipe-smoking old tar to learn how to join two ropes together or how to fasten a submissive down securely. However, a thorough knowledge of a few knots should be part of your repertoire.

Square or Reef Knot—This is one of the most common knots. It works best with two ends of the same rope or with ropes of the same size and material. It is simply two overhand knots, one in each direction. Millions of ex–Boy Scouts tie it every day, muttering under their breaths, "Right over left; left over right."

Slipped Reef or Safety Knot—This is a modification of the square knot, in which one end has been doubled back like a half-bow under the other rope. In an emergency, the dominant can give a good yank on the doubled-back end, and the knot will come apart.

Two Half-hitches—Because this knot can tighten, you should never use it directly on a submissive's body. However, it is an effective knot to attach a rope to a ring or other inanimate object. Run the rope completely around the object and then back along the rope. Loop it around the rope with the end coming out under itself. Go down the rope a bit and then repeat this.

Bowline—The bowline lets you make a loop in a way that is less likely to slip than two half-hitches. However, especially with nylon rope, you have to be careful to tighten the knot after you tie it. The classic description of a bowline is:"The rabbit (the end of the rope) comes out of the hole (the loop you have made), goes around the tree (the part of the rope above the loop), and then goes back in the hole." It sounds cutesy, but it is an effective memory aid.

Fisherman's Bend—This knot allows you to use rope as a less-effective substitute for bondage cuffs. First, wrap three or four loops of rope loosely around the submissive's wrist or ankle, leaving at least two feet of free end. Wrap the end around the rope, loop it through the loose loops, and then tie it off with a two half hitches. This makes the loops less likely to tighten independently and cut off circulation.

Sheet Bend—This knot is used to connect two ropes of different size or to connect a rope to an eye. Make a loop in the larger rope. Then run the smaller rope through the loop, around both portions of the loop, and then under itself.

That's it. There are many other useful knots, but these are the basics. If you want to learn about bottle knots, Spanish bowlines, or rolling hitches, read any book on knots.

When tying and untying a submissive, you should always be aware of the rope ends. More than once, I have seen enthusiastic novices inadvertently smacking the object of their attentions with the end of the rope while attempting to tie or untie a complex knot. When being pulled through a loop, a rope can move at substantial speed. As the end of the rope approaches the loop, it can easily be slingshotted to one side or the other. Under such conditions, 3/8-inch rope with a fused end can have a substantial impact.

Trying to work too fast can also lead to rope burns. While such burns are less common with the recommended cotton and nylon ropes, they can happen. Work slowly and carefully. When you must drag a rope across the submissive's body, put your hand under the rope so you are aware of the potential for burning and are partially shielding the submissive from it. If your submissive is rope-burned, clean the area with warm water and a mild soap. Then sterilize the affected skin with alcohol or Betadine.

A precise, careful dominant is a lot more impressive and gives far more pleasure than one who works fast but seems to be on the edge of losing control or, worse, actually injures the submissive because of ill-advised speed.

Bondage Positions

Of course, the tying is only part of a gestalt, the whole of which goes together to excite both of you. While a wonderful feeling of helplessness can be created simply by tying a submissive's hands behind his or her back, there are positions that amplify that feeling.

They can be as simple as adding an additional tie at the elbows to bring the arms closer together. This is particularly exciting with a woman because the position forces her breasts into greater prominence. However, there are two dangers with this position. The elbows should never be forced. While some people can bring their elbows together behind them, doing that with others can result in permanent shoulder injury. Also, a person should never be placed so that his or her body is resting on tied wrists for more than a very short time.

Another position that puts the submissive in a very erotic helpless position is with the hands up behind the neck. First, run a length of rope (climbing webbing is even better) behind the neck, bring it around in front of both shoulders and then back across the upper part of the back. With a female submissive, moderate tension on this rope will also make her bring her breasts into greater prominence. Then, with another length of rope, tie the hands together in front, with about a foot of rope between them. Leave another foot of each end of the rope loose. Bring the hands up and over the neck and tie them to the rope across the back and neck. This position leaves the submissive completely helpless, exposes the entire body, back and front, and can be used either standing or lying down.

A very versatile position is to have the submissive sit on the floor with her knees bent and leaning forward slightly. Tie the wrists to the ankles and the elbows to the knees. A spreader bar can be attached between the ankles but, in most cases, only the most flexible submissive will be able to bring the legs together in this position. Because the genitals are in forced exposure in this position, one of my submissives coined the generic phrase "naked-making."

Another position that many submissives find naked-making is to be placed horizontally on the ground or on a bed with their legs vertical and spread widely. I used to have ringbolts in my ceiling beam for just such a situation (among others). A spreader bar attached to a single line also works, but I have found that the feeling of helplessness is greater when each ankle is attached to a separate point. You may want him or her to wear boots (and nothing else) during this, both for erotic contrast and to protect the tendons. If the tendons are protected, the legs can be left up and spread for quite a long time.

The Fold is a very secure position. Tie your submissive's hands behind his or her back. The forearms should be horizontal, and each wrist should be tied to the opposite elbow. This folds the arms behind the back. Next, have him or her sit cross-legged—what in yoga is called the "lotus position," and tie each ankle to the opposite calf. Take a 10-foot rope, fold it in half, loop the middle under the already-bound forearms, and tie it off. This will result in your having two 4-foot-long (or so) lengths of rope tied to the submissive's forearms. Bring one length over the shoulders on either side of the neck. Lean the submissive forward until there is a bit of stretch, but no discomfort; then tie each length of rope to a calf or to the ropes connecting the wrists and the calves. He or she can be left in that position to "meditate upon sins" or tipped backward, an action that exposes the genitals for casual play. Because the arms are bound in the small of the back, there is less pressure on them than in the conventional wrist-wrist tie.

Hog tying is a classic position but should be used with care. It can put a lot of strain on the back and knees. Position the submissive on his or her stomach. Tie the hands behind the back, wrists together, with enough rope so that you have a 3-foot tail on either end after you have finished. Tie the elbows together with a number of coils of rope. Take care not to put pressure on the shoulders doing this. As I wrote before, some people cannot touch their elbows without severe injury; you want the submissive secure, not injured.

Tie the ankles together and fold them up against the thighs. Run the rope tails from the wrists and tie them around the ankle rope. Hog-tied submissives should not be placed on their backs, nor should any portion of the tie go around the throat. This is a popular photographic subject, but is much, much too dangerous for real play.

There is no hard-and-fast rule for how long a person can be left in bondage. Some positions are extremely stressful and should be used only for a few minutes. Others are so comfortable that sleeping in them is possible. Submissives' tolerances also vary. It should go without saying that you should carefully watch anyone in bondage, and he or she should never be left alone.

Aside from asking them how they are, you should check that their extremities do not become cold and that they can wiggle their fingers and toes on command. Blue skin is a good indication that circulation has been cut off, as is a complete loss of sensation.

This does not mean that a bit of circulation restriction can't be part of the bondage scene. Some submissives love the helpless feeling a numb limb gives them and glory in the pins-and-needles effect of returning circulation. However, this sort of scene must be monitored even more closely than conventional bondage.

For submissives who enjoy these feelings, I prefer to let gravity rather than ropes restrict the circulation. Anyone who has his or her hands held above the head can attest to how fast they go numb.

After around half an hour, most people begin to lose sensation in their elevated hands. Releasing them produces the sought-after tingling.

Decorative Bondage

Many women enjoy having their breasts singled out for special bondage attention. Some report that the reduction of the circulation by the bondage increases the sensitivity; others just like the way it looks.

There are several ways to do this.

An approach that is often the choice of bondage photographers is to encase each breast in a coil of rope. A thin rope, like parachute cord (1/4 inch), is easier to use for this than the thicker rope we have been using for immobilizing ties.

Have her lean forward, then begin with an anchoring loop over one shoulder and down under the arm. The rope then passes under the breast, up between the breasts, and down the outside. Each successive coil should go outside the previous one. The rope should be tight enough to that it gets a good grip on the skin but shouldn't be so tight that it will cut off circulation.

Repeat this for the other breast. Finally, tie the ends of each rope behind her neck for a very effective rope bra. As this will reduce blood circulation, it should not be left on for too long. In any case, many women report that the breasts lose the extra sensitivity created by the rope bondage after about ten minutes.

Some breasts are simply too small and firm to offer the rope a good grip. As this can be a very hurtful point for some women, your failure to achieve a solid decorative bondage with rope can have more impact than you realize. You can avoid this by doing a full chest binding.

One way to do this is to wrap several layers of plastic wrap around the chest. When the chest has been wrapped, take a pair of EMT or bandage scissors (do not use anything with a sharp point) and cut holes through which the breasts or just the nipples can protrude.

You can also use coils of rope around the upper chest to provide a similar experience, except that you can't simply cut holes in the coils. While you are wrapping, leave room between strands for the nipples to protrude.

Naturally, since both of these techniques have the potential to interfere with chest expansion—and therefore breathing—you must monitor the submissive very carefully while the bondage is in place and be ready to cut it off if she becomes disoriented or dizzy. Also, when a woman is menstruating or is about to begin her period, her breasts may be extrasensitive, and what would be pleasant at another time becomes very painful.

For the female dominant, men's cocks can provide hours of delightful fun. In the scene, this is often known as cock-and-ball torture or CBT, and bondage is an important part of this specialty.

Since this is a binding rather than an immobilization, you can use parachute cord or other relatively narrow twine. One scenario that parallels the previously described breast binding is to anchor the cord around the base of the genitals and then circle the scrotum with successive coils. The balls are forced farther and farther into the scrotum. The same approach can be used on the cock. However, its more uniform shape provides a surface for more artistic endeavors. At least one mistress preforms macramé with a thick yarn over her submissive's cock and balls until they resemble a teapot in its cozy.

Of course, eventually the cock will lose its erection and escape the bondage, providing an excuse for the mistress to punish her slave for this infraction.

Another approach is, after making the loop around the base of the genitals, to bring the cord around and between the balls, separating them and pulling them upward. This process is repeated until the a series of Xs are in place.

If your submissive has a tight little sack that makes getting a good grip difficult (fear often makes the balls retract), let them rest in a pan of moderately hot water. The reproductive system's temperature-control scheme will lower them right into your waiting hands.

Some leather shops and bondage magazine advertisements have clever little toys for binding, restricting, and clamping cocks and balls. The best of these lace rather than snap, providing a snug fit regardless of the size of the endowment.

As with any bondage that has the potential to interfere with circulation, you should undo or reposition cock-and-ball bondage every ten to fifteen minutes.

Whole-body Bondage and Mummification

A subspecialization of bondage is whole-body bondage. The goal is to extend the experience of binding over much of the body surface.

Japanese bondage is one technique that combines the whole-body experience with an aesthetic exercise. Because it is essentially a binding, you can use almost any smooth, flexible material including twine, parachute cord, or yarn. I tend to prefer my favorite—3/8-inch rope—but will admit that sufficient rope to do a proper Japanese bondage can be rather bulky.

Because this is a lengthy tie, you must have a pair of sharp bandage or EMT scissors handy. In an emergency, this type of bondage cannot be untied quickly and must be cut. Also, because it is usually done with the submissive standing up, you should make sure that at no time does the little rascal lock his or her knees. That makes it easier to stand still, but it also makes it likely that he or she will faint on you.

One easy approach to Japanese bondage requires a minimum of 50 feet of rope or cord. Double up the rope. About a foot from the bend which marks the center, hold the ends together and tie a simple overhand knot (half a square knot). Put one end of the rope over each of the submissive's shoulders. The knot should rest (not press) against the back of the submissive's neck.

Tie another overhand knot just below the rib cage and above the navel. The third knot goes about 8 inches below the clitoris or the cock. The fourth knot goes 3 to 4 inches below that.

Pass both ends of the rope through the submissive's legs and bring them up along the submissive's back and tie another knot about halfway up the back. Pass the rope through the loop made by the first knot (just behind his or her neck). Draw all the rope through this loop but don't pull it tight. It will get tight soon enough.

Pass each end of the rope around one side of the submissive's body. You can "trap" the arms at this time or pass the ends under the arms and secure the arms later. Both ends of the rope go through the loop between the first (behind the neck) and the second (below the rib cage) knot and then each end goes back around the submissive on the same side that it came forward. Thus the rope that came around the submissive's left side would go through the loop and then back around the left side toward the back. Do not tie the rope at this point. The whole point is that the rope is free to slide over itself.

Pull the rope moderately tight. The third knot should move above until it is just forward of the arse. Above the knot in the middle of the back, pass both ends of the rope through the two ropes and then bring the two ends back around again on the same side. This time they go through below the second knot and then go back around the submissive's body. This will bring the third knot on a woman right over her clitoris or on a man just under his cock. The other knot should be pressing on the arse.

By now, you see the pattern: an interlocking series of diamonds progressively tightening the entire pattern of ropes. At this point, you have plenty of rope remaining, and from this basic design, you can extemporize, looping and tying, until the submissive is a lovely piece of macramé.

Because there is not enough constriction to impede blood flow, a submissive can remain in Japanese bondage for an extended period and can, with some designs, actually don street clothes and venture out in public while remaining in this exotic bondage. When the entire pattern is completed, any strain should be distributed evenly across the entire body so the submissive can be lifted off his or her feet by attaching a hoisting rope to the web.

If the submissive's hands are tied to the web, this should be treated as an immobilization tie, and appropriate precautions taken. For example, it is acceptable to web the entire arm to the body web with twine or narrow cord because the pressure will be distributed across several loops. However, if you are doing a wrist tie with a single strand, you should use a wider rope and knot the rope with a fisherman's bend or use cuffs to protect the wrist from damage.

Another whole-body bondage technique is mummification. Again, you should not try this unless you have a pair of sharp bandage or EMT scissors handy in the event the submissive needs to be released quickly. Because there can be a gradual buildup of heat during a mummification, you should regularly monitor the submissive's alertness. Any faintness or disorientation is a danger sign. You must give him or her a cool drink and consider moving on to another activity.

The simplest approach to mummification is to dampen an ordinary sheet slightly and roll the submissive in it. The moist sheet will adhere to itself and to the submissive. The submissive's head should always be outside the roll.

A similar technique is to use plastic wrap. The kind you get from the grocery store is acceptable, but many dominants like to buy industrial shrink wrap in 36- to 40-inch rolls. Simply wrap your submissive like a large leftover. A hair dryer can speed up the shrinking action, but the submissive's own body temperature will activate the process in any case.

This material conducts heat, cold, and impact very well. You can whip or wax right over it, with the well-wrapped submissive getting the full stimulation; however, you may enjoy using your EMT scissors to create openings through which all sorts of nice things can pop and be played with.

Many dominants keep a supply of regular or elastic bandages available for whole-body bondage. The usual procedure is to start with a few turns around the upper body and apply the wrappings in overlapping turns. As each bandage is put in place, it is secured with butterfly clips (usually supplied with elastic bandages) or with adhesive tape. A figure-eight pattern is used over the nipples to leave them exposed, as you don't want to cut elastic bandages, and if regular bandages are cut, they tend to unravel at the most inopportune times.

There is some debate about whether it is better to wrap the arms at the same time as the body, either crossed over the chest in Egyptian style or along the sides, or to bind them separately. Those who prefer the same-time wrapping argue that it is more aesthetic to have a single package. The arms-separate school holds that keeping them separate allows more options in the continuing bondage process.

The most important thing to remember with whole-body bondage is that it usually cannot be undone quickly. You must have some means by which you can cut the submissive free if something untoward happens.

Self-bondage

I'm setting aside the last part of this chapter for submissives, in particular those who are thinking of self-bondage.

First, and foremost, this is dangerous. If you have read the sections on bondage carefully, you will notice that I emphasize the importance of being able to free a submissive on a moment's notice. In self-bondage, this is generally difficult, if not impossible.

The best thing is to find a dominant and have him or her tie you up. OK, I accept that it isn't all that easy, but please consider doing this.

The next best thing is to do only partial immobilization. Many submissives secure only their feet and one hand. The main incentive for this is that the hand is used for masturbation, but it is also available for getting out of bondage in the event of a fire, break-in, or other emergency. Others secure only their hands and, in an emergency, could escape from their homes or apartments.

However, I recognize that, for some people, nothing but complete immobilization will do. In most cases, they use a locking device with a system to withhold the key for a certain interval. Many of these systems are extremely dangerous. One, which has appeared in more than one bondage film, is a burning candle that cuts a cord, dropping the key within reach. Unless you enjoy being helpless in a burning building, I do not recommend this approach.

A less-dangerous approach uses keys suspended from a string which runs through a pulley and down to the minute hand on a CrayLab timer. When the hand approaches the zero position, the cord slips off, and the keys drop from where they have been hoisted.

A common technique is to freeze the keys into a block of ice. The keys are unavailable until the ice melts. The size of the block determines the length of the bondage, and submissives have used gallon milk containers as molds for their "bondage cubes."

It is possible to arrange a weak equivalent of the safe word in self-bondage. Put an extra set of keys into a valued vase on a high table. The logic is that in a real emergency, you won't hesitate to knock over the table, smashing the vase and making the keys available. If you lack a Ming antique, put the spare keys in a regular jar in the middle of the living-room rug—then fill it with vegetable oil. Again, knocking this over isn't something you will do casually, but it will provide you with a set of keys when you need them.

However, remember that you won't be able to get your extra keys with anything like the speed with which an attentive partner can free you. Self-bondage is only a choice if a trustworthy partner is not available and you feel you must be in bondage. It is not something that should be tried casually.

Bound by Love

Pat Califia

The fantasy of being restrained while a passionate and forceful Other overcomes all resistance and wrings pleasure from your helpless body is probably one of the most common erotic dreams—for men as well as for women. Although it's often labeled or scripted as a "rape fantasy," this scenario has little or nothing to do with wanting to be victimized by sexual violence. It makes much more sense to see it as a metaphor for overwhelming desire. If someone wants you enough to overpower and conquer you, it's obvious that you must be quite a hot little pheromone factory, and you probably have nice buns as well. Most of us are still dealing with the vestiges of being trained to feel guilty about sex. But if someone has you trussed up, what can you do? Anything that happens is not your fault. Let the panting, sweating, and grappling begin!

Many people who have no interest in the rest of the S/M repertoire of body-stress techniques are fascinated with bondage. Some of us are drawn so strongly to the sensation of being held in place by ropes as taut as violin strings that we started tying ourselves up when we were children. So it makes sense that most of us start experimenting with S/M by buying a package of clothesline or a pair of handcuffs. Of course, bondage is like any other dominant/submissive activity: If it doesn't appeal to you, no one has a right to pressure you into trying it. You don't have to be into bondage to have a good time or be part of the leather community.

From the outside, it may seem that tying somebody up is inherently less intense and much safer than, say, flagellation, but in fact that is not true. Placing ropes or chains on someone's body alters his or her emotional as well as physical state, and a caring bondage top should be aware of this and deliberately use it to enhance the experience. Carelessly used restraints can cause nerve damage, dislocated joints, or fainting, or interfere with the bottom's breathing. The information in this chapter will help you to avoid many mistakes that sometimes trip up or frighten beginners.

Allowing someone to deprive you of freedom of movement is an enormous gift of trust. To deserve that trust, the top must be ready to accept full responsibility for the bottom's well-being. In fact, this is the key to all ethical acts of sensual domination. It is immoral to accept power without the responsibility which (overtly or covertly) comes with it.

The Psychology of Bondage

The same set of leather bondage cuffs and chains can be used to create many different internal states. I have identified nine different types of bondage scenes. But there are probably many more waiting for you and your partner to discover and define.

First, there is *sensual bondage.* If rope is used, it will be silky, brightly colored. A chain body harness might be chilled before being placed on the bottom's body, or gently heated. The purpose of this type of bondage is to heighten the bottom's awareness of his or her skin, muscles, and body tone. Focusing on these here-and-now physical sensations results in shedding tension and anxiety left over from the outside world. The goal is to create a state of arousal in bottoms and then prolong it without allowing orgasm, so they float in a state of blissful need, craving the top's touch. A scene like this is insidious, subtle, bewitching, and very seductive.

Bondage can also be *physically stressful.* A position can be selected that causes anything from mild discomfort to outright pain. It takes expertise to do this without putting excessive pressure on nerves or joints. Long-term bondage scenes are often designed to challenge the bottom's pain tolerance. These scenes work well with masochists who want their endorphins released when muscles are stretched and aching, but do not enjoy being struck. The goal here is endurance, the bondage is a test, and the top is a watchful and demanding guardian.

Submission and bondage are immediately connected in many people's minds, and many of the devices used in bondage are also powerful signifiers of submissive status—the collar, the leash, the hood, wrist cuffs worn in lieu of bracelets. The goal during a scene of this type is to create a state of surrender and allow the bottom to go under and yield to your authority.

In this type of bondage, the top must assign meaning to any tokens which the bottom is allowed to wear. A collar, for example, should be presented with a bit of a speech. The Mistress might say to her kneeling male slave, "This is a nice, sturdy collar because you're a very big dog indeed. And it's important for dogs to know where they belong. You are my mastiff now, my guard dog and pet. You are to come when I call and take to the floor at my signal. If you ever forget your place, I will take back my collar and put you out, and for all I care you can be picked up by the public dogcatcher and taken to the pound."

Submissives can entertain the Dominant by performing service in restraints. There are few things prettier than a girl whose hands are joined behind her back with two feet of chain, trying to figure out how to pour a glass of wine or pick up your glove.

Sensory deprivation is another common bondage technique. The top exercises power by restricting the bottom's use of one of the five senses: sight, hearing, taste, smell, touch. Blindfolds and hoods, earplugs, gags, and mummification are often used in this type of scene. The goal may be to increase helplessness, thus creating an even deeper state of submission. Or the top may want to surprise the bottom with a variety of painful and pleasurable caresses. Not knowing how, where, or when you will be touched can induce a state of delicious anticipation. Near-total sensory deprivation can also send bottoms on an extended journey into their own silence and the center of their being. In this case, the techniques of sexual magic are used to reach a strange and wonderful place that is beyond sexuality.

One of the drawbacks of sensory deprivation is that a bottom who is hooded, for example, will lose eye contact with the top. So you must become adept at learning to read body language. Bottoms who are gagged obviously can't use safe words. Give them a marble to hold, which they can release if they need to take a break and talk to you out of role.

There is also *utilitarian bondage*, in which bottoms are restrained to make them hold still for another activity, like whipping or piercing. This type of bondage must be strong and escape-proof. Ornamental, fine chains or hooks that can be pulled out of the wall would ruin this sort of scene. However, it is almost impossible to immobilize someone completely, so he or she cannot move any part of the body, and still leave the skin accessible to the top's harsh or teasing touch. So the bottom must be schooled to use the restraints as a reminder to hold still. If the action is going to get rough, the bottom will need the security of stout rope and something to yank on. When a top places a bottom (usually a masochist) in utilitarian bondage, it is a token of mercy, and gratitude should be expressed by the one in harness.

Captivity is a very intense bondage modality which can be especially useful for training rebellious males who have trouble believing or entering fully into a bottom role. As with utilitarian bondage, the container (cage, cell, closet, casket, or kennel) must be well constructed and escape-proof. The first time someone is placed in captivity, expect a tantrum. The same man who walked laughing into a cage will erupt into a fury or panic when he realizes that the bars will not give way. Captivity scenes revolve around a dialectic of fear and security. The top becomes jailer, warden, trainer, kidnapper, or some other custodial type. Oddly enough, childhood issues about one's mother often come up for bottoms in captivity. Perhaps the container becomes a metaphor for the confining—yet nourishing—womb.

At leather events, bondage is often used as *costume*. Why bother to tuck a gray hanky in your back pocket (a gay-male signal for an interest in restraint) when you can simply wear a straitjacket or parade about in leg irons? Bondage tops may wear their handcuffs in a leather case on their belts or fashion an intricate knot to hang from keys or an epaulet. Bondage can also function as costume in a more private context. Bottoms who are taken out to dinner wearing a rope body harness beneath their clothing will be in a dither all evening. Bondage costume highlights the polarization of top and bottom.

It is often necessary to restrain bottoms who find that *resistance, frustration, or anger* come up when they try to play. Effective bondage can be reassuring for bottoms who are afraid that they might hurt themselves or their partner if they get so angry that they lose control. Bottoms who want a top to push them through a state of rage are asking a lot and must understand that many tops will not be willing to take that kind of risk. I have rarely seen bottoms go berserk. The anger is often a cover for another emotion that is more difficult to express. Tight bondage creates a safe space for these vulnerable feelings to emerge. Fear of being abandoned, grief over not receiving enough love, and shame about being sexually needy often spill out. This is when the top becomes a healer who mends broken hearts and comforts the psychically wounded. Not everyone is qualified to do this, and you should not hesitate to get assistance from an S/M-positive therapist if you feel overwhelmed.

Most of these scenes involve playing with much milder forms of anger, such as resistance and frustration. In this case, bondage is a useful training device for people who have trouble giving it up or spoiled brats who think they should be able to grab whatever they want. The scene may turn into a contest of wills, in which case, the top must remind himself or herself to stay within the bottom's stated limits and remain deaf to manipulation. While a little aggravation or irritation on the top's part can lend spice to the scene, if a bottom pushes you to lose your temper, it's time to take a break and recalibrate.

Finally, bondage is a metaphor for *trust*. A scene that embroiders this theme can create a powerful bond between the two players. Although one person may look helpless and the other may seem to be in control, these distinctions disappear rapidly as the bottom demonstrates strength and courage by placing absolute trust in the top. For example, a Master may lace a new girl to his bed and tell her she must remain there, motionless, until he returns and sets her free. The thought of being left alone fills her with panic. As he places the blindfold over her eyes, she almost pronounces her safe word. But then, because of her knowledge of this man's integrity and affection, she bites her tongue. She thinks, *My Master would never do anything that would put me in real danger.* And so she waits patiently, barely breathing, for what seems like hours, until he puts his hand upon her naked breast. After they make love and he has undone the knots, she learns that he walked only to the far end of the room, opened, and then shut the door. He knew it wasn't safe to leave a restrained person alone, so he waited and kept watch on her, to see how she would behave when she thought she was not being observed.

Of course, you don't need to restrict yourself to one of the above types of bondage scenes when you are designing an evening of entertainment for your partner. Good bondage scenes often alternate between modes, and sensations overlap. A toy (a feather, for example) that caused the bottom to purr one moment can easily make him or her struggle to escape in the next. Ropes that were friendly thirty minutes ago become fiendish as the body tires.

But it's always best to begin a scene by clarifying your motives and goals. It's easy to get caught up in technical issues and forget about the psychological mechanisms that really drive an S/M relationship. I encourage you to learn all you can about ropecraft, the history of bondage, knots, and restraining devices. On your way to becoming an expert on Japanese bondage or suspension, just remember: You can know a hundred knots and have a collection of antique fetters that's the envy of the Tower of London, but if there's no rapport between subject and Director, package and Wrapper, the scene will be a flop.

†††

Physical Techniques and Safety

There are four potential dangers when bondage is done improperly: fainting, nerve or tendon damage, dislocated joints, and strangulation. Some of the "simple" devices that beginners are most likely to try actually carry a high risk of causing counter-erotic damage.

For example, when many of us finally get up the courage to buy our first kinky toy, we rush down to the local leather shop or a police-supply store and purchase handcuffs. Novices often don't realize that it's important to buy well-made cuffs that have a locking device that prevents the metal ratchets from continuing to close after they are placed on someone's wrists. Excessive pressure from the thin bands of steel can cause nerve damage or tendonitis. Don't trust cuffs that lock in place with levers. The levers can be moved easily during play. Look for cuffs that have a tiny pin near the wrist chain which can be depressed with the end of the key to set it in place.

Someone who is in a safe pair of handcuffs can still get hurt if her or she is handled too roughly. For example, it's a bad idea to cuff someone's hands behind his or her back and then toss him or her up against a wall. Cops do it on television all the time, but in real life, the tender wrist joint bounces against the circlet of metal and is bruised or pinched.

When you buy handcuffs, try to order an extra set of keys. Before you put this (or any other toy that locks) on yourself or a friend, *make sure you have the key.* There are hundreds of different types of handcuff keys, so don't assume the cop on your beat or your pervy friends will be able to set you free. Your local fire department or a locksmith may be able to get you out if you've lost your own key, but this can be expensive, time-consuming, and embarrassing. If one key breaks off in the handcuff, use a magnet to remove the broken pieces, spray WD-40 into the jammed lock, and then *gently* try to open it again with your spare key.

It's also common for novices to try to tie their mate up with sash cord or imitate that tiresome cliché of soft-core porn and use silk scarves. Although these things look much less menacing than heavy chain, three-quarter –inch rope, or thick leather cuffs, they are actually quite a bit more dangerous. Sash cord is too thin to be wrapped tightly around unpadded wrists or ankles. Silk scarves can cut the skin or pinch nerves. You might as well use wire. Although it's possible to construct safe bondage from thicker, softer rope, this technique is best learned in person from an expert. Novices should never place rope against bare skin.

Your first purchase should be a pair of well-made leather cuffs for the wrists, lined with kid or suede, and another pair, padded with fur or wool, for the ankles. Wrist cuffs should be at least two inches wide. Ankle cuffs should be at least three inches across. You may have to get these cuffs custom-made to fit you. A good pair of bondage cuffs can cost up to $100, but they are indispensable. If you take care of them, they will probably last for years.

The person who is tied up is responsible for alerting the top if their hands or feet start to tingle or feel numb. If this happens, cuffs should be loosened, the bottom should be allowed to change positions to work blood back into the affected limb, and the bondage should be adjusted to prevent recurrence of the problem.

This will prevent most injuries. However, it is sometimes possible for the nerve that runs down the base of the thumb to get pinched before the hand feels like it is going to sleep, so make sure there is a finger's-breadth of slack in wrist cuffs. Never try to suspend someone by the wrists. These delicate joints were not meant to take the body's full weight.

If, despite all your best efforts, the bottom still has some loss of sensation in his or her hands after a scene, it will usually return within a few days. If not, seek medical attention. A bottom who is susceptible to this sort of injury may need to be placed in positions where pressure is not placed against the base of the thumb. A top who has to show this much ingenuity can, of course, expect to be rewarded suitably.

It's also a bad idea to bind hands together so that the bones in the wrist are touching. Wrists should be separated with a short length of chain or rope.

The nerve that runs along the armpit is vulnerable to pressure. Many people find that being tied in a standing position with their arms straight above their head is too fatiguing and causes loss of sensation or motion in the arms. It can also place too much stress on shoulder joints. It's much safer to allow bottoms to keep their upper arms straight out, at shoulder level, with their elbows bent. Standing bondage is still rather demanding, and some people cannot tolerate it for more than a half-hour or so.

Standing bondage increases the possibility of fainting. Someone who is very excited about playing may have forgotten to eat, indulged unwisely in alcohol or other drugs, or may just lock the knees. Being frightened or aroused also interferes with breathing and blood circulation. All of these things can lead to giddiness and loss of consciousness. You may sometimes get a little warning that the bottom is about to go limp—or you may not. Someone who faints in a standing position with arms restrained will suddenly place a lot of weight upon wrists or shoulders, and these joints may be dislocated. It is vital to be able to release the person quickly and lower them safely to the floor.

Panic snaps should be used as the center points for all standing bondage because they can be released even if there is a great deal of weight hanging from them. Double-ended clips, padlocks, and other devices for attaching cuffs to rope or chain are too difficult to undo in a crisis. Panic snaps can be obtained from most good leather shops. Stores that sell climbing gear or cater to livestock breeders will also sometimes have them. See the illustration below so you know what you're looking for.

When bottoms faint, they should be given ample time to recover. Make them lie down and elevate their legs. Do not give them any fluids until they can hold the cup or glass themselves—you don't want to make them choke. Make sure they are warm. When they are fully awake, it might be wise to get some protein and carbohydrates into their system. Tops and bottoms should also run through the activities that preceded the fainting and see whether the bottoms had a phobic reaction to anything that might have made them pass out.

Suspension (having the whole body lifted off the ground) is a logical extension of bondage that intrigues many of us. It may seem like the ultimate form of helplessness or sensory deprivation. It also conjures up visions of flying, swimming, and floating or being a child who is picked up, swung, and carried by a loving and playful adult caretaker.

If all of your information about S/M came from pornography, you would think it was easy as pie to throw a rope over a hook and hoist someone off the ground. In fact, suspension is difficult to perform safely and should not be attempted by novices. The hoisting equipment has to be installed with great care to make sure it will not break. The person who is being suspended needs to be in a specialized body harness, similar to a parachute harness, so that wrists and ankles will not be harmed. Some suspension experts will also use a pair of high boots, nailed to a board, which the subject puts on before being hoisted upside-down.

If you want to experiment with suspension, see a professional who has the appropriate equipment in his or her dungeon. S/M support groups (listed in the resources guide at the end of this book) offer educational workshops. If a workshop on suspension is scheduled, be there or be grounded. If you need reassurance about the quality of someone's setup, an inanimate object of appropriate weight should be lifted to test the equipment before a human body is entrusted to it. Enough people should be present to catch and safely lower the bottom if an accident happens.

Strangulation is the most serious consequence of unsafe bondage. Unfortunately, many people enjoy bondage positions which put pressure on the throat and restrict or limit breathing. For example, they may want to be hog-tied (on their stomach with hands and wrists tied together) and have a rope placed around their throat that is connected to their hands and feet. If someone passes out and blood flow to the brain is cut off, it takes very little time to die.

These games are always dangerous. You can reduce some of the risk by having another person present to spot you and cut you out of bondage if you pass out. Having a partner wrap his or her hand around your throat can be every bit as scary, and it is much, much safer. If you are determined to do this alone, please try to devise bondage that will release the pressure on your throat if you lose consciousness. Of course, this is very difficult to do, and every year a few people are killed accidentally by solitary erotic asphyxiation.

Before a scene, the top should check any gags to make sure there are no loose parts which might work free and block the bottom's throat. It is not safe to gag someone by placing a wad of cloth in their mouth and then taping or tying over it. A knot tied in a bandana can be placed in the mouth. Then the bandana can be tied behind the bottom's head and, if you like, you can use gaffer's tape (nothing stickier, or it may take off too much skin when you remove it!) over that.

Bottoms should not be left alone anyway, but it is especially dangerous to leave bottoms unattended if they are tied facedown on a soft surface. If they should pass out, they will not be able to lift their heads to breathe and could be smothered.

People who are drunk or high sometimes vomit and may choke if they inhale their own vomitus. This is one very good reason to avoid combining drugs or alcohol with S/M play. The small glass of wine that simply relaxes one player may impair another's judgment. It may be egotism, but I prefer to know that the bottom is responding to *me*, not the line they snorted in the bathroom or the pill taken before coming. And I think the bottom has a right to know that I am playing with all my wits about me. I can speak only for myself, but if the day ever arrives that the excitement that I derive from wielding the tools of my trade isn't enough, I will have problems that can't be solved by chemicals.

By now you may be thinking; *This is too hard. It sounds too scary. I can't deal with this!* In 99 percent of all S/M scenes, you won't run into any problems. Please understand that I am not presenting these warnings to discourage you from exploring your fantasies. Like Iggy Pop, you may think that "life should be/like Swedish magazines." But if you want to stop daydreaming and experience these things in the flesh, you have to learn how to do it safely. This is something you want to do again and again, remember? A hurt hand or a fainting spell can ruin an otherwise amazing evening. Knowing which handcuffs to buy or checking a hood before you lace it onto someone's head is part of being a responsible, sexually active adult. It's no different than deciding what method of birth control you're going to use or practicing safe sex. (*Nota bene:* If you still haven't gotten it together to deal with birth control or safer sex, you are far too immature to be doing S/M. Give this book to a more grownup friend, and restrict your sex life to jacking off to X-rated videos.)

Communication Exercises

Here are some ideas to help you and your partner start playing with bondage and learning more about each other.

1. Sit back-to-back with your partner. Each of you should have a pad of paper and something to write with. Set a timer. For two minutes, complete the sentence, "Being tied up makes me feel..." If you've never actually experienced bondage, complete the sentence. "I imagine that being tied up would make me feel..." When time is up, exchange lists. Then face each other and discuss them. This gives you important information about what kind of risks your partner is taking if they let you restrain them. It can also point to the most effective psychological grounds for a bondage scene.

2. Take a spool of ordinary sewing thread. Toss a coin to see which one of you gets tied up first. The one who is going to be restrained should undress and lie down on his or her back with arms and legs spread. Use one strand of sewing thread to tie your partner's thumbs and big toes to the appropriate corners of the bed. Then make love to him or her. The catch is this: If your partner breaks the thread, you stop, and take his or her place on the bed.

3. Buy three Ace bandages. When you get home, flip a coin to see who gets to be the first subject. Sit in a comfortable chair while

your partner uses the Ace bandages to wrap your head. Earplugs can be put in before you do this. Don't cover the nose! Set a timer for two minutes. Sit quietly, without being touched, until it goes off. When both of you have had this experience, share what happened to you (while "nothing" was happening). How did your body feel? Did you have any memories? Did time seem to stretch or compress?

4. Use three or four rolls of plastic wrap to mummify your partner. Start at the head, but don't cover the nose or mouth! He or she should be naked underneath the wrap. Earplugs or nipple clamps can be worn underneath it. Some people enjoy being mummified while they wear an insertable toy (dildo, ass plug, vibrator, ben-wa balls, etc.). You may want to leave your partner's genitals or nipples exposed. When you start wrapping the thighs, have your partner lie down before you finish wrapping the lower legs. People who are really mummified find it hard to lie down once you've wrapped their entire body. And it's not safe for them to try to stand up without support.

Leave the wrapping on for at least five minutes. If the bottom consents, experiment with a little spanking over the wrapping. What is it like to kiss somebody who literally can't lift a finger? Don't leave the plastic wrap on for more than an hour. When you remove it, make sure the room is warm. Give the person fluids to replace the liquid lost from perspiration. Bandage scissors (which have one blunt blade) are the safest tool to use for removing the mummification. You can get them at any pharmacy.

Both of you should experience being wrapped up. Then talk about this exercise. Did you enjoy doing the mummification more than being restrained? What would have made it more exciting?

Did you want more stimulation and interaction, or was it comforting to be swathed in several bands of restraining material? What was the first thing you wanted to do when you were let out?

Below are some erotic vignettes to throw a little more gasoline on the fire of your imagination.

WILLPOWER

"Tonight," he said, "I will test the sincerity of your submission."

They had been eating dinner at home. Gary had barely spoken to her since they sat down. He was wearing his paisley satin dressing gown. She was in a caftan. Lee put down her fork and gave him a startled look. Now she did not know if she could eat another bite. Her handsome husband, a fit forty-eight, with a neatly kept gray beard and luxurious mustache, had suddenly become her master.

Gary returned her look with a level stare until she blushed and dropped her eyes. Then he could admire her without being observed in return. After twenty-eight years of marriage, he knew every inch of this woman's body, but the twists and turns of her mind could still surprise him. "You aren't eating," he observed quietly.

"No," she agreed.

"Then kneel by my chair."

Lee did so without hesitation, lifting the skirt of her caftan so her knees rested on the floor. "Naked," he suggested, and she kept on lifting it until it was over her head and tossed over her chair. "Part your legs," he instructed, and watched her obey. "Now put your hands behind your back. And close your eyes." Gary fished an ice cube from his glass. "Don't move," he cautioned her and let it rest against her navel. She gasped, but did not flinch. He slowly trailed the melting bit of ice up her torso, drew a line from one nipple to the other. Goose bumps showed where it had passed.

"Now open your mouth," Gary whispered. Lee arched her

neck. Her lips parted. But instead of feeding her the ice, he fed her a dollop of whipped cream filched from his dessert. "See what happens when you're good?" he asked.

"Oh, yes," she murmured. "My Master is very good to me."

"Now go into the living room on your hands and knees," he said. "Keep your eyes closed. Go slowly."

It aroused him and touched his heart to see her carefully finding her way into the other room, obediently blind. He went after her and stopped her when she reached the hearth rug in front of the fireplace. He had already arranged the logs, and it took only a few minutes to set them ablaze.

"I am a very lucky Master," he told his compliant wife, still on all fours. The fire made strange, dancing shadows on her soft white skin. "I could display you on any stage in the world, and you would never disappoint me. It takes a very clever girl to understand that her true bondage is to her Master's will. If she wears a chain, it is only to symbolize His will. Now I want you to pretend you are a table, Lee. You cannot get up. You cannot move. You are an inanimate piece of furniture."

Kneeling behind her, Gary parted his dressing gown and entered her. She was eager to receive him and could not help moving back to take the last inch of his cock. For that, he gave her a stinging slap on the back of one thigh. "If you move again," he threatened, "I will stop. I will keep on fucking you, Lee, as long as you hold absolutely still in bondage to my will."

In a state of mixed terror (that he would stop) and delight (at being placed in such a pickle), Lee struggled to obey.

HER FAVORITE TOY

"Just exactly what do you-all think you're doin' in here?" Georgia demanded. Her normally soft Southern drawl sounded more like the angry hiss of a riled-up mountain lion. She had walked into their bedroom and caught Harley red-handed, doing the nasty with his fist and Miss April.

"Honey, I thought you were going to the show!" he protested. "I didn't expect you back so soon. Hey—don't you ever think about knocking?"

"Since when do *I* have to get permission to do anything around here?" she fired back.

"Now, just a minute—"

"No, I will not wait one minute more!" Georgia said, and swept his magazine off the bed with her tiny imperious hand. "Now I know why it's been so hard for me to get any decent lovin' out of you. You been wasting all your juice on make-believe girls in dirty pictures." She reached into her handbag and took out a device made out of leather straps and steel rings.

Before Harley could say, "The South shall rise again!" she had put it on his pecker. Now it looked like it would be a long time before his southern parts got to go anywhere at all.

But when Georgia started buckling cuffs on his hands, Harley decided it was time to put up a fight. It didn't do him much good. Georgia got his earlobe between her thumbnail and index finger and bore down hard. Harley hated that. His mama used to pull that trick on him when she wanted him to come inside. "Now are you gonna behave?" Georgia demanded, and Harley finally squeaked that he didn't have much choice, did he?

So Georgia got him staked out good. The whole thing made Harley feel pretty funny. This was different from the fooling around they had done before. He couldn't tell whether Georgia was really pissed off at him or not. Now she was taking off her dress, wearing nothing but some glossy dark-blue underthings. The fabric had little silver threads in it that made it twinkle. At the sight of Georgia's perky teacup-sized tits filling out the shiny fabric and her plump little sex in the tight, skimpy panties, Harley's hose tried to stretch itself out toward her, and was duly punished by the laws of physics it was trying to break.

Now Georgia was peeling off her panties. She sat on the bed, close enough for him to see her cleavage and not much else, and dragged them across his face. If the truth was told, Harley was a pussy-hound. He was kind of disappointed when Georgia quit saying no when he wanted to fuck her. It meant he didn't get to stick his face between her legs every time they had a date. Now that they were married and could legally do anything they wanted to do, but for some reason Harley didn't find it very exciting to just roll over with his tongue out.

"You like that, don't you?" Georgia whispered, and Harley whimpered.

"Baby, if you need some lovin', I'll be happy to help you out. Just let me get my tool out of hock," he pleaded.

"Oh, no, you don't get to use that tonight. Not yet, anyway. There's a million ways a big, strong boy like you can please a woman without stickin' his dick in her. Come on, Harley, use your imagination. You weren't havin' any trouble with your dirty mind when I walked in here and found your elbow clocking sixty miles an hour."

Harley couldn't help it. He bit down on the panties she was trailing across his cheek. Georgia gave him a cynical smile. "Okay," he confessed, "I like it. What do you want me to say? I like it."

Then she leaned forward and ran her fingertips along the edges of her brassiere. "And you like these, too, don't you, Harley?"

"More than Jesus," he said huskily, trying to get his head off the bed so he could lick her breasts.

"The road to hell is paved with good intentions, Harley. You're going to have to try harder than that," Georgia teased. She unsnapped her bra and let her breasts point right at him. But no amount of straining would budge her or the bed. She stayed just a half-inch out of reach. And she kept on teasing him until Harley was shouting for mercy.

"All right, now," Georgia said, cupping his imprisoned balls. "That's better. I think you've gotten some perspective on the situation. So who does this dick belong to, Harley?"

"You," he said, his teeth gritted. "It belongs to you."

"And what do I get to do with it?"

"Anything you want, Georgia. Anything you want."

"And what do you get to do with it?"

"Nothin'. Not one goddamned thing. I'm gonna get you for this, Georgia."

"Mmm. I can hardly wait." She gave his private parts a hard squeeze. "This is my toy, Harley, my very favorite toy, and I don't want you playin' with it when I'm not around. You're a real clumsy bubba, and you might break it. Then where would we be? And just to make sure you don't forget your lesson—"

Georgia straddled his face. Harley didn't care if he drowned.

Blue Sky Sideways

Alison Tyler

Being your slave, what should I do but tend
Upon the hours and times of your desire?
I have no precious time at all to spend,
Nor services to do til you require.

—William Shakespeare

From my position on the bed, I can see the window, partially opened to let in the late afternoon sun, and the wall, striped with lines of color from the shades. I'm on my stomach, with my wrists securely cuffed and fastened over my head to a hook in the wall. My legs are spread apart, my ankles bound to the bedposts of my Mistress' queen-sized canopy. She's not in the house. She tied me here and told me her plans for the evening. And then she left.

Now that she's gone, I wish she'd blindfolded me. Now that I'm alone, I realize that what I thought was a kindness is really another form of punishment. Deprivation of sight can be comforting. This is hell—able to see only a bit of the window, a bit of the fading light. I can turn my head the other way, though the movement is uncomfortable, but all there is to see on that side is a terrifying reflection of me in a wall-sized mirror. A confrontation I am not at this moment ready or willing to meet. How freaky, to look into my own eyes, to see the pain there. Or, more honestly, the desire for pain. Can't exactly describe it to you, if you don't already know. If you're not one of the cult who either revels in giving pain or relishes receiving it.

I'm of the latter crew, and I dream of my Mistress' tortures. The feel of her cold hands as she fastens the bindings in place. The movement, subtle, gentle, as she slips the blindfold over my eyes and ties it beneath my hair. I come thinking of her teeth finding purchase on one of the rings that adorns my nipples, my labia, and pulling, tearing at my flesh. I get the most joy when she makes me scream.

Hard to explain it to a novice. To one of the as-yet uninitiated. But I've got the time, if you've got the inclination to listen. My Mistress won't be back for hours, and I can whisper to you until then. After that, I'd advise you to hide in the closet and stay very still. If she catches you here, you'll be in for the same treatment that awaits me. And for a novice, for one as pure as yourself, that might be a bit extreme.

So, meant to ask you, but somehow got confused, are you one of us? Are you a dark horse that rides the fringe of society? Does the thought of a thin black collar around your pale throat make you wet? When you were pierced for the first time, did just the brush of your blouse against your nipples make you come?

That's how it was for me. I've always loved secrets, refuse to give myself up entirely for anyone, and the secret piercings were my first dance with darkness. I remember the smell of the place—the Gauntlet—the near-angelic smile of the black-haired demon as he cleaned me with alcohol before readying the needle. Addictive, it was, the rush of the pain. Not long enough. Over much too quickly. But my Mistress knew what I was thinking and she assured me that we would be back. And soon.

That's how it was for me. The desire to please her. And my pain pleases her. My pain makes me beautiful to her. My ugliness, the tears that mar my finely-cut features, the furrows that line my brow as I fight back the screams— these are the things that my Mistress loves best.

"Look at yourself," she hisses, grabbing fistfuls of my black hair, shiny as a colt's, and pulling me upright. "Look into the mirror and tell me what you see."

I close my eyes against this request. I don't want to see the reflection, the evil twin lurking beneath a frozen screen of mercury. I don't want to know the part of me that stares so calmly back through the glass.

The palm of her open hand slaps my cheek, bringing the welcome pain to my soul that makes it easier for me to obey her. I wish sometimes that I could obey her without the need to be punished. I've told her as much, but she just bares her teeth at me in the grimace that passes for one of her smiles, bares her teeth and strokes my hair and croons, lullaby-style, "Darling, if you didn't need pain, you wouldn't be my slave. I do so love to make you cry."

Staring at my reflection in the mirror, the tears that slide down my cheeks, the puffy hurt look to my lips—it's like staring at a stranger. And then her hand on my face again, slapping the other side this time, bringing a fresh rosy blush to my cheek, just to even me out. Watching that is like watching the start of a fire. The spark, the glow, before the raging blaze. Watching that is like buying a ticket to hell.

"What do you see?" she asks, biting off the words that could follow: "What do you see, cunt?" she could say.

"What do you see, slave?"

"What do you see, whore?"

I see a need, burning, engulfing. I see a yearning. A desire that only my Mistress can meet. She fills me. She holds me. She bends me until my will is broken. She scatters the pieces so far apart that I can never be whole again. How I long to submit to her.

How I long to please her.

"You see a sinful little fuck," she tells me, slapping me again as she lists the correct answers, not *A*, *B*, or *C*, but all of the above. "You see an evil soul. You see a sinner."

Yes. All of those things, Mistress. All of those things and more.

When we met, at a club in the Village, a dark hole that suited my needs perfectly, she slipped up behind me, wrapped one arm around my waist pulling me back against her, and she hissed, "I will break you."

Oh God. If you are a novice, I can't explain it to you. If you're normal—if you don't need pain (to give or receive it) then you won't understand. Then you'll think I'm a sick, perverted creature—which I am— and you'll leave the room, quietly closing the door behind you. That's fine. Go, if you need to. Go, if you can't take it.

I'll wait here by myself for her.

I'll wait here, with my wrists cuffed too tightly together, my legs pulled to their widest point possible, stretched until I feel that ache in every muscle, and I'll wait. Until my Mistress comes home and pulls her cane from the stand. I'll wait for her to position herself by the bed and use that thin bamboo cane to stripe me from my shoulder blades to the soles of my feet. I'll wait patiently for her to do everything she promised before she left—"I'm gonna mark you tonight. I'm gonna make you mine. I'm gonna break you."

Do you get it? If you're still here, then you must get it. You must be kin, a blood sister, to understand the waves of white-hot need that ride through me at all times. Place your hand against your throat and feel the lifeline of your blood pulsing there. C'mon, press a little harder now, I want it to be a struggle for you to breathe over the pressure. It's not scary, child. You're doing this to yourself. You have all the power. Honest. You can stop any time you want.

Next test. Take your blouse off, or at least unbutton the top three or four buttons. Nice little bra you've got on there. Black. I like it. My Mistress would like it. She thinks black bras are very sexy, especially when worn under good-girl clothes. I try to please her, I try to wear what she likes. But sometimes I forget. I'm glad you didn't forget, this being your first time with her. It's important that you show her your respect.

Okay, now, I want you to pinch your right nipple between your thumb and your finger. Harder. I'll tell you when you can stop. I want you to feel this, and I want you to think of your Mistress doing this to you. She'll pinch your nipples until they go numb. She'll clip clothespins on them. She use those nasty clamps with the ridges and the chain between them that will humiliate you by jingling every time you walk. But for now, you're to show your obedience by pinching them yourself.

Good girl.

Describe the sensation to me. C'mon. Just because I'm tied here, doesn't mean I don't have power. I do, child. I can stop talking to you. I can stop spinning my tales for you. And I know you wouldn't like that. I can tell by the way you're looking at me, the haunted look in your eyes. The desire. It comes off you in waves, my darling, like perfume, the sweetest scent. And mingled with it is the smell of fear. That's good, very good. You should be afraid.

Okay, now. Pinch the other. Harder this time. I want your nipples to be throbbing with heat and fire. I want you to bite down on your bottom lip to stifle the cry. That hurts more than you thought it would, doesn't it? But as soon as you release, the feeling is replaced, right? By something entirely different. A flood of sensations, sort of swollen, but tingling. It feels different, doesn't it, child? It feels...good.

Oh, yessss. Come closer to me. Sit yourself down right on the edge of the bed. I want you to look in the mirror, girl. I want you to stare at yourself while you take your blouse all the way off. Just throw it on the ground. Now your bra. Now pinch those nipples again. Both at the same time. Keep holding. I'll tell you when you can stop. Don't look down, girl. Stare right into your eyes while you're doing it. And tell me, tell me....

What do you see?

You see a naughty girl, don't you? You see a slut, a whore, someone who deserves to be punished. Of course you do. I can read it in your eyes. Even if you thought you were a Mistress. Even if you thought you were the one who'd be in charge. You're not in charge now, are you? You're not telling ME what to do, are you? See how easy that is? That switch of power. The slide, the shift, the subtle dance. Ahh, child, it doesn't matter that my limbs are fastened to this bed. Power is not in the body. It's in the mind.

(You can let go now. Mmmm, I wish I could put my tongue on those beauties and cool you down.)

Confused, aren't you? Don't worry. You're supposed to be. All I'm doing is giving you what you want. What you need. More than that. Darker than that. Deeper than that. Older than that. I'm giving you what you deserve.

You've known for a long time. I can tell. You've tripped with your naughty fantasies, slid your fingers under the sheets at night to find that throbbing little jewel between your thighs. Pressing, rolling, tickling it between your fingertips, you've thought of the most sinful desires. You've given in to them. Understand this, then, child. Understand that your chums, your mates, your gang—many of them would be disgusted if you told them what you want. They're thinking sweet thoughts. Happy thoughts. They're thinking of k.d. lang on a Harley zooming up to them at the prom and whisking them off into the sunset. And that's just naughty enough for their pure minds. A Harley, they're thinking. Ooooh. Bad.

But not you, slut. You're thinking of bending over the desk at school, having the professor bare your ass while she whips those tender thighs of yours with her thick leather belt. Gets worse, doesn't it? The whole class is watching, aren't they? All those eyes on you, watching as the edge your skirt is pulled up and tucked into the waistband, as your panties are yanked down your thighs and left to hang (left to humiliate you) down around your ankles. The whole class is watching as she reaches for a cane from the stand by the door, reaches for it and shows it to you before bringing it down on your bare haunches.

What does she want you to do, girl? Tell me. It's your fantasy.

Does she want you to kiss it before she punishes you with it? Does she want to let those first teardrops (caused solely by fear) to rain on the bamboo before the weapon marks your pale skin? What does she want you to do?

Does she want you to come? Is that what it's about? Would you come in front of your peers? Would you let them see you writhe in combination of pain and pleasure? Is that what you want, girl? Is that what it takes?

You think of them moving closer, of their hands on you, inspecting you, touching the welts as they bloom against your pale skin. Stroking the marks that she leaves—reminder marks. Poor thing. You want to feel them touch you. I know.

Ah, you're a bad girl. I knew you were. I can usually tell. Don't you love that, my darling? Don't you *come* to that image at night, those naughty fingers of yours moving in those tingling circles, 'round and 'round your pulsing clit?

Yes, you come to it, late at night, when everyone else in your house is asleep—wouldn't want to wake them with the sound of your bed shaking, would you? It's okay. I'll ease your troubled mind for you. It's okay to think the things you do, to want the things you do. It's even okay to do them...just look at me, tied so tightly to the bed that it's hard for me to move, thinking only of what my Mistress will do to me when she returns. Especially when she learns that I've been talking to you. I was supposed to be spending the afternoon contemplating my sins, my transgressions. You know that it's the anticipation that always makes the moment. It builds inside until you can't contain it. Until it's too strong. Too wild. Until it's screaming inside to get out.

And she'll be angry with me for wasting time talking with you. No, don't worry. I'm sure you wouldn't rat on me. But I will. I'll confess as soon as she walks through the door. I'll say, "Mistress Jane, I have something to tell you." For your sake, my darling, I hope that you're gone. Because she will want to take care of us both at the same time. So unless you're truly secure in your desire for pain, I'd recommend that you either hide or vanish.

What would she do? C'mon, cutie, do you really have to ask? No. I know you don't. I know that you just want to hear me say the words. It's much more real when someone else says the words, isn't it? When someone else says, "Lower your panties, child, and bend over my lap. You're gonna get a spanking." Mmm. I caught the look in your eyes when I said that. Has it really been that long, darling? Have you never scrambled over the lap of a displeased lover and felt her fingertips sliding beneath your underpants and pulling them down your legs? Poor thing. What you've been missing.

But I was telling you a story, wasn't I? I was telling you about

Jane, about the night we met. It was one of those bizarre circumstances. I'd decided that I didn't need anyone. I was tired of looking, tired of the quest to find a decent Mistress who wasn't completely psycho. In fact, I'd just plain given up, and I was taking myself out for a pre-slumber drink at the club down the street from my apartment. It always happens like that—love, I mean—when you don't need it, when you are totally secure with who you are and what you're doing, that's when it hits you.

Literally, in my case.

Jane came up to the bar in her panther-stride, silently stalking behind me and appearing at my right with a magician's ease. Now you see her, now you don't. She lit a cigarette and then, without saying a word, slipped it between my lips. I will never forget that feeling, her fingers pressed to the pucker of my mouth as she held the fag there for me to inhale. I did, took a nice long drag, and then stared at her as she brought the Marlboro to her own mouth and inhaled.

She hadn't even asked me if I smoked. She'd just assumed. (In fact, I'd given up the cancer-sticks six months before, but the taste was just as nasty and sweet as I'd remembered, and it stirred a longing within me that wasn't only for the nicotine.) Eyes still holding mine, she leaned forward again, but this time she didn't pass over the cigarette. This time she moved in closer and kissed me. Softly. Gently. Her lips brushing over mine like a silken handkerchief, like the colored ones I'd worn in my back pocket years before to let people know that, yes, I liked Victorian games and corsetry (white lace) and, yes, I would be tied down if so desired by lover (gray), and, yes, I would be whipped (black).

"Jane," she said as she pulled away, exhaling the smoke that still lingered in her lungs. My hand went out and caught hers, "Rice," I said.

"Last name?"

Shake of my ebony curls. "Nickname."

She left it at that. We weren't after small talk, neither of us.

"You done here?"

I waited a beat, staring into her eyes again, watching the colors within them shift and change in the dim light. She had chameleon eyes, now green, now blue, now grey. They stayed on this last color, going a dull metal hue as I watched, and then, deep within them, I saw the spirals of black. Veinlike, the way white marble is veined, the way the sidewalks crack after an earthquake. Swirls of black against gray, they cracked further, swallowing me up, promising me, promising me....

"Yeah, I'm done."

Her grip was iron-strong, firm around my waist, shuffling me out of the pub and down the block in a rapid, military step. No words again. Energy moving between us instead. I trusted her and I let her set the beat.

She lived in a brownstone then, up three flights of rickety wooden stairs, and she led me through her entranceway and to the bedroom without a single hostess-like word of welcome. No "Here's my living room" nonsense. No "Would you like another drink?" stall for time. Her hands were on me, all over me, leading, pushing, prodding me down the dark hall to her room, a quick heave and onto the bed. And then she stood a few steps back, her breathing hastened, and stared at me.

I wondered what she was seeing. Thin, college-type. Faded jeans, black velvet turtleneck. Bottle-black hair in glossy ringlets, so dark it had a mentholated blue, Elvis-style sheen to it. Pale gray eyes, rimmed with black lashes. Wild lips still stained with berry-gloss.

I wondered if she could see beyond that. *No fear. No fear. No fear.*

I have nothing left to lose. Take me. Use me. Break/abuse me. Sinful twisted fantasies are here for you to find. Cheap, free for the asking, no cover charge....

"Lie down. On your back."

Done. I closed my eyes to avoid staring at the nothingness of her ceiling.

"Lift your hips."

Her hands were on the waistband, unzipping my jeans, pulling them down to my ankles, leaving them there, held in place by my patent leather boots. My panties came down next, caught to the same place, a bit of white cotton that felt soft against my ankles.

"Would you prefer to be tied?"

Shake of my head, not bothering to move the curls away once they'd partially covered my face. I could feel the blush to my cheeks, but I didn't want to call attention to it. I didn't know what was driving her at this point, what I might inadvertently do to stop her, to anger her. I forced myself to be as still and as noncombatant as I could, hoping with all my soul that this wasn't a dream. A tease. A nighttime fantasy.

She was at my side on the bed, parting the lips of my pussy with both thumbs, opening me up and observing me there, the colors, the gradations of pinks, dark rose to pale petal. I could smell my scent already, and she could, too. This made her laugh, as did the gloss that came away on her fingertips when she removed her hands.

"You were wet in the bar."

A statement. I didn't know if she expected or required an answer.

"You were."

"Yes..."

"That's how I found you. I smelled you from across the room."

The flush to my cheeks grew darker, creeping along the line of my jaw and to my neck. I could feel the heat of embarrassment there, but also a new flood of honey that coated my thighs. Her voice was turning me on.

"You've been alone for a long time, haven't you?"

"Yes..."

"Long enough to have forgotten how to respond to one in charge."

There, stated easily for me to interpret. I now knew our game. ("But hold on," a tiny voice said inside me, "This doesn't feel like a game. Not like the kinds you're used to. This feels dangerous. And real.")

"Oh," out of my mouth before I could stop it, a sigh, dark with need, hungry with want. "Yes..." still unfinished, wishing I knew the correct answer, not caring about the consolation prize, I was going for what was behind door number one. "It has been a long time, Mistress."

Dark chuckle that didn't let me know whether I'd won the new car or whether I was about to join the ranks of the runners-up.

"That's better. Not perfect, but better."

This is not a game, I thought again. It's not a game with a capital "M" for her and a lower-case "s" for me. Thank God, thank you, God, I've waited much too long for this. Waited my whole life for this. Deep within myself, I was still sane enough to wonder whether it was truly God I should be thanking. If He is the creator of all, than He created me, with my multitude of sinful passions, wicked thoughts, harmful desires. But it just doesn't seem right.

She interrupted my thoughts with a blindfold, brought tight over my eyes and then slipped expertly behind my neck. I lifted up for her to make it easier for her to tie it. My eyes were closed beneath the smooth material, and in that new place there was no light.

"You don't need to be tied," she repeated to me. "But I will tie you. In the future, whenever I want to, I will tie you. For now, I'd like to see how much you can take. This is for your own sake, so I know where our starting ground is, what I have to work with. How far you want to go." A pause, "Though, you really must understand that it's not about your wants, your petty desires. It's about needs. Both of our needs. And I will take you beyond the edge of your world. I will take you into mine."

Then silence. And darkness. And I lay there waiting for it to begin. It takes some courage, you know, to wait like that without screaming, without begging. The pain is always better than the moments before. Better because you're already immersed. It's like dipping your toes into icy water—oh, how awful—it's always much better to be thoroughly drenched, that heart-stopping feeling of the icy waves surrounding you.

In horror movies I've heard it's described as 'the monster behind the closed door.' Your mind will always create a much more frightening monster than any F/X technician ever could. Why? Because you are the sole owner of your own fears. You have named each one, created each one. Once the door opens to reveal an actor in a silly costume, the fear is over. But those few precious moments before...those are worth cherishing.

As I cherish these...tied here and waiting for my Mistress's return. Yes, I still refer to her as such. But only when discussing our relationship. At the times that she beats me, she is nameless. At the times that she takes me higher, she is all things. And nothing. And I am the same.

I have no religion to get in the way of my worshipping her. Or, better yet, I have a religion that is of my own creation. I have a religion and she is my God. Does that surprise you? Does that make you quiver, make you want to stand out of the way to see if some lightning bolt will fell me? Don't worry, kiddo. Nothing can hurt me. I am already in hell.

What are you looking at now? The chest by the door? That's where she keeps her toys, her props, the tricks of the trade. Go ahead, open it up. It's not Pandora's Box, sweetheart. Nothing will fly out and scare you. Just open it up and poke around, see if you recognize anything. See if you like anything. I'll tell you my favorites as you reach them. There are some sweet toys there, some vibrators, pure pleasure enhancers. And some items of sole discipline.

You stopped when I said that word. Do you like it? Does it do something to you inside. Yesss, it does. I can tell. Oh, you are one of us, little one. And let me give you another reading—I'm not like one of those wacky psychic member hot lines, this reading is free, of course—this reading is of your future. And I see you in a lot of pain. Yes, just as I thought. Come here and look at your face in the mirror. Your eyes went down as I said that, your lashes fluttered and your cheeks grew hot. You want pain, don't you, darling? You crave it. You yearn for it. You deserve it.

Don't tremble like that, sweetheart. It's okay. I wish my hands were free so I could hold you. As it is, you'll have to snuggle up against me if you want comfort. That's it. That's the girl. Come lay by my side and whisper your fantasies to me. You can't say anything that would offend me. I'm much too far gone for that.

There, doesn't that feel better? Tell me, sweetheart. Tell me everything...tell me everything that you want.

No? Cat got your tongue? That's all right, too. Settle down against me, get comfortable, and listen to my voice. I will tell you stories....

Loony Ward

Cynthia Freeley

It was lights-out on the late shift at the hospital, and all the patients on the psycho ward had been secured and locked down. The guards had gone on tour, and the nurse at the receptionist's desk sipped coffee and went over the day's records.

Just on her first break, Francine sneaked into the supply closet for a smoke. She stood there taking a deep drag off the cigarette, enjoying the burning sensation of the smoke filling her lungs. It soothed her.

She heard footsteps right outside the door. She stubbed out the cigarette as the door opened. Waving the smoke from the air with her hand, she turned to face the intruder. It was Nick, the orderly.

Nick was a sweet and naturally gorgeous guy. He had a muscular physique from his daily workouts. It was important for an orderly to be strong in this hospital, and Nick was rarely remiss in his duties. He also always seemed to know where she was hanging out and tracked her down like a bloodhound. She didn't mind because they smoked the same brand of cigarettes and shared a sick sense of humor.

He locked the door behind him and placed a finger to his lips. He came closer and, to her surprise, feathered a light kiss on the tip of her nose. He removed her lab coat, still not saying anything. He put his arms around her and unzipped her dress, letting it fall to the floor. She was alarmed but excited. She knew she could trust him.

After he had folded the dress and put it neatly on a shelf, he opened a package of gauze, took her wrists, and tied them over her head to the steel shelves. Now she was amused, wondering what he would do next. His warm fingers brushed the skin on her stomach as he removed her panties carefully and pulled them down around her ankles. With his foot, he pushed her legs apart gently.

He stood face-to-face with her and grinned. He was holding two pairs of disposable forceps. He opened one and hooked it onto one of her hard nipples. She gasped at the sudden pain. When he did the same thing to the other one, she bit her lower lip to keep from crying out. Francine felt a wave of dizziness.

"Nick—that's too painful!" she hissed through her teeth.

He just placed his finger against her luscious red lips and, without saying a word, continued with his plan. He spread her pussylips apart and tickled her clit. The combination of pleasure and pain had her standing on her tiptoes, gasping for breath.

Nick dropped to his knees and began to lick her cunt. His tongue danced around the tip of her clit, teasing her. Without warning, he plunged his finger in and out of her asshole. Between his mouth and finger, Francine started to moan a little too loudly.

Her clit was throbbing under the onslaught of Nick's lips and tongue.

It was sweet agony not to be able to touch him. Nick would decide when Francine could actually lay her hands on his body.

He kept tracing every wrinkle and fold of her cunt and asshole with his tongue and the sharp edges of his teeth, until her juices were pouring out of her pussy like water from a faucet.

Suddenly Nick thrust three fingers up her tight pussyhole and pushed and turned until her body twisted and shook as if she were a rag doll. Francine was biting her lips to keep from screaming; only garbled moans managed to escape. Her climax was strong and intense. Her fluids drenched his hand.

Nick untied her wrists, removed the clamps from her nipples—which gave her a rush of renewed pain—and held her in his arms, feeling the warmth of her naked body. He kissed her lips and told her that it was time for her to thank him.

Francine dropped to her knees and took his stiff cock into her mouth.

She sucked hard, simultaneously yanking his shaft and squeezing his balls gently. Tracing every part of him with her tongue, repeating her motions in a quickening rhythm, she was getting him more excited than he'd ever been before. Before too long, Nick felt a profound heaviness deep within his balls, traveling up the shaft of his cock until it exploded from the tip, coating Francine's hands and wrists in hot, steaming sperm. She shoved his dick into her mouth quickly, sucking him dry.

She grinned up at him and wiped her face on his sleeve. She stood up and kissed his lips, and they embraced that way for several minutes, enjoying each other's scent.

After a few moments, they got dressed. Their break was over, and they were due back on their posts in less than a minute. They looked at their watches, and as they hurried out of the closet Francine reminded Nick that their next break was in four hours. Nick winked at her and told her that there was an empty room on the third floor. She smiled at him and walked away, thinking of all the possibilities.

Six-Handed Fugue

Anonymous

Los Angeles—a city full of stars. Who would have thought that I'd be one of them? Okay, so I was only a small star in a minor galaxy. But when the lists from publicists for event openings went to the media, my name was usually on them. And I was just as likely to have a camera pointed in my direction as any starlet. Admittedly, the footage wasn't likely to be aired, unless it was taken by our sister TV station.

But as far as my mother was concerned, I was Elizabeth Taylor, Jane Fonda, and Sophia Loren in one glorious package. She was so proud of me that she even stopped sending clippings of the wedding announcements of the girls who had attended high school with me. In her own way, Mother was getting her consciousness raised.

A year after I left San Francisco, she also decided that since she was already this far away from me, she could tolerate an even greater separation. I almost died when she announced over the phone that she was going to sell the house in the Marina and go live with her sister in Florida.

Oddly enough, I was disturbed by this change in the order of the universe. It would constitute a bona fide rite of passage for me. It wasn't that I felt any particular closeness to her. There'd always been a certain distance, no matter how much she'd invested in my life. Mother was a man's woman without a man, and wasn't at her best relating to another woman, even if it was her own daughter. She'd done her best, by her standards. Probably by everyone else's, too. And now her job was done. She was free, as free as she was capable of being. I felt happy for her. Weeks after the big move was over, I admitted I was relieved. At least I was free of the emotional shackles she'd bound me with.

I never quite unloaded my other emotional baggage—Dan Harrington. Big Dan and his midnight blue briefs.

Screw him, I told myself on more than one occasion. Only I kept wishing I could have. But he never called. And I'm proud to say I never did anything worse than hang up on his telephone answering machine. To this day, I'm convinced he did the same to mine. Modern technology opens so many new avenues in interpersonal relationships.

The next several years in L.A. were rewarding ones. I moved up to reporter, then was promoted to morning drive-time anchor, then advanced to a reporter's job at a local TV station. We weren't network-affiliated, but in L.A. you didn't have to be to gain celebrity. I had a career. I had men. I had marriage proposals.

I had...nothing.

Yeah, yeah, I kept carrying that stupid torch. I look back now and I understand that life was a great deal easier that way. My therapist helped me to discover that it was a lot simpler to love someone in absentia than to adjust to the day-to-day complications of an ever-evolving relationship.

Mother, on the other hand, met and married a retired raincoat manufacturer six months after she moved to Florida; she's still living happily ever after.

I wallowed in self-pity the first year AD—After Dan—felt lessening melancholy the second year, and thought I was really over him by the third. Then one day, I read something about him in the *L.A. Times*—he was in town arranging a merger. He had advanced to the tier just below the upper executive level of Netweb. It reopened the wound just when I'd begun facing the world without my "Closed for Repairs" sign.

I might have been pathetic, but I still had my pride. I was Elizabeth Renard. I'd been written up in the entertainment columns. I knew men who could buy and sell Dan Harrington and not even bother to count the change. So why shouldn't I avail myself of my opportunities? I was ready. I'd show the men of Los Angeles a thing or two.

Of course I fell into a relationship even dumber than the one I'd endured with Dan.

I just wasn't very good at finding Mr. Right.

By the time I was ready to commit myself once again to the quagmire of love, I had worked my way into my current specialty, entertainment coverage. In L.A. that's a genuine accomplishment. It was frivolous, too, and arduous. Every day I'd have to deal with egos of celestial proportions, both in the newsroom and on the beat.

But the good thing about doing my kind of work was that even the worst of egos, when they're being interviewed, want to show their best side. Illusions. People outside the business continue to ask me if this celebrity or that one is as gracious in person as he or she is on screen.

I used to answer in the affirmative. Then it dawned on me that these people were performers. Who the hell knew what they were really like?

What's more, I didn't care, just so long as I nailed down my story.

The year of my L.A. debacle began with a local scandal that was rife with interesting twists. No, there wasn't a murder involved. And it didn't involve a movie or television star. But it caught the romantic fancy, not only of the denizens of Smogville, but of the world...for the usual twenty minutes.

I covered some of it when it happened. And ten months later, I got caught in the aftermath.

Etienne St. Germain. He was in his early twenties at the time, I think. It was hard to be sure. Etienne was one of those Peter Pan-types who would look twenty-two when he turned forty-five, and probably have just about as much maturity. His features were black, his skin café au lait, his eyes blue, his hair a soft, golden brown, and curly.

I was never as impassioned with Etienne's hair as I was with Dan's ass, but I came close.

Then there was his voice—gentle, mellow, with a charming French accent that reinforced his continental aura. That voice was enticing at first, compelling so much of the time, cloying and annoying at the last.

According to Etienne, the story of his life was a great romantic tragedy. He seemed almost to revel in the sadness of it.

"My father was an American executive held in very high regard by his company. He was rewarded for his good work by being assigned the presidency of the Paris office. The women who was to be my mother, a black woman of extraordinary beauty, began as one of the secretaries in his office. They were drawn to each other almost from the start. Before long they were deeply in love."

This is, of course, an abbreviated version of the details. I'm not about to let Etienne become the central figure in my own drama.

"She left the company, for reasons known only to her and to my father. Their affair had remained discreet. A few months later, she and my father married.

"Their union put an end to further advancement in the company by my father. But the executive committee decided that firing him would cause too great a scandal. And after all, Paris was Paris. Wasn't it the birthplace of the romantic scandal?

"My father was very good at his job, but when clients came to France, the home office arranged whenever possible for them to meet with someone other than the division president. It was ludicrous how they made excuses for it. But my parents lived with the knowledge. That sort of nonsense is a trifle when a love between two people is so perfect.

Their greatest desire was to have a child. After three years and a difficult pregnancy, my mother gave birth to me. She wasn't healthy, and the doctors advised that she never have another.

"I was to be the ultimate symbol of their love. But this was not a simple thing. Even in Paris, I soon learned that I belonged nowhere. Not only because of my color, but because of my American father.

"I tried to prove that I was as French as anyone. I refused to speak English, even to my father, except when forced to in class. I tried to be like the other boys in my school. But I was never accepted.

"I resolved to stop trying to be. I remained apart. I withdrew more and more into myself. I felt alienated from everyone, even my parents. Between us there was love, but little understanding. Perhaps this was my fault; I cannot say.

"My one joy was music. I don't know what would have become of my life had I been deprived of it. By the time I was five years old, I could sit at a piano and play any music I'd heard.

"My schoolmasters were impressed. Of course, my skill set me apart even more from others my age. But I didn't care. They decided to structure a special course of study that would allow me to emphasize music. They became convinced that one day I would play the world's great concert stages."

As it turned out, Etienne's goal wasn't quite met. He enjoyed a career in music, but it was closer, I think, to the one I would have had if I'd pursued my goals in the art. He performed in concerts and recitals, but almost exclusively in churches and colleges. He achieved some small degree of fame, playing with second-rate orchestras in Europe. He was good, but good in the way that a thousand similarly talented people are who might or might not rise to stardom.

He could have fostered a romantic image that might have taken him to the pinnacle, but Etienne would have none of that, or was incapable of it. Critics pointed out that there was a certain coldness in his playing that emanated from even the most passionately composed passages. His technique was flawless, but when it came to feeling, Etienne was always slightly removed.

That's also how he made love.

He reached the height of his career with an opportunity to play with the Los Angeles Philharmonic. His timing was perfect. It was low tide in the social season. And the ladies of the symphony's auxiliary took to him one after another, basking in the reflection of their vanity in his shining blue eyes.

Etienne was very adept at making those eyes shine and dance in response to the interest of the woman before him. He was so very skilled it would take even smart, experienced women longer than it should have to penetrate the illusion and peer behind the mask.

There were, of course, ladies who didn't care, or who even preferred to live the illusion. One of them, as is often the case in such circles, had show business connections. She found Etienne a job as a musical consultant, whatever that is, with one of the studios. A suitable position was also created for him in her, um, heart.

"The ladies were so kind to me," Etienne would say. "I was flattered. But still I was empty. There were always women. I will not pretend that I don't know that they find me attractive. But what did I have when even the most skilled of them had left my bed?

"And then I met her. She was lovely, fragile, shy—not like the other ladies in Los Angeles who were so frightening in their cloak of brittle sophistication. She was many years older than I. But it didn't seem so when we were together. She had been married forever to a Philistine of a banker, and they had a daughter.

"But this woman was like a sweet, tender young virgin. She loved me in a way I had never known. Ah, to be loved so completely, so innocently.

"I met her at one of those ridiculous ladies' teas. It was in my honor, of course, and I did my duty. I smiled. I was kind to all of them. I kissed hands. I charmed. And then I met her. I was enchanted. I had to be with her."

He pursued her, seduced her, and for several months they basked in the flame of each other's passion in a series of discreet matinees at his beachfront apartment. Unfortunately for her, love for a woman was secondary to Etienne when it came to his career, even if he didn't quite like to admit it.

An important piece of music found its way into Etienne's hands, and the lady, his fair Louisa, became just a little less significant, although I don't doubt he still loved her very much. It was a concerto, modern in texture, but with romantic overtones. It suited the state of his emotions. He was sure it would be a masterpiece, that if he could premiere it at one of his concerts it would ensure him fame and fortune.

"Louisa was so caring, wanting me to have my dream made real. I didn't ever imagine the lengths to which she would go. She had an inheritance separate from the money she'd appropriated from her husband's account. Without my knowledge, she went to New York and arranged a commission, not with the New York Philharmonic, for that couldn't be done. But the orchestra was talented and the hall was an important one. The critics who mattered would be there.

When I received an invitation to debut the work I was ecstatic. This was everything I'd hoped for. I didn't ask questions. Maybe in my heart I knew what my Louisa had done, but I didn't, wouldn't acknowledge it. I knew only that it would be a magnificent night. I would be hailed as a new and major talent.

"My highest expectations were exceeded. The composer got his credits as well, but he was all but forgotten. The glory was mine. I tried to remind people that I was only the communicator of his genius. But it was the concerto and Etienne St. Germain that captured the imagination of the press. Soon, to everyone, the music was known as 'Concerto for Etienne.'

"But the price of this fame was the curiosity it aroused. The music world is a gossip-filled community. It took little trouble to track down the secret of the commission. The world learned what I had not really wanted to know. I felt that I would be regarded, and ridiculed, as a kept man. I loved Louisa for giving me my concert. And I hated her for making me look like a fool.

"Yes, I know it was cruel and stupid for me to think that way. But my mind was in conflict. I knew it was unlikely that I would have had the opportunity to play without her underwriting the concert. But now the triumph was forever removed, I thought, by the disgraceful position into which I had been placed.

"Then there was the added scandal of Louisa's subsequent divorce. I loved her. That didn't change. Nor did her love for me. She had given me so much, had ultimately surrendered her entire life. How could a man turn his back on that kind of love?

"I could not. And not for a moment believing that what I was doing was the right thing for either of us, I asked her to be my wife. She refused me. I admit now that I both was relieved and grateful. But she did agree to come with me to Europe."

What Etienne neglected to include in his melodrama was the fact that he was far from perceived as what he truly was—a man who had been, and would be, assisted in his livelihood by smitten women. Instead, he was portrayed by the media and perceived by a willing public as a romantic figure.

We loved it—our own modern-day Duke and Duchess of Windsor. All for love and that sort of thing. So romantic.

And so helpful to Etienne's career. Even though concert schedules in major halls are normally planned months and even years ahead, many were adjusted to include a special appearance by this new Valentino of the keyboard. There were radio and television appearances as well. He was the man...they were the couple...of the hour.

It was all so utterly compelling. But, as in so many romances, the librettists of operas having it right, such romances only work out if one or the other or both are killed or separated in some dramatic way. That way the passion and our adoration can live on and we don't have to watch the laundry get dirty.

Etienne did well at first, so long as he stuck to "his" concerto. But that could only last for so long. Critics were soon pointing out that he was a one-note pianist. So even during Etienne's glory days there was specter of trouble on the horizon.

He had his world, in which, for a short while, he was celebrated. Louisa was shy, out of place, even more so since her life became subject to public scrutiny. He began socializing without her. For her there was loneliness, for him as much guilt as he could muster. The whole thing steadily came apart.

The lovers quarreled, privately and in public. Etienne's temperament became increasingly erratic as important critical and social circles were less and less impressed with his talents or his charms.

"It all became quite hopeless. We were so sad. We loved each other. A part of me will always love her. Our souls touched. That is not easily forgotten. But we could not go on together. She could not live in the world to which I belonged. Once she had given me a great gift, but now that gift became an anchor that would soon drown us both. She went to England where she had friends. I think she lives in London still."

He returned to the United States. There were enough small-scale engagements to keep him going, and enough ladies to pay him his due. He survived.

How he loved telling his tragic tale. It was difficult for me to refrain from diminishing it with the harsh light of probing questions. But even with what I knew and suspected as a hardened reporter and a woman full of cynicism and disbelief, I was touched. Well, not in the way Etienne usually touched other ladies. I never contributed to his financial support. But I did find him attractive in a strange sort of way.

I met him briefly when he first hit the public spotlight. I interviewed the "happy couple." He did most of the talking in an accent so thick I was inclined to doubt its authenticity. Later I learned it was real, just thickly layered and practiced. A man would be a fool to lose a French accent in the United States, especially in the presence of women.

At the time, Etienne was mostly just a story to me. The romance of it all, the passionate conflict, the apparent love, at least on the part of Louisa, aroused in me a passionate jealousy.

Dan Harrington would only had to have told me to "stay" and I would willingly have done it. Etienne and Louisa, in the beginning, had done everything for each other, for their love.

It practically killed me.

Once they had departed for Europe, the scandal was old news. But I never entirely got it out of my mind. When, months later, I met Etienne at a party, I immediately asked about Louisa. He looked wonderfully tragic and told me they were no longer together. I am ashamed to admit how many emotions and hormones he stirred in me with that one beautifully spoken line.

I mean, this guy was good. Later, much later, when I regained my sanity, I of course realized that the story of his lost love was as well practiced as his accent.

Later, over drinks on the patio of his apartment overlooking the Pacific Ocean, he told me his heartrending story in its entirety. My sole thought was to comfort him, to prove to him and to myself that love still existed, that the two of us could find happiness in each other. We made our best effort that same night.

He seemed passive, almost shy, as I removed his shirt and drew down his pants and shorts. He wasn't quite so passive as I thought; his cock was *hungry* where it hung pendulous and swollen.

I kissed his neck and chest, then moved downward. My hair brushed all around his loins as I maneuvered around my target. I touched the tip of his cock with my tongue and felt him shudder.

I positioned my mouth to take all of him. Licking up and down the entire shaft, I varied my rhythm and intensity. I circled the head and swept down along the base. Etienne finally responded and pushed my head further down; his lance pricked the back of my throat.

He pulled back and positioned himself above me, putting my legs around his shoulders. With a single thrust he entered me, filling my pussy with his hard cock. His strokes were long and deep, coming faster and faster. His hands grabbed at my breasts, pinching the nipples, kneading the mounds. I felt him expand within me and I came at the same instant he did. He seemed to pump into me forever until he finished, then he slowly rolled off me. We fell asleep in each other's arms.

It was the beginning of our affair, although the pretense of love dissipated quickly. Still, being tenacious and not wanting to admit in my first post-Dan try at commitment that I'd made another huge mistake, I went on with it. I was faithful to him and functioned as a woman in love, without having the slightest illusion after the first weeks that he was in love with me. I needed someone in my life at that point, and I was willing to delude myself that Etienne was all I needed.

That he was never really there for me, that the emotional texture of our relationship evolved from his indulgence in his own sorrow, seeking my sympathy and warmth at the moments most convenient to him ... I ignored these things and told myself that he would come around in time. One day his pain would be gone. And then he would love me entirely.

All right, so I still had some illusions.

But it didn't matter. Etienne was never what I really wanted. I knew this.

I would have this dream that I was marrying Etienne. But I could only see as far as the wedding, never beyond.

There I was, breathtakingly beautiful in my white gown. My dark hair and eyes contrasted starkly with the fabric. The only splash of color was provided by my lips—ruby red. Etienne and I would be standing in the receiving line, joyously accepting congratulations.

Suddenly, Dan would appear. He'd take my hand, wish me well, and then impulsively kiss me on the cheek. As he did it, I would whisper in his ear, "I'll always love you."

I really hated my subconscious.

Etienne and I endured. My work continued at a breakneck pace. His agent was able to get him engagements with minor orchestras in small cities, usually with the stipulation that "Concerto for Etienne" be in the program. He had recorded it during the first flush of fame and it had continued to sell. So he was able to maintain a modicum of self-respect.

Los Angeles, however, was Etienne's bane. Each time he appeared, the same second-string critic, Andrew Byrd, would tear him apart. Each review would be more vicious than the last.

We would both dread the day after an opening. We'd get the morning paper, anticipating the worst and not even coming close to the reality. No matter how Etienne prepared himself, he was always devastated. I was consumed by sympathy for him and could offer him no comfort that he would accept, no matter how he seemed to demand it. When, at last, he would submit to being consoled, he would come to me as the arms of a loving mother. For days afterward, no matter what my libido craved, there would be little chance of satisfaction.

You can't fuck Mommy.

Naturally, the subject of my musical abilities and the presence of the Baldwin baby grand in my flat were things we tried to ignore. I strongly suspect that if I'd stayed at it, I would have been better than Etienne. Never in the time I knew him did I ever play the piano in front of him. Nor did he want me to. I was sensible. I didn't want to be as good as I thought I was and confront him with it. Then I'd have to cope with whatever vanity required him to do to diminish my abilities in his mind. It was a losing proposition either way.

Oddly enough, the man I did play for, without fear or pretension, was Andrew Byrd.

My L.A. beat covered mostly Hollywoodish stuff—glitz and glamour, tits and tinsel. But from time to time, someone would remember my musical background and assign me to a story that related to it. Sometimes it was marginal, like the Etienne-Louisa story. But sometimes it was more serious. That's how I met Andrew, by covering a reception for a visiting ballet company.

Having seen Andrew Byrd at performances around town, I recognized him immediately. Knowing my temper, I thought it would be best to ignore him or pretend ignorance of his presence. What would be the point of a confrontation, especially when lurking inside of me was a general agreement with his assessment of Etienne's limited abilities? Of course, that didn't excuse him for being a vicious bastard in print.

My luck was terrible, I groaned. He saw me and apparently knew who I was. He immediately came toward me.

"Whatever do you see in that never-was has-been?" was his opening line. Not bad. Andrew certainly knew how to make a strong first impression. But I was ready for him.

"What a surprise. You're just as nasty in person as you are in print. But not nearly as witty."

Need I say that this was a beginning that could only lead to one of two places—his or mine.

Mine.

He had a surprisingly large, firm cock. I made him lie down on the floor as I stood over him and removed my clothes. When I was naked, I made him watch me as I fingered my clit with one hand and fondled a nipple with the other. If it was possible, his erection grew even larger.

I stepped over him and lowered myself until my pussy lips met his mouth. He began to lick me. Being a sarcastic bastard wasn't the only thing he knew how to do well. He sucked on my clit for an indescribably long time as I bathed his face in my creamy juices.

When I tired of this, I reversed my position and licked my way down his chest and belly. I surrounded his cock with my lips and began to suck him off. When I figured he was going to lose control, I stood up once again, then lowered myself directly onto his pole. I fucked him by tightening my muscles around his penis, squeezing and relaxing, squeezing and relaxing, until his body started to shake. I raised myself off his cock so that I could see his great warm spurts erupting into the air.

In the morning, for some masochistic reason, I chose to play the piano for him. I suppose I had to prove to him the extent of my fearlessness. His response nearly floored me.

"If I were reviewing the entertainment, both of this morning, and if you'll forgive me, of the night before, which latter review I'll refrain from making because to do so would be a decidedly ungentlemanly thing to do, I would be tempted to say this: that after a stunning climax to what seemed to be the final aspect of the performance, this reviewer was delightfully surprised to discover yet another aspect of the young lady's apparently endless store of versatility and appeal. You really are quite a good musician. You shouldn't have been so quick to surrender your hopes for a career. If you'd kept at it you would have far surpassed your French friend.

My shock changed to elation. "Do you actually think I'm good, or are you just saying so to strike yet another blow at poor Etienne while pandering to my ego?"

I, too, could speak as if every brilliant word was waiting to be etched in stone for rediscovery at some later date.

"You wound me. I do think you're extremely talented. And you have feelings you aren't afraid to risk in your music. That's far more than your pet piano player is willing to do." He stood behind me, running his hands along my shoulders, then over my breasts. "Tell me, honestly, isn't he a bit of a passionless bore in bed?"

"I won't tell you anything," I sniffed indignantly, "any more than I would tell him what kind of lover you are."

"No, I don't suppose that you *would* tell him that I had been so presumptuous as to trespass into your boudoir and dared to caress your glorious flesh. I should think that would be our little secret."

"Are you thinking of telling him?" I couldn't believe what I was hearing. "Is that what this is all about, another blow you can strike at Etienne? Surely, even you wouldn't be that despicable."

"Come on," he said as he walked away, stopping before the window. "Let's be honest. You're a beautiful woman. We both know that. If I had seen you at the reception and known nothing at all about you, I would still have wanted you. But can't you also admit that a part of your participation in last evening's activities was related to the assumption of how devastating it would be to *cher* Etienne if he found out what we were doing? You've taken pleasure in knowing that you've just been fucked by his worst enemy. That attitude is so female."

"And you are a total bastard. That's so male."

"Bravo!" he applauded. "You've wounded me. And, to make it

so much the worse, you've done it by turning my own phrase. I'm impressed, even as much as you intended me to be. And excited, more than you can imagine. Let's go back to bed."

The man was like something out of a Noel Coward parody. And I have to admit I adored him more with each passing minute. Passion was clearly secondary to repartee as far as he was concerned, but I didn't care. With Andrew, I could virtually have a mental orgasm. If I was going to mind-fuck, he was certainly the ideal partner.

For several weeks, I alternated sleeping with both of them. Two nights a week I spent with Etienne in his beach apartment. One or two nights Andrew arrived with a flourish at my flat. Somehow, I felt safer with him on my own territory.

How he intrigued me. At that point, he was certainly a hell of a lot more fun then Etienne, who was spending increasing amounts of time enthralled with his own personal tragedy.

One man so tedious. The other so amusing.

I kept thinking that it would be much more honest of me to end my relationship with Etienne. But whenever I got close to doing it, he'd start telling me how much he needed me. Plus, the truth was that having both men were becoming increasingly necessary to me.

But only if I had them both.

Was it the beginning of perversity in me, or just the first notable outward manifestation that I was steadily progressing toward some great psychological revelation?

One night as Andrew and I were talking in bed, he said, "You know, I've never actually met yesterday's boy wonder. Wouldn't it be interesting if you introduced us?"

"It would be horrible," I retorted. "How could I do that to him? And why would I want to give you the opportunity to attack him to his face and probably tell him about us? How can you ask me to be a party to such cruelty?"

"Because cruelty is the farthest thing from my mind. I promise to be exceedingly charming and kind. I already feel much more gently disposed toward the lad than I have in the past. You have softened me."

"Somehow I hadn't thought that was the effect I have on you at all."

"Much too obvious a riposte, my dear. Definitely beneath your abilities."

"And of course, you prefer me beneath your abilities."

He waved his hands in mock surrender. "Enough, enough. One more double entendre and I shall have to attack you in retaliation."

"In print, or to my face or some other portion of my anatomy?"

"Bitch. You're trying to provoke me to your whorehouse level of repartee, but I shall neither stoop nor rise to the challenge."

But, of course, he did.

With the initial assault out of the way, Andrew began a campaign to meet Etienne. The subject dominated our conversations. I began to feel that it didn't really matter which one of them I was with, at least conversationally. Either way, we always wound up talking about Etienne.

And then my little demon of perversity elbowed me in the ribs again. Go ahead. Do it, the little voice urged. You know the very idea makes you wet.

I agreed to it, but only if we could make the meeting look accidental and if Andrew agreed that he would say nothing to Etienne about us.

About a month later, Andrew and I were invited to the same cocktail party and I agreed to bring Etienne. I couldn't resist anymore. I was dreaming of the two of them every night. I had always been fairly conventional in bed, although I'd been told I was a good lover. No illusion there; I'd always been easily carried away by pure, delicious lust. And as evidenced by my response to Etienne and his tale of woe, I could be terrifically caring and protective of the male ego. Mom would have been proud if she could have seen her little princess.

One of the things that intrigued me about Andrew was that I never did or was required to do any of the typical things with him. If we played the roles of bastard and bitch, at least we were equals. I fed his vanity with real delight at his wit and wickedness, doing my best to top him when I could. Sometimes I succeeded, although he was loath to acknowledge it.

I don't suppose that was the healthiest basis for a relationship. I didn't think so even then. But I was enjoying it. I left the analysis to my analyst, whom I was seeing less and less of as I saw Andrew more and more.

If Andrew was bringing out the darker side of my nature, then so be it. Obviously, it was something that was meant to happen. He was only the means of my deliverance.

Etienne and I arrived at the party before Andrew. How like him, I thought, to make me wait, anxious, on edge, wondering if he would come or not.

When he finally made his grand entrance, he flashed me a smile that said, "I knew you'd be waiting." Bastard, I thought. He read my expression, smiling with that conceit that was uniquely his. If there had been another exit, I would have ushered Etienne out of there immediately just to thwart the bastard and his evil intent.

No. I guess I wouldn't have.

I could feel the muscles in my face altering my own expression. I met Andrew's smile with my own. Oh, it was all so rotten.

So far I had told Etienne only that I had met Andrew at another event and spoken to him briefly. He wanted to know if I'd given him hell. I told him that I had not. To do so would not only have been unprofessional, it would probably have hurt his career even further.

"What more could he do to me?" Etienne whined, falling prey to what I thought was his most annoying mood. His agent had been coming up with fewer and fewer bookings of consequence. Despite this, I noted that Etienne not only succeeded in getting his rent paid, but each time I went to his apartment some significant new article of clothing or piece of jewelry had been added to his substantial collection. I suspected those were rewards and tokens of appreciation from ladies of greater means and less reluctance than yours truly.

I'm not saying that Etienne took money for his somewhat limited prowess in bed. At least he didn't take it directly. That would have made him a prostitute and would have horrified him beyond words. No, he was content to accept payment for being a sort of dancing bear of the keyboard, playing the piano at parties, ostensibly as a guest, the hostess pleading with him ever so gently to tickle the ivories, and then hers, for just a little while.

With a great show of reluctance, he would graciously acquiesce, the illusion of propriety preserved in his mind and the lady's. Ego once again protected from reality, he could accept his trinkets.

As to his prowess in bed with me...the sad truth was that my morose maestro was less and less competent as time passed. My interest waned as well. But I felt sorry for him and did my best to comfort him.

I remained willing to hold and caress him on long, sleepless nights, and I didn't want to desert him.

But the whole affair was depressing me and was taking its toll on my work. I found myself perpetually tired, worn out by the constant wringing of my emotions and the lack of sleep and my warring feelings for Andrew and Etienne.

Andrew, thank goodness, rattled my cage. He challenged and stimulated me. I looked to him to restore my psyche and deliver me from Etienne. No, I couldn't leave him when he so clearly needed me. But, as I'm sure my subconscious was aware, I could drive him away by doing something truly horrible—such as bedding Andrew Byrd and making sure that he found out about it.

Andrew circled us like some cautious hunting cat, prolonging his approach by stopping to talk to several groups who blocked his path. Etienne was so engrossed in conversation with a lady who was eventually to become yet another of his benefactresses that he wasn't even aware of Andrew's presence.

I could hear my heart pounding, feel my adrenaline flowing. I had never been so thoroughly aroused as I was at that moment with the smell of confrontation in my nostrils.

Andrew, when he greeted us at last, oozed snake oil salesman's charm. He was every bit as fascinating as the serpent in Eden. Only this time, it was Adam he was trying to tempt.

Etienne didn't know what to do. Prepared to dole out righteous anger, he was taken off-guard by Andrew's casual friendliness. Andrew didn't even allude to the spate of unfavorable reviews he'd written over the years. Instead, he talked generally about the music scene, asking Etienne for his opinions, listening politely, respectfully, to his responses.

Before Etienne knew what was happening, he was snared. He had fallen under Andrew's spell, completely forgetting, at least for that moment, that this man was responsible for many of his woes.

If there's one thing more powerful than the vanity of a man, it's the vanity of a male musician. All resentment was lost, all suspicion was suspended as Andrew courted Etienne with simple flattery. Initially I thought it was to goad him on to even greater displays of ego and foolishness, which Andrew would later turn against him. I was wrong...and incredibly naive.

Within an hour, the three of us—best friends—left the party in search of a place to dine.

It was in the restaurant that Andrew began his courtship in earnest. I call it that, because courtship was most certainly what it was. Lip-smacking, lascivious, obvious courtship. It hurt to think that two men in my life were more interested in each other than they were in me. But even in that I was mistaken.

I was more confused than anything else. Andrew and Etienne displayed unbridled passion for me in bed, actually surpassing anything we'd experienced previously. I struggled with the nagging belief that our relationship had become an exercise in sublimation. I wrestled with the thought that I was, for the moment, the closest they could come to bedding each other.

That coupling grew out of a tripling.

One night the three of us attended a very bad concert. Our eloquent trashing of the soloist reached new heights as we sipped cognac in front of the fire in Andrew's living room. It was terrifically cozy. We were all feeling the glow of the liquor, growing ever more enamored with our collective wit.

That's when Andrew looked at Etienne and said, not so cleverly, I thought at the moment, "The man is a passionless dolt."

There was one of those horrible, prolonged stretches of silence. It probably lasted only a matter of seconds, but the web of camaraderie that had been woven between us could almost be heard to snap.

"Are you talking about me?" Etienne said in a menacing voice, every blistering review clearly as fresh and festering as it had been before the meeting with Andrew.

And, I thought, Etienne, to whom I'd given little credit for vast intelligence, had perhaps not been Andrew's dupe at all. It was possible that he'd gone along with all of this to await the proper moment for his revenge.

I eyed the poker resting by the fireplace, wondering if I was about to become witness to a murder. The tension was palpable.

They were sitting in tan leather chairs, facing each other like gunfighters preparing for a showdown. Andrew reached across the figurative and physical breach and put his hand on Etienne's arm.

"Oh, no, dear boy. I was very wrong about you. I know that since we've become friends. I suspected that your greatness lay just beneath the surface, and wanted to goad you into becoming the artist that you were meant to be. In my glib cruelty, I failed. But now I know that your passion is there, ever present, waiting to be released, to become ecstasy."

The air was thick with lust, enveloping not only the two of them, but me as well. I was the link. Without me, what was growing between them could not be consummated. I had been used, but my usefulness gave me a certain power.

Even after we'd become a social threesome, none of us had ever discussed what transpired behind bedroom doors. Andrew and Etienne both must have known that I'd divided myself between them, but that unspoken knowledge seemed only to add fuel to our passions.

In bed Andrew was motivated by a creative as much as a physical drive, and yes, by vanity. And although he wasn't a handsome man, he was attractive enough in an academic sort of way. He was tall, on the lean side, graying at the temples, slightly myopic, and wore horn-rimmed glasses. He was so bright, so clever. And he intrigued me.

Andrew especially had risen to heights of extraordinary excitement.

Etienne, on the other hand, had always fucked by rote. Sometimes he was as mechanical as he was on the piano. But he was strong and athletic and technically very accomplished. Interestingly, his self-pity had largely evaporated during the formation of our social trinity, and his charm, although often cloying, once again predominated. I was sure he knew that I had taken Andrew as my lover. It seemed to have created a spirit of competition.

I would willingly accept the consequences.

I could see an erection straining the fabric of Andrew's trousers. The excitement was palpable, almost physically painful for me. I wanted both of them. And as much as they might have wanted me, they wanted each other. I was the catalyst, the force that would propel the inevitable.

I entered into my role, an utter slave to my raging desire. Rationality was forgotten. I knew what I wanted with frightening clarity of vision.

Wordlessly, I moved from the sofa. I sat on the floor between them and began stroking their legs, gently, using just the slightest touch. I didn't look at either of them.

In a moment, first Andrew and then Etienne brushed my arms with their fingertips. I looked first at one and then at the other. They were smiling.

In a moment, we were all laughing.

Andrew, who of course had to be the leader, stood up first and pulled me to my feet. Etienne followed. There was a brief pause, a final opportunity to regain sanity.

The moment passed. None of us felt the slightest hesitation.

Andrew's bedroom was an adolescent fantasy made real. The first time I'd been admitted to the inner sanctum I'd laughed out loud. Andrew had been so offended we almost never made it to the fur-covered, king-sized, satin-sheeted water bed. My whispered apology and a husky promise to make it up to him appeased his wounded pride, but thereafter I made every effort to sleep with Andrew in my more conservative surroundings.

This night, though, tackiness was the last thing on my mind.

I don't know quite how to explain the feelings I experienced. They weren't so much different from the moods that overtook me when I got screwed by Andrew or Etienne alone. But, perhaps, with the addition of another penis, everything increases proportionately.

I was probably the only one of us who retained a flicker of rational facility. It was probably the reporter in me. It kept me just slightly removed from the action so that I could observe, make mental notes, form phrases I could use later when it was time to describe the abyss of passion into which I'd fallen.

But, oh, I was so close to shutting down my faculties that night. Added to animal passion was the stimulation of exploration into a sexual domain where I had never been nor ever expected to be.

This was all before the AIDS epidemic, and I was of a generation that regarded sexual freedom as an inalienable right. But even then, such a step was foreign, forbidden.

Thrilling.

We came together, at first wordlessly, and began slowly undressing each other. We showed remarkable restraint, I thought, considering the heat of the situation. But that made it so much more exciting.

Nonetheless, this being real life, not a well-choreographed

film, there were moments when awkwardness would overtake us, when we weren't quite sure what or whom to reach for first.

But that became a part of the joy. We laughed as our efforts became more frenzied and hilarious. We were like innocent children playing with their first sexual discovery.

At one point, they both went at me as if I were some kind of inanimate, life-sized doll that had just been given to them for Christmas. I loved it. I stood still, moving an arm or leg only as they moved me. It was winter and layered clothes were fashionable. Even in warm Southern California, wool sweaters and boots suited the elements.

They pulled off my cardigan and then my turtleneck sweater. Then Andrew unhooked my bra, while Etienne slid it off from the front. My nipples, hardened and raised, beckoned to them. They responded readily, sucking at my tits. I moaned as they tugged with their teeth and ran their tongues over my sensitized skin. I felt like a mother who had just given birth to aberrant twins.

Their shirts were off by then. Etienne had his pants unzipped and they had begun to slip down his legs, making him look slightly ludicrous. Andrew was the most dressed, the most composed of the three of us. His pants were still closed; his belt was even yet to be undone.

How like him, I thought, in a fleeting fragment of thought. It kept him in control to the last. I reached for his belt buckle and loosened it in two swift movements. Then I opened the fly of his slacks, pulling them down to his knees so that he looked totally absurd.

I laughed uproariously at the sight of the two of them.

Retaliation was immediate.

They went at me as if I were a rag doll, pulling and tugging. I began to fear I'd be dragged about the room, a victim of children's' carelessness.

Their actions weren't violent or hostile, though—just silly and sexy.

They halted their mock attack of me long enough to remove their dangling trousers. They were free now. Wearing only their briefs, they came at me anew.

Etienne, the larger and stronger of the two, lifted me up under the arms, swinging me off the ground, while Andrew pulled off my skirt and burgundy satin slip. A lace G-string, knit black panty hose, and black leather boots were all that remained of my ensemble.

Etienne returned me to my feet. I stood there as they circled me.

"Isn't she pretty?" Andrew said, just within reach, touching me ever so slightly on the nipple of my right breast.

"Yes," said Etienne, "*très charmante*." He moved in just a little closer and brushed the inside of my leg.

"I think I like this best of all," said Andrew with a glancing touch to the area around my pubic hair.

Around and around they went, coming just a fraction of an inch nearer with each rotation, commenting on my body as if it were a thing independent of personality, touching me just barely, but with increasing intimacy.

I stood motionless, as if I were indeed a thing, a physical thing, bereft of will or intelligence.

Then, without further preamble, Etienne was in front of me, Andrew behind. Etienne caressed my inner thighs with his hands. Andrew massaged, no, *kneaded*, my buttocks, as if they were two rounded loaves of bread he couldn't wait to bake, then consume.

Jointly, they pulled off my panty hose and boots, flinging them to the side. Then, like a pair of groping schoolboys, they reached inside my panties. Their fingers began probing my pussy, separating the folds, darting in and out like single-minded snakes. I gasped, barely able to stand under the assault.

They stopped only long enough to remove their own briefs. They tore off my G-string, then lifted me into the air like a captive sacrificial virgin ready to be flung into a volcano.

They flung me onto the bed, surrounding me on either side. Hands, lips, tongues, touched me everywhere.

And then, because I was merely the appetizer, they went from me to each other. Reaching across my prone body they embraced, kissed, deeper, deeper, their mouths locked together.

I was fascinated.

Repulsed.

Aroused.

Jealous.

They separated, their hands reaching for the other's penis, fondling, stoking. I couldn't tear my eyes away from the sight of their stiffening cocks. They appeared larger than I'd ever seen them and they hung, throbbing in anticipation of what was to come.

Then, as if set off by some internal signal, Etienne climbed on top of me. Just as quickly, Andrew crawled behind and mounted him. Etienne groaned at the violation, but the expression on his face was one of ecstasy. I barely saw the angry purple head of his cock before he rammed his entire length into me.

I was engulfed, crushed by the weight of the two of them.

I was also excited beyond anything I could ever have imagined.

Our bodies moved as one entity, thrusting, undulating. Etienne plunged into me with pistonlike regularity in response to Andrew's motion, then drew back as the pressure eased in his anal canal. I was sure it must have been painful for him, but he uttered no complaint as he pounded harder into my frothing cave. I was rocked by one wave of pleasure after another.

There was no way to prolong beyond that moment the union that we shared. Within seconds, we all came screaming our joy to each other and to anyone else who could hear us.

We separated wordlessly, each of us falling into a deep sleep that didn't end until nearly noon the next day.

Always one to insist on the last word, Andrew woke me while Etienne still slumbered. Despite my sleepy protests, he insisted that I fellate him, and wouldn't give up until I relented and let him ejaculate in my mouth.

How quickly extraordinary things became the norm. Our little ménage à trois continued for several weeks, each time becoming a little less interesting than the last—for me, anyway. Our configurations varied only slightly from that of the first night. The preliminaries became increasingly predictable.

I suppose, for the sake of the illusion of virtue, I should say I ultimately put a stop to it because I was disgusted by such perversion, that I realized how disgusting and sinful it all was.

But I would be lying. I left because I got bored. I left because the novelty of seeing Andrew's prick penetrate Etienne's asshole became stale pretty quickly. I left because of the knowledge that they were far more enchanted with each other than they were with me. Now I wasn't so enamored of either of them that I cared overmuch about that. But since I no longer had my libido or my ego gratified by the situation, it made it nonsensical to continue.

I had become nothing more than a minor, and probably unnecessary, catalyst.

I gave them little. I got from them even less.

I wasn't angry, but I did prefer to leave them to themselves. When I told them how I felt, they made obligatory motions urging me to continue the relationship. But in truth, I think they were both relieved that I was withdrawing.

It was all so terribly civilized.

When I left them I consoled myself by coming to the conclusion that neither of them would have filled Dan's midnight blue briefs.

No, romance just wasn't my strong suit.

Cinderella
Titian Beresford

Victoria stood waiting in the tiny shop of the Calauverge harness-maker, savoring the cool Spanish tiles beneath her bare feet. The harness-maker stood at the window looking out into the haggling throngs.

"Is there more market day spectacle on the scaffold?" Victoria asked hopefully.

"No, and for that I am grateful. But Prince Steven's carriage has stopped and he appears to be mingling with the crowd as if looking for someone."

Victoria smiled to herself and imagined what it would be like if the prince were searching for her—a silly, impossible notion, of course—but one delightful to entertain. Victoria's senses had been stimulated by the lewd treatment of the pilloried prisoner and it was easy to imagine the prince sweeping her up in his arms and taking her to his royal chamber high in a palace tower. Her cheeks turned crimson as she thought of clasping the royal member in her hand, and then being slowly and deliciously impaled upon it.

"Three braided dog whips, then, and one Barcelonian pony tawse...." The harness-maker paused when he realized that the lovely barefoot girl in the green dress was lost in reverie.

Quickly collecting herself, she apologized with a blushing smile. The harness-maker handed her the narrow paper packet containing the whips, and she paid. She was still thinking of the prince as she walked down the steps and onto the street.

In her vision she lay on her back, legs bent at the knee and toes pointed. The prince knelt, thrusting vigorously inside her, his body bathed in sweat, his motions urgent and fevered. These pleasant fantasies occupied Victoria until she reached the sun-dappled garden wall of her home.

An old pensioner sat on a wooden bench, his wrinkled, pleasant face turned to the sunlight. Victoria smiled and crept up to him, pouncing at the last moment to throw her arms about his neck and kiss his weathered cheek.

"Ah, Victoria!" the old man murmured, delighting in her closeness. "You smell of the Market Square and of leather. For shame, Victoria! The bawdy scenes of market day could end your innocence!"

Victoria blushed and ruffled the old man's white hair. "I did not look."

She continued on to the wrought iron garden gate of her home through which she was quickly escorted by a conspiratorial maid who had been waiting for her.

Victoria's stepmother, Regine, wanted her always to send the houseboy, Lucas, on errands to the harness-maker's in Market Square. She said it was beneath the dignity of a family of nobility to take on such errands themselves.

But Victoria loved to go. She always went clad as a servant in a plain green dress to savor the sights, sounds, and smells of market day. She especially savored the sights on the scaffold when a pilloried prisoner was to be dealt with for the amusement of the crowd.

But now was the time for her and the pretty young housemaid to reward Lucas. He risked a prolonged caning from Victoria's stepsister Marcella if ever he was found to have let the young lady go in his place.

Victoria and the housemaid, Rachel, joined Lucas in a quiet garden nook. Lucas eagerly divested himself of all his clothes until he stood coltlike and naked on the grass.

"Will you suck me today?" he boldly inquired of Rachel, who blushed and rolled her eyes at the effrontery of the lad.

"No, Lucas," Victoria said firmly. "She will pleasure you with her hand, as usual, to reward you for risking a caning on my behalf, and I will show you my legs as she does so!" Victoria added this last with sudden inspiration.

Rachel stood by Lucas' side and, grasping his penis, began to fondle and caress it, even as Victoria sat impudently on a stone bench and raised her green dress until she well bared the smooth allure of her pretty thighs.

She then rested her lovely bare feet on the trunk of a shade tree and watched Rachel masturbate Lucas. Victoria smiled as she watched the young housemaid's hand work Lucas's foreskin back and forth in long, slow, pulling strokes. The young man spread his legs so Rachel would have complete and easy access to his genitals, and he leaned into her strokes. His face was placid with youthful ecstasy.

Victoria noted with amusement that Rachel, for her part, though pretending to be casual and even bored by the proceedings, took a secret delight in her handiwork which her parted lips and flaming cheeks betrayed. Lucas gasped as his scrotum flapped about between his legs, so influenced by the eager force of Rachel's hands. Victoria felt her breath come more rapidly as she watched, fascinated, as the masturbation continued. She knew that her stepmother Regine, and her stepsisters Ana and Marcella, would be revolted by a sight such as she now enjoyed. That realization made Victoria enjoy it all the more.

Lucas gazed worshipfully at the forbidden curves of Victoria's calves and thighs as he strained and finally ejaculated onto the trimmed grass of the garden lawn.

Victoria watched the thick arcs of his seed flip through the air and land with impromptu male conceit upon some flowers nearly a yard before him. The tip of his penis continued to disgorge a torrent of sperm to which Rachel's pistoning hand gave high trajectory.

At last Lucas went down on all fours on the grass, his shaking legs giving way under waves of pleasure, his fogged mind still full of the luscious vision of Victoria's legs. Rachel stood noting the exhaustion of her victim with smug satisfaction, attributing it to the expertise of her handiwork. She bent prettily to wipe her glistening hand on the grass and affectionately chided Lucas for soiling the flowers. Then the trio set themselves aright and went into the house.

Victoria's eldest stepsister, Marcella, awaited them, standing innocently in the kitchen door where she had been amusing herself by bullying the kitchen maids a moment before.

"Victoria, you are wanted upstairs, at once," she cooed, her voice velvet with gloating malice.

Marcella's otherwise lovely mouth had but the slightest petulant downturn at the corners of her lips—the effect of which was further enhanced by the hard, cruel set of her eyes. Many a household servant had learned to rue the day he failed to avoid Marcella when she was bored.

Lucas and Rachel quickly disappeared to attend to their household duties, and Victoria ascended the sweeping stairs to knock quietly on the paneled door of her stepmother Regine's suite.

Victoria's calm poise never left her and long ago she had become adept at steeling herself to face any bizarre tableau she might find in Regine's chambers.

Regine sat on a velvet upholstered dressing stool, naked save for a short luxurious fur wrap that hung low on her bare shoulders. Her dark hair was piled high in an elegant twist atop her head, giving her delicately lovely face a hint of haughty imperiousness. Victoria had not noticed their striking beauty before, but was certain now that Regine had the exotic, almost slanted, eyes of a cat. Regine's legs were bent at the knee, and her bare feet were tiptoed on the rich gold and crimson carpet of the floor. Her fingers, beringed with delicately jeweled bands, rested almost gently on the head of the young upstairs maid, Maria del Castillo.

Maria knelt naked on the floor before Regine and was gently licking her clitoris.

Behind Maria sat Victoria's youngest stepsister, Ana, fully clothed, her buttocks resting on a high-backed chair upholstered in striped satin. Ana smiled as her fingers lewdly caressed the moist shaven mount of Maria's sex.

"Ah, Victoria!" Regine purred smugly, gently chiding Maria for slowing the intimate work of her tongue. "I must inform you that tonight, once again, you have a good deal of work to do in our training rooms. Did Lucas purchase the whips and the tawse from the harness-maker as I desired?"

"Yes, Regine, Lucas has brought them from Market Square. He arrived just a moment ago."

"Splendid!" Regine exclaimed, her breath coming faster as Maria's tongue remained diligently employed and was now stimulating her clitoris with delightful little fluttering sweeps.

"To think, Victoria, that Maria is the daughter of what once was one of the wealthiest families in Lisbon, and would be penniless now but for my generosity in giving her a good situation of employment."

Ana now had the index finger of her left hand worked deeply within Maria's crinkled circlet while the fingers of her other hand teased Maria's genitals with soft butterfly caresses. Victoria could not tear her eyes from her stepsister's violating hands as they gently played with the young maid, delicately turning her to a near fever pitch of helpless and humiliated excitement.

Victoria realized that the caresses provided the young maid inspired her tongue, making it all the more a willing servant of Regine's jaded sexual appetites.

Ana laughed quietly as Maria del Castillo wiggled her curvaceous hips in helpless abandon, pleading with the motions of her body for Ana's teasing fingers to probe her vagina as well.

Regine, for her part, did look beautiful, her face suffused with the glow of sensual enjoyment. She leaned back and gave herself to the lapping, catlike tongue of the kneeling maid, even as Victoria's own sex swelled and moistened at the soft feminine sound of the gentle licking.

Regine presently recovered herself and spoke again to Victoria.

"The Comte de Languedoc will arrive by closed carriage tonight, and wishes to play a new game. He wishes to feel the sting of the Barcelonian pony tawse on his bared buttocks and be ridden about the training room. Then he wishes to be manualized to spending after suitable and lengthy humiliations are carried out upon him—the duration and type of these, Victoria, I leave as usual to your imagination. Suffice it to say that I require him so pleased when the proceedings are ended that he regards his payment as well-directed and even a small price, well worth such heady delight."

"Must I wear the leather hood, Regine?" Victoria asked. "It is stuffy and so confining!"

"Yes, I fear that you must, nor do I want you ever to perform your duties without it. Our clients have often told me how the mystery of their hooded abuser adds delight and intrigue to the games that you play, and several have said that they take pleasure in wondering of every women they meet—is she the one who enslaves me? Why deprive them of their crumbs of enjoyment and profane the mystery on which they have become so dependent?"

As Regine talked of Victoria's clients and male propensities, Ana's mouth curled into a expression of disgust even while she continued to masturbate Maria, now busily employing two of her slim fingers within the maid's vagina. Regine sighed as again the maid's servile tongue swept her to another summit of pleasure.

"You are dismissed, Victoria. Oh, and after the Comte will come the Vicomte Cevenne. He requests his usual game and sounds so eager for the sport to begin that I do wonder if the vicomtesse has been tending to her husband's intimate requirement."

"May Rachel assist me with the vicomte?" Victoria asked.

"Yes, of course, Victoria, now you are dismissed!"

Victoria paused just outside Regine's door after first gently drawing it closed. Her pretty, full-lipped mouth curled into a smile of satisfaction.

"Profane the mystery indeed!" she said to herself in a lighthearted mimic of Regine's suave tones.

Victoria knew then that Regine insisted on the hood as a jealous measure to conceal her loveliness. The thought was an angry reminder of her position in this home, and yet it flushed her cheeks with pride.

When Victoria gained the bottom of the stairs she headed for her own chamber. When passing the stillroom door she saw Marcella busy at her typical amusements. Elvert, one of the young household grooms, stood naked from the waist down in a posture of forced and rigid military attention. He watched Marcella use a glazing brush to apply fresh conserves about the cleft of a pretty, blushing, stillroom maid's buttocks.

The stillroom maid, a young apple-cheeked girl named Sonia, knelt on top of the table where the jams and jellies were stirred. Her back was to Elvert and Marcella, though she obediently displayed the saucy bare curves of her bottom by holding her skirts well up. Sonia bit her lip in vexation at the indignity of her predicament. But her glance darted back behind Marcella to note the girth and length of Elvert's penis.

Marcella worked delicately, applying the conserves about Sonia's circlet in unhurried swirling strokes. When occasion necessitated, Marcella brazenly spread Sonia's smooth, broad globes to apply the conserves to the crack of her bottom. She spread the sweet substance well down until some of it caught in the dark hairs about the pouting mound of Sonia's sex. Sonia gasped, and her cheeks reddened yet more.

Marcella laughed at Sonia's anguish and paid scant attention to Elvert for the moment.

Due to the placement of the doorway in the room, Victoria could watch the game while unseen herself.

Marcella then reversed the brush and dipped its polished wooden handle into the jar of conserves. "Brace yourself, Sonia dear!" she purred. "I'm going to make you sweet!"

With that the bored young woman slowly inserted the sticky, shining handle of the glazing brush up into Sonia's anus. Sonia squirmed and protested, but knew better than to protest overmuch. Marcella smiled as she twisted the brush about in Sonia's bottom to see that it had left a good quantity of conserves behind, then she abruptly withdrew it.

Victoria held her breath, unable to tear her eyes away from the bizarre sights of the stillroom.

Marcella next turned her attention to the groom and ringed his penis lightly in her soft grasp. "Before you are relieved, Elvert, I do expect you to kindly tend to Sonia's buttocks. She appears to have sat bare-bottomed in sweet plums and oranges!"

Marcella drew Elvert forward by his penis and pressed him down till his mouth was even with Sonia's sticky buttocks.

Elvert resisted having his face pressed forward—he resisted out of shame—but Marcella disdained to spare his dignity. She drew him back by his hair long enough to slap him soundly across the face. Then she smiled and pressed his face forward, bringing his nose to nestle in the sweet sticky cleavage of Sonia's bare bottom.

"Lick her well, you pathetic boy, and who knows? I may yet reward you despite your insolence."

Elvert trembled, and he began the soft, slow lapping of the conserves from the intimacy of the stillroom maid's bottom. Elvert's testicles hung low and pendant, swaying slightly with his efforts as he set himself to his task.

Marcella viewed the proceedings with her arms folded smugly across her breasts. She was most specific and demeaning in her verbal direction of Elvert's tongue. He started beneath her belly, near the downy bulge of Sonia's sex, and slowly worked toward her circlet.

Victoria watched as gradually Sonia's pretenses of outrage and disgust crumbled and Elvert's tongue gently persuaded her body's pretexts of modesty and chastity to give way. Soft sighs of pleasure broke almost unconsciously from Sonia's lips, even though her face still registered dismay at the indignity of her predicament. Elvert's organ thickened and throbbed, shifting slowly parallel to his splayed thighs, helpless to escape this humiliating erotic bondage.

Marcella slipped from her shoes, raising her skirts and exposing her pretty bare legs, and sat back on her heels to enjoy her contrived amusements.

"Yes, Elvert, yes! That's it! Very good, Elvert, and now thrust your tongue within her circlet. No, deeper. Harder! Yes, like that!"

Marcella's right hand found Elvert's penis while her left reached beneath him from behind to capture and squeeze his scrotum. Elvert's mouth was gleaming with the sweet conserves as his penis was ever so gently abused in Marcella's soothing palm. With a low, moaning sob he utterly abandoned himself to Marcella's whims and obeyed her every detailed instruction. He stiffened his tongue and repeatedly thrust it through the resistance of Sonia's circlet into the sweetness of her depths.

A moment later Sonia went rigid and trembled in the throes of a long, satisfying orgasm. Her nipples throbbed, hugely erect beneath her bodice as all her sensation became centered in her bottom. She felt weak as the flames of a base and perverse passion ignited her every sense in a firestorm of delight.

As Sonia's quivering subsided, Marcella turned her attention to Elvert and made him stand once again. Marcella smiled as she brushed her fingers over his lips and then thrust them, one by one, into his mouth, making him suck the sticky jam from each.

Marcella held Elvert by the scrotum and used it as a bridle to ensure that he cleaned her fingers well.

Victoria took special note that Marcella truly gloated with every degradation to which she subjected these poor household servants, and smiled despite herself at the thought.

Sonia had stood up, but seemed to be in a quandary as to what she should do next. She still held her skirts high, exposing her bare bottom, which, although Elvert had done his best, was still glistening with conserves. She dared not let her clothes down for fear of soiling them, and bit her lip in dismay.

Marcella noticed: "Turn about, Sonia. That's it. Now bend over well at the waist and hold your buttocks spread apart."

Then Marcella inserted the glazing brush once again, handle first, into the jar of conserves. This accomplished, she slid the handle into Sonia's anus and left it there. "See that it does not slip out, dear girl; tense your buttocks upon it and take care that it remains in place."

Sonia tensed herself and turned about. The brush quivered—but remained inserted. She drew up on tiptoe and strained to hold it in, her expression a reddening mixture of agony of embarrassment. Marcella smirked as she applied a handful of conserves to Elvert's penis. Then she pressed Sonia to her knees before him. Sonia took great care to keep the brush embedded, though it nearly slipped from her circlet once she settled on her knees.

"Now, Sonia," Marcella murmured in tones of aggravated sweetness. "It seems that Elvert has also been playing naughtily in a sticky mix of plums and oranges. Clean him well with your tongue!"

The vexed maid had no choice, and soon her lips formed a wet sucking ring that gently drew on Elvert's glistening tool. Sonia's eyes were expressive in their consternation as she felt Elvert's penis twitch and expand on the surface of her tongue. Sonia could not see that Marcella had two fingers of her left hand well embedded in Elvert's anus and was gently twisting them to and fro.

Elvert was excited beyond endurance, and though he did not wish to spend in the pretty maid's mouth, he could do little to stop the course of nature. After being forced to lick the bare bottom of the very maid that he had adored from afar for so long, and after having his penis stimulated by his mistress, her fingers probing in his bottom, and now after being suckled so deliciously—he surrendered.

Sonia's eyes widened in outrage, but she knew better than to take her mouth away and risk Marcella's wrath. As Elvert's tool jolted and twitched, filling her mouth with thick spurts of warm sperm, Sonia swallowed them all one by one. The tidy maid even kept the seal of her lips tight about his glans to prevent spillage. The tang of the sperm mixed with the sweet stickiness of the conserves Marcella had rubbed on his penis.

Marcella drove her fingers upward to the depths in Elvert's backside, forcing him up on tiptoe and goading his penis to spurt even more copiously.

Victoria watched the scene to its conclusion, then softly crept to her chamber, her face aflame and her clitoris swollen huge.

Minutes later, on her bed, the vivid erotic scenes of the day coalesced in her mind. The image of the pilloried prisoner squirming as the laughing pastry cook's girls masturbated him, Lucas straining as his penis jolted in Rachel's hand, Maria del Castillo—with Ana's fingers in her bottom—softly lapping Regine, and what Victoria had just seen in the stillroom, all conspired and beckoned her to solitary pleasure. Victoria raised her dress, her fingers found her clitoris, and she gently soothed away its intimate passion.

The Game
Alison Tyler

And her bosom lick,
And upon her neck,
From his eyes of flame,
Ruby tears there came;
While the lioness
Loos'd her slender dress,
And naked they convey'd
To caves the sleeping maid.

—William Blake

Angel called that first party, almost two years ago, a trial by fire—having to meet the entire band at one time. But, honestly, I preferred it that way, plunged into the group without a chance to step back, to move away from the flames.

Still, I was scared. I tried to control my nerves as I slid off her Harley, then waited while she set her gloves and helmet on the rack. We'd parked her bike in the circular driveway, already filled with other, more decadent bikes, and we walked past them to the front of the house.

"Guess we're the last one's here," Angel said, leading me up the stairs and into Deleen DeMarco's Hollywood Hills estate. "That's good. You'll get to know everyone in about five seconds flat—then you can stop trembling and enjoy yourself."

I nodded and gripped her hand. As a model, you'd think I'd be used to meeting celebrities—especially since I'm considered one myself. But at this point, I was fairly new on the scene. And meeting the members of Objects—the band with the most number one hits in the country—was disconcerting, regardless of how many fashion shoots I'd done.

Angel pulled me along behind her, whispering assurances to me: "You'll do fine. They'll love you." We brushed past the multicolored balloons that filled the entryway, lolling against the molded doorways and fluttering softly up to the ceiling.

A poster of the new album cover, "Objects of Desire," was taped to one wall. It showed Angel, Deleen, Beauty, and Arianna totally nude with Keith Haring-style arrows pointing to their breasts and cunts. Lola, the cherub of the group with her blonde ringlets and innocent smile, sat naked in her wheelchair, staring up at the rest of the band.

As I looked at the picture, I realized how each woman derived power through individuality, and this calmed me down slightly. Angel's tattoos were starkly severe in the black and white photo, as if they'd been carved into her body. Arianna had painted stars and stripes on her breasts to make them more patriotic. Deleen was like a mad sorceress. She winked at the camera with an almost evil smirk, and rubbed her hands together with glee. Beauty, who's half German and half Native American, had braided her thick, black hair into a solid rope—it made her look dangerous, mean. She stood sideways between Deleen and Arianna, and her braid hung down her back, past her shoulder-blades, almost to her waist.

"That's the uncensored version," Angel told me. "The public receives a model with black X's covering the indecent parts."

I stared, fascinated by the curves and dips of the women's

bodies, their unique shapes, intricate designs, but Angel pulled on my hand, leading me into the sprawling living room.

The lights were dimmed, and I almost stumbled over a white cat walking up to greet us.

"Hey, Shazzam," Angel picked up the kitty. "I'd like you to meet Katrina."

I shook a fuzzy paw, and Beauty, staked out on a nearby sofa said, "Where are your manners, Angel? You introduce your lady to a pussy before us?"

Angel shrugged, set Shazzam gently on the ground, and said, "Everyone, I'd like you to meet Katrina. Katrina, this is everyone." She looked around the room. "Well, almost everyone. Where are our hosts?"

Arianna, reclining on a matching red leather chaise-lounge with her girlfriend, said, "Somewhere in the kitchen." She was covered by a petite Asian beauty named Sara, draped casually over her like a shawl.

"You should check out the spread," Beauty told us. "Tessa got the Sleeping Buddha to cater."

Angel and I turned then as Tessa appeared in the doorway, caught beneath the iridescent light filtering through a gathering of balloons. Tess is a true Irish red-head, her ivory skin sprinkled with millions of freckles like golden confetti. They seemed to sparkle across her nose and shoulders and over her cleavage, and I wondered if they covered her entire body, then blushed at the thought.

Deleen came up behind her carrying a glass of champagne in each hand.

"Hey, Angel. Who's the babe?"

"Deleen, really," Tessa admonished. "You're frightening her."

"This is Katrina," Angel said, her arm behind me, pushing me toward them. I shook hands with Tessa. Deleen, passing the champagne on to Arianna and Sara, took one of my hands in both of hers and kissed my fingertips.

"Charmed," she smiled.

"Help yourself to food," Tessa said, ignoring her flirtatious lover, "We've got a feast spread out in the dining room, buffet style."

Angel and I piled our plates, then walked back into the main room and settled onto the floor against a flood of satin pillows.

Tessa came to sit by my side.

She had on a strapless dress with a black bodice and a short skirt of fluffy lace. Her slender waist was accentuated with a wide velvet ribbon. I complimented her on the look and she said, "Thanks. Easy on, easy off," and then leaned across me to ask Angel a question, rubbing her breasts slightly against my knees.

I wondered if she'd done it on purpose, and then looked at her startled as she asked me a question.

"I'm sorry, what?"

"Do you know Lola?"

"No. I know of her, but we haven't met."

"She should be here later," Tessa said, looking at Angel to include her in the conversation. "Lo was meeting with a publisher in New York about doing a book of photos. They say she's the next Herb Ritz." She paused, as an idea came to her. "You know, she ought to take some of you."

"The two of you together," Deleen interrupted. "Now, that would be a picture."

I saw Angel nodding in agreement, but turned when Arianna leaned up on the sofa, Sara moving with her lover's body as if she were another limb.

"Add Sara, too," Arianna insisted.

"And, um," Beauty fumbled as a gorgeous strawberry blonde strolled in from the kitchen holding a bottle of mineral water. She walked up to Beauty and snuggled against her.

"Liz," she purred.

"Yeah, and Liz," Beauty finished, lamely, and the rest of us laughed, transforming an awkward moment into a rather silly one. Liz didn't seem to mind. She curled her long limbs around Beauty's, protectively, like an owner.

"I wouldn't get too comfortable if I were her," Tessa whispered to me. "Beauty left her last girlfriend on the plane when she met this one," Tessa nodded to Liz who was now kissing Beauty's earlobe. "Beauty has always had a problem with the word 'commitment.'"

Angel excused herself, then, to get more food, and Tessa took this opportunity to lean even closer to me. Her body pressed against my side so that I could feel her fragile ribs, the warm, bare skin of her upper chest on my arm.

"How long have you two been hiding out?" she asked me when Angel was out of the room. "We haven't seen much of Angel since the recording ended."

"A month," I told her, thinking in my head that it was thirty days exactly since she'd come with Melanie to the fashion shoot at Zebra.

"And you met..."

"Through Melanie Samuel." I waited for the recognition to appear in Tessa's eyes.

"The journalist?"

I nodded.

"You're on the cover of Zebra this month, aren't you?" she said, getting it.

I nodded again, giving her a quick version of the smoldering look they'd had me do for the shoot—the one currently appearing on every newsstand. Lashes lowered, head tilted, lips pouting.

"You seem different in person," Tessa said, smiling at me. "So much younger."

"That's the makeup," I explained. "But it's what Angel said, too. It's what she liked about me, I think, the person beneath the image." Everyone in the business knows about it, but only a few people allow others into their shell.

Angel had said, "Can I talk with you?" And I told her, knees trembling at the thought of talking with Angel McMorrow, lead singer in the hottest band in the country. "Hang out until I get this makeup off." She'd waited, outside the dressing room, chatting with Melanie who kept yelling for me to hurry up. I came out in a T-shirt and ripped jeans, my normal attire, and Angel looked me over and shook her head.

"You're younger than all that, aren't you?" she'd asked, glancing toward the lights and the fancy dresses hanging from a metal pole in "wardrobe."

"I'm the same age underneath" I grinned, "You just have to look beneath the surface."

Angel had nodded, moving in close to me as Melanie withdrew to answer her cellular phone in private. "Yeah, I would like to do just that, Katrina. I would like to see what's lurking beneath your surface, peel you open, spread you out, learn each of your secrets for myself."

Then Melanie had returned and things continued as normal—at least until the next time Angel and I were alone. Still, I didn't say any of these things to Tessa. She would know all about duplicity, two-faced worlds, being the partner of Deleen DeMarco—someone whose little black book contained the number of every 'in' person in Hollywood.

Angel came back then, now sitting on Tessa's side, and she gave me a look over Tessa's head that I took to mean, "How are you holding out?"

I shrugged back at her and then said, "Please," as Deleen stopped in front of me, with a fresh bottle of champagne. It surprised me at first that there wasn't any "help" at the party, but I was glad for it, glad for the low-key atmosphere. I could tell that these people were for real—not needing the constant stroking of fans or media.

Their house—mansion, really—was as kickback as they were—set up for comfort, not appearances, although all was stylishly done. There were pillows everywhere, velvet and satin striped, with butter-soft leather sofas. I hoped to decorate my own place in a similar fashion someday, wanting to be able to walk into a room, eyes closed (or blindfolded), and enjoy the surroundings by touch alone.

By my third bubble-filled glass, I was leaning against cushions, listening to Montage croon on the stereo, drifting in a warm fulfillment. I paid scant attention to Angel and Tessa who were discussing the promotion for "Objects of Desire." I watched as Arianna and Beauty gossiped across the space between their sofas, Sara describing her latest nude centerfold in Planet X magazine, and Liz, a first-class cabin attendant, explaining how Beauty had stolen her heart at 32,000 feet.

I wondered what had happened to the girl Beauty had been with, and I thought about asking Tessa, but she left to fetch a joint. When she returned to the living room, she was tottering on her spangled high heels.

"Want some, Angel?" she asked, collapsing on the pillows on Angel's left side, turning my lover into a "person sandwich" with Tess and me the bread.

"Naw, I'm saving my voice."

"Katrina?" she asked.

"Sure."

Marijuana goes to my head quickly, especially when I'm drinking, so I only took one hit, but Tessa apparently had been smoking in the bedroom. She was flying, and while I lit up, she leaned seductively against Angel and said, "You have the most beautiful brown eyes, Angel. You know it?"

Angel tried to brush her off, nicely, by saying, "Deleen's the one with the killer eyes." Angel turned to me, "Did you know that Del's eyes have no color?"

I was more stoned than I'd thought, because this statement tripped a string of bizarre images in my mind. "What do you mean?" I finally managed to ask.

"They're almost perfectly clear. She usually wears shades or colored lenses to hide them. Del!"

Deleen looked over from her lazy-lioness position in the hammock chair.

"What's up?" She was gone, too.

"Come show Kat your eyes."

"Send the kitty over here."

I got up, also a bit unbalanced, and wove my way to Deleen's corner. She turned a floor lamp around so that the light shone directly in her eyes, and I drew in my breath. They were like glass, perfectly clear irises with liquid black pupils in the center.

Deleen smiled at me, and said, "I always wear contacts for public appearances. I wouldn't want to scare anyone."

She put her hand out to steady me, I'd been rocking in place, and her fingers were like flames licking at my skin. Startled, I stumbled back to the pillow corner. Tessa was now in Angel's lap, her dress hiked up to her thighs exposing the purple ribbons of her garters as she straddled my lover. Angel didn't seem uncomfortable, but I could tell she was humoring Tess.

"You don't mind, do you Katrina?" Tessa grinned at me. "Angel has the most inviting body. I wanted to be closer to it."

"Go ahead," I said magnanimously as I leaned against the wall, letting it support me as I slid to a sitting position. "Do what you have to." I wanted to see how far Angel would take it, wanted to know what I'd be in store for in the future. At the moment she seemed to be letting Tessa call the shots.

Deleen got up then to open another bottle of champagne, and I saw a frown on her painted lips.

"What are you up to, Tess?" she asked, her buzz obviously worn off. Deleen's demeanor surprised me, considering how she'd flirted with me when we'd met.

"Just goin' for a ride," Tessa slurred, leaving no doubts that Angel was to be her horse.

Deleen clicked her tongue against the roof of her mouth, and then sat down on the nearest sofa, forcing Arianna and Sara aside. They protested for a second before resuming their positions: Sara had undone Arianna's leather jeans and was very quietly sucking on the strap-on dildo that Arianna wore in a harness. The darkness of the room had concealed their activity, but they didn't seem to mind being revealed. Arianna's moans and Sara's kitten-like suckling noises testified to that.

"What is it with you, Tessa?" Deleen's voice was very softly menacing. "It's been three hours since you last came, is that too long for you?"

Tessa looked at Deleen through clouded eyes. "I'm just entertaining our guests, Del," she said.

"Uh uh, baby, I'm not going to play that game." Deleen slid her hand through her silvery hair, apparently trying to calm herself, slow herself down. Deleen's hair is completely grey and has been since her teens. She wears it combed off her forehead, and it falls like an old lion's mane straight down her back. "Get your little ass over here."

Tessa stood up quickly, a worried look replacing the lecherous one she'd worn only a second earlier.

"Now," Deleen ordered, when she saw Tessa hesitate.

Angel watched the whole scene with her features set. She appeared emotionless, a statue, but I could tell she was getting turned on. I was already able to read her expressions, the slight wrinkle in her brow or tightening of her jaw. I settled against her and she put an arm around me, gently turning my face to kiss my lips.

Tessa cautiously walked the rest of the way over to Deleen, as if condemned. As soon as Tess was in reaching distance, Deleen grabbed hold of her waist and threw Tessa over her lap. Tess struggled, realizing suddenly what her Mistress meant to do, but Deleen held her firmly, scissoring one leg over Tessa's two squirming ones to keep her in place. Deleen lifted Tessa's dress by the hem, pulling it up to reveal a lavender lace G-string and matching garter belt.

"Katrina, would you mind bringing me my Harley gloves?" Deleen asked me, her voice unreadable except for the power in it, the command. "They're on the table in the entryway"

I looked at Angel to see if I should, but all she said was, "Go ahead, Kit-Kat, it's Del's party."

When I stood up, Deleen added, "Oh, and get me some K-Y, too, won't you? It's in the bathroom cabinet—the one in the hall." My heart racing, I left the room, gathered the tube of gel and the leather gloves, and walked back to Deleen who still held the upended Tessa over her knees.

"Thanks, sweetheart," Deleen said as I handed her the items. I turned to sit down next to my Mistress again, feeling weak and confused. Angel pulled me to her, positioning me between her legs so that I could feel the wetness that pulsed through her jeans.

Deleen slipped Tessa's G-string down her thighs, but left the garter and hose in place.

"Better calm down, Tess," her voice was hypnotic, and I realized suddenly that everyone in the room had turned to see what was going on. Sara and Arianna, after struggling into semi-upright positions, were watching intently. Liz and Beauty, who'd been up to something on their own plush sofa, were now mellowly regarding Tessa, Beauty softly explaining to Liz how Tess and Del's relationship worked. I heard Beauty say, "Don't worry, Lizzie, it's just how it is."

Deleen had her worn leather gloves on, and she squeezed a generous supply of the jelly onto one finger and then spread Tessa's ass cheeks with the other hand. Tessa continued to fight, but her slight frame was no match for Deleen's more powerful build.

"I said, calm down, Tessa."

Although Deleen hadn't raised her voice, there was a note of danger in it, one that made me sure that if I were in Tessa's position, I would be still. Tess must have sensed it, too, for she was suddenly quiet, yet I could tell her muscles were tensed to escape if Deleen would give her the chance.

"Tessa wants to come," Deleen said, addressing the rest of us as a group for the first time. "She has an insatiable appetite." As she spoke, she worked the K-Y around and into Tessa's asshole. When she slipped a gloved finger inside her naughty lover, Tessa started to protest again. Deleen put her lips close to Tessa's ear, but we all heard her hiss, "Once more, baby, and I'll get the studded gloves."

Now Deleen had two fingers inside her, and moved them in and out with increasing speed. She used her thumb on Tessa's clitoris, and Tess moaned, an obvious sound of pleasure that set off titters from Liz and Sara.

"Like that, don't you?" my Mistress whispered to me, and I nodded, leaning against her, feeling the hard synthetic cock that she was packing beneath the soft denim. Angel put both arms around me, protectively, as we continued to watch Deleen's progress with Tessa. Del was making her come slowly—bringing her close to climax, then teasing her down. When she'd forced three fingers into Tessa's asshole, Tess started to move against her Mistress, fucking Deleen's gloved hand, working her body on it, but Del would have none of that.

"Tessa, don't," she said, a warning in her voice. It was obvious that Deleen did not want her lover to take any form of control, and I could tell that it took every ounce of Tessa's strength for her to follow this command.

"I'll make you come in my own sweet time," Deleen promised, before turning her attention to me. "Katrina? Tess was..." she cleared her throat before saying, "riding your property. Would you like to be the one to punish her?" She paused to look at me before continuing. "Because as soon as she comes, she's going to need to be disciplined."

The blood drained from my cheeks, and I turned immediately to Angel for help, but my Mistress shook her head, leaving the decision up to me, testing me, I thought. Flashes of conversations with Melanie replayed themselves in my head. "Leather," she'd said, "Bondage and Dominance. Sex Games. Wild, wild parties."

"I couldn't," I whispered.

"Another time," Deleen said, letting me off with a reassuring smile. Then, in a completely different voice, a darker voice, "Did you hear me, Tess? You'd better try to slow it down, because I'm going to spank your little bottom as soon as you come."

Tessa started crying, and I knew it was because she was close to orgasm. And that, humiliating though it might be to come in front of everyone, being spanked would be worse. Deleen continued finger-fucking her asshole, and stroking her clit. I noticed how gently she stroked Tessa there, and understood that Beauty was right, that despite what Deleen had said, this was a game, with Tessa a willing player.

And then, with everyone's attention focused on her, Tessa flushed, closed her eyes tightly, and let her body finally respond to Deleen's attention. She arched her back, tense with concentration, and came in a series of powerful shivers, electricity running through her body.

The roomed seemed lit by her energy, a shower of metallic sparks, alien green and copper, vibrating in the air. She was truly stripped, as if Deleen had peeled her layer by layer, leaving a nude and shimmering soul for us to see.

How awesome it must feel to be that free.

"I've got a present for you," Angel told me on the evening after the party when I arrived home from work.

I set my satchel down on by the door and looked at her expectantly. "Really, what is it?"

I was thinking lingerie, maybe, or jewelry—the choker I'd admired in Cupid's Garden on Melrose— Angel's always surprising me. But I probably should have known better. Her brown eyes were glowing with a secret that implied sin. I'd seen that look before, the moment she fastened my collar around my throat for the first time, the feel of the leash as it hung down my naked back and rested, in a puddle of cool steel, at the base of my spine. I'd watched her reflection in the mirror, a vague glow in her eyes that revealed more to me than the tone of her voice, than the slap of her hand.

That was the look she gave me. So, really, I should have known.

"What is it?" I asked again, softer this time, more hesitant.

I was rewarded with a grin, her berry-stained lips curving upwards in a wicked smile. "Not what," she corrected, "Who."

"Who?" I repeated, dumbly, as Tessa, pretty red-headed Tessa, all but scampered out of the kitchen. She had on a pair of apricot-colored baby-doll pajamas trimmed with lace, and she held a bottle of beer in each hand.

"Want a drink, Katrina?" she asked, handing one to Angel.

"Sure," I told her, but I kept looking at Angel, attempting to send her a telepathic question. I was certain that Tess was my 'present,' but I wanted to know exactly what that meant.

Tessa handed me the other bottle and returned to the kitchen to get one for herself.

"So, do you like her?" Angel asked, nudging me. I couldn't quite read the expression on her face. "Do you, Kat?"

"Yeah," I whispered, thinking about how Tessa had behaved at the party the evening before. Or misbehaved, really. I could still picture her over Deleen's lap, could see those gloved fingers stroking Tessa's pale, freckled skin. I would own that image for a long time.

"What's up, Angel?" I managed to ask—though somewhere in the back of my head, I knew.

"She's yours for the night," Angel told me, still smiling in that slightly evil way of hers. "I'm afraid this gift is non-returnable, but I know that she's your size. I didn't think you'd want an exchange."

"What does she think is going to happen?"

"Whatever you want."

"Does Deleen know?"

"It was her idea."

Tessa came back into the room, put her arms around me, and whispered in my ear, "I'm so sorry about yesterday, Katrina—about flirting with Angel, I mean. I hope I can make it up to you."

"Why don't you two go to the bedroom," Angel suggested, and, my mind still a little numb, I looked hard at Tessa and then took her hand.

Angel had decorated our bedroom for the occasion. Silver streamers hung from the lamp, and tiny confetti stars covered the floor and furniture, glittering in the light from a few well-positioned candles. On the dresser, stood various bottles of perfumed oils, flavored lotions, and several wrapped boxes. I stood regarding the display as Angel came into the room, waiting just inside the doorway.

"Open the packages, Katrina."

I unwrapped the first one, my hands shaking, to find a battery-operated silver-hued vibrator molded like an elongated bullet. I twisted the knob at the base and it came to life, moving in my hand and making a low purring noise. Quickly, I shut it off and set it down on the dresser.

The next box held a pair of satin-lined handcuffs and a matching blindfold. I stroked the smooth fabric and lifted the heavy cuffs from their resting place. The weight felt good in my hands. Satisfying. I had an instant flash of Tessa captured to the bed with the cuffs, fastened securely—but kindly—nearly unable to move. That is the way Angel ties me, and for the first moment in my life I was sure I was capable of mimicking the behavior of a dominant.

The next present made me feel less so...

The long brown cardboard tube concealed a dark blue riding crop from the MOMA catalog, with an attached card that said this was a present from Deleen. The riding crop was light in my hands, and it made a sharp sound when it cut through the air. That sound would have struck fear in my heart had Angel been wielding it. As the Mistress, now, I only felt confusion. Could I use this on Tessa? Could I do it convincingly?

The last package, another gift from Angel, contained a pair of soft leather chaps and a leather vest, both in my size. I slipped the chaps over my tight jeans and the vest over my velvet tank. Then I looked up at Angel and Tessa. My slave waited patiently, leaning against the corner of the bed. My Mistress waited just as patiently, a bemused smile playing over her lips.

"So, you're the main gift?" I asked Tess.

"Yes, Katrina," she stared at me with her pale eyes, allowing me time to let everything sink in.

"And I'm supposed to use all of this on you?"

"She's ready and willing," Angel assured me. "And I'd like to see you in charge, Katrina. I would really like to see that."

Her voice let me know that this was a serious fantasy of hers, one that she had not yet revealed to me. Our sexual relationship thus far had been based on my subservience to her desires, my willingness to receive her pain. My need for it.

"I don't know if I can," I told her. "Angel, I don't know if I have that kind of power."

She shook her head, a frown marring her handsome features. Then she ran her fingers through her coal-black hair and stared hard at me, as if coming to a great decision.

Finally, she said, "We're going to have a little talk outside, Tessa. You make yourself comfortable on the bed, and we'll be right back."

Roughly, she grabbed my upper arm and dragged me from the room.

"I know you want to, Kat. I can feel it. And Deleen sent her here for you to punish. She expects visible proof, especially after Tessa's spectacle last night. You've got to make Tess sorry, okay? Right now she thinks this is just a game—but it's not. She deserves to be punished, and you've got to be angry enough to do it. Now, think of something that makes you mad. Think of the way she behaved at the party."

I tried to be angry about that, but I couldn't. She'd been so pretty, riding Angel, fucking her through her clothes. The image only made me wet, picturing Tessa's rumpled party dress up around her knees. How could I be mad about that? I felt the same way when I looked at Angel, wanted to do her wherever we were. And the repercussions—watching Deleen pull Tess over her lap, slip on her Harley gloves, and give that precious bottom a thorough spanking. Hadn't that been punishment enough.

(And pleasure, too?)

"Think, Katrina. Or I'm gonna have to send Tessa home and break out that stuff on your ass." A pause. "Or maybe I'll have her stay...and let her watch."

There, that was a threat I could handle. Regardless of how much I need pain, the thought of being humiliated in front of Tess made me tremble. Tessa requires the spectacle of it all in order to come. She needs public sex and public discipline—Angel had explained this to me after the party. I am much more private in my fantasies of being hurt. I like closed doors and drawn curtains. Angel says she'll help me get over this...but we haven't yet.

My jaw muscles tightened at the thought of being whipped in front of Tess, and Angel, who'd been regarding me intently, pushed me back through the door of our bedroom.

Tessa pouted prettily at me. She was checking out the different presents that lay amidst the wrapping paper on the dresser.

"I thought Angel told you to wait on the bed," I said to her, my voice hard even to my own ears. My heart was racing but I realized that I was doing a pretty good job when Tessa's eyes flashed at me before she lowered her lashes. I could read the look in them; they were filled with a hunger, a need.

"I was just looking…"

"I know what you were just doing," I said. "Now, get on the bed."

She scrambled to obey me, and I reached for the new set of handcuffs and came over beside her.

"On your stomach," I ordered, feeling an all-consuming rush steal through my veins.

"Hands clasped in the small of your back." Now, she was quick to do as I said, and I slid the cuffs on her wrists and fastened them. I decided to pass on the blindfold because I wanted to be able to see her eyes, but I went back to the dresser to grab a few of the other items. I made Tess wait there helplessly for a moment, and I watched her body tense and relax—the muscles shifting beneath the pale canvas of her skin. She was pure beauty in her fear.

How I loved her for it.

How I knew I could make her pay.

"Katrina?"

She was unsure of where I was in the room, what I was planning to do to her. Her fear fed me—made me even more powerful. I thought for a second, then decided to start the evening off with pleasure, to save the pain for later. Silently, I climbed onto the bed beside her, scented lotion in hand.

She sighed at the feel of my fingers beneath the waistband of her ruffled panties. I pulled them down her slender thighs, knowing that she thought I would spank her. Her body arched upwards, offering me the gift of her ass. I denied her. Instead, I leaned against her leg, rubbing the cool leather of my chaps against her hot skin, and she moaned a second time. I had complete control over her, could do anything I wanted.

I spread the cheeks of her ass slightly, and slid two fingers inside her pussy, wanting to feel if I'd already made her excited. She moved against me, trying to hide her face behind her hair, but it was captured with a silver ribbon, leaving her totally exposed to my inspection. I could see her blush, knew it was because she was wet, and we'd hardly even begun.

I slid her panties the rest of the way down her legs, and positioned myself between her spread thighs, wanting to feed on her.

There is something in the way a submissive moves that is inherently feline—but it's house-cat tame, tabby-cat hungry. A Mistress, however, possesses the heart of a lioness. I could feel my house-cat soul grow and spread in my chest. I could feel the ripple of muscles I wasn't aware of as I stretched my body and prepared to feast. I was changing before the eyes of my own Mistress, Angel. I was transforming, feeling the claws of my fingernails as they dragged down the backs of Tessa's thighs. Delighting in the way my breathing pattern slowed and grew steadier, steadier, while Tessa's sped up to a frantic pace.

I bent down, deciding to eat her from behind, the way Angel likes to taste me: A snack, an appetizer, before the main course of pain created the honeyed nectar for a true dessert. I spread her legs even wider apart and touched my tongue to the soft lips of her pussy. I used my thumbs to hold her open, and began sliding my tongue in and out of her, probing her, delving inside her. I had not tasted another woman since dating Angel, and the subtle difference that is always surprising to me managed to shock me again.

Tessa tasted of sin and delight, of rage and heat. She was wet for me from the start, but as I continued to work her, she rewarded me with an ever-present flow of sexual juices. I lapped at her lips, pinched them together with two fingers and licked the sweet stream that flowed even still.

"You're delicious," I told her, using the same hushed voice that Angel uses from this position, mimicking my Mistress. "Like a ripe fruit." I stroked the backs of her thighs—stark white except for the angry rakes left by my nails—while going down on her, and I could feel tiny shivers running through her legs. "Tell me what you want me to do," I said, my mouth against her so that she could feel the vibration of my voice echoing through her. "I want to know what turns you on the most."

She was breathless, grinding her pelvis in circles on the bed. Just a few more flicks with my tongue and she would come. I savored her like a dessert, rich, luscious, and, until tonight, forbidden.

"Please..." she whispered.

I sat up, though I continued to stroke her.

"Please what?" I asked.

"Put your fingers inside me," she begged.

I slid two fingers into the rising heat of her pussy. She tightened her muscles on me, my hand transformed into a cock. I put three fingers inside her and she seemed to sob with relief. I leaned against her, my heart beating so fast, fucking her as hard as I could, wanting to bring her off, to make her crazy with pleasure. I was divided: The Mistress with the power in control, the slave knowing exactly what it takes to come. I was all-powerful, knowing what she needed and having the ability to give it to her. I was transported with emotion, and I kept my eyes glued to her face to witness the moment when she reached the top and crested, the moment she came.

When it happened, I didn't stop the motions, but I slowed down, keeping my hand inside her, pressing inside her. I turned so that I could kiss her face, drink the salty tears spilling from her eyes, run my tongue along her bottom lip. I moved her onto her side, shifting so that my arm lay against her flat stomach, my fingers still deep inside her.

We were face to face, our breasts pressed together, hers covered by the lightest silk, mine sheathed in leather. I kept my hand working inside her, my tongue busy in her mouth, sucking the heat from her. The handcuffs on her wrists pulled behind her back, forcing her to arch her breasts into me, into the leather that brushed her hard nipples.

"Wait," I sighed, moving away again, and she opened her eyes to watch as I stripped off my clothes, grabbed the key for the handcuffs and undid them. I pulled her top over her head and untied the ribbon in her hair. It spilled free, and she shook it out, an ocean of ginger flowing down her back.

"Now," I told her. "Anything you want."

"Together," she said.

I put my hand out straight and she placed her own against it, palm to palm. She slid her fingertips down my fingers, lightly caressing my wrist, running the length of my arm. I copied her, touching her body as she touched mine, exploring. She bent to kiss my breasts, and I ran my hands through her hair, holding her head in place, moving as slowly and as gently as I could. I felt that if I rushed I might break into a million pieces, break into sharp crystal shards that would scatter glittering and dangerous across the bed and floor.

We lay on our sides again, facing each other, tentatively touching, our hands not seeming to belong to our bodies, endlessly roaming, learning. I slid a leg over her hip and turned so that I was straddling her, riding her as she'd done Angel at the party. She smiled at me, and I knew the same image had filled her own mind.

"Like this, Kat," she said, starting to rock gently beneath me. I matched her rhythm, let the waves begin to wash over me, waves of silk and satin, the hot sun beating down, golden sand beneath us, that obscene musky smell of woman. For a second, I thought about my silver bullet toy, my vibrator, and I found myself wondering whether she would like that, whether I could better please her if equipped with tools.

But she seemed to know what I was thinking, for she said, "No, honey. Just us. Just you and me."

And I sighed, at peace, and I followed her lead— moving on the bed, shifting and sliding. For the first time I found myself in a situation where I was an equal with a lover, knowing what I wanted done to myself and doing it to her...then realizing that she was doing the same things to me. My mouth on her cunt, drinking from the well of it—then shift, slip, slide— her mouth on mine, the quick dance of our bodies into that favorite position.

A 69 begs for equality.

Tongue to clit, caressing it with the wetness of my mouth, feeling her do the same to mine. So perfect and gentle at first that I thought I might swoon. Then faster and harder when those sensations began to build, when the pressure grew stronger. How I loved the feel of her skin as it warmed beneath my fingertips. I stroked her ass, parted the cheeks and ran my fingers down the exposed valley. She did the same, taking the lead for a moment to dip her finger in my juices and then impale me with just the tip of it.

And I caught up and echoed her movements—causing multiple and simultaneous sighs from both of us. In and out—our fingers fucking—our mouths sucking—our tongues tickling. The rhythm was hypnotic, undeniable, but I tried to hold on, to slow myself down. I wanted nothing but to come with her.

Fingers moving faster now, in and out and hard...and then two, two fingers wet and deep inside each other—and tongues still stroking, and mouths smeared and wet with liquid sex.

Divine. A feast like never before, the coming overpowering us and cascading us into second orgasms, into third, and fourth, until we were wrecked by it, wracked with the shuddering vibrations that only worked to perpetuate the pinnacle, the point of no return. Tessa starting it, her body bent into an S curve by the intensity, and her contractions, her spasms, pushing me over the edge, and then mine building hers again, and hers setting off mine...

We held each other afterwards, and Angel came over and sat on the edge of the bed, a look in her eyes that told only of understanding.

"I couldn't do it, Angel," I told her.

"I know, Kat. I'm sorry I asked."

Tessa lay curled up in my lap, her hair spread around her head in a fiery halo. I felt good looking at her, knowing I'd pleased her, that I wasn't able to give her pain. Wouldn't use that riding crop on her. And I realized that although power was intoxicating, and submission exhilarating, equality was sexy as well.

The Initiation of Caroline

Paul Little

I heard a timid knock at my door, and I bade her enter.

She was still naked, apart from a pair of fine black pumps. Made up impeccably, with her hair neatly combed, as ordered under penalty of whipping. A little pale, her eyes violet-circled, her nervous hands betraying her anguish. Her lovely naked titties, rising and falling quickly, seemed to offer one their rosy nipples—involuntarily, needless to say!

I pretended that I hardly noticed her and gestured toward the little bench placed near my armchair. With a fearful air, she seated herself, her thighs tightly squeezed together, her arms over her bosom to hide her splendid titties.

I smiled with amusement, but said nothing, continuing to smoke my cigarette and read the book I held in my hand. Finally, I decided to hurl my thunderbolt. Turning toward her, I stared straight at her, inwardly enchanted to see the fear that leaped into them.

"You're not at a tea party at the vicarage, Caroline. So it's useless for you to sit like that, with your arms crossed in that ugly way, your legs pressed together like a virgin. You must learn to sit down in a suitable fashion in my presence. Now stand up! Good...now, you're going to sit down as every slave must do before her Master. Now sit down...very straight...hands crossed behind your neck, arms well spread on each side, so as to stick out those lovely little titties you've no reason to hide. Come now, better than that—stick out your titties! Good...now open your legs!"

A shiver that announced imminent tears passed over her pale face, but after a few seconds' hesitation, her knees opened slightly.

"Open them! Spread them better than that! Perhaps you'd prefer to have me take the switch and incite you to livelier obedience?"

Her lips began to tremble, but she opened her legs, revealing the secret of her cunt, which I knew she would have longed to hide from my gaze. "Now that's better. But so it will be perfect, sit on the edge of the bench and push out your darling little cunt!"

She could not suppress another sob, but squirmed forward and arched out that adorable little quim of hers.

I felt passion rise in my prick. As I was completely naked under a silken robe, I should have every license, when the whim took me, to exhibit my big prick to modest little Caroline. For the time being, I leaned toward her and caressed the fawn-hued moss of her armpits, her titties palpitating to the quickened rhythm of her breathing, her belly tensing under my fingers, and then the curly fur of her cunt, whose yawning lips no longer concealed the inside of a lovely hole, bright pink and sweet to fuck!

"You're very lovely and exciting, Caroline," I said, tickling her clitoris, which made her start. I stared at her a moment without a word; then, raising my hand, I slapped her twice, first her right cheek, then the left, wrenching a terrified cry from her.

"No! Master! Master!" she cried shrilly.

"Good! Continue to call me thus. Besides, to refresh your memory in case you don't, I've the proper stimulant," I told her reaching behind me and bringing out a superb martinet with ebony handle and long green leather thongs. I saw anguish and terror mount in her beautiful tear-filled eyes, and I felt my big prick rise to savor its joy.

"Caroline, we're going to proceed to the first stage of your education as a slave. I'm going to teach you certain words and expressions which will be necessary for you to know and employ at the opportune time. Perhaps you may even already know some of them, but we'll find out. However, I warn you once and for all that a slave must not—must never—lie to her Master. It is an unpardonable fault which is punished very severely. Now, then, consider yourself duly warned."

I then pointed a finger toward her jutting bosom and asked, "Do you know what one calls those lovely things?"

"I-I—I don't know," she stammered, red with confusion.

"They're titties, or bubbies," I said calmly. "And now, tell me what they're called."

"Ah—er—I—m-my—t-titties—my—b-bubbies." Her face was as red as a beet.

Without hesitation, I lifted my arm and slashed the thongs of the martinet over those lovely globes, which seemed to dance under the clinging kiss of the whip, while she fell backward, shrieking with agony, clutching her bosom. Long livid streaks encircled those darling titties, ornamenting them magnificently.

I pointed the martinet at her. "Good. Now, we'll proceed the same way for the other parts of your charming nakedness. The place which the Countess and I have already occupied ourselves a good deal with you is called the ass. But you knew that, didn't you?"

"Y...Yes...M-M-Master."

"Then say it!"

"It is...my...my ass...M-Master...my...a-ass."

And Caroline began to cry.

"Yes, my beautiful miss, it's your ass, your lovely girlish ass, for which I reserve many a surprise, I promise you. But that isn't all. That lovely ass is composed of two beautiful buttocks, and when one spreads them open, what does one see?"

"I—I d-don't know—"

With violent backhand blows, I whipped her titties furiously. A frenzied shriek tore from Caroline who again flung herself, crying and sobbing, on the rug.

"Back in your seat, back, at once!" I cried, slashing the cruel thongs right against her tender satiny belly.

Caroline leaped wildly to her place, crying, and painfully resumed her seat, thighs open, hands behind her neck.

I examined her titties, which had begun to redden and swell where the leather thongs had traced dark pink stripes. I took her nipples between the thumb and forefinger of each hand and squeezed them with all my might as I pulled on them.

Under the torture, Caroline began to totter. Leaving her position, she gripped my wrists to try to release those wounded tidbits, uttering clamorous shrieks.

"Answer me!" I roared. "What do they call what's between your buttocks?"

Choking with agony, Caroline uttered unintelligible cries, and finally managed to articulate:

"Aagghhh...no...noooooooo...oooggghhhh...aaaanus...m-my aaaanus!!"

I released her. "Little bitch, take the position at once. You see, you knew it, didn't you? I warned you not to lie to me!"

"Oooh...ooooh!" she sobbed. It was enough to move a stone statue—but not myself, I assure you! "P-Pardon...pardon...M-Master...but don't hurt me so...Oooh...oooahhh...my b-breasts... ohh, my breasts!"

"No pity for you if you lie again," I warned as I took up my martinet. "Repeat it now!"

"M-my anus, Master," she groaned, then began to sob hysterically.

"Yes, yes, dear Caroline, it's your anus. Your bunghole...your asshole...and I reserve for that dainty asshole of yours a special treatment all my own. It's a particularly sensitive spot, quite susceptible in training a disobedient girl like you. Do you know what one can do to a woman's anus?"

"Noooo, M-Master, I—I swear it—"

"I believe you this time, dear Caroline, for these are things which well-brought-up young ladies like you scarcely have occasion to learn, or at least to discuss. That is why I'm going to teach you what awaits you."

I let this sink in for a moment. "First, from the viewpoint of punishment, one can bury various stretching objects in the anus, or whip your bunghole with the aid of a special lash made of rubber, which, I must confess to you, is extremely painful. Or again, in case of refusal to obey, thrust in a cotton tampon soaked in hot eau de cologne, a punishment which causes much suffering."

Caroline stared at me, her mouth gaping with terror. Without taking note of her frightened stupor, I continued jubilantly, "However, before all else, your asshole, lovely slave, is made to be buggered! I mean that for a man—your Master—to bury his erect prick into it and take his full joy within its dainty depths!"

Caroline couldn't hold back a horrified exclamation. "Ooh! No, no!" she protested. "Ooooh! Why—Why do you tell me such horrible things? N-No-No, I beg you...I beg you, Sir!"

"Oh, but yes indeed, my dear! One day you will be bottom-fucked, yes, buggered, and I warn you that generally it hurts a good deal, especially if the slave is buggered as a punishment." I chuckled as she shrank from me. "Think now"—and I opened my robe to expose my enormous prong standing up like a stallion's cock—"think now, Caroline, what you'll feel when this huge thing buries itself pitilessly in your tight, sensitive asshole. Sincerely, I've almost pity for you, and yet, you must receive it all entirely, up to here." I pointed to my heavy balls.

But this time, it was truly too much for her offended modesty and for her pride as a young lady accustomed to the respect and adulation of her admirers.

"Oh, you ignoble brute! How dare you say such things to a young girl? You're low, a shameless creature—oh, I detest you, I hate you!" And she burst into sobs and despairing cries.

To tell the truth, I had expected that, for I had deliberately used crude, obscene words to excite her disgust. I sprang up and, gripping her by the hair, dragged her head back violently. With all my might, I began to lash her titties, belly, thighs, and arms, when these latter tried to protect the vulnerable and most tempting portions of her delectable anatomy.

My room was filled with the clamor of her suffering and terror; and the more she cried out, wept and complained, the more it excited me and the more I whipped her, till her titties jiggled from one side to the other under the terrible lashes of the martinet, which I applied pitilessly to their round, jutting curves, thrilling with delicious joy to cause her such agony that, at the same time, struck home at her prudery.

The correction was so severe that suddenly she went limp in my arms. She had fainted, for I had forgotten to give her a fortifying injection which would have prevented her losing consciousness under the mounting threshold of the pain I bestowed upon her so joyously.

My prick was on fire and agonized me, so violently had I been roused to a full hard-on, but I was quite able to restrain myself and occupy myself with my victim as I must do before taking my pleasure with her. I promised myself that pleasure for later in the afternoon. Till then, I preferred to remain in full erection so I might better train my beautiful pupil, for I was far from having finished with her.

I gave her a stimulant to revive her and avoid a new fainting spell. Afterward, when trembling with terror and half-choked by her sobs, she had recovered, I hectored her while she moved her trembling hands timidly over her poor reddened and streaked titties, marked by the vigorous lashing I'd inflicted on them.

"Filthy little bitch! Is that the way you profit from my lessons? Ah, you rebuff me! So you call me filthy and low, I, your trainer! Very well, my dear, I know what has to be done. This evening, I'll lock you up in the Silver Cage, and not for an hour, nor for even four or five, but all night long! That will teach you, I wager!"

Only her despairing plaints answered my pronouncements. As usual, I quite ignored them. "And now," I continued, "we shall pursue our lesson. Don't try that little comedy again, or you'll earn yourself a visit to the Room of Punishments."

I glared at her, smiled to see her recoil. "For now, it's necessary that you learn the art and manner of exhibiting your charms when your Master orders you to do so. You'll begin by kneeling and presenting me with your lovely naked ass!"

"Ooooh! No—n-noooo—oh, pl-please," she begged me, clasping her hands and lifting them toward me as in prayer.

I bent over her and terribly aroused, kissed her lingeringly on the mouth. I felt her stiffen with despair when my tongue slithered between her lips. Then she submitted passively to that further exquisite humiliation.

I stood up and moved away from her. "Do you want me to take you right away to the Room of Punishments?" I demanded.

"Nooo! Oh, noo!"

"Very well, then do at once what I told you to do. Get on all fours, and stick your lovely ass out toward me. Offer it humbly!" And making the martinet whistle in the air above her, I added, "Don't try to push my patience to the end, Caroline."

With a long groan filled with despair, she finally placed herself on her hands and knees.

"Hoist that lovely backside still more!" I threatened.

"Ooooh, please—ohh n-not that, pl-please," she kept supplicating, weeping with all her heart.

I approached her swiftly and applied two terrible strokes across her naked behind, which tore piercing cries from her.

"I told you to present your ass properly! You must obey me without reservation! Lift your buttocks still more, and present them the way they should be for my inspection!" I waited a moment, glowering at her, and watched her obey shudderingly. "There, that's already much better. Now, beautiful little slave, you're going to put your hands behind you and of your own accord open up your lovely buttocks so I may properly examine your little cunt and your asshole!"

She seemed to hesitate for a few seconds. Then—suddenly—

taking me by surprise, since I believed her mastered, she flung herself forward with a cry of rage and revolt: "No! No!" she began to shriek furiously, "you've no right to make me do that! Filthy swine, disgusting scoundrel, I won't do it! I won't do it, no, no, no!"

She ran toward the door of my room, and with all the strength of her revulsion and despair, sought to open it. Needless to say, I'd taken the elementary precaution of locking it. When she discovered there was no possible way out, she slumped against the wooden panel, sobbing and weeping with abysmal despair.

I flung myself on her, crying out in a hoarse, furious voice: "Filthy little slut! Ah, you wanted to escape, did you? So, you don't want to obey? Well, I'll make you pay for that! You've just earned yourself a trip to the Room of Punishments, and I beg you to believe that we shall both have fun there!"

Caroline threw herself down on the rug, kicking and screaming, "Help! Help! Oh, God, won't someone help me?"

I plunged one hand into her long, silky tresses, and slipping my other hand between her thighs, despite the maddened resistance she tried to oppose, dug three fingers into her vagina. Having thus harpooned her, I lifted her with a sudden thrust of my loins and bore her shrieking and wriggling toward the dungeon and the Room of Punishments.

Once there, I flung her on her belly over the heavy wooden horse and, overpowering her kickings and squirmings, buckled round her ankles the leather cuffs sealed into the back legs of the apparatus. Then I immobilized her wrists the same way. Next I encircled her waist with the broad leather strap, which pinned her belly against the punishment horse.

"Nooooo! Ohhhh! Help! Help!" she shrieked, absolutely terrorized now, for she was becoming aware that her rebellion was going to cost her dearly.

"Yes, cry out as much as you want, beautiful bitch! Here, no one will hear you, except myself. And the more you cry out, the more it will arouse my prick! Look at this!" I flung off my robe to show her my huge prick throbbing, swollen, ready to explode its jismic burden. And stark naked, my prick bobbing as I walked, I strode around the punishment horse.

Because of its special construction, the horse was higher and wider at the rear part than at the front, to raise and totally distend the bottomcheeks of the victim attached to it. Hence I had under my eager eyes the most intimate view of Caroline's maiden secrets. In the amber cleft of her behind, the delicious bunghole, a dark pink aureole with silky blonde hairs; and then beneath, framed by the rich profusion of silky tufts, her vulva, yawning to expose the humid, bright red interior of the vagina, that exquisite channel for fucking!

What a delicious, exciting spectacle it was!

"So, little whore," I laughed, "you didn't want to show me your cunt and your asshole? But do you know that at this very moment, I see them as clearly as a doctor examining you would be able to do? I see them, and you can't prevent me." Even so, she tightened her muscles frantically, groaning and sobbing, in the feverish hope of contracting her bottomcheeks. But the straddle imposed upon her by the contours of the horse was such that she could do absolutely nothing except remain there, opened, offered, powerless to avert whatever I pleased to do to her.

"I'm going to kiss your ass…I'm going to lick your asshole and your pussy—do you hear me, Caroline? You're going to feel my tongue in your vagina, in your lovely cunt! You're going to feel it dig into your dainty little asshole!" I pronounced delightedly.

"Noooooo! Ooooh! Nooooo!" she gasped in a horrified voice.

With a mocking laugh, I bent over her till my face brushed

the cheeks of her distended naked bottom. I kissed that dainty, crinkly little mouth, whose silky hairs tickled my lips most agreeably; then with my hardened, pointed tongue, I forced the tender petals to open, and I buried my tongue in the warm little canal of soft, quaking flesh. Her asshole rejected my tongue with a violent nervous spasm.

Without wanting to make an issue over this sign of ill will, this time I put my mouth right against her pussylips, and I took a long moment in sucking and licking that soft moist flesh. This time my tongue plunged its entire length into her vagina. My lips grabbed the nodule of her clitoris, which began to harden under that intimate caress.

"You've got a hard-on! You've got a hard-on!" I teased Caroline, who burst into tears of shame and confusion. "Now give me your sweet little bunghole," I ordered; once again, pointing my tongue as if it were a veritable prick, I tried to force my way through that narrow little slit of crinkly, rosy flesh, but once again a nervous reflex on her part repulsed my tongue.

At once my sadistic instincts took over! "Ah, you little whore, you squeeze your ass shut, do you? You don't want to let me train you? Well, we'll see!" I cried angrily. Then, posing the tip of my index finger against her asshole, which glistened with my saliva, I thrust forward violently, and brutally buried my finger—up to my very palm—inside her bunghole!

Caroline uttered a strident cry: "You're hurting meee! *Ahhhh!* You're hurting me!" she shrieked, trying to turn her head toward me.

"So much the better. I want to hurt you...a good deal more, you'll see!"

I tore my finger out of her anus, wresting a new shriek from the young beauty. But I hadn't finished. This time, I stuck out my index and middle fingers together toward that dainty orifice. I saw her asshole become deformed and distend hugely around my two fingers, which I forced into her recalcitrant rectum. Then, after twisting them about several times, I pulled them out savagely. Her asshole was already reddened and congested. Caroline shrieked and sobbed, but she could do nothing at all to prevent my vicious caresses.

Now I placed my index, middle and ring fingers all in line, forming a sort of cone, which I tried to bury into her dainty bunghole. Her howls of suffering rose louder and louder as my fingers advanced. Her asshole was stretched out abnormally now, as it was when, with an accentuation of wrist pressure, I almost managed to penetrate it to the base of my three fingers.

Caroline uttered pitiful cries; leaning forward a little, I could see her fingers clawing madly at the legs of the punishment horse under the crisis of suffering that was lacerating her tender behind.

I wished I could have buggered her right then and there, dry, to make her suffer and bellow a good deal more; but, alas, the time had not yet come for that, and so, regretfully, I slowly removed my fingers from her lovely backside, which spasmed frenetically in its owner's intolerable agony.

For a few indescribably delicious moments, I contemplated Caroline's swollen anus, agitated by nervous flexions. Then I went to the wall from which I unhooked the whalebone switch, and moved in front of the punishment horse to show it to my victim.

Her face bathed in tears, Caroline lifted terrified eyes to the instrument she already knew so well, alas, and which I waved sadistically in front of her.

"Well, Caroline, this is the first time your titties and belly are in contact with the horse, but you may be sure it's not the last—far from it, my beauty!" I announced. "And now, I'm going to give you a real whipping; I'm going to lash you without pity, which will teach you, my dear, to profit from the lessons and the warnings I give you. You're here to be trained, to be whipped, to be conquered, my beauty; and you can believe that from my experience in such matters, you assuredly will be!"

While I harangued her thus, I seized her hair to lift her head above the horse, and I amused myself with tapping her cheeks gently with the whalebone. When I let her go, her head fell back onto the arched punishment horse while she redoubled her sobbing pleas for mercy.

Every nerve in my body vibrated with pleasure. This is what I loved above all else: to have a girl at my mercy and whip her without pity. I had the erection of a stallion in full heat. My prick was enormous. If I had buggered her at this moment, I should have broken her backside for her! Alas, as I've already explained, the time for that kind of amusement was still in the future, so I had to content myself with flogging her.

I took my place before the apparatus and there, my legs planted astride to ensure my balance, my prick throbbing up toward my belly, I raised my arm with the supple whalebone and, with all the force of my wrist, I lowered it across her white bottomcheeks.

Instantly Caroline jerked up her head. A strident shriek sprang from her throat. She was tormented by the horrible searing that had bitten into her behind. A long livid weal encircled her lovely bottomcheeks, shuddering and trembling in spasms of pain. When at last she had regained her breath, it was to shriek aloud, her agony echoing from wall to wall. I pivoted and, with all my strength, dealt her a second stroke of the switch that was far worse than the first.

There was a sudden silence, for the excessive agony had cut off Caroline's breath momentarily. Then, suddenly, she burst into deafening clamors. I knew that, wielded in this fashion, the whalebone must hurt abominably, but that only excited me more. Without pausing, I lashed her lovely behind with all my might.

Spacing the lashes methodically from ten to fifteen seconds apart, I inflicted cut after cut. Caroline shrieked with all the power of her lungs. She was like a madwoman. Her gaping mouth dripped saliva onto her chin. It mingled with the tears that streamed down her cheeks. Her neck was stretched so much that the tendons stood out against her sweating skin, and her eyes were so enlarged by her suffering that they seemed about to pop out of their sockets.

Weal after weal, stripe after stripe...my strokes fell regularly...five...then ten...from ten to fifteen...from fifteen to twenty. Caroline was really bellowing with agony. You could hardly believe that a lovely young girl like her could scream so loudly! My prick was almost clinging to my belly, so exquisitely was I in rut.

Oh, the joy that shook me at each stroke I inflicted. Oh, the exquisite pleasure to hear and see the thin flexible switch bite into the tender flesh of those satiny bare bottomcheeks of hers! Oh, the delicious sensation of hearing her shriek and imagine how she must be suffering under the cuts I gave her!

Lash after lash, stripe after stripe, without pity or compassion. Hadn't I told her I was going to show her what a real whipping was like, so she'd remember it a long while?

By now, the pale flesh of her bare bottom had virtually disappeared under a network of swollen weals that painted her behind a dark pink. In my flagellatory excitement, I didn't notice at once that between the thirtieth and fortieth lashes, my victim had finally lost consciousness, despite the injection I had given her to prolong her resistance. I stopped, panting, my forehead dripping with sweat, and I went back to the wall where I hung up the switch that had done such yeoman service.

Then, too excited to hold myself back any longer, I bent over the burning backside of my victim and, pressing my huge prick between her scarlet bottomcheeks, I masturbated deliciously. I needed only a few strokes along the amber valley between those soft quivering globes to unleash my spunk. Suddenly—with cries and groans of ecstasy—I spurted copious jets of thick white sperm over the unconscious Caroline's martyred behind.

At last I straightened up. I rubbed my viscous white semen over her lovely ass, as if anointing her with a soothing balm. When the two globes were thoroughly impregnated with my sperm, I took a flask of smelling salts and held it under her nostrils. Then, when she was nearly revived, I left the Room of Punishments.

I wanted a drink to calm my nerves, as well as to give my pupil time to recuperate after the terrible shock she had just endured.

About two hours later, I returned to see how Caroline was enduring her captivity, for she had remained bound to the whipping horse.

When I entered the Room of Punishments, there was such a silence that I feared for a moment she might still be unconscious, but much to my relief, I realized that such was not the case. At the sound of my footsteps, I saw her start violently. Her lovely naked body began to tremble with terror.

Her face rested on the side of the forward section of the horse, and one of her eyes fixed me with the terrified expression of a rabbit fascinated by a snake. I heard her groan softly.

"How's your pretty little ass, Caroline?" I asked, feigning compassion.

She began to weep and turned her face away. I dug my fingers into her hair, making her cry out in pain. "You mustn't turn your face away when your Master or your trainer speaks to you. That's something you must know once and for all," I reprimanded her.

Stretching out my arm, I drew toward me a slender adjustable chain dangling from the ceiling with a rather wide ring at its free end. I thrust a sheaf of her silky, perfumed hair through the ring and knotted it all around, then hoisted up the chain. It lifted Caroline's head and forced her to remain with her neck stretched painfully and her face visible. The poor darling wept like a child who is crushed by grief. Big tears began to roll down her pale cheeks again.

"I'm going to leave you this way till it's time for your meal. I hope this will be salutary to you and that this afternoon, when we resume our lesson in obedience, you'll be a little more supple and docile, my beautiful little miss! Try to be good now."

I left the room, pursued by her lamentations, but not till I had caressed lingeringly and savoringly the sweet little cunt she offered me so prettily.

After the excellent meal I forced her to eat (for there was no question of restraining her as to diet; quite the contrary, it was important that she regain her strength), I generously allowed her three hours of rest, then went to take her out of the room and bring her back to mine, as I had done in the morning.

After having made her resume the initial position with hands crossed on her nape and thighs spread wide, I began the educational session that had been interrupted so annoyingly in the morning.

"We shall see if you know your lesson, Caroline. What are those called?" I asked calmly as I fondled her breasts.

"My...my t-titties...Master."

"Very good. And what do they call the little orifice of your behind?"

"I—m-my—anus, M-Master."

"And besides?"

"My b-bung-hole...my...my...ass...ass...asshole," she breathed, blushing and lowering her eyes.

"Good, that's very good. Now, name for me the slit that hides under those lovely curly hairs."

Caroline began to tremble a little and raised supplicating eyes to me. "M-My s-sex...my s-slit...or my v-vulva?"

"No, that's not it at all!" I said in a cold tone. "Yet you've heard me tell you enough what the word is! All right, I'm waiting!"

She cast me a terrified glance. "I—it's my...my...c-cunt...."

"Say it better than that, three times!"

"My cunt...my cunt...my cunt..."

Already, to my great pleasure, I saw her lips trembling and her eyes fill with tears. I untied the belt of my robe and took it off. Caroline started and lowered her eyes instinctively. Already, my big prick was half-erect, like the neck of a swan.

"And that—do you know its name?"

"It—It—It's your sex organ, M-Master," she stammered, turning her head away.

"Look at it! Look at it right away!" I commanded. "It's called a prick, a cock, a whang...all right, now, repeat all that!"

Her eyes fixed on my stiffening cock with apprehension and revulsion, Caroline Martin had to repeat clearly: "It's your prick, your cock, your whang."

"Repeat again! You must know those lovely words, and you must know them well!"

"The p-prick...the...the c-cock...the wh-whang...the...the whang..." Saying this, tears ran freely down her suffering face.

And so, for half an hour, ignoring her horrified stammering, I taught her and forced her to repeat a lengthy collection of erotic words and expressions. My pleasure was in seeing this young girl, whose lips till now had been so used to the most intellectual and sophisticated phrases, obliged to explain to me, suffocated with shame and humiliation, the meaning of such words as: fuck, bugger, shit, frig, brown, pull prick out of bung, spurt, fuck ass, French, a blowjob, suck balls, and so on. And Caroline was half-dead with shame when at last I judged the moment ripe to pass on to the next step.

"Despite your stilted attitude of a young lady of society, I'm certain you already know some of these words. "Besides, you aren't a virgin, so you must already have got yourself fucked."

She was speechless and could only weep in confusion.

"Come on, answer me when I ask you a question—and above all, pay attention not to lie, because you know what it costs you!"

"Y-Yes."

"Yes, what?"

"I—I—g-got my-myself...f-fucked." As she stammered this, she burst into touching little sobs. It was easy to see that such a confession was not easy for a debutante like Caroline Martin to make.

I stared at her for a moment, caressing my cock slowly as her horror-filled eyes watched my obscene gestures. "And you love to be fucked. Tell me, Caroline, you love to feel a big hard prick dig into your cunt, don't you?"

"Oooooh! Ooooohh!! Ooooohhh!!!" She didn't answer but went on weeping without restraint.

"Look at my prick!" I ordered. "Look at it! Doesn't it make you hot? Wouldn't you love to have a long, thick, hard prick like that in your nice little cunt? Look at that juicy piece—tell me, does it please you?"

"Ooooooh! S-Sir...please-n-n-ooooh—n-no!"

"What? It doesn't please you?" I feigned anger.

"Y-yes...Ohhhh! Yes...it-it's l-lovely...it-it's...lovely," she blurted, her words interspersed with hot tears and choking little sobs.

"And why does this prick of mine please you so much? Tell me, lovely little fucker that you are," I went on, without pity for her modesty.

She knew what she had to say to please me, or the whip would enter into play; so she forced herself to explain to me in a voice broken by sobs: "It...it's b-because it...it's v-very b-beautiful...very big...it...it's enormous...it...it's an en-enormous p-prick...th-that's w-why I love it." And she burst into heartrending sobs.

"And my balls, do they please you too?" I demanded imperturbably.

"Y-y-yes, y-y-your b-balls...a-are...e-enormous, also."

"I see," I said with a mocking laugh. "I see you're a vicious little whore, who loves big whangs. Well, be satisfied, my beautiful Caroline. You shall have it—you shall have it soon, I promise you, and right up to the balls! You'll have it in your cunt and also in your ass! I think your ass is still virgin, isn't it?"

"Ooooohhh...M-Master...S-Sir."

I went on, ignoring her horrified expression. "Well, my little one, I shall take charge of deflowering that sweet ass of yours. And when you've received my big cock in your asshole, believe me, Caroline, you'll no longer fear suppositories!" I exclaimed as I frigged my huge cock to let her see what she was going to have to swallow when the time came.

She was ready to be sick from the horror that rose up in her, but I was far from finishing with her, and so I resumed my little discourse: "I understand very well that you're impatient to be buggered by such a handsome shaft, but your little hole must wait and content itself for the moment with my tongue or fingers, for the taking of your asshole virginity, my dove, is to be done before the Countess, who dearly loves to witness such a spectacle."

Hearing these last words, the poor little debutante was ready to faint. She redoubled her despairing groans.

"However, while waiting, we may occupy ourselves in another way," I said to her as if I did not notice her despair. "Stand up and come kneel before me." As I gave her that command, I sat down on the edge of my bed, my legs spread wide. Caroline came over and kneeled before me.

"Come closer," I told her, and she crawled forward a little on her knees, her hands still crossed on the nape of her neck.

"Closer still! Between my legs!"

"Pl-please...n-no...please," she cried, but she nevertheless obeyed. She was now kneeling right between my thighs, petrified before my huge prick as a mouse before a hungry cat. My prick was not more than an inch from her lovely contorted face. Its glistening, taut skin was so swollen that anyone would have thought it was on the verge of spurting.

"Although you may already be acquainted with fucking," I explained pedantically, as a schoolteacher might to a most attentive pupil—which she was!—"you've lots of things to learn. Things that your future Master will demand of you for his own pleasure. First of all, you must know that a slave must not content herself just to receive her Master's prick, though of course it may be for him one of the major pleasures. There are, for example, many delicious preliminaries, tasty perversions, and it is a slave's duty to know how to practice them in order to bring the Master's joy to the zenith and to spice it with infinite variety. I hope I make myself clearly understood?"

A groan escaped poor Caroline's throat. I knew she would certainly have given a great deal to be anywhere else in the world at this moment.

"Stop sniveling!" I ordered. "Otherwise, I'll give you something to really cry about! I'm going to teach you now one of the perversions of which I've just spoken. Nature has endowed you with a pair of lovely titties, soft, supple and firm all at once, delicious to touch and to look at. However, they are not only two splendid polarities of erotic attraction, they can do something else. Notably, they can provide a deliciously soft and satiny sheath for the Master's prick. That is what you're going to do—right away!"

Caroline stared at me as if she did not comprehend a single word. Smiling cruelly, I went on: "Approach a little more now, and then lift your titties a bit and bring them together. Then lower yourself slightly so that my prick no longer lodges between them; press them tightly together to pinch my prick between them. After that, you'll make them stir gently, while moving your bosom up and down, so as to frig my cock with your two lovely titties!"

While I thus instructed her, Caroline's face took on a look of horrified revulsion.

"No! Ohh! No...no...no!"

"Come on now, approach and do what I've just explained!" I glared at her.

"Oh, pl-please, Sir...I couldn't...I couldn't... Oh, I beg of you!" she choked, staring at me in the most appealing way you can imagine.

"I shall give you exactly ten seconds, Caroline."

"Oooohh! No...ohh! No...I can't...no, not that...it—it's frightful!" She began to cry and half-rose.

As you can imagine, I was in a state of ferocious excitement. With feverish impatience, I awaited that contact which I divined would be so infinitely soft and caressing: the clutching pressure of her two beautiful titties against my huge throbbing cock.

To be sure, I hadn't really counted on an immediate realization of my desire, nor one that would take place at once, docilely and without discussion. But the very notion that my haughty new pupil might perform that erotic perversion on me without hesitation was so stirring that I absolutely wanted her to do it to me right away.

However, Caroline didn't seem to be so disposed; half-risen, half-squatting, she stared at me with the frightened eyes of an animal caught in a trap.

My frustration was too great; I leaned over her quickly and, seizing her by her long hair, I dragged her violently toward me, making her cry out and struggle, while I gloatingly rubbed her face against my huge penis and my hairy balls.

Then, as she kept struggling and even clawed my thighs, rage overcame me. Tugging her hair back ferociously, I stuck my face up against hers, my gaze plunging into her terrorized eyes. "Very well, little bitch; you asked for it, you're going to get it!"

"Pity—pity—" She began to sob while I forced her to rise. Dragging her up by her hair and forcing her over to a leather chair, I flung her over the arm. To be sure, she struggled wildly, but quite in vain. I twisted one of her arms behind her back and began to apply a hail of dry, crisp smacks on her lovely naked backside, using all the strength of my arm.

Her buttocks were still severely reddened and swollen by all I had made them endure that morning. Soon they turned as burning a scarlet as hell itself.

Caroline yelled and screeched with all the power of her youthful lungs, and her long, sensually exciting legs waved wildly in empty space as she tried to kick free. Her bottomglobes bounded under the beating, sometimes contracting till the shadowy groove leading to her virgin asshole almost disappeared, then yawning to expose that dainty, hairy little hole and the base of the plump slit of her cunt, all in the vain hope of minimizing the burning fire that punished her voluptuous backside.

Without letting myself be softened by her endless plaints and shrieks, I continued to give her a spanking of exemplary vigor. "I've already told you that a slave must obey, Caroline," I lectured as I pitilessly beat that beautiful ass which was now as red as a ripe tomato. "And if you don't obey, you shall be chastised severely!"

But soon my hand began to burn and hurt me, so I halted the correction, to Caroline's great relief. She believed I had finished with her. What an error that was on her part!

Leaving her to sob and cry over the arm of the chair, so crushed that she didn't even try to rise, I strode to my dressing table and seized an oval hairbrush with a rather long handle. Holding it like a tennis racquet, I returned to my disobedient pupil and, placing a hand at the hollow of her loins to immobilize her, I raised my arm and applied the back of the brush to her crimson buttocks.

It smacked like a pistol shot on that burning skin, and it must have hurt a great deal, for my pupil kicked frenziedly and uttered a piercing shriek. My prick gave a convulsive jerk of pleasure, and I applied a second blow as biting as the first on that swollen bottom.

"Well, Caroline, have you changed your mind? You'll tell me when you'll agree to using your big titties to give me pleasure. But take your time—I'm in no hurry." And I applied another smack with the hairbrush, this time right at the base of her behind, near the thighs.

The pain was so scorching that it cut off her breath, but as soon as she had regained it, she resumed wailing out her torment. I gave her another good smack with all my might right over the lower curves of those fiery bottomglobes. And through the shrieks that filled the room, I gathered she was trying to tell me something.

I stopped beating her. Recovering my own quickened, panting breath, I waited for more coherent words. But almost with haste, terrified at the idea of receiving more blows from the hairbrush, Caroline continued to sob heartrendingly and gave involuntary vent to her physical reactions from that thrashing. Her scarlet buttocks relaxed, yawning to reveal to me her dainty pink bunghole wreathed with fine hairs.

Decidedly, there's nothing like the whip or a good spanking to master the most recalcitrant and modest pupil.

I bent over to take better note of Caroline's intimate furrow while I slowly rubbed my fiercely swollen cock. Then, with a lubricious smile, I straightened up over her yawning backside. This time I turned the brush to the side with its long nylon bristles. With a sudden deft turn of my wrist I brought the bristles down right into the girl-slave's asshole!

A veritable bellow of agony rose from the armchair. Under that hideous suffering which seemed to tear her anus to shreds, Caroline lunged out of my grasp and fell onto the rug, gripping her bottom with both hands and crying like one possessed.

I let her assuage her torment as best she could; then, when her cries began to diminish, I ordered her to kneel once more, hands again behind her neck.

Still overwhelmed by punishment, the young English beauty nevertheless hastened to obey. She took the indicated position.

"If I still get only disobedience from you, Caroline," I told her gruffly, "I warn you that I'll take you back to the Room of Punishments and administer a whipping that you'll remember till the end of your life. Is that understood, Caroline?"

"Oh! Y-yes...S-Sir...y-yes.... I promise to obey you."

"Very well, my darling, then let's go back to the bed and do what I explained to you: give me pleasure with your lovely titties!"

A moment later, Caroline found herself kneeling between my naked thighs, trying to keep her face as far as possible away from my huge prick, which dangled heavily before her desolate eyes. However, the fear of the whip made her act against her very visible revulsion and the obscene affront to her innate modesty. What an exquisite moment when her two soft, warm titties were pressed against my cock, providing a wonderfully satiny sheath for it!

"Very good!" I complimented her to encourage her. "Now, frig me up and down, keeping your titties nicely squeezed together. All right, go ahead! Unless, of course, you don't think your bottom has had enough yet?"

Her eyes closed to shut out the sight of my enormous prong, which emerged obscenely between those two white globes. Sobbing with powerless shame, she began to manipulate her breasts gently in a soft friction and to undulate her body rather jerkily at the beginning, then according to a slow rhythmic cadence.

I spread my thighs to give her more room, and I leaned back on the bed to relish the better these marvelous sensations that, through my huge throbbing cock, invaded every fiber of my being.

As inexperienced as Caroline's first titty-manipulation showed itself to be, it nonetheless did not take very long before I felt the infallible tickling that announced the approach of orgasm.

The soft warmth of her body pressed between my thighs. The fact that I was able to compel her to perform that obscene ritual increased my pleasure, as much as did the fact of hearing her sob with useless revolt and feel her tears moisten my big prickhead. By the by, they helped, much as an unguent would, my rubbing along that resilient, soft, warm sheath. Soon my gasps of lustful ecstasy mingled with her groans of shame and horror.

Suddenly, to prevent a too-rapid termination of the rut I felt surge along my prick, I pushed her away. I didn't want to go off so quickly—not this first sweet time with the haughty Caroline! She remained squatting on her haunches, trembling violently.

"It will be better soon," I told her, my voice hoarse and panting. But of course she didn't answer, for the situation held nothing joyful for her. I allowed my passion to ebb a little; then I ordered Caroline to resume caressing me with her titties. She showed a rather perceptible hesitation. But soon I felt those sweet warm globes squeeze around my cock voluptuously. Then she resumed her undulations, pressing her titties together with both her slim soft hands against the burning stiffness of my massive ramrod.

Her head down, she seemed hypnotized by the enormous, glistening cockhead that emerged rhythmically from between her bubbies and whose large jism-slit exuded thick, viscous drops as testimony of the intensity of my rut.

Suddenly I felt it mounting inexorably; I abandoned myself and cried out with my orgasmic crescendo. But I suspected that Caroline was not yet sufficiently trained to endure that culminating moment of my pleasure without rebelling. I was certain she could not endure it, in spite of all the threats with which I had confronted her.

And so, when I felt my moment was at hand, I suddenly gripped her between my knees and, plunging both hands into her disheveled hair, pressed her viciously against my belly, while I jerked my loins back and forth to bring about the orgasm.

Maddened, Caroline began to cry out and struggle, but in vain; suddenly, braying out in glorious rut, I felt myself spurt my essence.

My spunk spattered forcibly against Caroline's titties and neck, and, most of all, full against her face. Almost ill and beside herself with abhorrence, she felt my thick warm splashings moisten her eyes already wet with tears, besmear her nose, and enter her mouth as she opened it to cry out her horror.

After that sensational discharge, I remained a long moment on the bed, mulling over the intense delight I had known, while at my feet, Caroline, plunged into abysmal shame and disgust, sobbed heartbrokenly, her face glistening with tears, saliva, and jism.

A Woman of Passion

Martine Glowinski

Germaine Boller was a woman who had risen by strength of purpose to become a successful journalist in Paris. She was now an editor at one of the large daily newspapers. She no longer roamed France as a correspondent, but she was still young and much admired by her colleagues for both her intelligence and her beauty. She was half Algerian, with dark hair and dark eyes and a chic figure the envy of women half her age. For many years she had been the mistress of Albert Kleber, the man who owned the newspaper where she was employed, and although the liaison had certainly assisted Germaine in her career, her attachment to her chief was governed more by pleasure than expedience. For Albert Kleber was a skillful lover, sophisticated and adventurous. Even if these days their passion seemed to have mellowed a bit, Germaine always found an evening with Albert enchanting. Unfortunately, the enchanted evenings were too infrequent for Germaine. She did not blame Albert because, after all, she was nearly twenty years older than when they had first met. It was understandable that a man's passion might wane. She recognized that his interests may have naturally turned to younger women. She was a realist, priding herself on her direct attitude toward life. Albert still considered her his mistress, as evidenced by the many presents and attentions he bestowed upon her, but Germaine suspected that before long he would no longer demand that she be his and his alone. She had never married, and she had no intention of marrying, but she hoped that after Albert there might be another man of consequence to replace him. She was not certain of it, and at times she felt depressed as she contemplated an unknown future.

One day, in the Café des Deux Magots on the Left Bank, Germaine encountered Irma, an old friend. They had known each other during Germaine's younger years, when Germaine had lived for a brief time in Bordeaux. Irma had apparently married a successful factory manager, and she now lived in Paris with her husband and son. The reunion of the two women was casual but pleasant, extending longer than either expected. Eventually, a young man entered the café and approached the table. "Hello, Maman." Irma introduced her son to Germaine.

His name was Lucien and he was quite handsome. Germaine, in fact, thought him a beautiful young man, barely twenty, tall, slender, with dark passionate eyes and lips that occasionally curled with a look of half amusement and half arrogance. Irma had been waiting for Lucien, and now that he had arrived, she bade goodbye to Germaine with a casual promise to telephone her soon for another meeting. Germaine did not expect her to telephone. Their lives were quite different, and she suspected Irma was not that comfortable with women who had successful careers.

Germaine's intuition was correct—Irma did not telephone. But nearly a month later, as Germaine sat waiting for a friend in a café in Montparnasse, a young man approached her table.

"Don't you remember me?" he said.

It was Lucien, Irma's son. He sat at her table and they chatted awhile. She learned he had developed an interest in a career as a journalist, and they talked of the possibilities. Then Germaine said: "I'm meeting someone here. But why don't you visit me some afternoon when you finish classes at the university. Would you like that?"

"Yes!"

She gave him her address in the Montmartre district, and they agreed he would come to her apartment the following Wednesday.

As he left her, Germaine was again struck by his appearance, his youthful vibrant masculinity. Would he indeed visit her? She hoped he would; she wanted to see him again. He was half her age, but he had maturity in his eyes—and he had certainly stared at her breasts. Did she dare consider a flirtation with a boy like this one? The son of an old acquaintance? The idea amused her.

Late Wednesday afternoon, Lucien came calling at Germaine's flat. She had been working on an article, and she had actually forgotten about her invitation. When she opened the door, she was surprised to see Lucien standing at the threshold, and then she remembered and she smiled.

"Well, you came after all."

"Is it inconvenient?"

"No, of course not. Please come in. I'll make tea and we'll talk about your studies."

He seemed ill at ease at first, but soon his equanimity returned and his lips were again curling with that delicious arrogance she had noticed the first time they had met.

"Are you always at home?" he asked. "Don't you have an office?"

Germaine laughed. "Yes, of course. Would you rather we meet there?"

"I suppose it would be too public."

"And you don't want that?"

"I don't know."

They sat on the sofa and talked about his studies. His eyes were constantly on her breasts, her knees, her ankles. Did she want him? She wasn't quite certain. He was so young. Perhaps he would be too clumsy. But his appearance was magnificent. Yes, he was beautiful. Several times she found herself glancing at his lap.

After she poured their second cup of tea, he leaned toward her and kissed her. He caught her by surprise, his lips merely touching the side of her mouth.

"Don't be rash," she said.

"You're the most beautiful woman I've ever known."

"That's absurd."

"No, it's true."

He kissed her again, but this time she expected it. She did not push him away. "My dear boy, I'm old enough to be your mother."

"I've thought about you for days."

"Are you lying?"

"Every day and every night."

"What do you think will come of this?"

"I don't know."

"Kiss me again." His lips were hot, moist, passionate. For a moment she welded her mouth to his as though to eat him alive. Then she broke away. "This is ridiculous."

"No, it's not. I think it's perfect."

She knew she could not resist him—he was too tempting. When

he kissed her again, she took one of his hands and moved it to her breasts. He fondled the contours of her breasts from outside her dress, and then his fingers hesitated at the buttons.

"Go on," she said. "I want it." She held still as he undid the buttons one after the other. His eyes were hot as he pushed the dress off her shoulders to expose her full breasts firmly encased in a lace brassiere. "It opens in front," she said. He fumbled with the clasp at first, but then finally the hook was freed and her brassiere fell away from her breasts like two shells uncovering their treasures.

He kissed her, and as he did so, she dropped her hand to find the warm flesh of his already rigid manhood. As he continued kissing her, his hands caressing her breasts, she unzipped his fly and released the rock-hard proof of his masculinity. She took hold of it and manipulated it, pulling her fist slowly up and down. He was well-made, of ample proportions, a perfect instrument. Then she removed her lips from his, and she adjusted her body on the sofa so that she could take the shaft of his penis in her mouth.

As her lips slid over the end of his organ, she had the feeling he expected it, that he knew from the first flirtation that this would be the outcome, that he was not surprised that she now had his penis in her mouth, her tongue swirling over the fat knob. Perhaps she ought to have been bothered by his arrogant expectation that she would yield so easily, but she was too consumed by the thrill of having her mouth filled with his hard flesh. Sucking a vigorous penis always provided her the most intense ecstasies, and at this moment she had no concern for what he might think or not think. He was handsome, young, and virile enough to excite her.

As she sucked, her tongue licked and savored his tumescent flesh. Her lips pulled back and slid forward over the head and shaft. She could feel his hand on top of her head gently easing her this way or that way to afford him the maximum pleasure. He was only twenty, but he was obviously old enough to know what he wanted.

"That's good," he sighed.

She grunted, pleased that she was giving him pleasure. She slipped his penis out of her mouth, but continued licking at the head with her tongue. "You have a lovely cock."

"Does the taste please you?"

"It's delicious!" She took the head in her mouth again, rolled her tongue around it and sucked hard enough to pucker her cheeks.

Then she heard him gasp, and a moment later the flesh in her mouth snapped and spurted its load of milky liquid down her throat. He urged her to suck, gently pushing her face more tightly against his crotch, almost forcing the head of penis against her tonsils. She sucked and swallowed until she was certain she had consumed the last drop of his ejaculation. He arched his hips one last time, and finally it was over.

And so Germaine began an affair with young Lucien, the son of her friend Irma. They met two or three times a week, sometimes in a café, more often in her flat. When they were together, they passed long afternoons and evenings in a leisurely sexual romp. Sometimes they made love in a frenzy, with a complete absence of the languor she usually enjoyed. One day he arrived at her apartment only a few minutes after she herself had returned home. While they were both dressed, she quickly opened his trousers and exposed his penis. In the living room, he leaned against a table as she sat on a chair at his side and bent to engulf his thick organ with her mouth. Her fingers made a tight ring around the base of the organ as she slid her lips up and down over the head and the upper part of the shaft. The organ seemed enormous in her mouth, a swollen pole of masculine flesh. Because of the way he slouched against the table, he was able to press his face against her coiffeur. She could hear his heavy breathing as she sucked him, each sound of pleasure, each groan in response to what her mouth accomplished with his penis. Finally she pulled her mouth away. "Stand up," she said. And when he did so, she hurriedly unbuckled the belt of his trousers and tugged his trousers down to his knees. Now she sat on a low ottoman as he stood before her with his magnificent organ curving upward from the vent in his white briefs. She took him again, arching forward, her right hand clasping the base of his penis as her mouth worked on his hot flesh. She sucked with art and experience, her head bobbing, her lips tightening each time she pulled back to the fat tip. Then she wanted him naked. She herself now stripped her clothes off, everything except her blouse and shoes. As he leaned against the wall with his hands behind his hips, she crouched with one knee on the floor and the other knee raised, her body extended forward, her hand grasping his organ to point it upward as she filled her mouth with the tip. He moved his loins, thrusting gently into her mouth, pulling back, thrusting again. Later he took her on the floor, her legs raised high, his hands grasping her ankles as he squatted to penetrate her with his thick scepter. In this position, she felt each thrust as an incredibly deep penetration piercing her vitals. She came long before he did, then came again when he finally spurted. Her mouth slack and wet from all the sucking she had done, she cried out as she felt him gushing in her channel.

Lucien was not an innocent. His life revolved around the women he knew, and he found each of them a happy antidote to boredom. When he was not with Germaine, he devoted himself to one girl after another. A classmate named Anne, a strange beautiful girl with haunting eyes, was ready to make love whenever he wished it. They would lie on the torn sofa in her filthy little room in Rue

Mouffetard, listening to records, kissing, smoking, fondling each other. She was like an immature gazelle compared to Germaine. Lucien liked to have Anne seated on his lap when they were both naked. She would sit with her back against his chest, her thighs straddling his legs, her sex filled with his thick penis. Across the room, leaning against the opposite wall, was a tall cracked mirror that showed their coupling. He would fondle her small breasts as she used the fingers of both hands to caress herself. The base of his penis looked like a pink truncheon stuffed inside her body. His balls dangled, one testicle lower than the other.

One day as they sat connected this way, Anne suggested he put his penis in her ass.

"I've never done it," she said. "I want to see what it's like."

"You're perverted," he teased.

"And you? Have you ever done it?"

"Yes, of course."

"To whom? Tell me!"

But Lucien did not want to talk about his other women. He was afraid Anne's jealousy would ruin his pleasure. Instead, he asked if she had any olive oil, explaining it could not be done without a lubricant. "The pain would be too much for you."

"Oil? No, there's no oil here. But I have some lip ointment."

They used the entire tube of lip ointment, Anne with a flushed face as she carefully applied it to Lucien's rigid penis.

"I think this will kill me. If I die, promise me you won't tell anyone how it happened."

Lucien assured her she would not die. He helped her mount him again, and this time he held his penis with his hand as she positioned her anus over the tip. She pressed down, grunted, pressed down again, and gradually her anus engulfed all of his penis until her buttocks came to rest on his belly.

"It's awful," she said. "I feel as though I'm about to be split apart."

"Does it hurt?"

"No, not any more. But don't move. I'm afraid if you move I'll die."

But when Lucien gazed at their images in the mirror, he could not help moving. He did it gently at first, merely squirming his hips, each movement causing his penis to slide a bit further in or out of her stretched anus. Anne groaned but she did not complain, and soon he was able to move his organ more directly, his eyes fixed on the mirror, Anne leaning back with her head draped over his shoulder and her face lifted to the cracked ceiling. When she felt him spurting in her bowels, she gave a long wail and desperately rubbed her clitoris to provoke her own orgasm. For a long time, they lay connected on the sofa, unwilling to separate their genitals.

The Champs Elysées, the city's highway of glass and gold, was a dazzling spectacle of *la vie mondaine*. A living stream poured by, one vehicle hardly flashing past before another followed, almost touching it. The very atmosphere was that of buoyant abandon and exhilaration, as though people had taken wings to fly joyously through space.

In the darkness of the cinema, Lucien put his left hand on Germaine's knee. "I like being with you," he whispered.

She gripped his shoulder. "I adore you, darling."

He shifted his body towards her, slid his left hand behind the small of her back and moved his right hand under her skirt and along her thigh. "The legs of a goddess," he murmured. His hand slowly moved above the top of her stocking until his fingers touched her belly. Germaine felt safe in the darkness, and she slid forward slightly on the seat and spread her thighs. Immediately, his fingers caressed her sex through her panties.

She moaned softly. "Darling, be careful. We don't want to be arrested!"

Lucien could feel the prickly hairs of her sex through the damp nylon. He could also smell her. She was the first woman he had known who could tantalize him with her scent. Was it because she was old enough to be his mother? The smell of her sex rose in delicious waves to his nostrils. He was unable to get his fingers beneath the legband of her panties, so instead he slid his hand up to massage her lower belly. Germaine sighed deeply, then exhaled, drawing her belly in, loosening the waistband to allow his fingers to get under it.

"Pull them down," she whispered, her voice husky with passion. "If you do it carefully, no one will notice."

It was true. The nearest person in the cinema sat three rows in front of them. The old woman who had led them to their seats was nowhere to be seen.

Germaine lifted her hips, enabling Lucien to pull her panties down to her thighs. Then she used her own hands to pull them down her calves and off her feet. After stuffing the panties inside her purse, she leaned back and spread her thighs again. Lucien's hand returned under her dress, and his fingers at once moved to play in her humid sex. He cleverly searched out her clitoris, and Germaine moaned as he gently rubbed it.

"What a scandal!" she whispered. "I haven't done anything like this in years!" She pushed her pelvis forward on the seat a bit more, allowing his fingers to reach everywhere. With her right hand, she fumbled with the zipper tab of his trousers. "You'd better have a handkerchief ready, darling." She unzipped his trousers and brought his turgid penis out to fondle it. "Mmm, you're marvelously stiff."

"And you're like a lake," he whispered. "I wish I could get my nose in it!"

"Later, darling. We'll do everything when we get home."

She slid her buttocks back and forth on the seat, making love to his fingers without moving her shoulders, her hand slowly stroking his penis at the same time. She came quickly, grinding her sex against his hand, moaning and sighing in the darkness. As he continued the pressure on her clitoris, she came again.

"Oh Lucien!" she cried softly. "I wish we were in my bed. Are you close, darling? Never mind the handkerchief, I'll take it with my mouth."

Her audacity shocked him. "Better do it now...Oh God!"

He moved back from her, and immediately she dropped her head down to engulf his penis. She sucked it greedily, and in a moment he started spurting in her mouth.

They left the cinema long before the end of the film, causing the old woman outside the door to glare at them for making a disturbance. Tugging at Lucien's hand, Germaine hurried him into a taxi and ordered the driver to Place de Clichy.

"Stay with me tonight," she said to Lucien.

He smiled. "Do I have a choice?"

"I'll make sure the maid wakes you in time for your class." Germaine kissed him. She would not tolerate a refusal. She wanted him in her bed all night.

When they arrived at her house, he put his arm around her as they walked to her bedroom.

"Let me undress you," he said.

"Yes!"

Her eyes glittering with love and passion, she watched him as he fumbled with zippers and removed her dress. She turned to give him access to the fasteners on her brassiere, then turned again into his arms, pressing her belly against his thumping penis as he fondled her breasts. He bent his head to kiss and lick her nipples, his wet tongue sliding upward to the side of her neck and into her ear.

Germaine trembled with joyous expectation. Together they pulled the covers down to the foot of the bed, and she lay in the center, watching him as he stripped off his clothes. When he lay beside her, he ran his fingers over her belly as he kissed her eyes and ears and lips. His fingers probed her sex, his thumb circling the base of her clitoris. She moved against him, shifting her buttocks off the bed to pump her sex against his hand. She was now in a state of sustained ecstasy, a delicious orgasm warming her vitals. "Put it inside me, darling! Please..."

But he refused. He wanted to caress her first. While he mouthed her breasts, he pulled two pillows under the small of her back. He slid his wet mouth over the slopes of her breasts and down to her belly. Her body responded to his warm lips with spasms of delight. He kissed and licked her navel, then moved again until his mouth reached the hairs of her sex. Sliding over her outstretched leg to lie between her thighs, he kissed the top of her sex and worked his tongue beneath the clitoral hood.

She moaned, urging him on, telling him how much she adored the feel of his tongue on her flesh. Her body seemed filled with a joyous warmth radiating out from her sex. She tangled her fingers in his hair, pulling his face more firmly against her sex, working her ass up and down to aid his foraging tongue. She marveled at his skill. He was so young, and yet he knew so much! Raising her legs in the air, she pressed her knees against her breasts and opened her inflamed sex to his mouth. A great shiver of excitement swept up her thighs and into her belly as his tongue fluttered downward to the sensitive area between her sex and her anus. He kissed her there, directly on the tight opening, his tongue making small circles around the ring, then jabbing inside the sphincter. She moaned in anguished joy. “Oh Lucien!” His hands slid around her hips, over her belly and onto her breasts. His fingers kneaded her nipples as he continued the intimate caress.

Finally, he pulled his tongue away from her anus and he moved back to her sex. “Now I'll suck you,” he said. “Will you come?”

“Yes!”

His tongue worked into her wet slit, circling her clitoris several times before he started sucking it. Her buttocks jerked upward as she came, raised in the air for a long moment, then broke into wild gyrations. He maintained contact with her, continued to suck her clitoris as the orgasm peaked to a crescendo of sheer rapture.

At last it was finished and she lay quietly. With his face still near her sex, he raised one of her legs and separated the outer lips with his fingers. He thrust his tongue into the interior. He sniffed and tasted and lapped at her juices. He inhaled deeply, savoring her female scent. Then he held his head back and studied her sex. He could see everything. He thought her anus looked less delicate than Anne's. Anne's anus was like a tiny mouth puckered for a kiss. Germaine's dark ring was a round rubbery band of tough muscle.

Germaine opened her eyes, and when he glanced upward, their eyes met. “You brought me to heaven,” Germaine said.

“I love you. You have the most beautiful cunt in Paris.”

She blushed, but she did not close her legs. Reaching down, she took hold of his erect penis and pulled it toward her sex. She moved the head up and down in her juices. “And this is the most handsome cock in the world. Big and thick and lovely! Like a bull! The most satisfying cock I've ever had inside me. It's true, darling.” She held his penis at the mouth of her sex, then raised her buttocks off the bed to impale herself on the swollen crown.

“What time is it?” she said.

He glanced at the clock. “Almost eleven.”

"Let's see if we can make it last an hour. Or at least until midnight. If I do come unexpectedly, try to hold yours. Will you do that? I'd love to have an orgasm and come out of it and still feel you hard and ready inside me."

He promised. She released the grip of her sex on the head of his penis. She put her legs over the small of his back, locking her ankles as he moved inside her. Her buttocks moved up to meet his inward stroke, and she felt the head slide into her depths. She worked her internal muscles, milking his organ and then releasing it.

To Lucien it felt as though his penis were gripped and caressed by a velvet glove. He lay with his penis buried to his balls while Germaine rotated and bucked her hips in agonized delight. He was amazed that he could hold back. Surely the interlude in the cinema had helped.

"You're still hard!" Germaine said. "Oh darling!" She hugged him to her, kissing his lips and his eyes and his cheeks as her hands moved over his back in an affectionate embrace. "I want to keep you forever! Make love to me, darling! Make love to me!"

Their bodies moved again in unison, Lucien's thick penis sliding back inside her sex like an oversized piston in a well-greased cylinder. Except for the weight on her shoulders, her body was supported by Lucien as she moved her buttocks. Their combined juices drenched their pubic mats, their bellies, their thighs, dribbling into the crack between Germaine's buttocks, and covering his balls with a slick coating. Their bodies were alive and tingling, waves of warmth engulfing them both. The air was filled with the sounds of their wet bellies meeting, and the acrid scent of their juices. Germaine came again, biting her lip to keep from crying out. Lucien could feel her inner muscles gripping him again as she worked her sex against his stroking shaft. She cried out, urging him on, her body trembling. Then she bucked and rolled and rotated her hips in a wild and savage thrashing that quickly brought him to a climax. He grunted as he came, his hips pumping, his balls erupting as she held onto him.

Germaine collapsed beneath him, causing his deflated penis to slide out of her sex. Her legs slipped off his back.

Lucien lay on top of her, his heart beating rapidly, pounding against his rib cage, thumping at the yielding flesh of her breasts.

After some time, Germaine opened her eyes and slid her arms around his neck. "I love you."

"I love you too," he said.

"What time is it?"

He looked at the clock. "A quarter past eleven. We lasted twenty minutes."

"Marvelous!" she said. "Most men can never last that long." Then she added: "I'm dripping, darling. Let me repair myself."

But he would not allow it. He insisted that she climb over him so that he could use his mouth on her sex. She was amazed, thrilled at the idea of it. Facing his feet, she mounted him on her knees, her thighs straddling his chest, her sex hovering over his mouth.

Lucien looked up into the hairy sex over his face. The lips were swollen, wet and distended. Viscous gatherings of their juices hung from the mouth of her vagina. He put his hands on the globes of her ass to pull her sex down. At the same moment, he felt her hot breath on his soft wet penis, then her tongue lapping his organ. Opening his mouth, he sucked in the drippings from her sex, rolling the drops around on his tongue, tasting the mixture. He put his lips directly on the opening and sucked with more force to gather what was inside her. He could feel her elbows under his knees as she forced his legs up and apart, and her lips kissing his balls, then sucking one ball inside her mouth. Then her mouth moved again, and he grunted with pleasure as he felt her tongue and lips at his anus. He did the same to her, pulling her down further onto his face, burying his mouth against her anus to suck at it and drill his tongue inside.

As if driven by the same mainspring of lust, they tongued each other relentlessly. Lucien felt spasms of delight swirling in his loins and tickling his balls. He sensed Germaine's pleasure through the movements of her body and the moaning sounds she made. She came again, moving her ass back and forth, but not vigorously enough to make him lose contact with her anus. He waited until she had quieted down, then he pulled his face back and gently spread her buttocks with his hands in order to look at her sex and anus again. He had never looked at Anne like this, not in this position, but now he was determined to do it soon.

Suddenly, Lucien was aware that Germaine was sucking his penis again. She had all of it in her mouth. He began a humping movement of his hips, pushing his organ deep in her mouth, then withdrawing it as he dropped his buttocks. The end came quickly, the sperm shooting out of him in needle-like jets, and when it was over, Germaine collapsed on top of him with her mouth still clutching his penis.

What a bitch! Lucien thought. What a hungry bitch she is!

Lucien's favorite way of making love to Germaine was to use his loins to push his penis in and out of her mouth. Germaine would lie on the sofa, and Lucien would suspend his belly over her face, supporting his weight with his hands and knees as though he were doing push-up exercises. Germaine would capture his long organ in her mouth, and Lucien would then move his loins up and down. In this position his balls hung down along the shaft of his penis, and each time he pushed himself completely into Germaine's mouth, his balls came to rest on her chin. Germaine would hold his buttocks as he moved, and she greatly enjoyed the feel of his muscles as his body moved up and down.

One afternoon, as Lucien made love to her this way, Germaine slipped her fingers into the groove between his buttocks and she caressed his anus, only on the outside, her fingertip rubbing back and forth. He was silent as he continued to pump his penis in her mouth, but then he said: "What are you doing? I don't like to be touched like that."

Unable to respond because her mouth was stuffed with his penis, she gently forced him to withdraw.

"Are you sure?" she said, her fingertip still touching his tight little opening. "You've had my tongue in there."

"A tongue is not a finger. I'm not a woman."

"Of course not, darling. But if you have my finger inside you while I'm sucking you, you'll see how much nicer it will be."

Lucien was dubious, but she persuaded him to try it. She first wet her fingertip with her saliva, and when he dipped his penis again into her mouth, she found his anus with her wet fingertip and she carefully worked it inside him. He stopped moving and she felt him tremble. Then his loins moved again, more vigorously than before, and it was obvious that his excitement had increased. She stretched his opening with her finger, prodding, probing, sliding the finger in and out, and when he finally ejaculated in her mouth she was certain the quantity of sperm was more than ever before. After that, whenever she sucked him, he welcomed her finger in his rectum. His movements were always more forceful, which gave her great enjoyment, because when she sucked a penis this way she liked to have the piston-like sliding of the penis be strong enough to be almost brutal. She wanted to be thoroughly possessed by the male organ. She wanted a complete ravishment.

† † †

One day Germaine said: "All love is fantasy."

"What do you mean?" asked Lucien.

"When people make love, they each have their enchantments."

"And you? What are your enchantments?"

"I adore sucking you. I adore having you in my mouth. Do you mind?"

Her fingers slid lightly up and down his thighs. Her fingertips brushed over the sac holding his balls, descended and probed the flesh between his legs while her palm gently massaged his testicles. As she shifted her position, she allowed her robe to fall open to reveal her breasts and belly.

As Lucien admired her body, his penis grew more firm under the touch of her hands. She cupped his balls, squeezed and released them repeatedly in a series of caresses. Their eyes met, and she smiled as she placed her hand directly on his penis.

"Do you want me to bring you off, darling?"

"And after that?"

"After that I'll take you to dinner. And after dinner we'll talk of possibilities."

"Magnificent possibilities."

"Yes, darling yes..."

While one hand covered his balls, the other slid slowly and gently up the length of his pulsing organ. She formed a tight circle with her thumb and forefinger and squeezed the base of his penis. Her fingers moved up half the length of the shaft and then pulled the skin back sharply. Then she relaxed her tight grasp immediately, and she began rolling the skin up and down in a slow sensual manner. She massaged his balls with a circular movement while continuing to masturbate his turgid penis. He watched her, his eyes on her fingers as they slid the loose skin back and forth over the shaft and the head of his cock.

He reached out to support the weight of one of her breasts on his palm. "Your technique is perfect."

"Practice, darling. I've had years of practice."

"Not too many years."

"More than enough, I'm sure."

She placed her finger at the end of his penis and probed the moist opening. She gathered the leaking fluid with her fingertip and painted the smooth helmet with it until the purplish surface gleamed. Then she grasped the organ and began to masturbate him. She grasped him tightly, stroking slowly at first, then she increased the tempo, her hand slamming into the base of the organ and then pumping up the full length of the shaft before rapidly slamming back down again.

Of course, he could not last too long under these ministrations, but she did not want that anyway. Faster and faster she jerked at his penis, his balls bouncing with the movements of her stroking hand. Supporting his balls with just the fingertips of her left hand, she continued the rapid pumping until she felt his penis swell and jerk and the first bubbling white froth appeared at the tip. As he came, she leaned over to catch the white stream on her breast. She continued pumping him until the last drop oozed out of his penis to flood her hand and nipple.

"Was it good, darling?"

His head tossed backward, he groaned. "Perfection."

"Look at me."

And as he watched her, she cupped her sperm-soaked breast in both hands and lifted it to lick the juices from her skin. She lapped at his white sperm, her tongue wiping her nipple clean. Then she sucked the nipple between her lips and tongued it until the last remnants of sperm were gone.

"I've never seen you do that," he said.

"Does it excite you? Here, you can have it now." She stroked his forehead as she fed her breast into his waiting mouth.

After dinner one evening, she said: "What would you like to do, darling? Would you like to watch television?" She rose and walked to a small wall mirror to pat her hair.

"I'd rather watch you than watch television."

Her back to him, she playfully wiggled her hips. "Like you're watching me now, eh? This way or without clothes?"

"Both."

Deliberately teasing him, she lifted her skirt while she was still facing the mirror and exposed her buttocks to his eyes. She peeled her panties down her hips and legs and stepped out of them.

"What a sight!" he muttered.

"Do you like my *popo*?"

"I adore it."

"And I adore yours too, *chéri*."

He left the sofa and moved to stand behind her. He kissed her neck, his hands on the bare cheeks of her bottom. Germaine squirmed, pressing back against him, murmuring her approval as he squeezed the globes of her derriere.

Lucien whispered in her ear: "What about something new, something we haven't done yet?"

"Oh? Like what?"

"I haven't put it in your behind."

Germaine quivered. "Does the idea excite you?"

"What do you think? I've been dreaming about it."

"You need to be gentle with a woman when you do that. Especially you, since you're so big. We can try it tonight, but you must promise me to be gentle. It hurts too much if one tries to rush things. Do you understand?"

"I promise. Anyway, I've done it before."

"You have? With whom?"

"One or two girls."

She felt a ridiculous jealousy. "Did they like it?"

"One of them did."

She did not want to think about his girls. She turned in his arms and kissed him. "What would you like to do now? Would you like some wine?"

"No, let me undress you. That excites me."

"And me too, *chéri*!"

She remained standing while he unzipped her dress. He helped her peel it off and unhooked her bra. Baring her heavy breasts to his hands made her tremble with desire. Her dark nipples were thickly extended. Lucien lowered his head to kiss her creamy breasts and lick her stiff nipples.

"Turn around," he said softly. "Let me see your ass."

She gave him a coy look, then swiveled on her heels to show him her bottom. Leaning forward a bit, she slid her hands back to her buttocks and lewdly pulled them apart. "Have a good look, chéri. Does it make you hot?"

"What do you think?"

She laughed and turned around to face him again. "Let me undress you."

When she had him stripped naked, she held his thick cock on the palm of one hand and used the other hand to fondle his balls. His organ was erect, hot and throbbing under her fingers. Wetting her lips with the tip of her tongue, she lowered her head and took the meaty penis into her mouth. She licked and sucked it, swirling her tongue over the blue-veined underside of the shaft. Then she made a wide ring of her lips and she began bobbing her mouth up and down.

His hips gradually took up the rhythm. They had done it often enough, and his movements were perfectly coordinated with hers.

"Be careful," he said. "I don't want to come now."

She pulled her mouth away and looked up at him. "Yes, you're right."

"Can we do it now?"

"In my *popo*?"

"Yes."

She smiled. The idea made her shiver with desire. It was probably a good time. But she wanted to do it on her back, on a bed, to make it easier to control him while he penetrated her. The size of his organ could not be ignored.

"In the bedroom," she said. "Come along and I'll show you how I want it."

As she lay stretched out on her bed, he climbed over her and started kissing her body. Fluid dripped off the end of his penis to wet her belly. She squirmed with pleasure as he slipped his fingers into the wet mouth of her sex.

"Yes, do it with your hand!" she said.

Lucien could smell her pungent odor and it excited him. She humped her mound at his hand, forcing his fingers deeper into her tunnel. He slipped a finger down to her anus and gently rubbed the ring of muscle. Her juices had oozed down to the crack between her buttocks, and he no difficulty pushing his finger inside the lubricated sphincter. The orifice was hot and quite elastic, and he was amused as he imagined all the stretching the ring had endured during the years. The girls his own age were always too fearful of having it in their backsides, too fearful to properly let him in. Germaine showed no fear at all. He imagined she'd had countless lovers. What a delicious slut!

"Gently," she said, pulling her legs up and holding the backs of her knees with her hands. "Do it gently with your finger until the opening relaxes."

"Don't you want some jelly?"

"In a few moments. Just do it this way first."

He slowly slid his finger in and out of her anus. He could feel the passage and ring of muscle clamping his moving finger in a tight grip. He imagined how the clenching muscles would feel when they were wrapped around his penis. He gazed down at the sliding digit, at the sucking orifice with its border of fine damp hair, at the cunt above it opened like a red mouth and oozing a milky syrup.

"Enough," Germaine said. "Now we can use some jelly. There's a tube in the night table drawer."

He had to pull his finger out in order to get the jelly, and when he did so he looked at it surreptitiously and was relieved to see his finger was clean.

Germaine, meanwhile, was worried about his cock. He was big enough to hurt her. Although she enjoyed the feel of a cock stuffing her back passage, she did not relish the idea of a painful encounter. But the risk was worth it: if he learned how to do it the way she liked it, she would have better times with him in the future. What madness! Her ass abandoned to a boy his age! Albert, of course, had done it often. She was thrilled at the idea of yielding her smallest opening to this young Adonis.

He brought the tube of jelly.

Germaine said: "Put some on my *popo*." He squeezed some out on his fingertips and rubbed it over her anus. Still holding her legs up, she squirmed her hips. "Inside, *chéri*. Make sure you get some of it inside." She watched him as he pushed some jelly inside her back passage. "Now put some on your cock." He applied some of the jelly to his penis, smeared it on the knob and all along the shaft. The organ glistened now, and she thought it looked even lovelier than before. She slipped a pillow under her buttocks and told him to get between her legs. "Go on, *chéri*, I'm ready now." She wiggled her hips provocatively as he pushed the tip of his organ at the ring of her anus.

"It's exciting," he said, his face flushed, his eyes fixed on their contact.

"Yes, of course it is. Go easy, but keep pushing."

The fat knob slowly stretched and spread the tight ring. Germaine craned her neck, and she could just see it as it pushed in. He pushed again, and five centimeters of his penis slid into her rectum.

She groaned and urged him on. "More, darling, more. Go out a little, and then inside again." She now had her knees pulled all the way back to her breasts, and she closed her eyes and focused on the sensation as he slowly, centimeter by centimeter, worked the full length of his tool into the tight confines of her bowels.

Lucien had never done it to a woman this way. This position was almost like the ordinary way, except for the incredibly tight feeling as he pumped slowly in her ass. He reached down to caress her cunt as he moved, rubbing her clitoris. Each time he pinched her clitoris, her anus clamped more tightly around his sliding penis. She looked so wanton, her legs raised, her plump ass wide open, her anus sucking at the shaft of his shining cock. It was nothing like what he had done with Anne. He was drunk with lust.

Germaine groaned and pushed her legs further upward.

His thrusting became more forceful. He thought he might be hurting her, but when he looked at her face he saw nothing but pleasure in her features. Nevertheless, he asked: "Am I hurting you?"

"No, darling, no.... It's heavenly!"

She suddenly had an orgasm. He held still as her body convulsed. He was nowhere near his own climax. He remained motionless until hers was finished.

Germaine finally calmed down and looked at him with adoring eyes. "That was wonderful! And you're still hard!"

She moved her hips slowly, churning her ass, pushing her rectum all the way down on his organ. She adored the feel of him in there. He was so huge! She relaxed the ring as much as possible, pushed out and then took even more of his length. His hands grabbed her hips, and his hot organ slid through the relaxed ring of her anus to bury itself full-length in her passage.

"Yes, Lucien, yes.... It's delicious.... I love the feel of you in there.... Do you like it too?"

"It's marvelous!"

"Ouf! Don't stop moving.... But do it slowly." She slid a hand down to her poor abandoned cunt and pushed two fingers inside the gaping hole.

"Do you want me to do that?"

She shook her head. She would rather do it herself. She urged him to keep his penis moving in her ass. She wanted him to have a powerful orgasm. She wanted to feel the sperm shooting inside her bowels.

When it finally happened, it was better than she expected. He rammed her like a bull, not fast, but with slow hard thrusts that shook her bones. And when she felt the sperm splashing in her rectum, she rocked her knees and cried out and came again.

A week later Lucien seemed distracted, indifferent to her, and Germaine found that intolerable. She did everything she could to make him at ease, to force him to think only of her and of being inside her, making love to her, holding her in his arms. He had another world apart from hers, and she had to compete with it. She wanted him to forget about everything else except their time together. Was he already tired of her? She could not bear it.

In the living room, she walked over to him and ruffled his hair as if he were a small child. She sat down, crossing her legs in a manner that showed her knees provocatively.

"It must be pleasant to come here," she said. "It's so close to the university, but yet so far away from all the pressures you have there."

Lucien nodded. "Yes, it's convenient to be so close."

"I'd like it if you were much closer."

"Forgive me, my mind is on other things."

Germaine took him by the hand and led him into her bedroom. "Just stand there awhile," she said. She removed her blouse and dropped it on a chair. Next, her skirt fluttered down and Lucien could see the dark triangle of her sex bulging out against the nylon of her briefs.

Germaine said: "Relax, darling, it gets better."

She unhooked her bra and allowed it to slide down her arms and off her body. She smiled as his eyes remained on her breasts. She cupped them with her hands, pushed them into her chest before leaning over and hooking her thumbs into the elastic that held up her panties. She drew her hands down, tugging her panties over her thighs and then her calves before she stepped out of them. With her fingers, she spread her sex apart. "I want your mind on this. Now come to the bed."

She sat on the edge of the bed, and when he came to her she reached out to his trousers, undid them and tugged them to the floor. She took his limp penis and held it in the palm of her hand before she opened her mouth to take it. She kept it there, thrilled by its bulk, by the gradual stiffening of his flesh. She rubbed his balls to encourage him, and soon his penis was at its full extent, large enough so that she had to pull her mouth back to the tip in order to breathe. Then she started to suck him in earnest, squeezing the thick shaft with her lips as she skated her fingertips up and down over the backs of his hairy thighs. She removed the penis glistening with her saliva out of her mouth, and she held it and tried to force the tip of her tongue into the tiny hole. Then she engulfed the head again and sucked it with relish. Now she did not care about what occupied his mind—she cared only about the feel of his cock in her mouth, and about how it would feel later on when it was inside her. But of course with his penis in her mouth like this, she gave him no choice in the matter—he could not think of anything else. He became more and more excited, and finally he pulled back so that he could strip off the rest of his clothes.

She lay down on the bed, spread her legs and waited for him. He quickly climbed over her and found the right opening without help. He was obviously impatient, pushing his penis inside her, hurting her a bit. She hoped he would not come too soon, at least not before she had her own climax. But he rushed her along, slamming his body hard against hers. It was good for her nevertheless, and she was ready for anything he liked. She reached around to touch his balls, caressing them with her fingers. When he kissed her, she opened her mouth as he mashed his lips against hers. She found his tongue and sucked on it. She wrapped her arms around his back and crushed him down against her body, her breasts flattened by his chest. She gyrated her pelvis to make the head of his driving penis hit various places far up in the innermost recesses of her vagina. She gasped as he made love to her, moaning as he cleaved her sex with his organ. With each thrust, he pushed as far inside her as possible. She had to pull her mouth away in order to breathe. His face dropped to one of her breasts and he sucked on the nipple, whipping it with his tongue, causing her breast to fill with warmth. Her excitement swelled, her pleasure becoming more and more intense. She writhed furiously beneath him, fighting her orgasm, wanting him to tear it out of her, to purge her body. She used her muscles to squeeze the thickness of his penis as he drove it in and out of her sex. Then her head burst, and she suddenly felt light and airy and free of pressure. She started to come, a giant orgasm that caused her to spasm and shake. "Come in me, come in me!" she panted.

But he suddenly pulled back. "Not this way." He pulled his penis out of her sex and urged her to roll over onto her belly. With his hands, he spread the cheeks of her buttocks far apart to reveal her anus.

"I'll put it in your ass," he said.

"Please, darling, use some jelly."

"You're loose enough to take me without it."

"No! You must use something!"

He finally agreed. She remained face down while he prepared himself. She waited for it. Then the head of his penis was at the center, and he pushed in, slowly filling her up, providing her with a delicious pleasure. Her hands clutched the sheets as she accepted him inside her body. Finally, she felt his hairy crotch grinding against her buttocks. He withdrew slowly, then pushed inside her again with more force. He did this again and again, pounding into her like a wild animal, or as though to punish her. But everything he did only added to her pleasure. She managed to raise herself up a bit, rising halfway to her knees to make it better for her. Lucien rose on his own knees, clutching her waist, holding her tightly as he jabbed her bowels with his rigid penis. His buttocks swung back and forth like a fulcrum, methodical, machinelike, uncaring. Germaine did not mind it. All she cared about was the next orgasm she knew was on its way. She wiggled her buttocks from side to side to change the angle of penetration, to stretch the flesh of her anus and add to her enjoyment. She felt no discomfort—nothing but the marvelous pleasure produced by his sliding penis.

Then she came. She panted loudly, her moans filling the otherwise quiet room. Lucien continued to pump her as she came and came and came. He reached around to push two fingers inside her sex, stretching it, scratching at the walls with his fingertips. She tried to clench her sex around his fingers, but her position would not allow it. He increased his pace, and she knew he was about to come. A moment later she felt a stream of hot sperm gush into her bowels, one spurt, another spurt, and still another. She moaned as she felt it.

He emptied himself quickly, and when he was finished he stopped his movements abruptly, pulled out of her and lay down. She turned around and hovered over him, gazing at his penis as it started shrinking. Without caring what he thought, she bent forward to take his cock in her mouth and taste it. She ran her hands up and down its length and over his balls. She stopped and smiled at him. "Good, wasn't it?"

He looked at her. "How many men have had you there?"

Her eyes widened with surprise. "In my ass?"

"Yes."

"You should never ask a woman such a question."

He shrugged. He had to leave. He rose and dressed without saying another word.

Eddies of pleasure lingered in her body as she watched him pace back and forth in the room. "Say something," she said.

But he simply walked out.

It won't last, she thought. She was certain now she would not be able to keep him. She felt miserable. Lucien would abandon her. Even Albert was ignoring her these days.

Albert Kleber considered a life without amusements not worth living. If his wife was aware of his women, she never made a sound. This afternoon Albert's mood required his secretary, Suzanne Blanchot, a capable young woman who had advanced to be something more than a mere assistant. Suzanne was always a delicious antidote to a boring day. He pushed a button and called her into his office. "I need your calming influence," Albert said. He heard her chuckle. She knew his intent.

In a few moments, Suzanne entered. After she locked the door, she unbuttoned her blouse and removed it. Albert sat on his swivel chair and watched her strip. She wore no bra under the blouse, and she was soon completely naked, her small breasts bouncing gently in front of him as she stood on the other side of his desk.

"Don't forget about tomorrow," she said, her hands fondling her breasts.

"Tomorrow?"

"You're flying to Lyon tomorrow."

"Ah yes. Well, that's tomorrow, isn't it? At the moment I think there's something more important than Lyon."

She laughed as she walked around the desk to where he sat. Albert reached out to grasp her buttocks, his fingers tweaking and kneading the soft skin as he drew her into him. His lips grazed her white belly and nuzzled down among the fine blonde hairs of her sex. She was more like his wife than like Germaine, but yet different than either of them. Suzanne had her own charm, and of course his wife was long past the age when she could interest him sexually. He liked his women firm-fleshed and energetic in bed.

Even Germaine would soon pass her prime and be of no further interest to him. She was a marvelous sexual companion, but her best years were certainly behind her.

He sniffed at Suzanne's sex. "Delicious," he said, trailing his tongue over the firm mound and fluttering it lightly over her clitoris. His fingers curled around under her buttocks and then moved in front to gently spread the moist lips of her sex. His lips and fingers joined together and massaged the tight little bud above the entrance to her juicy opening.

She rocked back and forth on the balls of her feet, pushing her sex against his fingers and lips. Then she stepped back. "Wait, let me put you in form." She dropped to her knees in front of him, opened his jacket, unbuckled his belt, and tugged his trousers and shorts down to his ankles. His penis reared up to meet her fingers. She stroked the shaft with a delicate touch, rubbing her thumb over the head, coaxing the organ into an erection. He gradually became erect, his cock fattening beneath her fingers. She put a hand to her lips and drew off some saliva on her fingertips. She applied the saliva to his penis, slowly massaging the straining organ with a technique that made him shudder with pleasure.

"Ouf! You do that well," he said.

"Yes, it's nice, isn't it?"

"Superb."

He could not wait. He made her rise, and he pulled her legs over him until she straddled his rigid penis. She sighed, rubbing the wet lips of her sex back and forth over his erection. Then she lowered herself onto his organ, taking the first few centimeters with ease. She cork-screwed her body, rotating her hips as his thick penis slipped deeper into her sex. His hands on her buttocks, he guided her body down on top of him. Her tight wet sex fit him like a glove. That was one reason why he liked his women young—he liked a firm hot sex, one that gripped his penis and throbbed so that he could feel the internal muscles twitching. Germaine had marvelous control of her internal muscles, and she could grip him delightfully even if in its relaxed state her sex was loose. Suzanne was naturally tight, with narrow hips and a tight channel. He sat back on his swivel chair and allowed her to do the work. She was truly an expert. Bending her knees, she moved up and down easily, sliding her sex along the full length of his penis, always careful not to rise high enough to lose the penetration. When she was all the way down, she managed a short corkscrew movement that drove him wild.

His mouth worked on her stiff nipples, tonguing them, squeezing the buds between his lips. He loved the hard pert nipples of young women, as well as their tight sexes. And with this one, he especially delighted in her rear opening. His finger tickled and toyed with the tight little orifice as she moved up and down on his penis. When he slipped his finger deep inside her anus, he could feel the excitement run through her lovely body. Her breasts heaved and her hips rotated more quickly on his cock. She moaned, pulling her thighs tight, murmuring with pleasure. He pushed his finger further inside her anus until he could feel his penis through the thin wall separating the two channels. He had an urge to take her there, but there was no time. He had a dinner engagement in an hour, and it was imperative that he leave the office.

Suzanne moved up and down with more vigor now, approaching her climax. Albert allowed her to have it without coming himself. He wanted to come in her mouth, empty himself between her pretty red lips.

She cried out as she came, and he thrust his penis upward as he jammed his finger deep inside her rear opening. He could feel her insides twitching, spasms in both channels.

After the last throb had left her, the spasm of her orgasm spent, he helped her dismount and then pushed her down between his legs.

"Your mouth," he said with urgency. "Give me your mouth."

She quickly took his penis between her lips and began sucking him. Her tongue rubbed the underside of the shaft, swirling over the head. Then she took him more deeply, and he could feel the soft touch of her throat against the tip of his organ. At that moment he erupted, his sperm gushing inside her mouth, his hands holding her head as he emptied his balls.

Albert was not only Germaine's employer and lover, he was also her mentor in amorous attitudes. He was a man of complicated sexuality, the man who taught her that in physical love the refinements are most conducive to maximum pleasure. When they dined together, if circumstance permitted it, he liked her to sit beside him in a booth and fondle him beneath the tablecloth. Germaine, as well, found these surreptitious caresses exciting, her pulse quickened by a suspicion that either the waiters or other patrons realized their game.

One evening, only a few hours after a rather vigorous afternoon with Lucien, Germaine found herself dining in a restaurant with Albert. He had telephoned at the last moment and insisted she have dinner with him, and unwilling to cause him an annoyance, Germaine had agreed. She was not certain she could cope with Albert this evening, since Lucien had succeeded in exhausting her, but she thought if she refused his invitation, Albert would not only be annoyed but also suspicious she had another lover.

So now they sat in a booth in a restaurant near the Louvre, sipping their champagne, dipping into their salad, chatting, and all the while, under the table cloth, Germaine had her left hand in Albert's lap and her fingers pinching and stroking his penis through his trousers.

"Are you despondent?" Albert asked.

Germaine shrugged. "A bit harried at the office."

"Ah. I was concerned my dinner invitation might find you indisposed."

"Darling Albert, for you I'm never indisposed."

Yes, it was true. In the dozen years she had been his mistress, she had never refused him when he wanted her. She wondered if he remembered all the occasions when other women might have pleaded they were *hors de combat*.

As if answering her thought, he said: "Valmont may be leaving us."

"Really?" Valmont was the editor-in-chief and Germaine's direct superior.

"He may move to *L'Express*. Do you think you could handle his job?"

"Yes!" She said it without thinking, uncertain whether it was true, but nevertheless if there was a chance....

"All right, we'll see. I can't promise anything at the moment, of course. The directors will need to be satisfied. But we shall see."

Germaine felt a great excitement. The idea that she might be promoted to editor-in-chief of the newspaper thrilled her. She would be the first woman in Paris to have such a post. A great coup, certainly. The possibility was delicious. If it happened, she would certainly thank Albert appropriately with a night he would long remember. She felt a bit guilty now as she remembered Lucien, her young lover. If Albert discovered her affair with Lucien.... No, she would not think about that. She devoted all her attention to Albert, particularly to the thickening organ she felt beneath her fingers. She traced the outline of the knob, and then the length of the shaft. Sliding her hand down further between his thighs, she probed the warmth of his large balls.

The waiter arrived. The salad plates were removed, the main course was placed before them. With perfect aplomb, Germaine kept her hand on Albert's balls.

After the waiter left, Albert chuckled. "I think he knows."

"Shall I remove my hand?"

"Definitely not."

"I'll unzip you."

"They'll have us thrown out on the sidewalk."

"I don't care."

She found the tab of his zipper, and she deftly pulled it all the way down. Her fingers quickly slipped into his trousers to bring out his erection.

"Like the trunk of an elephant," Germaine said.

"You exaggerate."

"Darling, you have the most marvelous prick in Paris."

"You exaggerate and you're a liar."

Later, in the taxi, she extracted his penis again, and under cover of his coat she began a skillful masturbation.

"Do you want to come, darling?"

"No, definitely not. I'm going to have you in your bed. On your knees, my pet, with my belly pressed against your lovely bottom."

Germaine's anus was quite sore from her earlier bout with Lucien, and she did not relish the prospect of Albert ravishing the same channel that Lucien had visited twice in two hours. She hoped she could find some way to divert Albert's attentions elsewhere. Now she dipped her head to briefly take the head of his penis in her mouth. He allowed the caress for only a brief moment before urging her to cease.

"No, no," he whispered. "Not here in the taxi."

When they were finally inside her apartment, she kissed him and said: "Will you give me a moment to change my clothes?"

"I'll smoke a cigar."

"Yes, that's perfect. Ten minutes, darling."

She would take more than ten minutes, but Albert seemed particularly mellow this evening and she expected he would not complain. She went to her bedroom, stripped off her clothes, and walked into the bathroom to wash herself at the bidet. Her anus was definitely still unusable, and now she wondered how she might prevent Albert from even looking at it. She was afraid that if he looked at it he would deduce the tiny orifice had recently been penetrated.

In the bedroom, she quickly rummaged through various drawers. What should she wear? How should she present herself to distract his attention from her buttocks? She finally decided to wear nothing, or almost nothing, no more than the barest minimum to keep his attention on her sex. She chose a minuscule suspender belt, dark stockings, and black sandals with high stiletto heels. She hoped he would be too busy admiring the front of her body to think of attacking her from the rear. But nevertheless she prepared both openings, delicately rouging the lips of her sex and applying an ointment just inside the ring of her anus. Albert was an unpredictable lover, and she thought it wise to be prepared.

When she rejoined him in the living room, wearing only the suspender belt, hose and shoes, Albert, seated on the sofa with his cigar, gazed at her with obvious admiration.

"Exquisite!" he exclaimed. "What a lovely vision you are!"

She poured herself some champagne and approached him. She deliberately positioned herself in front of him, her belly no more than half a meter from his face. "I've been wanting you all evening," she said, her fingers toying with one of her nipples. She moved closer to him, close enough to feel the heat of his breath on her belly.

With a soft laugh, he leaned forward to press his nose against her triangle. He sniffed at her, his fingers stroking the insides of her thighs. Then his hand moved upward, and his fingers probed the hot wetness of her sex. As he kept his nose buried in her bush, she arched her pelvis forward to encourage him. "Albert..." she murmured.

He did not respond. Instead he slipped from the sofa to the floor and sat there waiting. With a smile, Germaine glided forward to place her sex on his mouth. There would be no dangerous attack at her rear this evening. She knew Albert's predilections. For the next hour or two, he would take his pleasure with his mouth at her sex. Gently rolling her hips, she pressed her conch against his face.

One day Lucien asked Germaine if he could borrow some money from her. "I need five thousand francs," he said.

Germaine was surprised. The subject of money had never arisen before. She always paid for everything, but he had never requested anything. "Have you asked your mother?"

His face reddened. "Why should I ask my mother? Aren't we lovers? Don't you love me?"

"Lucien, I don't know why you need five thousand francs, but I don't think I can give it to you." She would not bend. She did not want to imagine herself buying his affections. Five thousand francs was a considerable sum, and he would certainly never pay her back. "No, it's impossible," she said.

Lucien's response was to smash one of the lamps and storm out of the apartment. Germaine was shocked, realizing the affair might be over. Did she want that? Had she committed an irrevocable error by refusing him?

A week passed, and then finally a letter from Lucien came in the mail:

> Dear Germaine:
>
> I understand now that our friendship is not good for either of us. We shall not see each other again. Adieu.
>
> Lucien

Germaine felt miserable for an hour, and then she pulled herself together. So it was finished. Lucien was a darling lover, but sooner or later their liaison would have ended anyway. He was too immature, too petulant. And also too unimaginative in bed. One had to be an optimist and look to the future. She had made a success in her life because of her willingness to be strong. She told herself these things, but she suddenly felt defeated again. What an absurdity! She needed a diversion. Albert? No, Albert was much too serious. It was Robert Desnoel who came to mind, a former lover, an actor, totally uncomplicated. Robert lived only for pleasure, and that was what she needed to make her forget her fiasco with Lucien. After twenty minutes telephoning one place after another, she finally located Robert at one of his haunts on the Left Bank. Yes, he would meet her. Germaine was satisfied. She had not seen Robert in quite some time. Yes, the evening would be interesting.

She had a bath and she passed an hour choosing the clothes she would wear. She found it exciting to be on her way to a rendezvous with a lover she hadn't seen in some time. She stood before the full-length mirror in her bedroom and aroused herself by running her hands over her body. Her breasts looked swollen, her nipples thick and succulent. As she always did when she was unhappy, she felt an intense desire suffusing her mind and body. She slid her fingers over her mound, teasing her labia with her fingertips. She held one breast with her free hand as she slipped her fingers inside her wet sex. She moved her legs apart to give her hand more room, slowly stroking herself, one hand fondling her breasts and buttocks as she watched it all in the mirror. How delicious it was to be so wanton! She brought her fingers to her mouth to taste her juices. She dabbed some of the syrup on her nipples and rubbed it into her heavy breasts.

She thought of Robert Desnoel, remembering their previous interludes. Enough! she thought; enough of these fantasies!

An hour later, Germaine met Robert Desnoel in a café near the Odéon.

"Hello, darling," he said as she slipped into the booth beside him. "Are we in the mood for a party this evening?"

He was still a handsome devil, suave, always carefully dressed. Germaine smiled. "I don't think I'm here to discuss the repairs of Notre Dame. You had better be in the mood, darling."

"For you, Germaine, any man is always in the mood."

"In a short while you may show me the proof."

"Has Albert Kleber been falling asleep on your pillow?"

"What do you think?"

"I think the woman now sitting beside me is as exquisite as always. Let's leave this place and find some privacy."

As they rode a taxi to his apartment in Rue de Rennes, Robert had his fingers tickling the insides of her thighs. By the time they arrived at his flat, Germaine's sex was flooded and her legs trembling. Robert quickly stripped her dress off her shoulders to get at her breasts. Germaine remembered how adept he was at exciting her during the preliminaries. He was a talented lover. He kissed her breasts now, pinching her long nipples, sucking her breast-flesh into his mouth until she moaned at the feel of his hot lips on her tender skin. He licked her swollen nipples, suctioning her breasts one after the other deep into his mouth. When he finally pulled his mouth away, she looked down at her breasts and groaned with pleasure at the sight of her nipples fat and wet with his saliva.

"My God, you do know how to suck a woman's breasts!"

Robert laughed, his hands holding her breasts, his fingers tugging gently at her nipples. He seemed in no hurry to get to the bedroom. "What are you wearing under the dress?" he said.

"Nothing. Does that excite you?"

"Show it to me. Let me see the garden of delights."

Germaine quivered, stepped back, her heavy breasts dropping away from his hands. She slowly raised her dress over the tops of her stockings until the dark hairy bush covering her sex was revealed. "Do you like it, darling?"

"*Formidable*! Open it, open it with your fingers. I want to see your color."

Holding her dress up with one hand, Germaine pried her labia apart to show him the inside of her sex. She adored the lust in his handsome eyes.

He stepped forward and gently probed her sex with his fingertips. "You're dripping, chéri."

"Put your fingers inside. Yes, like that!"

He slowly thrust two fingers in and out of her wet opening. She closed her eyes, moaning softly. She could hear the delicious wet noises made by his fingers as they slid in and out of her drenched channel.

At last he pulled his hand away and playfully pinched her ass as he asked her to remove the dress. "Just the dress," he said. "I want you to suck me while you're still partly dressed."

Germaine trembled with excitement as she peeled off her dress. This was just what she needed to forget her troubles. She was thankful she had succeeded in finding Robert this evening.

When she was ready for him, he stripped his clothes off until he was naked. His neatly circumcised penis soared upward like a knight's lance, and Germaine's mouth watered at the sight of the fat purplish head.

Robert made her sit on a velvet-covered footrest that put her at just the right height to suck his throbbing organ. He closed his fingers around the shaft, rubbed the head over her mouth, smeared his leaking juice over her face and finally on her eager lips. By this time she was feverish for it, her nostrils filled with his masculine scent. She knew what he liked. She ran her tongue over the bulb of the head, teasing his flesh without taking him in her mouth. She tickled the tiny opening with the tip of her tongue, sucking at the leaking fluid. She licked down his thick shaft, nuzzled his balls, and licked and nipped at his scrotum, at the tight leathery sac. She lapped his testicles with her tongue, coating them with her saliva, and then finally sucking them into her mouth one after the other.

At last she dropped his balls out of her mouth and she moved her lips up to the head of his penis. Cradling his balls with one hand, she squeezed the base of the shaft with the other hand and closed her mouth over the swollen knob.

Robert grunted with pleasure at the feel of her warm mouth on his penis. He looked down at her, watching the way her mouth moved as she sucked his turgid organ. She was a lusty woman, a marvelous *suceuse* with delicious breasts and a hot sex. Out of bed she was much too cerebral for him, but with her clothes off she was a spicy diversion. *Sacristi*, what a mouth she had! And those breasts. Her nipples were like thumbs. He had special plans for her this evening, plans that his instinct told him Germaine would adore.

Her eyes closed, her nostrils flaring as they filled with Robert's mansmell, Germaine sucked like a gourmande. Nothing was more wonderful to her than a mouthful of hot masculine flesh, a tasty penis with a fat head throbbing on her tongue. Again and again she swallowed his organ until the knob pressed the back of her throat. Her saliva drooled thickly over his rampant cock. One hand squeezing and fondling the hard muscles of his buttocks, she fluttered her tongue along the underside of the shaft as she pumped her mouth back and forth.

She pulled her lips off his penis and smiled up at him. "Do you like this, darling?"

"You're wonderful! Are you as good with Albert Kleber?"

"That's the second time this evening you've asked about Albert."

"I'm curious. I met him a few weeks ago at some ceremony at the Ministry of Culture."

"So that's it. I should never have told you about him."

"Darling, I swear myself to secrecy. Does he make love to your ass?"

Germaine chuckled, her hands still fondling Robert's penis and balls. "Sometimes. Do you have ideas of your own, *chéri*?"

"You've never allowed me to do that."

"Not now. Do it in my mouth a little. I like that."

Robert was happy to oblige her. One hand holding her head, he slowly pushed the full length of his penis into her open mouth.

Germaine held his balls as he began stroking his tumescent flesh in and out of her lips. She adored having her mouth penetrated in this manner. She loved the feel of a thick penis sliding in and out of her mouth, over her tongue and down to the back of her throat, then pulling out again until she had his bloated glans stretching her lips.

Robert continued thrusting until he felt himself dangerously close to a climax. He pulled away and said: "Bend over that arm chair, darling."

"I don't want it in my ass."

"Have no fear, you'll get it all in your cunt. Just bend over."

She knelt on the seat of the arm chair and offered him a rear view of her treasures. Robert was impressed. She had luscious buttocks, dark hair growing into the crack. Her puffy labia pouted like a ripe hairy fig. Her anus was adorable, dark brown and appearing as tight as a drum. He had an urge to pull at the fine hairs surrounding it with his teeth, but his penis was too impatient. Caressing her buttocks with one hand, he ran the knob of his organ up and down between her labia until he found the opening and pushed inward. They both groaned with pleasure as the full length of his penis slid forward to stretch her passage. He gave her everything he had, pushing the last centimeter inside with a roll of his hips that brought his balls swinging against her clitoris.

"How is that?" he asked.

"*C'est bon*!"

"Listen, darling, I have a girl coming here in a little while, a rendezvous I couldn't cancel. You can stay or go, whatever you like. If you stay, I think we can have a delightful time. What do you think?"

Germaine was silent a long time. "You're a *fouteur*."

"We'll have a wonderful little *partouze*."

"All right, I'll stay. Now do it to me hard and make me come."

Grinning, Robert grabbed her hips and began slamming his penis in and out of her dripping sex.

Claire was a tall slender blonde, not yet thirty, with small breasts and long legs. She had the sort of lithe figure Germaine had always desired, and Germaine liked her immediately. The blonde seemed totally unsurprised to find Germaine with Robert, and it soon became apparent to Germaine that Claire not only understood Robert's intentions but she accepted the idea of a partouze enthusiastically. Germaine, who had never become accustomed to the ease with which people in certain quarters engaged in these combats of the flesh, now found herself totally aroused at the prospect. She felt primed by Robert's lovemaking, ready for anything no matter how wild it might be. She looked at Claire with intense interest. Germaine and Robert had covered their bodies with robes before Claire had arrived, but Claire was still fully dressed. Germaine imagined all three of them completely naked. Particularly Claire. She had an urge to have a look at those pert breasts and that adorable bottom. She felt no jealousy at all. Robert, after all, meant nothing to her—she was here only to enjoy herself.

A few glasses of champagne were enough to provoke boldness. Germaine watched as Robert slowly undressed Claire. He soon had her breasts exposed. The blonde wore no bra, and with her blouse pushed to each side, her lovely little breasts quivered deliciously, her pointed pink nipples already stiff with excitement. Robert continued undressing Claire until she wore only her stockings. Her beige nylons had elastic welts that made a suspender belt unnecessary. Dressed in nothing but her stockings and high heels, Claire presented a delightfully erotic appearance. She was one of those blondes with dark sex hair. She had a lovely sex with neat pink lips protruding at least two centimeters. Robert amused himself by making Claire spread her thighs to show Germaine her little treasure.

"What do you think? Is it pretty?" he said to Germaine.

Germaine nodded. "Everything about Claire is pretty. From her pretty toes to the top of her pretty head."

Claire smiled as she accepted the compliment. "He likes the cunt," she said to Germaine. "He collects pictures of them. Did you know that? The first time we made love, I fell asleep posing for his photos. Does he have pictures of you?"

Germaine admitted it. "I allowed him to take a few."

"Of course you did! How could you resist? I certainly could not."

The sight of Claire naked with her sex exposed had aroused Germaine, and her excitement now increased even further as the attractive blonde, seated in a chair and facing Germaine, casually slipped her hands between her thighs and began caressing herself.

"It excites me when people watch me," Claire explained. "Do you mind?"

Stunned, Germaine shook her head. Her blood raced as she sat beside Robert and watched Claire caress herself. Claire's fingers probed between the pink lips of her sex. She explored the opening with a forefinger, gathered some of the syrup and brought it to her clitoris. Germaine was fascinated, thrilled to watch Claire pleasure herself. Claire squeezed her breasts with her left hand as she pushed three fingers of her right hand inside her wet sex. The air was heavy with sexual potential—and total decadence. But Germaine decided she had no time for stupid moralizing—she was tremendously excited and nothing else mattered. She was certain Claire would be interested in the two of them doing more than merely looking at each other. She was more than willing to amuse herself with Claire. The blonde looked delectable. Germaine imagined the younger woman's head between her thighs, Claire's lovely mouth sucking at her sex. Yes, I'm ready for it, Germaine thought; she was certain Claire would be a superb lover.

Now Claire sighed. "Robert says I caress myself too much. But

I think it's healthy, don't you? I don't know why men have such ridiculous ideas about it. I adore using my fingers. And you, Germaine?"

"Yes, it's pleasant."

"It's lovely," Claire said, her wet fingers stroking in and out of her wet sex. "And Robert obviously likes to watch. Look at him!"

Robert had an enormous erection rising from the opening in his robe. He had his hand around the shaft, his glans swollen above his fist. Germaine felt her sex twitch as she looked at it. She ran her hands over her thighs, and Claire immediately caught the movement.

"You ought to remove your robe," Claire said to Germaine. "It's not fair that you remain covered."

Germaine agreed. She rose, slipped out of her robe, then sat down again. She slowly opened her legs to show Claire her sex. Claire's eyes glittered with excitement as she gazed at Germaine's belly. Amused at the blonde's ready response, Germaine opened her legs further. For several moments, the two women were totally preoccupied with each other. Then their attentions turned to Robert. Claire left her chair and went to kneel at his feet. She helped him remove his robe, and then she slid his penis over the side of her face. He moved his hips as she licked his shaft with her tongue. Closing her lips over the fat glans, Claire began pumping her mouth up and down on his turgid organ.

Germaine watched them, her fingers idly toying with her labia. She watched Claire's mouth working on Robert's penis. She found it thrilling to watch another woman suck a male organ. Claire had a wide sensuous mouth that seemed made for it. And perhaps made for other things too, Germaine thought as she imagined Claire's mouth on her sex. She wanted the blonde's head between her legs. Meanwhile, she found it impossible to remain aloof. Claire welcomed Germaine as she knelt on the rug to share Robert's penis. The two women worked together, running their lips up and down his shaft at the same time as Robert leaned back and grunted with pleasure. Saliva drooled out of the mouths of Claire and Germaine as they licked his hard flesh. They took turns licking the head. They licked his balls, their tongues occasionally touching, their lips chasing each other. They finally divided the spoils, Germaine sucking on his knob while Claire worked her mouth over his bloated testicles. Before long they switched, Claire taking the head as Germaine sucked his scrotum. When Germaine had his penis in her mouth again, Robert announced he was about to discharge. "*J'arrive*!"

"Go on, take it," Claire said to Germaine, her fingers trailing like feathers over one of Germaine's breasts. This was the first time Claire had touched Germaine, and Germaine quivered in response.

Germaine took the effusion of sperm. She felt Robert's penis swelling in her mouth, his shaft throbbing beneath her fingers. An instant later his hot sperm foamed and bubbled and his organ suddenly spurted jet after jet into her waiting mouth. She milked his balls with her hand as she sucked hard on the knob.

Robert needed to rest after that, and the two women went off to the bathroom to repair themselves. Germaine offered to let Claire have some privacy, but the blonde insisted that Germaine remain with her. "Kiss me," Claire said, her hand gently stroking one of Germaine's breasts.

Germaine kissed her mouth. When they broke apart, she admired Claire's slender body, the long legs sheathed in nylon. She ran her fingers over Claire's thighs, touching the elastic tops where they indented Claire's tender skin. "These are too tight. Doesn't the elastic bother you?"

Claire laughed and said no, and then she abruptly sat down on the toilet and began pissing. "You use the bidet first," Claire said.

But Germaine wanted something else. Overcome by a sudden impulse, she said: "No, I want to watch you."

Claire smiled and opened her legs to show more of her sex. "Do you like my little *minou*? Can you see it coming out?" She gazed down at her sex as she continued pissing.

Germaine trembled with excitement. "Yes, it's pretty."

Their eyes met, and Claire said: "Let me touch your breasts. I've wanted to do that since I arrived."

Germaine moved across the intervening space to stand in front of the seated blonde. Leaning forward, Germaine offered the heavy globes of her breasts to Claire's hands.

"Formidable!" Claire said, her eyes hot as she lightly ran her fingers over Germaine's hanging breasts. She rubbed Germaine's nipples with her fingertips. "I adore large breasts."

Germaine's excitement increased. Holding one of her breasts with her hands, she offered the nipple to Claire. The blonde immediately opened her mouth and began sucking. Germaine finally pulled her breast out of Claire's mouth, fingered her sex and said: "Would you like to suck me here?"

"But of course!"

"Later," Germaine said. She had an idea how she wanted it done to her, and the bathroom was not the place for it.

When the two women returned to Robert, they found him seated on the sofa waiting for them. "A *tête-à-tête* in the bath?"

Germaine said: "We were getting acquainted, darling. Claire wants to suck me, and I thought you might like to watch."

"*D'accord!* Claire must like you. She doesn't do that to every woman she meets, you know. Isn't that so, Claire?"

Claire nodded, her pretty mouth curled in a weak smile. "I

have a feeling I'm about to be the goose, but I suppose that's what I want." She looked at Germaine. "How do you want it?"

Germaine pursed her lips. "If you stretch out on the rug, I'd like to ride your face."

Claire flushed. It was not her favorite way to suck a woman, but she felt compelled to go along with it. Then, as she stretched out on the thick rug, whatever reservations she had vanished as she felt an intense excitement at the idea of being dominated by this sultry brunette.

Germaine's excitement was also intense. She hadn't expected Claire would yield to this position so easily. She straddled the blonde's body, her legs on either side of Claire's shoulders. For a moment she merely stood there, running her hands over her breasts and down to her sex. She looked down at Claire and said: "There's time to change your mind."

Claire shook her head. "No, give it to me."

"I like to be kissed all over."

"Give it to me."

Germaine slowly squatted, lowering her sex to Claire's upturned face. She avoided actually sitting on Claire. She held her sex suspended some distance away from the blonde's mouth.

Robert chuckled, his hand stroking his penis as he watched them. "Claire, darling, I think Germaine understands precisely what you want!"

Germaine's eyes met Claire's. Yes, she did know what Claire wanted. Germaine trembled with excitement. "Smell me," she said quietly. "Smell my sex."

Claire seemed in a daze as Germaine lowered her sex another few centimeters. The blonde's nostrils flared as Claire sniffed the aroma of Germaine's garden. Germaine weaved her hips, teasing Claire by avoiding contact, then suddenly she lowered her sex once more and for the first time she pressed herself against Claire's mouth. "Suck it!" Germaine hissed.

Claire's face soon glistened with Germaine's leaking juices. The blonde's tongue was deliciously active, licking everywhere, pushing into the opening. Germaine squirmed until she had Claire's nose rubbing her clitoris. Then she shifted forward and shuddered as she felt Claire's nose pushing against her anus. She wanted that too. She wanted all of it. Whatever misery she had felt about losing Lucien had now disappeared. The feel of a hungry face feeding at her was exhilarating. She groaned with pleasure as Claire shifted her mouth and began licking her anus.

Later, in Robert's bedroom, Germaine opened her eyes after a deep sleep to see Robert pushing his penis into Claire's rear portal as Claire knelt on all fours. Germaine watched it awhile, and then she closed her eyes and slept again.

A week later, Albert announced that Germaine would indeed succeed to the post of editor-in-chief. The journalistic community in Paris, many of whom were Germaine's friends, sent flowers and telegrams of congratulations.

"Don't fail me," Albert said.

"Albert, I adore you. Let me thank you."

"How?"

"Come to my apartment this evening."

Albert chuckled. "An irresistible invitation."

In the evening Germaine prepared herself for Albert. After a shower, she powdered her breasts and belly. She applied perfume between her breasts, in her navel, and in her pubic hair. She combed her hair out, and then pinned it high on her head in an elaborate chignon. She selected a sheer peignoir and slipped it on. Stepping back to admire herself, she saw that with the light coming from behind her, the peignoir was transparent. Her nipples were two tight little protrusions pressing against the sheer material, and the swell of her belly and pubic hair showed faintly. She was certain Albert would be aroused by her appearance.

Just as she was putting the finishing touches on her hair, she heard the sound of the doorbell. Albert had arrived. The maid was long gone, and Germaine would have to let him in. She quickly fixed the last hairpin and walked to the front door to open it.

"You look marvelous," Albert said, after she closed the door behind him and led him into the living room. "I adore it when you wear your hair up like that."

Germaine deliberately walked near the window in order to have the late afternoon light shining through her peignoir. "And this gown? Do you like it? It's a new one."

"Fabulous!"

His eyes glittered as he gazed at her body only barely hidden by the sheer peignoir. She wore mules with high heels, dark stockings and pretty pink garters. She looked like the complete cocotte, which was precisely what she wanted, for she intended to ravish him and make her promotion an absolute certainty. She reached up and cupped her breasts suggestively, squeezing the globes through the peignoir. "I've been thinking about you for hours, darling."

His eyes did not leave her as she walked slowly towards him with her hips swinging, her eyelids fluttering. She knew what Albert liked. She stopped about a meter in front of him, then slowly opened her peignoir and allowed it to slip off her shoulders. She removed it completely, and she stood there naked, wearing only the dark stockings and shoes, a slender gold necklace, and the drops of perfume she had applied earlier.

Albert's face appeared flushed. "You're exquisite."

"As your new chief editor or as a woman."

"Both."

"I want this to be a special afternoon," she said, her full breasts rising and falling gently. When he reached out for her, she stopped him. "No, I don't want you to do anything, not yet. From this moment, everything is to make you happy." With that, she stepped forward and reached for his swelling member already jutting forcefully in the leg of his trousers. She ran her hand slowly over the bulge, gazing down at it, then looking up at his face. His penis throbbed under her fingers, pushing against the cloth. "I think this part of you is no more than twenty years old."

Albert's eyes were hot. "Perhaps you overestimate my capabilities."

"But it's true, darling! Don't I know you well enough?" Keeping one hand on his penis, she removed his jacket and tie, her movements slow and deliberate. She peeled off his shirt, tossed it over the jacket on a nearby chair. She slowly rubbed her cool hand over his chest, her fingertips tangling in the coarse hair. He looked dumbfounded. A long time had passed since she had played this sort of role with him, not since the early days when she had first become his mistress. He was now a dozen years older. He seemed a bit confused, but he was obviously enjoying it. He shuddered visibly as her hands went to his belt and slipped it out of the loops. She pulled the zipper down with agonizing slowness, with short teasing jerks. She placed both hands on his hips and pushed his trousers and shorts down to his ankles.

"Ah yes!" she said, smiling as she gazed at the organ that jutted straight and hard at a horizontal angle. Albert's penis lacked length, but it had an impressive thickness, a broad circumcised helmet with a faint bluish tinge. She took hold of the shaft, squeezed it, and bent over to kiss the head, her lips leaving an imprint of lip rouge. Then she released his penis, lowered her body, ran her hands along his thighs and calves, and without hurry removed his shoes and socks. Starting at his ankles, she rubbed her lips up his legs, dragging her tongue along the hairy skin. She remembered doing this to Lucien. She pretended now it was Lucien's legs she caressed. She kissed Albert's thighs and the insides of his thighs, planting long hot kisses everywhere. Her nipples grazed against his shins and knees. First with her hands, then with her lips, she worked carefully all around his crotch. She kissed and licked his pubic hair and the creases between his legs. She ran her tongue lightly over his balls, playfully flicking the hairy sac with the tip of her tongue. But she did not touch his penis. His thick organ jerked each time her mouth moved close to it, but she did not touch it.

Finally, with Albert panting and sweating, she lifted her eyes and said: "Don't you want to get more comfortable, darling? I have more than this to do." She took hold of his penis to lead him to the bedroom, and he followed her obediently like a horse being led to water.

Albert, perhaps, suspected the delights she had in store for him, but he said nothing. He behaved as if he were mesmerized.

She had him lie down on the bed with his knees wide apart. His penis reared up like a short thick flagpole. Stretching out beside him on the bed, she lowered her head to his loins. She slipped one finger inside her mouth, wetting it with her saliva, sucking on the finger a bit and watching his hungry eyes. Then she traced the wet finger around his genitals, making fine wet lines on his skin. She put more saliva on her fingers and ran them lightly over his tumescent organ. He shivered with pleasure as he felt her warm wet fingers stroke his flesh. She slid her fingers over the smooth head, polishing it. Her fingers moved down to the edge of the helmet, then over the entire length of the shaft.

Albert groaned, his hips rocking up and down. "You're making me crazy."

"Do you want me to stop?"

"Never!"

She tickled his balls, running her wet fingertips along the wrinkled skin. She bounced his testicles lightly in the palm of her hand, as if testing their weight. Then she moved her finger behind his balls and edged it toward his anus. Tantalizing him, she lingered at the soft skin between his scrotum and the opening, her fingertip making tentative little jabs at the orifice. He grunted with impatience, wanting more, knowing full well her capabilities, since this was not the first time she had attended to this part of his anatomy.

But she continued teasing him. She drew her finger back, leaving only the suggestion of what would follow. Now she went to work on him with her mouth, following the same route she had traveled with her fingers—first just his pubic hair and the insides of his thighs, then at last, when he was seething with need, she slid her tongue over his steaming penis. She licked slowly and carefully, dragging her tongue over the veins and around the thick rim of the helmet. She remembered what he liked. Years ago, when she had first become his mistress, it was always the agile work of her tongue on his organ that had driven him wild.

He groaned now. Her tongue swirled across the inflamed glans. She licked the smooth skin, reveling in her skill. On several occasions she had made Lucien come like this without ever taking his penis inside her mouth. Albert, of course, was less prone to have a climax this way, but she could still tantalize him to the maximum, keeping him at her complete mercy.

She took one of his balls into her mouth, encasing it in a soft sucking embrace. Her lips pressed gently against it, her tongue jiggling the orb, pushing it around in its hairy sac. He lay there panting, his body oozing sweat. She buried her nose in the musky man-smell, savoring it, inhaling the aroma deeply. She adored that pungent odor of the male sex. It drove her wild. Her hands reached under him to spread his buttocks wide with the tips of her fingers. With a groan he raised his knees, offering himself. The tight little opening stared back at her like a brown eye. She slid her tongue down over his balls and licked close to the eye without actually touching it.

"Do it...do it!" he grunted. He cursed as he rocked his knees.

She pulled back a bit and teased him. "It's awful, Monsieur Kleber. Quite awful to have your editor-in-chief about to..."

"Feuille de rose!"

"Yes."

"Germaine, I'll fire you!"

She laughed. "I don't think you will."

She knew she would do it. She had done it to Albert before, but in fact with him it always repelled her a bit. He was really too old for her. With Lucien it was different; with Lucien she could do almost anything and find it exciting. She slowly extended her tongue toward the little hole. She curled her tongue into a funnel shape and grazed the very tip against the tight opening. He writhed with pleasure as he felt the caress, raising his hips to get more of it. She went on with it, the tip of her tongue sliding into the ring. Now she could feel the hot suction pulling at her tongue, drawing it in deeper. She moved her tongue around, darting it in little circles as he began thrashing his hips wildly, grunting and shoving his ass at her as if wanted to suck up all of her tongue with his clutching anus. Her tongue still curled, she moved it in and out of the opening like a small penis. As his anus became more wet, she slid more deeply inside it, until finally her lips pressed against the anus itself.

This caress, which she only rarely performed, always made her feel weak and vulnerable. She thought of it as the ultimate in submission, and she was always amazed at the way it excited her. She was now a complete slave, ready to do anything for Albert Kleber, even suck his ass, this man past sixty who meant nothing to her except as the source that sustained her bank account. You're a whore, she thought, you're no better than the women offering themselves on the boulevards. How much did a man have to pay for this? But Albert had already paid many thousands to her. What more did he want from her? What more could she do? All he needed to do was ask her and she would oblige him. That was the way it had been from the beginning with him. That was her mission with Albert, her supreme pleasure—to oblige. She rammed her tongue in as far as it would go, feeling the tight hot skin pressing in on her, sucking her in even as she sucked him. He writhed in anguished ecstasy, thrashing his arms and legs against the mattress. Now she grabbed hold of his penis and jerked it with her hand as she sucked deep in his anus. His organ felt as hot as his rectum—hot and full of juice. She sucked harder and harder, driving him, making him cry and thrash and whimper like a small boy. Lucien had never been as wild as this, never so dissolved with passion. She slid her tongue in and out, faster and faster, doing it like an expert, this beastly act that maddened her with lust. She felt his penis swell and thicken. She drilled his anus with her tongue, while with her hand she pumped his organ. This dual action was too much for poor Albert. He thrust his hips high in the air and grunted loudly as she pulled his penis as hard as she could. The first jet of hot sperm landed on her forehead as she bent over him with her mouth still sucking his anus. She kept her tongue working as his penis spit gobs of sperm all over her hair and face. With sperm dripping down her eyes and nose, she gave his anus a final few strokes with her tongue before falling exhausted on his belly.

Desert Diary

Alexander Trocchi

It is dark where I am lying, alone, in a tent, on a few sheepskins that they provided for me. They have taken my clothes away from me and have given me the clothes of an Arab woman.

Outside, I can hear them speaking but I cannot understand their language. They are watering their camels. Soon, I suppose, someone will come in. But I am not really afraid. In the past I have always found that to be a woman is enough. I have only to wait. Eventually we must reach a town where someone speaks English or French and then I will be able to explain. They will have to give me up. It may take a long time, but I shall plan, and I shall have my revenge.

How terrified I was when I saw the camels of Youssef's caravan move off in single file! And Youssef himself, the only living soul to whom I could speak, turning his eyes away as though I no longer existed!

One day I shall make him pay for all that.

Meanwhile I am going to go back to the beginning and write it all down—oh, I regret nothing! Not even this. Or what happened on the sand dunes a few hours ago. And Youssef, the poor fool, thought he was humiliating me! How like a man! I have met many men, and some of them have been fine, strong, beautiful men, but at bottom, I'm afraid, all men are fools.

It seems a long time ago now since I bathed in the coral-spined water in the little cove below our village. That was where life began for me, I suppose. It was, anyway, almost the beginning...

How difficult it is to explain the terrible mute hunger in our bodies! If I touch my thigh here in the near-darkness of the tent my whole body is again suffused with the driving urge that brought me here, and I cannot explain it. As always, it is stronger than fear. For me it has always been that way. It is as though my whole history were contained in the touch, asserted again in the pressure of fingers, all my life laid out with the smooth curves of my body, maturer now, but young still, and waiting silently, yes, waiting, on these hard sunbaked sheepskins that they threw in after me. Oh, I could laugh! For I have only one feeling. I have only to touch the smooth slab of my thigh again and I feel triumphant!

And it was the same then, I suppose, as it is now. I was lonely. I climbed down over the rocks to the little cove.

In the northwest of Australia there is a long stretch of beach, wild and desolate, that gives on to the Coral Sea. This part of the Pacific is so called because of the vast pink stretches of coral reef, which spread for hundreds of miles like pale wounds in the smooth turquoise shimmer of the sea. From the window of my room I could look out right across the sea shelf. The scores of coral were sometimes almost scarlet and sometimes, in the evening, almost black. Few boats came there except those of the fishermen of our own village, and most of them belonged to my father, who owned four boats and employed ten men.

The village itself was small and was situated high over the water and high over the little cove which, for a number of years, I had regarded almost as my private property. I had swum there since I was twelve years of age and had seldom been disturbed. No stranger ever came there, only sometimes a courting couple from the village, but, as that sort of thing was severely looked upon, not even the villagers came often.

By the time I was fifteen I had taken to going into the sea naked. That first time it was a sudden decision, no sooner thought than acted upon. The idea, for reasons I was unable to analyze, seemed to explode through my entire body, becoming a sensation of weakness at my flanks and excitement at my navel. I remember standing there at the edge of the water, my toes pressing into the sharp shingle, flexing the muscles of my calves and thighs, and looking for the first time downward at the slim yellowish twist of my body. There, though the delicate hollow of my half-formed breasts, I glimpsed the beginning of a chevron of silky hairs, damp to the touch from the sweat of my young body, from which my long slender legs seemed to radiate like spokes. I realized then that in some mysterious way this was my body's center, the axis of my desires, the mercurial fulcrum around which all my movements would henceforth pivot, and in whose ecstasy my female limbs, bared at that moment to the light sea wind, would find fulfillment.

Then, with my eyes closed, the victim of my sudden obsession, I moved like a sleepwalker into the sea that rose upwards over the finely-haired skin of my legs until, with my knees submerged, the water became a circle of cool fire at each thigh. All the world was extinguished save for my own flesh and the softly pervasive flesh of the sea.

Gradually, I opened my knees and felt the hot center of myself pulled downward into the water as though by a gravitational pull, and as the lips of the water swung coolly between my buttocks and took my lower belly within itself, all the tension in my body was released and I sank ecstatically backwards beneath the surface of the water.

How long I remained there, bobbing like a cork beneath the surface, I don't know. Every muscle and sinew was relaxed, so that my splayed limbs and the white curve of my torso, in sinking, were abandoned like flotsam to the relentless will of the water.

I count the sea my first love and, in a sense, the most immaculate, for there was no percussive sentiment between us to pollute the elemental tremors of our union; unlike the liaisons to which I later consented, the passion that fed it was an impersonal one.

When I came out of the sea I found I was bleeding. I must have gashed myself during my plunge on a sharp splinter of coral, for there was a small cut just above the knee on the sleek concave surface of my inner thigh. By the time I had waded ashore the blood had trickled down as far as my ankle. I sat down on the shingle, drew my knees apart with my hands, and allowed the sun to strike the wound on which the blood had already begun to congeal.

My father, a narrowly religious man, forbade the hired hands to keep company with me. He viewed my approaching maturity with a mixture of fear and pride; fear, because among the menfolk in our village there was not one whom he would willingly have accepted as a son-in-law; pride because, widower as he was, he found himself once again possessed of a desirable young woman who drew the glances of all the young men in the village. For my part, I despised the young men of the village, partly, I suppose, because of my father's constant admonitions, and partly because, having read widely from childhood of the world beyond the bleak sunstruck desert of the interior of Australia, I despised the mute fatalism of men who would live and die in an isolated village like ours. The world of the villagers led to abrupt limits on all sides. Although I had little opportunity for comparison, I knew intuitively that the men of our village had in some way, doubtless because of the inflexible pressure of non-conformist religion, allowed their manhood to go from them. They were vulgar creatures and, like most vulgar creatures, suspicious and afraid.

This was probably the real reason why I avoided the beach where most of the village girls bathed. Although I would have been protected there by the strict conventions of the community, I was reluctant to exhibit the bold outline of my torso to the prurient eyes of the village men. I waited for the day when my father would be dead and I would be able to leave the village for the last time.

Such were my thoughts when, on the eve of my eighteenth birthday, I climbed once again down over the rocks to the isolated little cove below the village where I had spent my short life.

On the very next day I would be eighteen. I stood looking out far across the coral-studded sea for a long time, conscious again of the dull excitement at my roots that came to exist in me at the moment I decided to come there. For it was almost a ritual by this time. Without haste, I would remove my clothes until every shred of my being was exposed to the impersonal gaze of the sun and the sea. My lissome body, light like a blade of grass in the wind, exuded a pinprick sweat of excitement so that the slow surfaces of my belly and my flanks glistened like dull sequins in the sunlight. The hairs of my lower abdomen had spread by this time, and a tenuous filament of sleek hairs connected the strong jut of my mound to the deeply indented whorl of my navel. My breasts, grown hard with desire, were dully painful in their arched-up position, and the lilac putty of my nipples was as heavy and ambiguous as mercury.

As I came out of the sea, I moved my hands briskly against my limbs to remove the salt water that clung there. But I was unsatisfied. For the first time the sea had failed to bring relief to my limbs. In exasperation I threw myself down on the shingle and lay there on my front with my cheek pressed against the shells. I do not know what I expected other than to feel the thrust of the earth against me, perhaps nothing, for I was conscious only of the tension in my muscles and of an oblique dilation at my roots.

As I lay there, I caught sight of the log. It had been there for some days, washed in by the sea. It was half-rotten, fat, with a portion of the rough bark still intact. For a moment I looked only, and then gradually, the knowledge of what I was about to do came over me like a sickness, the familiar weakness at my thighs, the hard little rotation of pleasure somewhere deep under my navel.

A moment later I was standing, looking down upon it, and then sinking to my knees, I bought my sex close to the rough bark. My whole body quivered and, with a sob, I collapsed on top of it, crushing it against my crotch by the pressure of my knees, and against my breasts with all the force of my arms. So violent was the convulsion of my body that the log rose under me and my body toppled sideways, bringing the waterlogged weight of the wood directly on top of me, rough and damp, and bruising the delicate sun-dusky skin of the front of my torso. Meanwhile, my back and buttocks were ground against the cutting shingles that crackled like china chips at my buttocks, riven by an irresistible arrow of lust, tightened spasmodically to bring my flailing legs round the log to grip it with the force of a vice against the hungry jaws of my sex.

When the agitations of my body ceased, I lay quite still under the heavy hulk of the tree, and I opened my eyes and stared straight above me at the unchanging cobalt depth of sky that fell upwards into infinity without cloud and without horizon.

My body was painful from the superficial wounds the weight and the rough texture of the tree trunk had inflicted upon me. I could feel the sting of broken skin at my knees, at the cleft in my thighs, and at my delicate breasts, but I could feel no hatred for the thing that had hurt me. Almost reluctantly, I moved from underneath it. The whole front of my body was red from its abrasive contact, and here and there the trickles of blood mingled with the muddy liquid that had exuded from the bark and with the green smears that were evidence the tree had once been rooted in a fertile soil.

I returned to the sea to wash my wounds. The salt nipped them painfully and my clothes when I put them on chafed the tender skin. Soon, however, I was dressed and, without further thought for the pain, I turned to go home.

At that moment, the sound of a man's laughter came to me. For an instant I froze with fear. What if someone should have witnessed my actions? But then I realized that the laughter came from the far side of a line of rocks more than twenty yards away and that the rocks cut me off completely from the sight of whoever was there. I might have gone straight home then had I not heard a woman's voice call out in fear: "No... please... I can't...let me go!"

Without further thought, I moved quickly toward the rocks. The panic in her voice excited me. Tired as my body was, it was aroused by the urgent secrecy in the woman's voice. My heart was beating fast as I scaled the rocks and brought my eyes to a level from which I could look down on them.

I saw them at once. They were lying close under the shade of a strangely shaped rock that was suspended over them like a stalactite, the woman—I recognized her as one of the village girls who had been in my class at school—with her skirt disarranged above her knees, a sharp crescent of plump white flesh apparent between the top of her stocking and the hem of the displaced skirt, and her face red from the struggle with the man—I did not recognize him at first—who was straddled on top of her, his arms pinioning hers to the ground. Occasionally, leaning the weight of his body on top of one of her arms, he released his grip with one hand, reached down, and clawed at the swelling white orb of one buttock that stuck out from the frilly lace of her knickers like the gleaming knob of a boiled egg from a tattered eggshell. But every time he did so, the girl bucked violently underneath him and he was forced to bring his hand back to her wrist again to prevent her escape. Suddenly, during one of these maneuvers, the girl succeeded in toppling him over on to his side, and at once, before he had time to regain his balance, she had lifted a large pebble and struck him a glancing blow to his forehead. He uttered a cry of pain and brought his hands to his head while she, hesitating no longer, made good her escape. I watched her run quickly between the rocks and disappear from sight.

The man sat up, still rubbing his head, and at last I was able to recognize him. It was Tom Smith, one of the young men of the village who had been to the war and who had returned when he was demobilized. As a matter of fact, he was employed by my father, who looked upon him as a blackguard and had threatened to fire him on more than one occasion. He was a dark-skinned young man of more than medium height, well-built, and he seldom appeared in public without a cigarette between his lips. Evidently he had decided not to give chase because now he lay back on the shingle and lit a cigarette. He held it in his right hand while his left, stretched out at ninety degrees to his body, lifted a heap of shingle and allowed it to trickle from his tilted palm back on to the ground.

I hesitated. An idea was beginning to dawn upon me. Smith had at least been in the outside world. With his help I might be able to escape sooner than I had expected. Was that all that decided me? I don't know. I had seen him lying heavily on top of my schoolmate and my body, in spite of its cuts, was already eager to succumb again to the primal turbulence I had lately experienced. I suppose I wanted him as well. I wanted him immediately. His flesh hard as the tree had been, but warmer, and with more resilience. I had never seen a naked man.

Boldly, I climbed into view and walked towards where he was lying. He sat up quickly at my approach and I felt his eyes studying the nervous movement of my walk. When I was within speaking distance, he addressed me with a sneer.

"I thought your father told you not to speak to strange men?" he said.

"It was you who spoke," I said.

"So it was!" he replied.

We looked at one another. And then I saw his eyes which, in his reclining position, were on a level with the hem of my skirt, move downward to my calves, which were almost gold from the sun, and remain there for a moment before he threw a glance upwards and said: "Why don't you sit down?"

I did so without replying.

Suddenly he knitted his brows.

"How long have you been here?" he demanded.

I looked at him. He was wearing his shirt open at the neck and the muscles of his chest were well-outlined beneath the dark hairs.

"Tell me something first," I said. "Why did you come back here—to the village, I mean?"

He threw his cigarette against the rock.

"God knows!" he said.

"Why don't you go away again?"

He laughed bitterly.

"It takes money," he said.

"I could get money."

"What do you mean?"

I noticed that his eyes had once again fallen to the small triangle of cloth where my skirt rucked up against my mound. I raised one of my knees, casually, but so that the white skirt fell away, leaving the heavy surface of one thigh exposed. For a moment he stared at the bare flesh and then he looked quickly at me.

"Together?"

I nodded. "I can take the money from my father's safe," I said.

"You mean it?"

"I was watching you when you tried to make love to Peggy," I said.

He grinned. And then suddenly his face relaxed and, as though he were making a tentative bargain, he laid one of his brown hands on the dull opaque skin of my thigh. A quiver ran through me. I was now beyond my own decision. I slithered on the shingle into a position so that his hand came into contact with the moist and tremulous hairs of my sex. A moment later, his shadow blotted out the world for me, his lips, slightly open, came against my own, and his hand moved upwards over the smooth skin of my belly, tracing a hundred contours of my thighs and buttocks, while I, losing the thread of all thought, arched my torso against him and waited for the inundation of relief.

Beyond the edges of myself, I existed at my lips, at the twin excitements high and hard beneath my shift against him, and atop the finger which, with slight pressure, broke the frail webs of sweat that my body exuded in its delirium. And again, most fiercely, at my woman's pole to where eventually his fingers came, opening like scissors inside me, flooding my virgin body with pain and pleasure until suddenly, my skirt high above my waist and the lower part of my torso abandoned to his will, his hard male core broke through between my cloven hair, and his angry movements culminated, his body rigid, in a javelin thrust that seemed to cleave me in half. The tension in my thighs relaxed. My lean, outspread legs twitched nervously for a moment and then came to rest like long plantshoots on the shingle. The hard concentration that had existed in my flesh became liquid and the relief moved like a sensual lava through my limbs.

Smith had opened the front of my blouse and his firm lips sucked voraciously at my left breast. The pliant flesh shaped itself to the ring of his mouth and I breathed more heavily again as, with the slickness of a camera shutter, a small needle of desire pricked through my loins. I moved my fingers through his dark hair, at the same time pressing the back of his head so that his face was almost buried in the fleshy part of my breast. Then, with my other hand between our bodies, I pressed against the flatness of his belly, downward, mingling my fingers with the hairs of his crotch, until, his spirits reawakened by my caress, his buttocks tightened and his power moved again at the wet richness between my thighs. This time, one of his hands came round under my trembling buttocks and his middle finger slipped surely into the downy rut that ran like a gully between them. There, torso thrust against torso and my plump golden thighs spread-eagled under the tufted white rectangle of his moving front, all the radiant juices of my young starved body mingled with the pearly male stream that marked the consummation of our union.

A few moments later, he drew away from me. I rolled over, bringing my thighs, which were hot and smeared with our love, together tightly as though to contain the strange male emission that I knew then for the first time. He meanwhile had rearranged his clothes and was seated cross-legged, smoking a cigarette. His first words were:

"Did you mean what you said?"

I was lying on my front, perfectly composed, my skirts decent once again, leaning on my elbows.

"We must go to Charleston," I said. "We can go south from there."

"When?"

"Tonight," I replied. "Before my father takes the money to the bank."

"And we can be married in Charleston," he said, as though he were talking to himself. "He won't be able to do anything then."

Fortunately, he could not see my face. What a fool he was! The thought of marriage had never crossed my mind. To be a house-slave as my mother was, to lose my freedom and adapt myself to his absurd male requirements! That was my first experience of this kind of idiot male presumption—why do they assume that because we have need of their bodies we will be willing to submit ourselves to the drab pattern of their everyday existence? If a man is poor and must work, what an overbearing impertinence to expect a beautiful woman to harness herself to his venal and constricted existence! Such men should be housed in a stable after their toil, and, if it is a woman's pleasure, they should be loaned to her for her occasional enjoyment. I had to suppress the impulse to laugh in Smith's face.

"We go tonight then," I said. "You must borrow a motorcycle and wait outside the house at midnight."

He laughed.

"Don't worry," he said. "I'll be there."

I had just written those words Smith spoke to me when the heavy tent-flap moved. I crammed the paper out of sight under the sheepskins. The man stood in shadow looking down at me where I lay.

For a few moments he said nothing and then, suddenly, he pointed his finger at himself and said something I could not understand. Perhaps he was telling me his name. When I did not answer, he continued to gaze down at me.

Under his impenetrable gaze, I felt something stir in me. It was as though some delicate plant inhabited my loins and was at that moment thrusting its roots and shoots into the darkest reaches of my flesh. I acted quickly, or rather, found myself acting quickly, for I did not consciously decide to play the part I did in the mute pantomime that followed. I was stripping myself of the robe they had given me. And then I was lying naked on my back in a prone position a few feet away from the man who looked down at me. My legs were heavy and apart. And then I was raising myself on my elbows, my body bristling in a tawny arch, my heels tight on the sand beyond the sheepskins, so that the hot halter of my loins rose like a snake about to strike at the man in the shadows.

For a moment he hesitated, and then, falling on his knees, he thrust his bearded face voraciously against my sex.

The straight hairs of his bearded face intermingled with the curly hairs of my pussy. I watched as his black beard forced its way into the lightness of my blond forest. His swarthy skin, burnt almost black by the desert sun, contrasted sharply with my milky white flesh, as his face worked its way between my thighs. I felt his tongue lick at my inner thighs. Licking first one side, then the other. His tongue splayed out, covering the outside of my aching vulva. He lapped at me in this manner until I had been brought to a heightened sexual tension. He narrowed his tongue into a moist hot shaft and began to probe the pink lips of my pussy. He flicked it teasingly in and out. I wanted to grab his head and force his face into me, but that might terminate this pleasure too soon. Thankfully I resisted, for he was soon to show how skillful he was with his mouth.

He removed his robe, exposing a hard, muscular body, gleaming with sweat. Going down on me again, he neatly changed tactics with his tongue. Instead of flicking it like a snake, in and out, he now slowly ran it along the length of my warm pink trench. Up and down, up and down, ever so slowly. When his mouth reached the top of my fleshy folds, he used just the tip of his tongue to flick at my clitoris. This oral teasing had an immediate effect. My clit became engorged with erotic tingling and began to protrude through my pussy lips, like a little pink nipple. It was ecstasy. I tried to hold his mouth on my cunt by clamping my legs around his head, but he wasn't about to let me be fulfilled that easily.

He gripped my legs behind my knees with his strong, dark, rough hands, and pressed them back towards my chest. Holding my taut legs back in this manner, he exposed me fully, from the top of my pussy hairs to the base of my spine. My entire cunt and asshole were laid open to his gaze and desires. He then used his left forearm to pinion my legs against my chest, freeing his right hand to stroke my smooth silky legs and ass.

Starting at the base of my spine, be began running his tongue along the valley between my buttocks. Just as his mouth reached my pussy, he opened the crevice of my juicy cunt with the fingers of his free hand and blew his hot moist breath gently into my vaginal core. Returning to the rift between the cheeks of my ass, he licked upwards towards my pussy as before. Once more he opened me, to gently force his hot breath into my dripping orifice. He repeated this sensuous torture again and again.

I couldn't believe his tongue was capable of more lasciviousness, but it was. As his tongue licked the inside of my rear valley, he stopped halfway along this path, where my puckered asshole had been hidden by my buttocks. Forming his tongue into a tunnel-shaped probe, he moistened his oral spear fully. Pausing at the rim of my puckered tan portal, he slowly began penetrating this secret passageway. His firm tongue curled into a narrow tip and having been lubricated with the moisture of his mouth, found little resistance to its probing. His fleshy oral limb, pushed deeper and deeper into my recess. I was being overcome by the stimulation he was exposing me to.

His rigid tongue then began going in small circular motions. When I relaxed, he started to widen the movement of his tongue, expanding my anal opening in a manner most exquisite. I could feel his hot breath inside the valley of my buttocks, as his tongue did its naughty work.

After enlarging me in this manner, he allowed his tongue to go from a narrow probe to a full-fleshed ramrod. He then began to give me a new lesson in the use of his talented tongue. Separating and holding my buttocks apart with the thumb and fingers of his right hand, he began to penetrate my asshole with the thick fullness of his wonderful tongue. Slowly at first, he began to force it further and further into me. I couldn't ever have fancied pleasure this marvelous or exciting. I could feel his coarsely bearded face when it brushed past the insides of my soft tender buttocks, while it moved up and down on its lewd indecent mission, forcing his enthusiastic tongue in and out of my dark recess.

While his tongue was engaged in its remarkable explorations, I felt his fingers move up towards my vaginal gash. Working their way past the curly guardians of my pink opening, I felt the most fantastic sensations. Two fingers entered the tunnel to my cunt. He moved these two strong, dandy digits in and out of me in the front, while his tongue was pursuing its penetrations of me in the rear.

Just when I thought I had experienced all the erotic sensations possible, he opened me to new ones. When his tongue was inserted to its maximum, his fingers pressed down against the thin wall of flesh separating my cunt and rectum. I could feel these two firm intruders fully inside both my passageways at the same time. His fingers were pressing against his tongue, and I was between them. He then began to shake his two fingers in a vibrating movement. Rapturous waves of sensuality went through me. My entire body quivered with erotic exaltation, but I wasn't to obtain final release just yet. The lessons were to continue.

He removed his tongue from the smooth, dark, anal tunnel it was servicing and replaced it with a finger that only moments before had been in my pussy. He thrust his tongue fully into my wide-open and pulsating front fissure. I felt his firm oral projection in my fleshy love corridor and his finger filling my asshole. He opened his mouth wide, covering my sex trench, pressing his lips against me. His tongue began a rhythmic thrusting in and out of my cunt. I grabbed his head and tried to force it into me, as my own head rocked from side to side in glorious bliss.

I needed more, I wanted more, I had to have more. As if responding to my overwhelming cravings, he released my legs from where they had been pressed against my chest, allowing them to lie prone and open on the rug. Raising his head up from its position between my thighs, he looked into my blue pleading eyes and seemed to understand my urgent unquenched desires.

Slowly and gently, he began removing his hands from their present splendid location, while he continued driving his tongue into me. His dark brown hands began moving upwards along my body. When his hands reached my opaque white breasts, he began to gently but firmly squeeze their firm fleshiness. His fingers began manipulating my tits, causing my hardening nipples to reach full erectness; all the while his delightful tongue continued probing my insides.

My upper body was heaving from the pleasure he was bestowing upon me. His hands gripped my shoulders and he pulled himself up towards me until we were face to face. I could smell the secretions from my cunt in his beard and it excited me even more. I could feel the turgid fullness of his cock at my pussy, where, only moments before, his face had been.

I threw my arms around his dark head and pulled him towards me. I felt the muscular strength and heat of his body on mine. I could smell the musky odor emanating from his sweaty body, the sharp, pungent aroma arousing me even more. I kissed him with passion and felt his rough tongue enter my mouth, while at the same time, I felt his firm thick cock enter my cunt below.

His rigid, firm-fleshed phallus entered my well lubricated channel easily, yet filled it completely. When his tongue passed through his bearded lips and entered my mouth, I could taste myself on him. While he pumped and plunged into me with his swollen cock below, I imagined that I was experiencing a woman on my face. At that moment, I wished I could be experiencing both. The thought drove me to the edge of rapture.

With his left hand, he grasped my breasts and began to roughly squeeze them. His other hand went under my milky white hindquarters, gripped my buttcheeks tightly and drove his long slender forefinger into my rectum. So many sensations, so many erotic feelings. His prick surging into me below, his tongue thrusting out of his bearded face into my mouth. My breasts being voluptuously clutched and pressed. A finger probing my buttocks and then plunging down and in. I held his head tightly with my left hand, and with my right hand I encircled his fleshy dark penis where it was entering my heated cunt. It felt so wonderful. I put my forefinger into my pussy and felt his cock slide past, as it went in and out on its lustful mission. I gripped his dark muscular buttocks as he held mine, and forced my now lubricated finger into his asshole. I could hold back no longer, nor could he. As waves of sensation, pleasurable pain and orgiastic release passed through every cell of my body, I could feel his cock give up its hot release of come within me. His entire body became taut, and I clasped his firm ass tighter with my left hand, in order to pull him even closer into me. I forced his face fully against mine. Using my lips, I grasped his tongue, which was covered with my cunt juices, and sucked it into my mouth.

While locked in our licentious embrace, my entire being shuddered with total ecstatic release. I felt his body give a full prolonged surge and his prick a final staccato spurt of semen into my inflamed cunt.

Before I could fully recover from my exertions, he roughly pulled me to my feet. Using leather thongs and forcing me to bend over, he tied my left wrist and ankle to a stout tent pole. Keeping me bent over, he spread my legs and arms and bound my right wrist and ankle to another sturdy tent pole. He had allowed a bit of slack in the thongs holding me, giving me a slight freedom of movement, but I was now securely tied in a bent over, spread-eagled, indecent position. My tits were hanging down seductively, and my cunt and anus were exposed to the gaze of anyone who might pass by. Bent over like this, I was looking directly at my blond crotch. I watched as the Arab's glistening semen trickled down my thighs. I was able to turn my head and body enough to see the swarthy Arab slip on his robe and sandals, open the tent flaps, and walk quickly away.

As I hung, spread open in this humiliating position, I smelled a sharp pungent odor and heard movement at the opening to the tent. A slim, young, Bedouin goatherder had wandered in, and with what seemed a keen interest, stared at my exposed hindquarters. I felt my heartbeat speed up and sensed a sharp twinge in my cunt. I watched this mangy, smelly, son of the desert move towards me, and I involuntarily bent over further, making my openings even more accessible to this hairy beast of a man.

The sweating goatherder approached my exposed rear and began sniffing me, much as one of his animals might do. I could feel his nose as it bumped into the inner cheeks of my ass. The hairy man, smelling of the goats he kept, must have liked what he found, because he started lapping at my gash with his long, harsh tongue. I could feel my pussy juices begin to flow and this seemed to spur him on. His coarse tongue licked quicker and deeper at the slit between my legs and along the inside of my ass. I was being driven to a frenzy.

Since I was bent over, I looked between my legs and saw his inflamed red cock begin to rise from his crotch. It was long and pointy, just like that of the goats he tended. The randy man-beast was in full heat and he quickly mounted me from the rear. I wanted to wrap my arms around this hairy lover, but I was frustrated in my desires by my leather bindings. Since I had some freedom of movement, I pushed my ass backwards as far as I could go in an effort to help his hard probing cock enter my overheated cunt. The herdsman's beautiful long red prick entered my moist vagina easily. As he began to hump into me, I could feel his hairy thighs rub against my wiggling butt. I felt hot panting breath. Foaming drool from his excited mouth fell on my silky smooth back as he began fucking me vigorously, pounding into my swollen pussy, faster and faster. I felt prickling excitement all over my body, but before I could come, the over-excited male ejaculated into my fleshy chamber, flooding me with an immense amount of hot sticky animal-like semen. I could feel his long cock soften and slip out of me.

I was still in the throes of excitement and desire from the fucking I had been given, but which ended too soon. With my cunt and asshole still exposed, I looked with glazed eyes at the young Bedouin, hoping he would somehow complete the ravishment he had begun.

His response was to pick up a slim bamboo cane he used for herding, and exposing his white teeth, he smiled an evil grin. Suddenly, he whipped his cane around and brought it down across my helpless buttocks. The sting of the cane sent shock waves through me, but the lash did not break my skin. The momentary bite of the bamboo switch heightened my excitement and I moaned gratefully. Again and again, he scourged my ass with his flogging cane, pricking but not cutting my firm round butt. He could see my ass move up to meet this new source of pleasure and he changed the angle of attack. He now brought the bamboo pole upwards from below my parted legs and with a softer force, let it lash into my pussy. It was the most joyous pain I had yet experienced. With short, almost gentle strokes, he repeatedly thrashed my aroused cunt. When the bamboo branch had struck my clit a few times in succession, I could contain myself no longer, and climaxed in one body-shaking spasm after another. I soon hung limply down, restrained from falling only by the leather thongs that still bound me to the tent posts. For the moment, I was whole again, without fear for my sanity or safety.

Once again, I experienced the terrible joy of annihilation, the deliverance of my whole being to the mystery of sensual union, and this time with a male whom I would not recognize in daylight.

There is perfection in that. I want nothing more of him. I rejoice again in my separateness, in the vital isolation that makes it possible for a human being to collide, to coalesce, and for a short while to coexist with another. That is the essence of it. I am not like those weak women who want to be owned by a man, body and soul, and who, having submitted to such an indignity, seek in retaliation to hedge him in, to have him belong. What would I do with a man for twenty-four hours in a day, for seven days in a week, and for months, years? This would be a kind of slow poison. My life is my own. That is a truism. But in saying it I assert the fact that I am not like those women, devitalized by convention, who will mutilate their own personalities because they will not accept the fact that all great lust is impersonal, a drive in the very mineral part of us whose gleaming ore can only be tarnished by sentiment.

My limbs are at rest. The man is gone, as quietly and obliquely as he came. I do not suppose I will be disturbed at least until dawn. I am anxious to record everything, to break through the shameful shell of civilized expression and to penetrate into the pulsing recesses of my primal being. I want to have what I want to say said before they discover, and perhaps destroy, my record.

Midwestern Holiday

Lyn Davenport

I keep the determined smile on my face the first couple of days of school. Having to listen to everyone's commiseration about not receiving the position of principal is worse than not getting the job. Especially since half of them are silently gloating inside and do little to try and hide it. On top of that it always makes me realize how narrow their world is and how terribly dull and boring my life has become.

My quaint little town in the heart of Iowa has lost its charm. One incredible, hardly believable, secret summer has ruined my old comfortable world for me. I'm no longer the person I was. I'm no longer content with what I have. I view it all through wide-opened eyes now. What had been a satisfying, cozy life now drags along at a snail's pace as I wait impatiently for next summer to arrive.

How will Grant arrange for us to be together to travel and explore new worlds? I can't even begin to imagine, but I don't doubt for one moment he will contrive it. He's a wealthy, determined man. A manipulative man. A man who has turned my life completely upside down within a short seven-week period. A man who wants to do it all over again next July.

And I want it too. Desperately. More so as each long day passes with a sameness that smothers me. I have been whisked from one continent to another and tasted forbidden fruit that before that time I'd hardly dared to fantasize about, never mind ever expected to experience, to come to love, to crave, to need. Now I slowly stagnate and smolder as the yearnings build hotter each day, yet remain unfulfilled.

The sharp memories both entice and haunt. I find myself daydreaming, reliving, desperately trying to recapture parts of last summer at the oddest times. One Sunday in church I found myself tuning my brother-in-law's sermon out, and once again I was high above the Mediterranean, Grant's hands working their magic on my naked body as I stared out over the watery expanse. My happy sigh caused a few heads to turn my way, and I shamefully tried to cover it with a hasty yawn. Is it a sin to sit in church and recall such decadent behavior? My mother looks at me curiously a lot lately. Maybe I should think of getting my own place.

Would Grant come to me if I did? No. I know he won't. He'd been adamant about us not knowing each other in public. Not that we ever meet, even by accident. His age, reputation, and position would stand the titillating scandal that would sweep though my small community. I would be doomed and, knowing his thoughts about the subject, so would our relationship.

I miss Grant constantly but the nights are the worst and seem to be getting more so. My hand has once again become my lover and a very poor substitute it is indeed, especially since I now know what another's is capable of doing to me.

The summer days hadn't been all total pleasure, but even so, no matter what had occurred each time, they had ended in my being consumed by the raging fires of Grant's passion. The good parts, the yearning for more, have made many of the other memories fade and become insignificant. I'd gladly endure all the bad moments again for one blazing night in Grant's arms. Even his rage and retribution would be preferable to this nothingness I now live through, each long day slowly, tortuously passing to bring me one day closer to seeing him. But that is not to be for another nine months. How will I ever endure it?

The school bell rings and almost at once the students begin to pour into the classroom. Noisy. Boisterous. Sullen. Expectant. They're just at the age where they are desperate to appear more worldly. More macho. More sophisticated.

I notice some of the boys seem to scrutinize me closely. Assessing me. Weighing the odds of who knows what in their minds. Do they tune me out and daydream about their fantasies with me? Do they wonder what it would be like to love an older woman? Do they stare more this year or is it that I'm more aware of the strong. steady, sexual undertone that seems to hum and vibrate from their young, vibrant bodies?

Am I different? Do my experiences proclaim themselves in my expression? My demeanor? Does my yearning show? Can some of the more mature boys tell I'd be an easy target? Would any of them dare? Do I wish they would? Are they just fantasizing about their own forbidden dreams as they struggle through the end of puberty or do they wish I was a part of it? Do they have any idea how many different ways there are to make love? Would someone so young, so eager, so open to new ideas make a good lover?

I stand quickly and force myself to concentrate on the lesson that the state demands I teach. Thoughts like that will lead to nowhere but trouble.

I swear each minute becomes an hour as the day progresses. The teenagers have as little interest in learning as I do in teaching. They're still reliving their summer vacations and aren't ready to buckle down and concentrate on the day-to-day routine. Neither am I. Will I ever be again?

I rush down the steps of the porch knowing I've hurt my mother's feelings, but I'll start screaming if I listen to her tell me about Mrs. Carroll's stroke one more time. How have I stood it for so many years? Has my life been so meaningless that someone's misfortune was the topic of conversation for weeks at a time? Mom's hurt eyes haunt me and guilt invades my soul, but now it's not enough to stop me leaving. I've learned to be a little selfish when it comes to my needs and desires. I've learned, too well, that I have needs and desires.

The seats in my car are hot. The backs of my thighs tingle and burn. I feel the stinging high up. Immediately it reminds me of the hot passionate days on board the yacht. Sun, heat, the burning of my buttocks and thighs, the burning of my insides always before the sweet relief of rapture.

A drop of perspiration drips off my chin. The air is stifling. Summer is lingering this year. I flip the switch for the AC as soon as the car starts and back out of the gravel drive without glancing at my mother on the porch. I have to get away. Everything is closing in around me.

The street is straight and wide open to the sun. Not a shadow appears. Not a spot of shade to protect the smallest of creatures, never mind man. The air shimmers with heat, distorting the horizon I'm heading for. I imagine standing naked on the hot pavement and feeling the heat shimmering, humming along my body like a thousand infinitesimal invisible hot vibrators. Prickles of sweat break out on my brow even as the cool air hits my face. I step on the accelerator and drive aimlessly.

The roads are empty. I steer automatically with no thought of direction as my mind wanders back and forth between today and last summer. Everything is dry and dusty. It makes me feel old, used up. The farmers will begin to harvest their crops soon, and the cooling fall breezes may then flow over the land.

A long while later a patch of blue beyond some trees catches my eye and I slow down. A small lake glistens in the distance. I pull over to the side and stare at it. It's so cool looking, inviting. An obscure dirt track leads from the road to it. White-tipped prairie grass waves gently to and fro in the hot breeze as if beckoning me, defying me to trespass, to do what I never would have done a few months ago. Daring me. Challenging me with its inviting color and promise of coolness to bury my guilt and make myself happy.

Opening the door, I ignore the blast of heat that hits me. Standing, I see nothing but fields of crops stretching far into the distance, the spot of blue with a few trees around it looking more remote than before, more tempting. There is no sign of the farm that I know is probably just over the rise. There is no sign of life in any direction.

To be in the midst of someone's vast property but so totally alone is both thrilling and intimidating. My heart beats faster. The fields of crops and grass go on forever, the gently waving tops seeming to offer caresses if one should choose to walk amongst them.

What would it feel like to walk naked through the undulating fields? Would the tips caress with feathery touches, reminding me of long, languid caresses? Or would they be sharp and stinging, reminding me of harsher, keener moments with Grant? My nipples harden with need and I look out over the never-ending fields with both trepidation and yearning.

The magnitude is staggering. I feel like a tiny speck in the universe. The only friendly thing in sight is the inviting blue of the lake. I heed its call. I'll stay with Mrs. Carroll a few nights to relieve my mother of the burden and me of my guilt.

I stop the car under the largest tree and shut off the engine. Immediately, the car becomes hot, and I quickly open both windows, the thin, hot breeze slightly cooler in the shade of the tree. The water ripples softly, the almost nonexistent waves lap the shore, and I envision myself once again on Grant's island.

I can almost feel the sand beneath me, cool in the summer night. My nakedness is caressed by the silent, balmy breeze. My legs are open and the gentle waves lick and lap at my source. It was such a gentle climax. A necessary one that calmed and soothed so I was finally able to let Grant love me as he wished to.

I jerk from my reverie when my arm touches the burning-hot metal of the car. Rubbing my arm softly, I stare at my dress. Light blue. Thin. One that Grant bought me. Then, I was forbidden to wear undergarments. Here, I don't dare not to. It took me a long time to get used to the confines of bra and panties again. And I'm still not used to it completely.

I throw the keys in my purse and open the door. My eyes scan the horizon in all directions. I'm so alone. So deliciously alone with all that cool water in front of me. It's impossible to resist its allure, and I don't even try.

The dress falls onto the soft grass, the bra and panties following. The cushioning grass is soft beneath my feet. The air whispers around me, slightly cooling my sweat-soaked body. Insects hum.

Time seems to slow down. A bird lands on a high branch and sings me a song as I step into the silky liquid.

This is heaven. I toss my short tresses and stretch my arms high above me. The breeze kisses me with featherlight breath. I wade deeper and then plunge. Cool, heavenly water laves my body, and I stay below in its delightful embrace as long as my lungs allow.

This is bliss. Grant would like this. It's not as exotic as the oasis on his island, but he'd appreciate its beauty. I float on my back, hands languidly propelling me along. The oasis had been a place of pain and pleasure. Of storm and calm. Of raw sex and fiery passion. I wish I were there. Will we return next summer?

I hear a buzz that grows louder than the insects that whirr and buzz as they pester me occasionally. Shading my eyes I see a small plane high up in the sky. A sly, devilish smile curls my lips. Is it the owner of the lake? Can he see me? Do I want him to? What would he think to find a naked woman in his lake, breasts bobbing merrily above the water, my once-again-thick thatch peeking up at him?

Will he land and come storming over here? To what? Throw me out? Throw me down and ravish me? I can't help laughing at myself. The plane is so high I'm sure he can't see me. Wishful thinking has lately been unfulfilled and this time will be no different.

I dive, relishing the silkiness of the liquid on my skin. The water is so still, so silent. Nothing at all like the pounding of the ocean on Long Island's east end. I clasp my legs tightly together and relive the first time I swam in the ocean. Grant had made it a memorable occasion. But all my times with Grant have been memorable.

I open my eyes and my world is now a silent, cool, shimmering green. Grass grows on the bottom, its swaying dreamy movements hypnotic. Erotic. I rise, gulp in a breath of air and dive down, swimming low and letting the blades tickle and tease my breasts and belly as I skim them lightly. Silky, slick edges of green make me yearn anew for the strong, steely fingers that used to caress me. I'm gasping for breath by the time I give in to my body's demands and surface.

A cloud has covered the sun and my mood of decadent naughtiness fades. The magic dissipates and the too-familiar gloom intrudes. How sad to have something so wonderful and no one to share it with.

I drag myself from the water and shake my head like a shaggy dog. My hands roam over my body, flicking the water beads from it. They linger on my breasts but I stop myself. That is less than satisfying lately.

The shade of the tree is cool, and I shiver slightly before stopping dead in my tracks. Wide blue eyes twinkle with amusement as they watch my progress. He's sitting cross-legged where my clothes and purse had been. Youngish, early twenties perhaps, almost platinum hair and the most roguish smile I've ever seen.

Instinctively I cover my breasts, then my mound, then try to do both at the same time. I feel my belly churn with want even as the blood suffuses my cheeks. His smile is beguiling. I'm torn between warring emotions. His chuckle breaks my silence. He's too superior.

"How dare you spy on me!" What an inane, spinsterish thing to say. His roving eyes make my body tingle.

"I believe you're trespassing, ma'am."

"That has nothing to do with your despicable behavior. Would you please leave and I'll be off your land as soon as I can get dressed." My attempt at outraged haughtiness is having little effect on him. He grins wider and rises slowly to his feet in one fluid movement. I hate myself for being so weak. He has such a nice body.

"Not my land. You can stay as long as you like as far as I care. I kinda like the view myself."

Too many emotions rage within me. I feel no fear of him. It's myself I worry about. His total maleness is so obvious. I have to leave quickly or I won't want to leave at all. My eyes flick around but I can't spot my clothes anywhere.

"Did you move my clothes?"

"Hid them." He grins at my startled expression, and my mouth goes dry as he begins slowly to remove his shirt. He's tan and muscular. His hands are large and rough from whatever work he does. His eyes continually slide up and down my body. And my body is responding. My breathing is ragged and irregular. My nipples are harder than stone.

I don't know what to do. I should run. I want to stay. It's exciting and adventurous. Risky and scary. And by the look in his eye I'll have very little to say about it.

That's what makes me finally turn and try for the car. I don't want to be under anyone's control again. I'm surprised he doesn't try to stop me till I reach for the door handle. It's jammed. I can't lock myself in. I just stare at it stupidly till I sense him behind me and turn. I'm a little frightened but still don't think he'll hurt me. His grin is so confident, so wonderfully wicked.

"I think we'll be more comfortable on the grass. Your car is on the small side, ma'am."

I can't take my eyes from his. They probe and seem to read my thoughts. His grin widens and he raises his hand for me to take. It all has such an unreal quality about it. Like a dream one once had and can just scarcely remember. Like a dream I've had too many times since Grant and I parted. He takes my hand when I don't take his.

His touch is light but firm and his skin is rough. He leads me to a soft grassy knoll and kneels, taking me with him. I haven't uttered a sound or made any attempt to get away from him. Is this really happening? His eyes are so blue, so knowing.

Rugged hands frame my face and then firm lips slant to mine. The touch of his probing tongue breaks my trance and I give a jerk of resistance but he holds me. My hands push against an unyielding granite chest. He doesn't seem to notice. His tongue is making my head spin. It seeks and investigates the recesses of my mouth. It searches and soothes. My tongue is sucked into his mouth, and his teeth nibble it gently. My hands are holding onto his shoulders. I'm drawn close. His coarse chest hair tickles and teases my heaving breasts. I rub them against it in delight. I feel my hardened peaks skim over his tiny, equally hard nipples. His penis is thick and solid. It slaps against my belly.

And I want him. I want a man so desperately. Grant has spoiled me and I won't deny myself this unexpected opportunity. I pull him close and rub against him. His hands release my head. They skim my shoulders, tickle my ribs. My breasts ache for his touch, but he teases me. Sides, waist, belly. I arch into him. I want to feel the tube against my mound. He pulls back slightly. I moan with frustration. His tongue traces a path along my collarbone. I raise my breasts for his mouth. He ignores them. Neck, shoulder, chin, jaw, eyes, and then back to my mouth. I groan and seek his hardness. My hands are taken and held behind me. Gently he pulls me backward till his hands hold mine on the ground. I'm stretched before him on my knees, legs wide, breasts thrust out. I'm pleading with him with my eyes. He ignores me. My breath is ragged, my chest heaving.

"Please." I hate myself for begging.

His eyes watch me silently for a long moment. "When I'm ready."

And then I know. He won't harm me. He'll get his kicks out of tormenting me. I want him desperately and he's going to use it. My body is screaming with frustration, and I'll do anything to find my release. And he knows that, too.

My hands are released, and he leans back from me and watches me. It takes everything I have not to reach for myself. He knows it, too. I can see it in his eyes. I hate him and he grins wider. He knows that as well, and he's enjoying it.

I raise up till I'm kneeling in front of him. His sandpaper hands reach for my breasts. He takes the nipples and squeezes them gently. I can't stop my gasp of pleasure. The pressure increases and I lean toward him, seeking his mouth. His hands push me back by my breasts. I'm to be touched, to be toyed with, but not allowed to touch. I would give anything to have the strength of character to leave, but I need him too much.

His hands knead and stroke, over and over. My mouth is slack, my breathing tortured. I would clamp my legs tight but his knees are between them. My hands reach for him, but he gently smacks them down. My clit is throbbing, pulsing with need. My hands seek it. They're taken and raised. His eyes bore into mine.

"Put your hands behind your head."

I hesitate.

"Now, or I leave." No raised voice. Just the effective, quiet threat. I do as he says. My breasts thrust out more. He flicks the turgid peaks with his tongue. I almost swoon. My legs grip his knees hard. I hear his chuckle. Feel his tongue glide from one tip to another. My body is trembling with need.

A finger touches my lips. "Suck."

I do.

"More."

I do.

A rhythmic pinching on my left nipple. I bite my lip with yearning. If he would just keep doing that I know I could come. I want him to touch me between my legs. The finger leaves my mouth. He leans toward me, teeth grab and worry my right nipple, his finger jams into my ass. I grunt and fall forward against him. My hands grab his shoulders. His mouth leaves my breast. His finger slides in and out steadily. His other hand kneads and molds my ass in time with his probing finger.

I'm a mass of sensation. I'm almost there. My belly heats up and then he stops and stands up. I collapse in a sobbing heap. My hands cup my mound.

"Do it and I leave." His words stop me cold. I lie panting, staring up at him. He's broad and tanned; the dark green leaves above silhouette him perfectly.

"Why are you doing this?" My voice is strangled as I fight the need to help myself.

He stares at me for a moment and then grins wickedly. "Because I've never in my life seen a woman more desperate for a man."

I wish I could stand and defy him. I wish he couldn't read me so well.

"Get on all fours."

I do. Slowly. Reluctantly. He kneels in front of me.

"Suck it."

I do. He's thick and short. It stretches my mouth but doesn't make me gag. I can sense him watching my lips close around his shaft. Why do men like to watch? I never want to see a man make love to me. I want to feel the man make love to me. He stays perfectly still. I move up and down steadily. I feel it swell.

"Turn around."

I do.

"Back into me."

I do. I slowly crawl backward till I feel his hard knob nudge my sphincter.

"If you want it do it."

And much to my shame, I do. I push against him till I feel the muscle give and slide onto his cock. He stretches me but doesn't fill me. It's another tease and I know I won't be able to climax this way. How could he possibly know it too?

He works me back and forth with his hands on my hips. If he'd only touch my clit. Just once. Just for one minute. I'm so far gone it wouldn't take much. Why can't he fondle my breasts? Why do men love to torture women this way?

I'm pushed forward and he pulls out. He hasn't come. I still have a chance.

"Stand up. Hands behind your head."

I do. I thrust my chest out proudly. I suck in my belly slightly and part my legs. Grant has taught me to be proud of my body. Grant loves my small, perky breasts and boyish hips.

The man reaches out and draws me close to him. I can feel his breath on my mound. He blows on the hair and parts it delicately. My legs tremble. My clit is engorged. It peeks boldly out of the swollen lips. I know he can see it. Please touch it. Please. I feel myself sway. His hands tighten around my thighs and then, with no warning, his mouth devours me and I'm screaming in ecstasy, my fingers digging into his hair, holding him to me as spasm after rapturous spasm shakes me to the core.

But he doesn't stop. His tongue licks and teases. His teeth nibble lightly. His finger seeks and invades my tighter tunnel. Heat, incredible heat, seems to engulf me, and I rock and grind myself into his feeding mouth. Only his strong arms around my thighs keep me upright as he continues his assault. I'm spent, done, but still he continues and the sensations become hotter and hotter. I'm trembling like a leaf in a storm. My head whirls, my body shakes, my senses no sooner recuperate from one orgasm and he's bringing me relentlessly toward another.

"No." The word is so weak the gentle breeze carries it away. His tongue refuses to stop its invasion of my body. It's intense, not quite painful, but mind shattering in its ferocity when it takes me. I sag, a finger pushes harder into my anus and still the tongue probes my inside depths. It's too tender but he won't listen and continues on as if obsessed.

My body is limp. I'm almost draped over his head. He lays me down and pins my hands to my sides and still he ravages me with his mouth. Sucking, licking, nibbling. I'm moaning with yearning. This is the worst kind of torture. Tender, aching deliciousness.

My clit is sucked in and chewed lightly. Bolts of painful pleasure travel up my body. My hands are released. My nipples grabbed, pinched, pulled, and twisted, but so gently it does nothing but make me want him to continue his onslaught. And he does until I finally scream in aching bliss.

I have less than a moment to try to regain my senses. He drops on me and enters me fast and furiously. His pounding is harder on my hips than my cunt as he grinds away, but he's finished in a scant minute and rolls from me. He's gone when I wake.

My clothes are exactly where I left them. The door handle is back in place. If not for the soreness of my pelvis and the dried semen on my thighs I'd have wondered if I'd dreamt it. My body is stiff as if I've been pummeled, and I only walk normally after a long, cool swim in the lake. I feel calmer than I have for a long time but it's still not Grant. He's the one I ache for.

Alice

Anonymous

I, the Man, will not take up the time of my readers by detailing the circumstances under which Alice, the Maid, roused in me the desire for vengeance which resulted in the tale I am about to relate. Suffice it to say that Alice cruelly and unjustifiably jilted me! In my bitterness of spirit, I swore that if I ever had an opportunity to get hold of her, I would make her voluptuous person recompense me for my disappointment and that I would snatch from her by force the bridegroom's privileges that I so ardently coveted. But I dissemble! Alice and I had many mutual friends to whom this rupture was unknown; we were therefore constantly meeting each other, and if I gave her the slightest hint of my intentions towards her it would have been fatal to the very doubtful chances of success that I had! Indeed, so successfully did I conceal my real feelings under a cloak of genuine acceptance of her action that she had not the faintest idea (as she afterwards admitted to me) that I was playing a part.

But, as the proverb says, everything comes to the man who waits. For some considerable time, it seemed as if it would be wise on my part to abandon my desire for vengeance, as the circumstances of our daily lives were such as did not promise the remotest chance of my getting possession of Alice under conditions of either place or time suitable for the accomplishment of my purpose. Nevertheless, I controlled my patience and hoped for the best, enduring as well as I could the torture of unsatisfied desire and increasing lust.

It then happened that I had occasion to change my residence, and in my search for fresh quarters, I came across a modest suite consisting of a sitting room and two bedrooms, which would by themselves have suited me excellently; but with them the landlord desired to let what he termed a box or lumber room. I demurred to this addition, but as he remained firm, I asked to see the room. It was most peculiar both as regards access and appearance. The former was by a short passage from the landing and furnished with remarkably well-fitting doors at each end. The room was nearly square, of a good size and lofty, but the walls were unbroken, save by the one entrance, light and air being derived from a skylight, or rather lantern, which occupied the greater part of the roof and was supported by four strong and stout wooden pillars. Further, the walls were thickly padded, while iron rings were let into them at regular distances all 'round in two rows, one close to the door and the other at a height of about eight feet. From the roof beams, rope pulleys dangled in pairs between the pillars, while the two recesses on the entrance side, caused by the projection of the passage into the room, looked as if they had at one time been separated from the rest of the room by bars, almost as if they were cells. So strange indeed was the appearance of the whole room that I asked its history and was informed that the house had been built as a private lunatic asylum at the time that the now unfashionable square in which it stood was one of the centers of fashion, and that this was the old "mad room" in which violent patients were confined, the bolts, rings, and pulleys being used to restrain them when they were very violent, while the padding and the double doors made the room absolutely sound-proof and prevented the ravings of the inmates from annoying the neighbors. The landlord added that the sound-proof quality was no fiction, as the room had frequently been tested by incredulous visitors.

Like lightning the thought flashed through my brain. Was not this room the very place for the consummation of my scheme of revenge? If I succeeded in luring Alice into it, she would be completely at my mercy—her screams for help would not be heard and would only increase my pleasure, while the bolts, rings, pulleys, etc., supplemented with a little suitable furniture, would enable me to secure her in any way I wished and to hold her fixed while I amused myself with her. Delighted with the idea, I agreed to include the room in my suite. Quietly, but with deep fore-thought and planning, I commissioned certain furniture made which, while in outward appearance most innocent, as well as most comfortable, was in truth full of hidden mechanisms planned for the special discomfiture of any woman or girl that I might wish to hold in physical control. I had the floor covered with thick Persian carpets and rugs, and the two alcoves converted into nominal photographic laboratories, but in a way that made them suitable for lavatories and dressing rooms.

When completed, the "Snuggery" (as I christened it) was really in appearance a distinctly pretty and comfortable room, while in reality it was nothing more or less than a disguised Torture Chamber!

And now came the difficult part of my scheme.

How to entrap Alice? Unfortunately she was not residing in London but a little way out. She lived with a married sister and never seemed to come to town except in her sister's company. My difficulty, therefore, was how to get Alice by herself for a sufficiently long time to accomplish my designs. Sorely I cudgeled my brains over this problem!

The sister frequently visited town at irregular intervals as dictated by the contingencies of social duties or shopping. True to my policy of *l'entente cordiale* I had welcomed them to my rooms for rest and refreshment and had encouraged them to use my quarters; and partly because of the propinquity of the rooms to Regent Street, partly because of the very dainty meals I invariably placed before them, but mainly because of the soothing restfulness induced by the absolute quiet of the Snuggery after the roar and turmoil of the streets, it soon became their regular practice to honor me with their company for luncheon or tea whenever they came to town and had no special engagement. I need hardly add that secretly I hoped these visits might bring me an opportunity of executing my revenge, but for some months I seemed doomed to disappointment: I used to suffer the tortures of Tantalus when I saw Alice unsuspectingly braving me in the very room I had prepared for her violation, in very touch of me and of the hidden machinery that would place her at my disposal once I set it working. Alas, I was unable to do so because of her sister's presence! In fact, so keenly did I feel the position that I began to plan the capture of both sisters together, to include Marion in the punishment designed for Alice, and the idea in itself was not unpleasant, as Marion was a fine specimen of female flesh and blood of a larger and more stately type than Alice (who was "petite"). One could do much worse than to have her at one's disposal for an hour or two to feel and fuck! So seriously did I entertain this project that I got an armchair made in such a way that the releasing of a secret catch would set free a mechanism that would be actuated by the weight of the occupant and would cause the arms to fold inwards and firmly imprison the sitter. Furnished with luxurious upholstery and the catch fixed, it made the most inviting of chairs, and from its first appearance Alice took possession of it, in happy ignorance that it was intended to hold her firmly imprisoned while I tackled and secured Marion!

Before, however, I resorted to this desperate measure, my patience was rewarded! And this is how it happened.

One evening, the familiar note came to say the sisters were traveling to town on the next day and would come for lunch. A little before the appointed hour Alice, to my surprise, appeared alone! She said that after the note had been posted Marion became ill and had been resting poorly all night and so could not come to town. The shopping engagement was one of considerable importance to Alice, and therefore she had come up alone. She had not come for lunch, she said, but had merely called to explain matters to me. She would get a cup of tea and a bun somewhere else.

Against this desertion of me I vigorously protested, but I doubt if I would have induced her to stay had not a smart shower of rain come on. This made her hesitate about going out into it since the dress she was wearing would be ruined. Finally she consented to have lunch and leave immediately afterwards.

While she was away in the spare bedroom used by the sisters on their visits, I was in a veritable turmoil of excitement! Alice in my rooms by herself! It seemed too good to be true! But I remembered I yet had to get her into the Snuggery; she was absolutely safe from my designs everywhere but there! It was imperative that she should be in no way alarmed, and so, with a strong effort, I controlled my panting excitement and by the time Alice rejoined me in the dining room I was my usual self.

Lunch was quickly served. At first, Alice seemed a little nervous and constrained, but by tactful conversation, I soon set her at ease and she then chatted away naturally and merrily. I had craftily placed her with her back to the window so that she should not note that a bad storm was evidently brewing: and soon, with satisfaction, I saw that the weather was getting worse and worse! But it might at any moment begin to clear away, and so the sooner I could get her into my Snuggery, the better for me—and the worse for her! So by every means in my power, I hurried on the procedure of lunch.

Alice was leisurely finishing her coffee when a rattle of rain against the window panes, followed by an ominous growl of thunder, made her start from her chair and go to the casement. "Oh! just look at the rain!" she exclaimed in dismay. "How very unfortunate!"

I joined her at the window: "By Jove, it is bad!" I replied, then added, "and it looks like it's lasting. I hope that you have no important engagement for the afternoon that will keep you much in the open." As I spoke, there came a vivid flash of lightning closely followed by a peal of thunder, which sent Alice staggering backwards with a scared face.

"Oh!" she exclaimed, evidently frightened; then, after a pause, she said: "I am a horrid little coward in a thunderstorm: It just terrifies me!"

"Won't you then take refuge in the Snuggery?" I asked with a host's look of concern. "I don't think you will see the lightning there and you certainly won't hear the thunder, as the room is sound-proof. Shall we go there?" and I opened the door invitingly.

Alice hesitated. Was her guardian angel trying to give her a premonitory hint of what her fate would be if she accepted my seemingly innocent suggestion? But at that moment came another flash of lightning blinding in its intensity, and almost simultaneously a roar of thunder. This settled the question in my favor. "Yes, yes!" she exclaimed, then ran out, I closely followed her, my heart beating exultantly! Quickly she passed through the double doors into the Snuggery, the trap I had so carefully set for her was about to snap shut! Noiselessly I bolted the outer door, then closed the inner one. Alice was now mine! Mine!! At last I had trapped her! Now my vengeance was about to be consummated! Now her chaste virgin self was to be submitted to my lust and compelled to satisfy my erotic desires! She was utterly at my mercy, and promptly I proceeded to work my will on her!

The soothing stillness of the room after the roar of the storm seemed most gratifying to Alice. She drew a deep breath of relief and turning to me she exclaimed: "What a wonderful room it really is, Jack! Just look how the rain is pelting down on the skylight, and yet we do not hear a sound!"

"Yes! There is no doubt about it," I replied, "it is absolutely sound-proof. I do not suppose that there is a better room in London for my special purpose!"

"What might that be, Jack?" she asked interestedly.

"Your violation, my dear!" I replied quietly, looking her straight in the face, "the surrender to me of your maidenhead!"

She started as if she had been struck. She colored hotly. She stared at me as if she doubted her hearing. I stood still and calmly watched her. Then indignation and the sense of outrage seized her.

"You must be mad to speak like that!" she said in a voice that trembled with concentrated anger. "You forget yourself. Be good enough to consider our friendship as suspended till you have recovered your senses and have suitably apologized for this intolerable insult. Meanwhile I will trouble you only to call a cab so that I may remove myself from your hateful presence!" And her eyes flashed in wrathful indignation.

I quietly laughed aloud: "Do you really think I would have taken this step without calculating the consequences, Alice?" I rejoined coolly. "Do you really think I have lost my senses? Is there not a little account to be settled between us for what you did to me not very long ago? The day of reckoning has come, my dear; you havc had your inning at my cost, now I am going to have mine at yours! You amused yourself with my heart, I am going to amuse myself with your body."

Alice stared at me, silent with surprise and horror! My quiet determined manner staggered her. She paled when I referred to the past, and she flushed painfully as I indicated what her immediate future would be. After a slight pause I spoke again:

"I have deliberately planned this revenge! I took these rooms solely because they would lend themselves so admirably to this end. I have prepared them for every contingency, even to having to subjugate you by force! Look!" And I proceeded to reveal to her astonished eyes the mechanism concealed in the furniture, etc. "You know you cannot get out of this room till I choose to let you go; you know that your screams and cries for help will not be heard. You now must decide what you will do. I give you two alternatives, and two only: You must choose one of them. Will you submit yourself quietly to me, or do you prefer to be forced?"

Alice stamped her little foot in her rage: "How dare you speak to me in this way?" she demanded furiously. "Do you think I am a child? Let me go at once!" and she moved in her most stately manner to the door.

"You are no child," I replied with a cruel smile, "you are a lusciously lovely girl possessing everything that I desire and able to satisfy my desires. But I am not going to let you waste time. The whole afternoon will hardly be long enough for the satisfaction of my whims, caprices, and lust. Once more, will you submit or will you be forced? Understand that if by the time the clock strikes the half-hour, you do not consent to submit, I shall, without further delay, proceed to take by force what I want from you! Now make the most of the three minutes you have left." And turning from her, I proceeded to get the room ready, as if I anticipated that I would have to use force.

Overcome by her feelings and emotions, Alice sank into an armchair, burying her face in her trembling hand. She evidently recognized her dreadful position! How could she yield herself up to me? And yet if she did not, she knew she would have to undergo violation! And possibly horrible indignities as well!! I left her absolutely alone, and when I had finished my preparation, I quietly seated myself and watched her.

Presently the clock chimed the half-hour. Immediately I rose. Alice quickly sprang to her feet and rushed to the far side of the large divan-couch on which I hoped before long to see her extended naked! It was evident that she was going to resist and fight me. You should know that I welcomed her decision, as now she would give me ample justification for the fullest exercising of my lascivious desires!

"Well, Alice, what is it to be? Will you submit quietly?"

A sudden passion seemed to possess her. She looked me squarely in the eyes for the first time, hers blazing with rage and indignation: "No! no!" she exclaimed vehemently, "I defy you! Do your worst. Do you think you will frighten me into satisfying your lust? Once and for all I give you my answer: No! No! No! Oh, you cowardly brute and beast!" And she laughed shrilly as she turned herself away contemptuously.

"As you please," I replied quietly and calmly, "let those laugh who win! I venture to say that within half an hour, you will not only be offering yourself to me absolutely and unconditionally, but will be begging me to accept your surrender! Let us see!"

Alice laughed incredulously and defiantly: "Yes, let us see! Let us see!" she retorted contemptuously.

Forthwith I sprang towards her to seize her, but she darted away, I in hot pursuit. For a short time she succeeded in eluding me, dodging in and out of the furniture like a butterfly, but soon I maneuvered her into a corner, and, pouncing on her, gripped her firmly, then half dragged and half carried her to where a pair of electrically worked rope-pulleys hung between two of the pillars. She struggled desperately and screamed for help. In spite of her determined resistance, I soon made the ropes fast to her wrists, then touched the button; the ropes tightened, and slowly but irresistibly, Alice's arms were drawn upwards till her hands were well above her head and she was forced to stand erect by the tension on her arms. She was now utterly helpless and unable to defend her person from the hands that were itching to invade and explore the sweet mysteries of her garments; but what with her exertions and the violence of her emotions, she was in such a state of agitation that I deemed it wise to leave her to herself for a few minutes, till she became more mistress of herself, when she would be better able to appreciate the indignities which she would now be compelled to suffer!

Here I think I had better explain the mechanical means I had at my disposal for the discomfiture and subjugation of Alice.

Between each two of the pillars that supported the lantern-skylight hung a pair of strong rope-pulleys working on a roller mechanism concealed in the beams and actuated by electricity. Should I want Alice upright, I had simply to attach the ropes to her wrists, and her arms would be pulled straight up and well over her head, thus forcing her to stand erect, and at the same time rendering her body defenseless and at my mercy. The pillars themselves I could utilize as whipping posts, being provided with rings to which Alice could be fastened in such a way that she could not move!

Close by the pillars was a huge divan-couch upholstered in dark leather that admirably enhanced the pearly loveliness of a naked girl. It stood on eight massive legs (four on each long side), behind each of which lay, coiled for use, a stout leather strap worked by rollers hidden in the upholstery and actuated by electricity. On it were piled a lot of cushions of various sorts and consistencies, with which Alice and Marion used to make nests for themselves, little dreaming that the real object of the "Turkish Divan" (as they had christened it) was to be the altar on which Alice's virginity was sacrificed to the Goddess of Love, the mission of the straps being to hold her in position while she was violated, should she not surrender herself quietly to her fate!

By the keyboard of the grand piano stood a duet-stool also upholstered in leather and with the usual mechanical power of adjustment for height, only to a much greater extent than usual. But the feature of the stool was its unusual length, a full six feet, and I one day had to satisfy Alice's curiosity by telling her that this was for the purpose of providing a comfortable seat to anyone who might be turning pages for the pianist! The real reason was that the stool was, for all practical purposes, a rack actuated by hidden machinery and fitted with a most ingenious arrangement of steps, the efficacy of which I looked forward to testing on Alice's tender self!

The treacherous armchair I have already explained. My readers can now perhaps understand that I could fix Alice in practically any position or attitude and keep her so fixed while I worked my sweet will on her helpless self!

All the ropes and straps were fitted with swivel snap-hooks. To attach them to Alice's limbs, I used an endless band of the longest and softest silk rope that I could find. It was an easy matter to slip a double length of the band 'round her wrist or ankle, pass one end through the other and draw tight then snap the free end into the swivel hook. No amount of plunging or struggling would loosen this attachment, and the softness of the silk prevented Alice's delicate flesh from being rubbed or even marked.

During the ten minute grace period I mentally allowed Alice in which to recover from the violence of her struggles, I quietly studied her as she stood helpless, almost supporting herself by resting her weight on her wrist. She was to me an exhilarating spectacle, her bosom fluttering, rising and falling as she caught her breath, her cheeks still flushing, her large hat somewhat disarranged, while her dainty well-fitting dress displayed her figure to its fullest advantage.

She regained command of herself wonderfully quickly, and then it was evident that she was stealthily watching me in horrible apprehension. I did not leave her long in suspense, but after going slowly 'round her and inspecting her, I placed a chair right in front of her, so close to her its edge almost touched her knees, then slipped myself into it, keeping my legs apart, so that she stood between them, the front of her dress pressing against the fly of my trousers. Her head was now above mine, so that I could peer directly into her downcast face.

As I took up this position, Alice trembled nervously and tried to draw herself away from me, but found herself compelled to stand as I had placed her. Noticing the action, I drew my legs closer to each other so as to loosely hold her between them, smiling cruelly at the uncontrollable shudder that passed through her, when she felt the pressure of my knees against hers! Then I extended my arms, clasped her gently 'round the waist, and drew her against me, at the same time tightening the clutch of my legs, till soon she was fairly in my embrace, my face pressing against her throbbing bosom. For a moment she struggled wildly, then resigned herself to the unavoidable as she recognized her helplessness.

Except when dancing with her, I had never held Alice in my arms, and the embrace permitted by the waltz was nothing to the comprehensive clasping between arms and legs in which she now found herself. She trembled fearfully, her tremors giving me exquisite pleasure as I felt them shoot through her, then she murmured: "Please don't, Jack!"

I looked up into her flushed face as I amorously pressed my cheek against the swell of her bosom: "Don't you like it, Alice?" I said maliciously, as I squeezed her still more closely against me. "I think you're just delicious, dear, and I am trying to imagine what it will feel like when your clothes have been taken off!"

"No! No! Jack!" she moaned, agonizingly, twisting herself in her distress, "let me go, Jack; don't...don't..." and her voice failed her.

For an answer, I held her against me with my left arm around her waist, then with my right hand I began to stroke and press her hips and bottom.

"Oh...! Don't, Jack! Don't!" Alice shrieked, squirming in distress and futilely endeavoring to avoid my marauding hand. I paid no attention to her pleading and cries, but continued my stroking and caressing over her full posteriors and thighs down to her knees, then back to her buttocks and haunches, she, all the while, quivering in a delicious way. Then I freed my left hand, and holding her tightly imprisoned between my legs, I proceeded with both hands to study, through her clothes, the configuration of her backside and hips and thighs, handling her buttocks with a freedom that seemed to stagger her, as she pressed herself against me in an effort to escape from the liberties that my hands were taking with her charms.

After toying delightfully with her in this way for some time, I ceased and withdrew my hands from her hips, but only to pass them up and down over her bosom, which I began lovingly to stroke and caress to her dismay. Her color rose as she swayed uneasily on her legs. But her stays prevented any direct attack on her bosom, so I decided to open her clothes sufficiently to obtain a peep at her virgin breasts. I set to work unbuttoning her blouse.

"Jack, no! No!!" shrieked Alice, struggling vainly to get loose. But I only smiled and continued to undo her blouse till I got it completely open and threw it back onto her shoulders, only to be balked as a fairly high bodice covered her bosom. I set to work opening this, my fingers reveling in the touch of Alice's dainty linen. Soon it also was open and thrown back—and then, right before my eager eyes, lay the snowy expanse of Alice's bosom, her breasts being visible nearly as far as their nipples!

"Oh!...oh!..." she moaned in her distress, flushing painfully at this cruel exposure. But I was too excited to take any notice; my eyes were riveted on the lovely swell of her breasts, exhibiting the valley between the twin globes, now heaving and fluttering under her agitated emotions. Unable to restrain myself, I threw my arms 'round Alice's waist, drew her closely to me, and pressed my lips on her palpitating flesh, which I kissed furiously.

"Don't, Jack," cried Alice, as she tugged frantically at her fastenings in her wild endeavors to escape from my passionate lips; but instead of stopping me, my mouth wandered all over her heaving delicious breasts, punctuating its progress with hot kisses that seemed to drive her mad, to such a pitch, in fact, that I thought it best to desist.

"Oh! my God!" she moaned as I relaxed my clasp and leaned back in my chair to enjoy the sight of her shame and distress. There was not the least doubt that she felt most keenly my indecent assault, and so I determined to worry her with lascivious liberties a little longer.

When she had become calmer, I passed my arms around her waist and again began to play with her posteriors, then, stooping down, I got my hands under her clothes and commenced to pull them up. Flushing violently, Alice shrieked to me to desist, but in vain! In a trice, I turned her petticoats up, held them thus with my left hand while with my right I proceeded to attack her bottom, now protected only by her dainty thin drawers!

The sensation was delicious! My hand delightedly roved over the fat plump cheeks of her arse, stroking, caressing, and pinching them, reveling in the firmness and elasticity of her flesh under its thin covering, Alice all the time wriggling and squirming in horrible shame, imploring me almost incoherently to desist and finally getting so hysterical that I was compelled to suspend my exquisite game. So, to her great relief, I dropped her skirts, pushed my chair back, and rose.

I had in the room a large plate glass mirror nearly eight feet high that reflected one at full length. While Alice was recovering from her last ordeal, I pushed this mirror close in front of her, placing it so that she could see herself in its center. She started uneasily as she caught sight of herself, for I had left her bosom uncovered, and the reflection of herself in such shameful *déshabille* in conjunction with her large hat (which she still retained) seemed vividly to impress on her the horror of her position!

Having arranged the mirror to my satisfaction, I picked up the chair and placed it just behind Alice, sat down in it, and worked myself forward on it till Alice again stood between my legs, but this time with her back to me. The mirror faithfully reflected my movements, and her feminine intuition warned her that the front of her person was now about to become the object of my indecent assault.

But I did not give her time to think. Quickly I encircled her waist again with my arms, drew her to me till her bottom pressed against my chest; then, while my left arm held her firmly, my right hand began to wander over the junction of her stomach and legs, pressing inquisitively her groin and thighs and intently watching her in the mirror.

Her color rose, her breath came unevenly, she quivered and trembled as she pressed her thighs closely together. She was horribly perturbed, but I do not think she anticipated what then happened.

Quietly dropping my hands, I slipped them under her clothes, caught hold of her ankles, then proceeded to climb up her legs over her stockings.

"No! no! for God's sake, don't, Jack!" Alice yelled, now scarlet with shame and wild with alarm at this invasion of her most secret parts. Frantically she dragged at her fastenings, her hands clenched, her head thrown back, her eyes dilated with horror. Throwing the whole of her weight on her wrists, she strove to free her legs from my attacking hands by kicking out desperately, but to no avail. The sight in the mirror of her struggles only stimulated me into a refinement of cruelty, for with one hand I raised her clothes waist high, exposing her in her dainty drawers and black silk stockings, while with the other I vigorously attacked her thighs over her drawers, forcing a way between them and finally working up so close to her cunt that Alice practically collapsed in an agony of apprehension and would have fallen had it not been for the sustaining ropes that were all that supported her as she hung in a semi-hysterical faint.

Quickly rising and dropping her clothes, I placed an armchair behind her and loosened the pulleys till she rested comfortably in it, then left her to recover herself, feeling pretty confident that she was now not far from surrendering herself to me, rather than continue a resistance which she could not help but see was utterly useless. This was what I wanted to effect. I did not propose to let her off any single one of the indignities I had in store for her, but I wanted to make her suffering the more keen, through the feeling that she was, to some extent, a consenting party to actions that inexpressibly shocked and revolted her. The first of these I intended to be the removal of her clothes, and, as soon as Alice became more mistress of herself, I set the pulleys working and soon had her standing erect with her arms stretched above her head.

She glanced fearfully at me as if trying to learn what was now going to happen to her. I deemed it as well to tell her, and to afford her an opportunity of yielding herself to me, if she should be willing to do so. I also wanted to save her clothes from being damaged, as she was really beautifully dressed, and I was not at all confident that I could get her garments off her without using a scissors on some of them.

"I see you want to know what is going to happen to you, Alice," I said. "I'll tell you. You are to be stripped naked, utterly and absolutely naked; not a stitch of any sort is to be left on you!"

A flood of crimson swept over her face, invading both neck and bosom, which remained bare; her head fell forward as she moaned: "No!...No!...Oh! Jack...Jack...how can you..." and she swayed uneasily on her feet.

"That is to be the next item in the program, my dear!" I said, enjoying her distress. "There is only one detail that remains to be settled first and that is, will you undress yourself quietly if I set you loose, or must I drag your clothes off you? I don't wish to influence your decision, and I know what queer ideals girls have about taking off their clothes in the presence of a man; I will leave the decision to you, only saying that I do not see what you have to gain by further resistance, and some of your garments may be ruined—which would be a pity. Now, which is it to be?"

She looked at me imploringly for a moment, trembling in every limb, then averting her eyes, but remaining silent, evidently torn by conflicting emotions.

"Come, Alice," I said presently, "I must have your decision or I shall proceed to take your clothes off you as best as I can."

Alice was now in a terrible state of distress! Her eyes wandered all over the room without seeming to see anything, incoherent murmurs escaped from her lips, as if she was trying to speak but could not, her breath came and went, her bosom rose and fell agitatedly. She was evidently endeavoring to form some decision, but found herself unable to do so.

I remained still for a brief space as if awaiting her answer; then, as she did not speak, I quietly went to a drawer, took out a pair of scissors and went back to her. At the sight of the scissors, she shivered, then with an effort, said, in a voice broken with emotion: "Don't...undress me, Jack! If you must...have me, let it be as I am...I will...submit quietly...oh! my God!!" she wailed.

"That won't do, dear," I replied, not unkindly, but still firmly, "you must be naked, Alice; now, will you or will you not undress yourself?"

Alice shuddered, cast another imploring glance at me, but seeing no answering gleam of pity in my eyes, but stern determination instead, she stammered out: "Oh! Jack! I can't! Have some pity on me, Jack, and...have me as I am! I promise I'll be...quiet!"

I shook my head, I saw there was only one thing for me to do, namely, to undress her without any further delay; and I set to work to do so, Alice crying piteously: "Don't, Jack; don't!...don't!"

I had left behind her the armchair in which I had allowed her to rest, and her blouse and bodice were still hanging open and thrown back on her shoulders. So I got on the chair and worked them along her arms and over her clenched hands onto the ropes; then gripping her wrists in turn one at a time, I released the noose, slipped the garments down and off it and refastened the noose. And as I had been quick to notice that Alice's chemise and vest had shoulder-strap fastenings and had merely to be unhooked, the anticipated difficulty of undressing her forcibly was now at an end! The rest of her garments would drop off her as each became released, and therefore it was in my power to reduce her to absolute nudity! My heart thrilled with fierce exultation, and without further pause, I went on with the delicious work of undressing her.

Alice quickly divined her helplessness and in an agony of apprehension and shame cried to me for mercy! But I was deaf to her pitiful pleadings! I was wild to see her naked!

Quickly I unhooked her dress and petticoats and pulled them down to her feet thus exhibiting her in stays, drawers, and stockings—a bewitching sight! Her cheeks were suffused with shamefaced blushes; she huddled herself together as much as she could, seemingly supported entirely by her arms; her eyes were downcast and she seemed dazed both by the rapidity of my motions and their horrible success!

Alice now had on only a dainty Parisian corset that allowed the laces of her chemise to be visible, just hiding the nipples of her maiden breasts, and a pair of exquisitely provoking drawers, cut wide especially at her knees and trimmed with a sea of frilly lace, from below which emerged her shapely legs encased in black silk stockings and terminated in neat little shoes. She was the daintiest sight a man could well imagine, and, to me, the daintiness was enhanced by her shamefaced consciousness, for she could see herself reflected in the mirror in all her dreadful *déshabille*!

After a minute of gloating admiration, I proceeded to untie the tapes of her drawers so as to take them off her. At this she seemed to wake to the full sense of the humiliation in store for her; wild at the idea of being deprived of this most intimate of garments, she screamed in her distress, tugging frantically at her fastenings in her desperation! But the knot gave way, and her drawers, being now unsupported, slipped down to below her knees where they hung for a brief moment, maintained only by the despairing pressure of her legs against each other. A tug or two from me, and they lay in snowy loads 'round her ankles and rested on her shoes!

Oh, that I had the pen of a ready writer with which to describe Alice at this stage of the terrible ordeal of being forcibly undressed, her mental and physical anguish, her frantic cries and impassioned pleadings, her frenzied struggles, the agony in her face, as garment after garment was removed from her and she was being hurried nearer and nearer to the appalling goal of absolute nudity! The accidental but unavoidable contact of my hands with her person as I undressed her seemed to upset her so terribly that I wondered how she would endure my handling and playing with the most secret and sensitive parts of herself when she was naked! But acute as was her distress while being deprived of her upper garment, it was nothing to her shame and anguish when she felt her drawers forced down her legs and the last defense to her cunt thus removed. Straining wildly at the ropes with cheeks aflame, eyes dilated with terror, and convulsively heaving bosom, she uttered inarticulate cries, half-choked by her emotions and panting under her exertions.

I gloated over her sufferings and I would have liked to have watched them—but I was now mad with desire for her naked charms and also feared that a prolongation of her agony might result in a faint, when I would lose the anticipated pleasure of witnessing Alice's misery when her last garment was removed and she was forced to stand naked in front of me. So, unheeding her imploring cries, I undid her corset and took it off her, dragged off her shoes and stockings and with them her fallen drawers. During this process I intently watched her struggles in the hope of getting a glimpse of her Holy of Holies, but vainly, then slipped behind her; unbuttoning the shoulder-fastenings of her chemise and vest, I held these up for a moment, then watching Alice closely in the mirror, I let go! Down they slid with a rush, right to her feet! I saw Alice flash one rapid stolen half-reluctant glance at the mirror, as she felt the cold air on her now naked skin. I saw her reflection stark naked, a lovely gleaming pearly vision; then instinctively she squeezed her legs together, as closely as she could, huddled herself cowering as much as the ropes permitted—her head fell back in the first intensity of her shame, then fell forward suffused with blushes that extended right down to her breasts, her eyes closed as she moaned in heartbroken accents: "Oh! oh! oh!" She was naked!

Half delirious with excitement and the joy of conquest, I

watched Alice's naked reflection in the mirror. Rapidly and tumultuously, my eager eyes roved over her shrinking, trembling form, gleaming white, save for her blushing face and the dark triangular mossy-looking patch at the junction of her belly and thighs. But I felt that, in this moment of triumph, I was not sufficiently master of myself to fully enjoy the spectacle of her naked maiden charms now so fully exposed; besides which, her chemise and vest still lay on her feet. So I knelt down behind these garments, noting, as I did so, the glorious curves of her bottom and hips. Throwing these garments onto the rest of her clothes, I pushed the armchair in front of her, and then settled myself down to a systematic and critical inspection of Alice's naked self!

As I did so, Alice colored deeply over face and bosom and moved herself uneasily. The bitterness of death (so to speak) was past, her clothes had been forced off her and she was naked; but she was evidently conscious that much indignity and humiliation was yet in store for her, and she was horribly aware that my eyes were now taking in every detail of her naked self! Forced to stand erect by the tension of the ropes on her arms, she could do nothing to conceal any part of herself, and, in an agony of shame, she endured the awful ordeal of having her naked person closely inspected and examined!

I had always greatly admired her trim little figure, and in the happy days before our rupture, I used to note with proud satisfaction how Alice held her own, whether at garden parties, at afternoon teas, or in the theater or ballroom. And after she had jilted me and I was sore in spirit, the sight of her invariably added fuel to the flames of my desire, and I often caught myself wondering how she looked in her bath! One evening, she wore at dinner a low-cut evening dress and she nearly upset my self-control by leaning forward over the card table by which I was standing, and unconsciously revealing to me the greater portion of her breasts! But my imagination never pictured anything as glorious as the reality now being so reluctantly exhibited to me!

Alice was simply a beautiful girl and her lines were deliciously voluptuous. No statue, no model, but glorious flesh and blood allied to superb femininity! Her well-shaped head was set on a beautifully modeled neck and bosom from which sprang a pair of exquisitely lovely breasts (if anything too full), firm, upstanding, saucy and inviting. She had fine rounded arms with small well-shaped hands, a dainty but not too small waist, swelling grandly downwards and outwards and melting into magnificent curves over her hips and haunches. Her thighs were plump and round, and tapered to the neatest of calves and ankles and tiny feet, her legs being the least trifle too short for her, but adding by this very defect to the indescribable fascination of her figure. She had a graciously swelling belly with a deep navel, and, framed by the lines of her groin, was her Mount of Venus, full, fat, fleshy, prominent, covered by a wealth of fine silky dark curly hairs through which I could just make out the lips of her cunt. Such was Alice as she stood naked before me, horribly conscious of my devouring eyes, quivering and trembling with suppressed emotion, tingling with shame, flushing red and white, knowing full well her own loveliness and what its effect on me must be; and in dumb silence I gazed and gazed again at her glorious naked self till my lust began to run riot and insist on the gratification of senses other than that of sight!

I did not however consider that Alice was ready to properly appreciate the mortification of being felt. She seemed to be still absorbed in the horrible consciousness of one all-pervading fact, namely, that she was utterly naked, that her chaste body was the prey of my lascivious eyes, that she could do nothing to hide or even screen any part of herself, even her cunt, from me! Every now and then, her downcast eyes would glance at the reflection of herself in the faithful mirror only to be hastily withdrawn with an excess of color to her already shame-suffused cheeks at these fresh reminders of the spectacle she was offering to me!

Therefore with a strong effort, I succeeded in overcoming the temptation to feel and handle Alice's luscious body there and then, and being desirous of first studying her naked self from all points of view, I rose and took her in strict profile, noting with delight the arch of her bosom, the proudly projecting breasts, the glorious curve of her belly, the conspicuous way in which the hairs on the Mount of Venus stood out, indicating that her cunt would be found both fat and fleshy, the magnificent swell of her bottom! Then I went behind her, and for a minute or two, reveled in silent admiration of the swelling lines of her hips and haunches, her quivering buttocks, her well-shaped legs! Without moving, I could command the most perfect exhibition of her naked loveliness, for I had her back view in full sight while her front was reflected in the mirror!

Presently I completed my circuit, then standing close to her, I had a good look at her palpitating breasts, noting their delicious fullness and ripeness, their ivory skin, and the tiny virgin nipples pointing outward so prettily, Alice coloring and flushing and swaying uneasily under my close inspection. Then I peered into the round cleft of her navel while she became more uneasy than ever, seeing the downward trend of my inspection. Then I dropped on my knees in front of her and from this vantage point I commenced to investigate with eager eyes the mysterious region of her cunt so deliciously covered with a wealth of close curling hairs, clustering so thickly 'round and over the coral lips as almost to render them invisible! As I did so, Alice desperately squeezed her thighs together as closely as she could, at the same time drawing in her stomach in the vain hope of defeating my purpose and of preventing me from inspecting the citadel wherein reposed her virginity!

As a matter of fact, she did to a certain extent thwart me, but as I intended before long to put her on her back and tie her down with her legs wide apart, I did not grudge her partial success, but brought my face close to her belly. "Don't! Oh, don't!" she cried, as if she could feel my eyes as they searched this most secret part of herself; but disregarding her pleadings, I closely scanned the seat of my approaching pleasure, noting delightedly that her Mount of Venus was exquisitely plump and fleshy and would afford my itching fingers the most delicious pleasure when I allowed them to wander over its delicate contours and hide themselves in the forest of hairs that so sweetly covered it!

At last I rose. Without a word, I slipped behind the mirror and quickly divested myself of my clothes, retaining only my shoes and socks. Then suddenly I emerged and stood right in front of Alice. "Oh," she ejaculated, horribly shocked by the unexpected apparition of my naked self, turning rosy red and hastily averting her eyes—but not before they had caught sight of my prick in glorious erection! I watched her closely. The sight seemed to fascinate her in spite of her alarmed modesty, she flashed rapid glances at me through half-closed eyes, her color coming and going. She seemed forced, in spite of herself, to regard the instrument of her approaching violation, as if to assess its size and her capacity!

"Won't you have a good look at me, Alice?" I presently remarked maliciously. "I believe I can claim to possess a good specimen of what is so dear to the heart of a girl!" (She quivered painfully.) After a moment I continued: "Must I then assume by your apparent indifference that you have, in your time, seen so many naked men that the sight no longer appeals to you?" She colored deeply, but kept her eyes averted.

"Are you not even curious to estimate whether my prick will fit in your cunt?" I added, determined, if I possibly could, to break down the barrier of silence she was endeavoring to protect herself with.

I succeeded! Alice tugged frantically at the ropes that kept her upright, then broke into a piteous cry: "No, no...my God, no!" she supplicated, throwing her head back but still keeping her eyes shut as if to exclude the sight she dreaded. "Oh!...you don't really mean to...to..." she broke down, utterly unable to clothe in words the overwhelming fear that she was now to be violated!

I stepped up to her, passed my left arm 'round her waist and drew her trembling figure to me, thrilling at the exquisite sensation caused by the touch of our naked bodies against each other. We were now both facing the mirror, both reflected in it.

"D-don't touch me!" she shrieked as she felt my arm encircle her, but holding her closely against me with my left arm, I gently placed my right forefinger on her navel, to force her to open her eyes and watch my movements in the mirror, which meant that she would also have to look at my naked self, and gently I tickled her.

She screamed in terror, opening her eyes, squirming deliciously. "Don't! oh, don't!" she cried agitatedly.

"Then use your chaste eyes properly and have a good look at the reflection of the pair of us in the mirror," I said somewhat sternly. "Look me over slowly and thoroughly from head to foot, then answer the questions I shall presently put to you. May I call your attention to that whip hanging on that wall and to the inviting defenselessness of your bottom? Understand that I shall not hesitate to apply one to the other if you don't do as you are told! Now have a good look at me!"

Alice shuddered, then reluctantly raised her eyes and shamefacedly regarded my reflection in the mirror, her color coming and going. I watched her intently (she being also reflected, my arm was still 'round her waist holding her against me) and I noted with cruel satisfaction how she trembled with shame and fright when her eyes dwelt on my prick, now stiff and erect!

"We make a fine pair, Alice, eh?" I whispered maliciously. She colored furiously, but remained silent.

"Now answer my questions: I want to know something about you before going further. How old are you?"

"Twenty-five," she whispered.

"In your prime then! Good! Now, are you a virgin!"

Alice flushed hotly and painfully, then whispered again: "Yes!"

Oh, my exultation! I was not too late! The prize of her maidenhead was to be mine! My prick showed my joy! I continued my catechism.

"Absolutely virgin?" I asked. "A pure virgin? Has no hand wandered over those lovely charms, has no eye but mine seen them?"

Alice shook her head, blushing rosy red at the idea suggested by my words. I looked rather doubtingly at her.

"I include female eyes and hands as well as male in my query, Alice," I continued. "You know that you have a most attractive lot of girl and woman friends and that you are constantly with them. Am I to understand that you and they have never compared your charms, have never, when occupying the same bed..." She broke in with a cry of distress. "No, no, not I, not I, oh! how can you talk to me like this, Jack?"

"My dear, I only wanted to find out how much you already knew so that I might know what to teach you now! Well, shall we begin your lessons?" And I drew her against me, more closely than ever, and again began to tickle her navel.

"Jack, don't!" she screamed, "oh, don't touch me! I can't stand it! really I can't!"

"Let me see if that is really so," I replied, as I removed my arm from her waist and slipped behind her, taking up a position from which I could command the reflection of our naked figures in the mirror, and thus watch her carefully and noted the effect on her of my tender mercy.

I commenced to feel Alice by placing my hands one on each side of her waist, noting with cruel satisfaction the shiver that ran through her at their contact with her naked skin. After a few caresses, I passed them gently but inquisitively over her full hips which I stroked, pressed, and patted lovingly; then bringing my hands downward behind her, I roved over her plump bottom, the fleshy cheeks of which I gripped and squeezed to my heart's content, Alice the while arching herself outwards in a vain attempt to escape my hands. Then I descended to the underneath portion of her soft round thighs and finally worked my way back to her waist running my hands up and down over her loins and finally arriving at her armpits.

Here I paused, and to try the effect on Alice, I gently tickled these sensitive spots of herself. "Don't!" she exclaimed, wriggling and twisting herself uneasily. "Don't, I am dreadfully ticklish, I can't stand it at all!" At once I ceased but my blood went on fire, as through my brain flashed the idea of the licentiously lovely spectacle Alice would afford, if she were tied down with her legs fastened widely apart, and a pointed feather-tip cleverly applied to the most sensitive part of her—her cunt—sufficient slack being allowed in her fastenings to permit of her wriggling and writhing freely while being thus tickled. I promised to give myself presently this treat together with the pleasure of trying on her this interesting experiment!

After a short pause, I again placed my hands on her waist, played for a moment over her swelling hips, then slipped onto her stomach, my right hand taking the region below her waist while my left devoted itself to her bosom, but carefully avoiding her breasts for the moment.

Oh! what pleasure I tasted in thus touching her pure sweet flesh, so smooth, so warm, so essentially female! My delighted hands wandered all over her body, while the poor girl stood quivering and trembling, unable to guess whether her breast or cunt was next to be attacked.

I did not keep her long in suspense. After circling a few times over her rounded belly, my right hand paused on her navel again, and while my forefinger gently tickled her, my left hand slid quietly onto her right breast, which it then gently seized.

She gave a great cry of dismay! Meanwhile my right hand had in turn slipped up to her left breast, and another involuntary shriek from Alice announced that both of her virgin bubbies had become the prey of my cruel hands!

Oh, how she begged me to release them, all the while tossing herself from side to side in almost uncontrollable agitation as my fingers played with her delicious breasts, now squeezing, now stroking, now pressing them against each other, now rolling them upwards and downwards, now gently irritating and exciting their tiny nipples! Such delicious morsels of flesh I had never handled: so firm and yet so springing, so ripe and yet so maidenly, palpitating under the hitherto unknown sensations communicated by the touch of masculine hands on their virgin surfaces. Meanwhile Alice's telltale face reflected in the mirror clearly indicated to me the mental shame and anguish she was feeling at this terrible outrage; her flushed cheeks, dilated nostrils, half-closed eyes, and panting, heaving bosom all revealing her agony under this desecration of her maiden self. In rapture, I continued toying with her virgin globes, all the while gloating on Alice's image in the mirror, twisting and contorting in the most lasciviously ravishing way under her varying emotions!

At last I tore my hands away from Alice's breasts. I slipped my left arm 'round her waist and drew her tightly against me. Then, while I held her stomach and slowly approached her cunt, Alice instantly guessed my intention! She threw her weight on one leg, then quickly placed the other across her groin to foil my attack, crying: "No, no, Jack!...not there...not there!" At the same time she endeavored frantically to turn herself away from my hand. But the close grip of my left arm defeated her, and disregarding her cries, my hand crept on and on till it reached her hairs! These I gently pulled, twining them 'round my fingers as I revelled in their curling silkiness. Then amorously, I began to feel and press her gloriously swelling Mount of Venus, a finger on each side of its slit! Alice now simply shrieked in her shame and distress, jerking herself convulsively backwards and twisting herself frenziedly! As she was forced to stand on both legs in order to maintain her balance, her cunt was absolutely defenseless, and my eager fingers roved all over it, touching, pressing, tickling, pulling her hairs at their sweet will. Then I began to attack her virgin orifice and tickle her slit, passing my forefinger lightly up and down it, all the time watching her intently in the mirror! Alice quivered violently, her head fell backwards in her agony as she shrieked: "Jack don't!...for God's sake, don't!...stop!...stop!" But I could feel her cunt opening under my lascivious titillation and so could she! Her distress became almost uncontrollable. "Oh, my God!" she screamed in her desperation as my finger found its way to her clitoris and lovingly titillated it, she spasmodically squeezing her thighs together in her vain attempts to defend herself. Unheeding her agonized pleading, I continued to tickle her clitoris for a few delicious moments, then I gently passed my finger along her cunt and between its now half-opened lips till I arrived at her maiden orifice up which it tenderly forced its way, burying itself in Alice's cunt till it could penetrate no further into her! Alice's agitation now became uncontrollable; she struggled so violently that I could hardly hold her still, especially when she felt the interior of her cunt invaded and my finger investigate the mysteries of its virgin recesses!

Oh! My voluptuous sensations at that moment! Alice's naked quivering body clutched tightly against mine! My finger, half-buried in her maiden cunt, enveloped in her soft, warm, throbbing flesh and gently exploring its luscious interior!! In my excitement I must have pushed my inquisitiveness too far, for Alice suddenly screamed: "Oh!...Oh!...you're hurting me!...stop!...stop!" her head falling forward on her bosom as she did so! Delighted at this unexpected proof of her virginity and fearful of exciting her sexual passions beyond her powers of control, I gently withdrew my finger and soothed her by passing it lovingly and caressingly over her cunt; then releasing her from my encircling arm, I left her to recover herself. Though visibly relieved at being at last left alone, Alice trembled so violently that I hastily pushed her favorite armchair (the treacherous one) behind her, hastily released the pulley-ropes and let her drop into the chair to rest and recover herself, for I knew that her distress was only temporary and would soon pass away and leave her in a fit condition to be again fastened and subjected to some other torture, for so it undoubtedly was to her.

On this occasion, I did not set free the catch that permitted the arms of the chair to imprison the occupant. Alice was so upset by her experiences that I felt sure she would not give me any trouble worth mentioning when it became time for her torturing to recommence, provided, of course, that I did not allow her too long a respite, and this, from my own point of view, I did not propose to do as I was wildly longing to play again with her naked charms!

I therefore let her coil herself up in the chair with her face buried in her hands, and greedily gloated over the voluptuous curves of the haunches and bottom she was unconsciously exhibiting, the while trying to make up my mind as to what I should next do to her. This I soon decided. My hands were itching to again handle her virgin flesh, and so I determined to tie Alice upright to one of the pillars and while comfortably seated close in front of her, to amuse myself by playing with her breasts and cunt again!

She was now lying quietly and breathing normally and regularly, the trembling and quivering that had been running intermittently through her having, by now, ceased. I did not feel quite sure she had recovered herself yet, but as I watched her, I noticed an attempt on her part to try and slip her wrists out of the silken nooses that attached the ropes to them. This settled the point, and, before she could free her hands, I set the ropes working, remarking as I did so: "Well, Alice, shall we resume?"

She glanced at me fearfully, then averted her eyes as she exclaimed hurriedly: "Oh, no, Jack! Not again, not again!" and shuddered at the recollection of her recent ordeal!

"Yes, my dear!" I replied, "the same thing, though not quite in the same way; you'll be more comfy this time! Now, Alice, come along, stand up again!"

"No!" she cried, fighting vainly the now fast-tightening ropes that were inexorably raising her to her feet! "Oh, Jack! no!...no!!" she pitifully pleaded, while opposing the upward pull with all her might but to no avail! I simply smiled cruelly at her as I picked up a leather strap and awaited the favorable moment to force her against the nearest pillar. Presently she was dragged off the chair, and now was my time. I pounced on her and rushed her backwards to the pillar, quickly slipping the strap 'round it and her waist and buckling it, and thus securing her. Then I loosened the pulleys and, lowering her arms, I forced them behind her and 'round the pillar, till I got her wrists together and made them fast to a ring set in the pillar. Alice was now helpless: the whole of the front of her person was at my disposal. She was securely fastened, but, with a refinement of cruelty, I lashed her ankles together and bound them to the pillar! Then I unbuckled the strap 'round her waist and threw it away, it being no longer needed. Placing the armchair in front of her, and sitting down in it, I drew it so close to her that she stood between my parted legs and within easy touch, just as she did when she was being indecently assaulted before she was undressed, only then we both were fully clothed, while now we both were stark naked! She could not throw her head back because of the pillar, and if she let it droop, as she naturally wanted to do, the first thing that her innocent eyes would rest upon would be my excited prick in glorious erection, its blushing head pointing directly towards her cunt as if striving to make the acquaintance of its destined bride!

Confused, shamefaced, and in horrible dread, Alice stood trembling in front of me, her eyes tightly closed as if to avoid the sight of my naked self, her bosom agitatedly palpitating till her breasts seemed almost to be dancing! I leant back in my chair luxuriously as I gloated over the voluptuously charming spectacle, allowing her a little time in which to recover herself somewhat, before I set to work to feel her again!

Before long, the agitations of her bosom died away; Alice's

breathing became quieter. She was evidently now ready for another turn, and I did not keep her waiting, but gently placed my hands on her breasts.

"No, Jack, don't!" she pleaded piteously, moving herself uneasily. My only response was to stroke lovingly her delicious twin-globes. As her shoulders were of necessity drawn well back by the pull of her arms, her bust was thrown well forward, thus causing her breasts to stand out saucily and provokingly; and I took the fullest advantage of this. Her flesh was delicious to the touch, so smooth and soft and warm, so springy and elastic! My fingers simply reveled in their contact with her skin! Taking her tempting bubbies between my fingers and thumbs, I amorously pressed and squeezed them, pulled them this way and that way, rubbed them against each other, finally taking each delicate nipple in turn in my mouth and sucking it while my hands made as if they were trying to milk her! Alice all the while involuntarily shifted herself nervously as if endeavoring to escape from my audaciously inquisitive fingers, her face scarlet with shame.

After a delicious five minutes of lascivious toying with her maiden breasts, I reluctantly quitted them, first imprinting on each of her little nipples a passionate kiss that seemed to send a thrill through her. As I sank back into my chair she took a long breath of relief, at which I smiled, for I had only deserted her breasts for her cunt!

Alice's legs were a trifle short, and her cunt therefore lay a little too low for effective attack from me in a sitting position. I therefore pushed the chair back and knelt in front of her. My intentions were now too obviously plain to her and she shrieked in her dismay, squirming deliciously!

For some little time I did not touch her, but indulged in a good look at close quarters at the sweet citadel of her chastity!

My readers will remember that immediately after I had stripped Alice naked, I had closely inspected her cunt from a similar point of view. But then it was unsullied, untouched; now it had experienced the adoring touch of a male finger, and her sensitive body was still all aquiver from the lustful handling her dainty breasts had just endured! Did her cunt share in the sexual excitement that my fingers had undoubtedly aroused in her?

It seemed to me that it did! The hair seemed to stand out as if ruffled, the Mount of Venus certainly looked fuller, while the coral lips of the cunt itself were distinctly more apart! I could not see her clitoris, but I concluded that it participated in the undoubted excitement that was prevailing in this sweet portion of Alice's body, and of which she evidently was painfully aware, to judge by her shrinking, quivering movements!

I soon settled the point by gently placing my right forefinger on her slit and lovingly stroking it! An electric shock seemed to send a thrill through Alice, her limbs contracted, her head fell forward as she screamed: "Don't, Jack!...oh, my God! how can you treat me so!!" while she struggled frantically to break the ropes which lashed her legs to the pillar to which she was fastened!

"Don't you like it, dear?" I asked softly with a cruel smile, as I continued to play gently with her cunt!

"No, no," she shrieked, "oh, stop!...I can't stand it!" And she squirmed horribly! The crack of her cunt now began to open visibly!

I slipped my finger in between the parted lips: another despairing shriek from Alice, whose face now was scarlet! Again I found my progress barred by the membrane that proved her virgin condition! Reveling in the warm moistness of her throbbing flesh, I slowly agitated my finger in its delicious envelope, as if frigging her: "Jack! don't!" Alice yelled, now mad with distress and shame, but I could not for the life of me stop, and with my left forefinger, I gently attacked her virgin clitoris!

Alice went off into a paroxysm of hysterical shrieks, straining at her fastenings, squirming, wriggling, writhing like one possessed. She was a lovely sight in herself and the knowledge that the struggling, shrieking girl I was torturing was Alice herself and none but Alice added zest to my occupation!

Disregarding her cries, I went on slowly frigging her, but carefully refrained from carrying her sexual excitement to the spending point, till I had pushed her powers of self-control to their utmost. I did not want her to spend yet, this crowning humiliation I intended to effect with my tongue. Presently, what I wished was to make Alice endure the most outrageously indecent indignities I could inflict on her virgin person, to play on her sexual sensitiveness, to provoke her nearly into spending, and then deny her the blessed relief. So, exercising every care, and utilizing to the utmost the peculiarly subtle power of touch I possessed, I continued to play with her cunt using both my hands, till I drove her nearly frantic with the sexual cravings and excitement I was provoking!

Just then I noticed certain spasmodic contortions of her hips and buttocks, certain involuntary thrusting out of her belly, as if begging for more close contact with my busy fingers; I knew this meant that her control over her sexual organs was giving out and that she would be driven into spending if I did not take care. Then, most reluctantly, I stopped torturing her for the moment, and, leaning back in my chair, I gloatingly watched Alice as little by little she regained her composure, my eyes dwelling delightedly on her trembling and quivering naked body so gloriously displayed!

She breathed a long sigh of heartfelt relief as she presently saw me rise and leave her. She did not, however, know that my object in doing so was to prepare for another, and perhaps more terrible, ordeal for her virgin cunt!

From a drawer, I took out a long glove box, then returned and resumed my seat in front of her with the box in my hand. She watched me with painful intensity, her feminine intuition telling her that something horrible was in store for her, and she was not wrong!

Holding the box in such a way that she could see the contents, I opened it. Inside were about a dozen long and finely pointed feathers. Alice at once guessed her fate—that her cunt was to be tickled. Her head fell back in her terror as she shrieked: "Oh, my God! not that, Jack!…not that!…you'll kill me! I can't stand it!" I laughed cruelly at her and proceeded to pick out a feather, whereupon she frantically tugged at her fastenings, screaming frenziedly for mercy!

"Steady, dear, steady now, Alice!" I said soothingly, as if addressing a restive mare, then touched her palpitating breasts with the feather's point.

"Jack, don't!" she yelled, pressing herself wildly back against the pillar in an impotent effort to escape the torture caused by the maddeningly gentle titillation, her face crimson. For response, I proceeded to pass the tip of the feather along the lower portion of her glorious bubbies, touching the skin ever so lightly here and there, then tickling her maiden nipples! With redoubled cries, Alice began to squirm convulsively as much as her fastenings would permit, while the effect of the fiendishly subtle torture on her became manifest by the sudden stiffening of her breasts, which now began to stand out tense and full! Noting this, I thought it as well to allow her a little respite; so I dropped my hand, but, at the same time, leaned forward till my face touched her breasts, which I then proceeded to kiss lovingly in turn, finally sucking them amorously till they again became soft and yielding. I then made as if I would repeat the torture, but after a touch or two (which produced piteous cries and contortions) I pretended to be moved by her distress, and again dropping my hand leaned back in the chair till she became less agitated!

But as soon as the regular rise and fall of her lovely bosom indicated the regaining of her composure, I proceeded to try the ardently longed for experiment: the effect of a feather applied to a girl's cunt! And no one could have desired a more lovely subject on which to test this much-debated question than was being offered by the naked helpless girl now standing terrified between my legs!

Pushing my chair back as much as was desirable, I leant forward, then slowly extended my right arm in the direction of Alice's cunt. A great cry of despair broke from her as she noted the movement, and she flattened her bottom against the pillar in a vain attempt to draw herself back out of reach. But the only effect of her desperate movement was to force forward her Mount of Venus, and thereby render her cunt more open to the attack of the feather than it previously was!

Carefully regulating my motions, I gently brought the tip of the feather against the lowest point of Alice's cunt hole, then very softly and gently began to play up and down, on and between its delicate coral lips! Alice's head had dropped onto her breast, the better, I fancy, to watch my movements; but as soon as the feather touched her cunt, she threw her head backwards as if in agony, shrieking at the top of her voice, her whole body twisting and contorting wildly. Not heeding her agonized appeals, I proceeded to work along her slit towards her clitoris, putting into play the most subtle titillation I was capable of, sometimes passing the feather all along the slit from one end to the other, sometimes tickling the orifice itself, not only outside but inside; then ascending towards her clitoris, I would pass the tip of the feather all 'round it, irritating it without so much as touching it. The effect of my manipulation soon became evident. First the lips of Alice's cunt began to pout, then to gape a little, then a little more as if inviting the feather to pass into it—which it did! Then Alice's clitoris commenced to assert itself and to become stiff and turgid, throbbing excitedly; then her whole cunt seemed as if possessed by an irresistible flood of sexual lust and almost to demand mutely the immediate satisfaction of its cravings! Meanwhile Alice, firmly attached to the pillar, went into a paroxysm of contortions and convulsions, wriggling, squirming, writhing, tugging frantically at her fastenings, shrieking, praying, uttering incoherent exclamations and ejaculations, her eyes starting out of her head, her quivering lips, her heaving bosom with its wildly palpitating breasts all revealing the agony of body and mind that she was enduring! Fascinated by the spectacle, I continued to torture her by tickling her cunt more and more scientifically and cruelly, noting carefully the spots at which the tickling seemed most felt and returning to those ultra-sensitive parts of her cunt avoiding only her clitoris—as I felt sure that, were this touched, Alice would spend—till her strength became exhausted under the double strain! With a strangled shriek Alice collapsed just as I had forced the feather up her cunt and was beginning to tickle the sensitive interior! Her head fell forward on her bosom, her figure lost its self-supporting rigidity; she hung flaccidly, prevented from falling only by her wrists being shackled together 'round the pillar! There was nothing to be gained by prolonging the torture, so quickly I unfastened her, loosed her wrists and ankles from their shackles, and carried her to the large divan-couch, where I gently laid her, knowing that she would soon recover herself and guessing that she now would not need to be kept tied and that she had realized the futility of resistance.

Richard's Correction

Anonymous

It was only the following afternoon when Bridget tapped at the schoolroom door.

"What is it, Bridget?" Harriet's eyes had begun to glitter

The old woman beckoned and Harriet went to the door, where they conferred for a few moments. A piece of paper changed hands. The governess came back.

"Come in, Bridget," she said, "and close the door." She turned to Richard; her expression ominous. "Something has arisen that calls for an explanation. Perhaps you have already guessed what it is?"

His expression was black. "N—no, miss..."

She looked at him closely. "Then I will begin by asking you a question. Have you been playing with yourself lately? Come now, speak up."

He had grown as red as fire. He did not know what may come. He gave an agonized glance towards Bridget, then in mute appeal to Harriet.

"Have you? Speak up, I said."

"No, miss. Oh, no."

"No? You are quite sure," she consulted the old woman again.

"Yes," he lied.

"Bridget, you hear what Master Richard says?"

"Indeed I do, ma'am," said the old woman. Her tone was one of outrage, but did not hide a hint of mockery and malice.

Harriet spread her billowing skirts and sat down. "Come here, Richard. Stand in front of me. So. Now, you have already said you have not indulged in that filthy habit of yours lately. Bridget and I have both heard you deny it. Before we go any further, I wish you to know there is only one fault I abominate as deeply as immorality, and that is lying. And I am accustomed to punishing both with equal severity. Therefore, Richard, if you are guilty of the one, do not risk doubling your punishment by persisting in the other. Is that clear?"

The boy's face had become livid. Only too conscious of his guilt, only too well aware that his governess had known of it for some time, he now found himself in a position where to admit his indulgence was impossible—above all in the presence of the servant. The real question was: What did she know? And if she did know, how had she found out? He was silent.

Harriet looked at him calmly, but at her side her hand clenched triumphantly.

"Very well, sir. You persist in your denial. And in that case, will you kindly explain how this came to be in the toilet?"

With these words, she held out the crumpled paper in her hand, in which the evidence of an ejaculation was clotted in a small gluey pool. The pallor of the boy's cheeks became leaden. He was still unable to speak.

Harriet remained motionless, her hand outstretched. When she spoke again her tone was dry. "You have no explanation then? You cannot tell us how this disgusting proof of sensuality came to be where Bridget found it this morning? Come now, my boy, you must know something about this. Answer me."

He tried to reply, but his emotion was so great that he was seized with a violent fit of coughing which left him as red as he had been pale an instant before.

Harriet waited patiently until his coughing ceased and then repeated her question. "I am waiting for your answer," she added quietly.

"M-m-miss," he stammered, "I—I don't know how it happened."

Harriet's gaze became terrible. "Indeed? You do not know! That is strange. That is altogether strange." Her lip curled scornfully. "See now, there are only the two of us who use that room, Richard. I hope for your sake that you are not implying this stuff has any connection with me. Answer! Is that what you mean?"

Richard, distracted with shame and confusion, wrung his hands while the tears poured down his cheeks. "Please, miss," he managed to say at last, "I—I tried not to. Really, I did—"

"Then you disobeyed me last night, even after my clear warning?"

"Oh, I—I couldn't help it..."

"Exactly. You couldn't help it. In other words, you wantonly abused yourself last night, even after I had warned you about what would happen if you did. And now, to crown your horrible sensuality, you have just tried to lie your way out of it. Very well, Bridget, you may go. Master Richard will be whipped."

The old woman remained where she was. The malicious look she had worn throughout the scene gave way to open-mouthed astonishment. "Whipped?"

"Certainly. Do you consider, by any chance, that he has not deserved it?"

"Oh, no ma'am. I—I certainly," said Bridget. "But I didn't think, at Master Richard's age—well, that ..."

Harriet smiled slightly. "His age makes no difference. I shall whip him this evening after dinner. I am telling you now, Bridget, so that you need not be alarmed when you hear us upstairs tonight. You may go."

When Bridget had gone the lesson was resumed as if nothing had happened. But now Richard, covered with shame, hardly dared raise his eyes to his instructress. Harriet, however, remained as calm as she had been before the old woman's appearance, speaking to her pupil with all her customary evenness of tone, attending as usual to the smallest points of detail that arose in the course of their work.

The study period came to an end and she dismissed him with a pleasant smile. The dinner hour arrived, and she took her place as usual opposite him at table. Neither during this time, nor at dinner, did she make any further allusion to the correction awaiting him. But when he had folded his napkin, risen and spoken the short prayer that followed every meal, Harriet also rose, opened a drawer and drew out the cane, which she presented to him silently. His features suddenly became terribly discomposed.

"Take the cane to your room, Richard," she said. "Leave it on your bedside table and go to bed at once without saying your prayers. You will say them with me as usual, after I have whipped you. Go!"

Whimpering slightly, he took the instrument of his approaching torment from her and left the room. On his way to his room he gripped it in a sudden access of childish rage, thinking for a moment he would like to break it across his knee, to throw it out of the window or into the fire. But the next moment he was seized by a sickly, shrinking curiosity that made him examine it carefully.

The cane was of the finest and almost flexible rattan, thinner than those used in English schools and reformatories, and also slightly longer. The greater length, Harriet had found, gave this instrument an increased elasticity that enabled her to inflict maximum pain with least effort.

Richard struck his palm lightly with it, wincing at the cruelty of its bite. Then, throwing it on the table in the middle of the room, he dropped face downwards on his bed with a groan of mingled fury and despair. But almost immediately he leapt up again in fear, lest Miss Marwood surprise him in this posture.

Not for an instant did he entertain the idea of resisting his governess. Not only was such an idea foreign to his soft and passive disposition, but the strange sensual weakness which swept over him at the sight and even thought of this woman's anger would have prevented him from putting it into practice. And so, breathless, his flesh twitching nervously, with a prickling sensation of the skin and a tingling in his fingers and toes, he found himself unable to do anything but wait, in terror mingled with anticipation, for the arrival of the young tyrant.

The period of waiting lasted a long time.

Several times, he heard the sound of her footsteps approaching his door, and his emotion mounted to a pitch of intensity. But each time the steps receded and died away, bringing him a momentary relief that was soon swallowed up by his returning trepidation. The hours went slowly by.

Harriet Marwood, as we may already suspect, was mistress of all the refinements of punishment. She was quite conscious of her pupil's state of mind, and in thus prolonging his suspense she not only made sure of reducing him to absolute docility but also ministered to her own taste for the infliction of a subtle and delicate species of torment.

From each visit she paid to the boy's door, in the intervals of her leisurely progress of undressing, she returned to her own room with a heightened color and a brighter eye. Looking in her mirror, she could admire the face whose diabolical beauty was sensibly increased by her imagination of the effect produced on the boy by each of these tantalizing trips. When she was at last ready for the business before her she parted the long cape she wore and examined the image of her own magnificent nudity in the glass with a sensual and speculative eye. Her hands lifted and caressed the points of her breasts, then passed down slowly and luxuriously over her belly...

It was ten o'clock before Richard saw the door of his room open. At that instant he felt nothing but a boundless surge of relief for the ending of his suspense, which was immediately followed by a paralyzing shock of fear as he saw his governess herself.

She was clad in a long, dark dressing cape whose straight severe folds, falling unbroken from her shoulders to the floor, concealed altogether the outlines of her figure, giving her a stark conventual air. It was in no way dispelled by the effect of her beautiful arms, bare to the shoulder, emerging from two long openings on either side, a display in which there was a suggestion of intimacy and the assurance of the greatest freedom of movement. A small hood, hanging loosely on her back, added a further touch of the bizarre.

This cape, we must remark in passing, obviously meant much to

Harriet, though its actual associations we have as yet no means of knowing. But her choice of it on this occasion would suggest that she had worn it many times before and in situations similar to the present—that it was in fact the costume appropriated by her for all ceremonial and exceptional severities. This is the only explanation we can furnish for her voluptuous gestures a few minutes before—as if there were concealed in its long heavy folds, like some exquisite and troubling perfume, the fancied echo of screams, the whistle of cane and whip, and the sight of helpless and writhing flesh.

Richard was gazing at her, sick with terror as he grasped the significance for himself of this costume. The next moment he was seized by a violent shudder as the appearance of this figure in his room irresistibly recalled that of the medieval torturer, smocked, hooded, bare-armed, whip in hand, pictured in an old illustrated book in the library: from Miss Marwood's pale hand hung a thin, curling brown leather strap.

She closed the door behind her, turned the key in the lock, and advanced to the bed beside which he was standing. Her face was pale, her eyes aglitter, and her expression one of extraordinary severity.

"Why are you not in bed?" she asked.

He made no reply. He remained standing before her, his arms dangling at his sides, trembling in every limb.

"I told you to be in bed," she said. "Once more you have disobeyed me. It appears I shall have to whip you every day before you learn the habit of obedience. Get undressed at once!"

He turned on her an imploring look, clasping his hand as he stammered, "Miss, I—I'm sorry for what I did. If you please, forgive me—"

She shook her head. "No, Richard. I will not tolerate sensuality and lying! Hurry and do as ordered."

With a moan of despair he began to take off his clothes. When only his shirt remained, Harriet reached out to take his hand and draw him towards her. He avoided her grasp and took a step backwards.

Harriet's nose wrinkled with sudden rage. She controlled herself with an effort: "Ah, this is too much," she said, throwing the strap on the chair. "After all that has happened, you still dare resist me. You shall smart for this, sir."

With a swift movement she raised her hands and drew the close-fitting hood over her head, confining her long, heavy hair. Thus prepared, she stepped forward.

The effect of the gesture made the boy turn pale. He shrank from this hooded figure, now even more terrifying, crying out, "Miss, please! I'm sorry—I won't move..." But still, as she came towards him, he backed against the wall beside his bed in terror.

Harriet raised her bare arm and slapped his cheek with such force that he reeled and fell sideways over his bed.

He staggered to his feet, his fists at his temples, half stunned. She pulled one of his arms down and another slap, still harder than the first, threw him back on the bed.

"So, you will resist me!" she repeated.

He slipped off the bed to his knees, shivering, turning on her a look of terror-stricken incredulity.

"Now will you obey me?" She was almost out of breath, as much from her exertions as from the heady sensation she experienced from an act of purely physical domination.

He stared at her in silence, like a beaten animal.

"Get up!"

He rose slowly to his feet, his arms raised defensively before him.

"Put your hands down! And look at me."

He obeyed. She drew a deep breath and bent her gaze on her pupil's wide eyes, terrified and filled with tears. They remained looking at each other silently for a few instants. Then a strange smile parted the governess's lips. "Now kiss me," she said. "And promise me you will submit in the future."

Looking at the beautiful gray eyes now suddenly grown soft and swimming, the boy emitted a deep sob, a moan of pleasure. A veritable ecstasy flooded him as he abandoned himself entirely to the woman's will. He put his arms around her neck and pressed his trembling lips to the severe mouth.

"Oh, miss, I promise..." he murmured.

"Very good," she said, pushing him away. "Now we will continue. You know why I am here, Richard, and that I mean to whip you without mercy. We have delayed too long already. On to the bed with you now—face down, please."

With the calm of despair, he obeyed, the muscles of his buttocks already contracting spasmodically under his shirt at the prospect of the pain to come.

But Harriet was not yet ready to begin. From the inner pocket of her cape she produced four bracelets of thick braided leather, each terminating in a strap and buckle. "Give me your hands," she said.

"Miss!" he cried, struck with panic at the idea of being fastened to his bed. "Oh, please—no! I promise you, I'll—I'll lie still!"

"No, Richard." She slipped the bracelets over his unresisting wrists, drew them tight, and buckled the straps to the posts of the heavy iron bed. Then she fastened his ankles in the same way, drawing the straps taut so that the boy's body was straight and secure. When this was done she raised his shirt and pulled it over his head.

This was the moment for which she had waited ever since she

saw him almost three weeks ago. The boy's swelling buttocks were now displayed before her, naked, beautiful, and at her mercy, as she had always desired them. She paused for a few delicious moments, savoring her anticipation, feasting with somber satisfaction on the sight of this virgin expanse of puerile flesh now at last ready for her to whip as long and severely as she wished. Then, with a deep voluptuous sigh, she picked up the leather strap...

Downstairs in the dining room, through which she was passing, Bridget heard the muffled cries from overhead. She stopped in surprise, then remembering, nodded her head and remained listening eagerly.

The cries continued, mounting steadily in shrillness and frequency, accompanied by the slow, regular sounds of the descending strap. A minute went by, then another, and another, and still the rhythm of the blows and cries continued inexorably. The old woman's expression changed gradually from smiling approval to admiration, to amazed incredulity, and at last to simple awe. "Lord," she muttered at last, "that young woman don't believe in doing things by halves!"

The sounds died away and were succeeded by faint groans. The old woman remained standing in the darkness of the dining room, listening intently. Soon the cries recommenced, now more agonized than ever...

In the room upstairs, Richard was being subjected to punishment of a rigor he had never dreamed of.

Here, indeed, we may say that the extent of an English governess' severity sixty years ago is almost inconceivable to those brought up in the softer educational climates of Europe or America. Only the upper-class English child of that period knew what it was to be flogged in slow and leisurely stages to the utmost limits by a firm and experienced woman, further than would be believed possible. Richard Lovel was now receiving his first taste of these English methods, which would be applied to him with stern and loving care in the years to come.

Harriet had just finished strapping him. He was still moaning weakly from the ordeal. His thighs as well as his buttocks, all the flesh from his knees to his waist, were now a sheet of uniform glowing scarlet, testifying to the merciless skill with which the instrument had been applied. She looked at her work impassively for a few moments, then uncovered the boy's head, noting with satisfaction that the muscles of his face and neck were still working convulsively.

Richard's great dark blue eyes, wide with fear, were lifted to hers. He tried to speak, but was prevented by the sobs that kept rising to his throat.

Harriet looked at him with a faint smile, drawing the strap caressingly through her fingers. "That was not pleasant, was it, Richard? I think if you had known of the effects of this strap of mine you would have thought twice before giving in to that habit of self-abuse again. I daresay you are also getting to know me a little better, and how I deal with boys like you. At any rate, I promise you that before I am through with you tonight you will know what a good whipping is."

His eyes filled with horror. "Then—then, miss—it's not finished?"

Harriet's thoughtful smile deepened. "No, Richard. I am afraid your poor buttocks must suffer still more punishment this evening." She laid down the strap, and picking up the cane, made it whistle through the air several times, studying her pupil's frightened face and wildly shaking loins with a dreamy, rapt expression. "You have still to taste this new cane, you know."

"But, miss—please! Please—I—I can't stand any more..."

Her only answer was to cut him sharply across the thighs. As he screamed, she studied his face intently, her eyes glowing softly.

"Ah," she said gently, "you will just have to stand it, I am afraid. Keep telling yourself that you are being whipped for your own good." Deliberately, she drew the shirt over his head again. "That may help you to bear the pain more manfully..."

Then, pressing a hand to her breast, which had begun to palpitate deliciously, she began lashing the boy's swollen loins with short, vigorous strokes of her powerful wrist. The sharper pain caused by the cane, in contrast with that of the strap, was at once manifested by shrill screams and an almost epileptic writhing of the buttocks as they sought to escape the bite of this famous instrument of scholastic discipline...

"Hark now, Arthur!"

Mr. Lovel, dozing beside his mistress in his own wing of the great house, returned to consciousness at the sound of her low vibrant voice. He raised himself in bed and listened for a few moments to the sounds coming to him faintly.

"Good heavens," he said, laughing. "Is that Richard? Our Miss Marwood is certainly taking her duties to heart, isn't she?"

"She surely is," replied his mistress. "Only listen to the boy! You'd think he was being murdered. Ah well, it's all for his own good, isn't it?"

"Hm-mmm, yes," he said, and then paused, cocking his head as another scream of particular intensity bored up through the thick walls and flooring, "What can she be beating him with, do you think, to make him howl like that?"

"Oh, that will be a cane or horsewhip, Arthur. It is what they use on a grown boy, you know."

"A horsewhip! By Jove, you women are cold-blooded creatures at times, Kate."

She laughed. "No, it's only that we cannot bear a habit that's likely to stint us of our due." Her hand automatically strayed to her protector's genitals. To her surprise she found his own hand ahead of her. "Saints defend us, Arthur—what are you at there? Why, you'll be needing the whip yourself at this rate! Ah, leave off that stroking of yourself, my dear. It's a woman's office to do that for her man..."

Arthur surrendered his member to her hands and lay back in the bed again, a prey to disturbing but delicious impressions, listening to the sharp cries from the room beneath while Kate's fingers teased and tickled and massaged his slowly stiffening member.

"Oh," she said after a few moments, "that is bringing you up now, isn't it? Or is that all that's doing it, tell me?"

"By God, Kate," he murmured softly, "I hardly know..."

Kate laughed indulgently. "Well, give yourself no trouble if it is. I've known many a man to get an erection when there's any kind of whipping going forward. God knows why, but it's a fact. And in that case I had best suck you out now, for you'll be wanting to spend before that Miss Marwood is finished flogging the poor boy. It cannot be long, I'm thinking, for surely the poor child cannot stand much more. Come, let me suck you now, and you just lie back and listen."

"No, Kate." Arthur sat up suddenly, and his hands sought her thighs. "By God, I want you as a woman tonight. Get on your back, and let me into your womb..."

"God in heaven above," Kate cried, laughing as she obeyed, "what's this that has taken you, that you are reforming your ways altogether! You've not taken me like this for more years than I can remember, Arthur. Oh, but it's good, it's wonderfully good for a change, isn't it?"

Mr. Lovel made no reply but to drive his member deeply into her. As the screams far below continued steadily in an agonized crescendo he kept thrusting with a stroke as insistent and regular as the blows that were falling on the writhing young body in the room beneath.

Harriet, too, was being carried to the heights of pleasure. The clear whistling of the cane, the shrieking of the boy, and the sight of the helpless flesh now crossed with the long welts she had raised with the skillful lash of the cane, afforded her at last the special, savage enjoyment her peculiar nature craved.

She had become rather pale. Short, languorous sighs escaped her with every stroke. The bridge of her nose was furrowed with a small wrinkle, her nostrils quivered, flaring widely as if she were breathing some intoxicating perfume, and her tight-lipped mouth was twitching with emotion. She struck hard, her arm descending evenly, methodically, with a superb mastery of aim and effort. Had it rested with her own appetite alone, she would have continued the punishment indefinitely. But her self-possession, which in the midst of her wildest excesses never deserted her, made her cease at last. By then, indeed, it was time for the chastisement to stop. Richard, at the end of his strength, had ceased to cry out at all.

She unfastened him, ordered him to remain as he was, and then, wetting a towel in the basin, laid it gently on the burning flesh. After a few minutes she took the boy in her arms and sitting on the bed, made him stand before her. He was sobbing with exhaustion, barely able to remain on his feet.

Harriet looked at his distress with entire satisfaction. This was how she liked to see a boy! She smiled into his still distorted face.

"I hope that will help cure you of that practice of playing with your genitals, Richard. Do you think it will?"

"Y-yes, miss," he groaned weakly.

"Come, come! You are making too much of an old-fashioned whipping, my boy. No more of this nonsensical whining, please! Kneel down in front of me."

He sank to his knees, his hands imprisoned in hers.

"Now say, 'Thank you, miss, for having corrected me. I ask your pardon for the trouble you have taken, and I promise to try not to abuse myself any more.'"

He repeated the humiliating words with docility.

"Very good," she said, the ghost of a smile curving her full lips. "And now—prayers!"

In a voice at first choked with sobs, but which towards the end became firmer and more controlled, he recited the evening prayer as he stood before her in his shirt.

"Now take off your shirt and go to bed."

As he did so she gave an exclamation, and the flush her cheeks had worn since the beginning of the punishment became deeper. The boy's penis had already begun to swell. He turned on her an agonized look; but she appeared to pay no further attention to this circumstance. He got into bed swiftly.

She drew the covers over him gently, then bent over and kissed him, softly and voluptuously, on the mouth. He did not close his eyes, but kept his gaze fixed in ecstasy on the beautiful flushed face, framed in its shirred hood, that was brought so close to his own.

"You are forgiven," she said, smiling at him. "But I advise you, Richard, to behave yourself in future. You will try, won't you?"

He said nothing, staring at her in fascination.

"Good night, Richard."

"Good night, miss."

And the governess regained her room, where she sank into an armchair facing the mirror which gave back a reflection of her caped and hooded figure. Luxuriously she opened her cape and parted her thighs. Her mouth was now soft and humid, her eyes glistening...

Upstairs, Arthur Lovel was still panting in the utter exhaustion induced by the most violent and pleasurable orgasm he had ever known. In the darkness of his room, his son was already rubbing his wildly erected member in a veritable ecstasy of pain, humiliation, and rapture.

Kibbles and Bits

Molly Weatherfield

A few days after our night at the opera, the phone rang in Jonathan's study. He picked up the receiver, listened for a minute, and started talking loudly. "Doug, that's ridiculous, the ventilation works fine, it's a minor adjustment that I've planned for already. No, they don't need me. I can walk them through it over the phone, I don't have to be there for the whole damn week while they install. Because I'm busy. No. No, personal things. No, I can't tell you."

He waited a bit, pushing me off his lap to a kneeling position on the floor, then rubbing my head distractedly. They were probably putting him on a conference call; his quality of life would take a turn for the worse, I thought, when those things all had video components built in.

Anyway, he argued with Doug, and then with Doug and Stan

and Carol, for about fifteen minutes, speaking that horrible singsong whiny yuppie-ese he could do so well: "But we've already completed that deliverable, Stan," and "Yes, Carol, I understand that your comfort level is not high." And by the end of it, he'd promised to go to Chicago the following evening, though he was adamant that he was right and they were wrong and that it was stupid for him to go. But the deal was that he'd walk them through the installation, whatever that was, in person, and then he'd be entirely done. No more calls, and no way were they going to mess up his trip to Europe in ten days—that was the auction, though of course they didn't know it.

I figured I'd finally get to go to Chicago, though I didn't really see that fantasy making much sense at this point, or how he'd fit it into our current intensive training schedule. But just then an alarm went off on his Mac to remind him that it was time for me to go for yoga, so he unbuckled my collar and shoved me out of the room.

He was very quiet and intense that evening, though, and didn't mention any changes—not that I'd expected him to. In fact, he was oddly affectionate, if you can call fucking me just about every way possible affectionate. I was exhausted and in a swoon, and although he did beat me, it was rather lightly, with his belt, before he sent me to bed early.

The next morning, however, after I'd brought him breakfast and eaten some myself at a plate at his feet, Mrs. Branden brought a man I'd never seen before into the study. He was different from anyone I'd ever seen visiting Jonathan, I thought. He was fat and late-fiftyish, in a buoyant, Sydney Greenstreet kind of way, and he wore corny light blue polyester pants and a yellow alligator shirt. Jonathan made me kiss his shoe—white loafers!—and called him "Sir Harold." Oh, right, I got it. This was one of his porn movie friends, or something like that anyhow. One of those silly-looking guys he respected so much. Well, the man was for sure silly-looking. As for what this was actually about, well, we—or I, really—would just have to wait and see. Of course there wasn't much I could do about it anyway.

He sat down in Jonathan's armchair. Jonathan sat in the straight chair opposite, and I knelt at attention, my shoulders in front of Jonathan's knees. Mrs. Branden brought in coffee and rolls. Sir Harold dunked his rolls, wolfed them down, and talked. He was expansive, affectionate, fatherly almost, toward Jonathan, and Jonathan was very, well, respectful toward him. There was some chatter about "business," about how the good old days were, of course, better than these benighted times, about how Kate was doing in Napa. I couldn't tell much from the conversation, until finally it seemed to turn to the matter at hand, which seemed to be me.

"Anyway," Jonathan was saying, "it's wonderful of you to help at such short notice. I would have had to take her with me, which wouldn't have worked out at all, or send her to Kate."

"Would've been fine to send her to Kate, you know," Sir Harold rumbled, finishing the last of the rolls. "Don't know why you're so set against that."

Jonathan winced. "Well, she's busy. She's got some big deal going this week. Some emir or a senator, or both maybe, I don't know."

"Don't give me that, Jon," the fat man said. "Kate can always handle one more little girl, no matter what she's got going. You don't want to send her, fine, I'm glad to help. But that's your call. Anyway, let me have a look at her."

Jonathan patted my shoulder. "Stand up, Carrie," he said. "Let Sir Harold look at you."

I stood up and walked over to where Sir Harold was sitting. "Turn around, girlie," he said. I did, slowly.

"Legs look okay," he said. "Rides a bike, you said? And ass, too. Well, more than okay, poetic, even. Kind of ass that talks to you across a crowded room." Block that metaphor, I thought, and I could see that Jonathan was a bit nonplused by it as well, even as he nodded, somewhat shyly.

"How's the mouth?" Sir Harold continued.

"Pretty good, I think," Jonathan said. He'd regained his cool. "Try it, why don't you? Kneel down, Carrie."

"Unzip me, girlie," Sir Harold said, "and put it in your mouth." His cock wasn't totally erect, but it grew rather spectacularly as I sucked on it, and he pushed insistently for the back of my throat. He made some guttural, moaning noises, but I could tell that he was seriously checking me out all the while. I could tell that Jonathan was nervous. I did the best I could, though I was nervous myself. What was all this about?

Rather than come, though, he pulled out and grabbed my shoulders. "Turn around," he said roughly, pushing me as he said it. He was very strong, and his big hands were very sure; quickly he had me turned around with my ass up. I was surprised, but Jonathan clearly wasn't, because he was ready with the ottoman. And when I was quickly positioned on it, he parted the cheeks of my poetic ass himself.

Sir Harold finished fucking me up the ass, groaning and bellowing. It hurt, and I had tears in my eyes by the time he was done, but I figured I'd done all right.

When he'd pulled out of my asshole and was zipping himself up, relaxing, catching his breath, Jonathan signaled to me to return to my original kneeling position, at attention. I did, and both of us waited silently a few minutes, our eyes on the fat man in Jonathan's armchair.

"She'll do," Sir Harold finally said. "You've taught her a few things, I guess. I'll take her with me."

Jonathan made a relieved sound, and bent to kiss my shoulder blade. "Get a coat, Carrie," he said. Take me with him where?

When I had put my coat on, and some shoes as well, we walked out to the front of the house. There was a pickup truck parked there, and attached to the back was one of those carrier vans that they use to transport horses. You know, you see them on the freeway sometimes. They're usually somewhat open, so you can see the back part of the horse, but this one was closed over. The shape was the same, though. On the side was lettered "Sir Harold's Custom Ponies." My knees began to wobble, and I wanted to turn and run, but Jonathan put a hand at the small of my back, steering me toward the curb at a steady pace.

Sir Harold opened the back of the van, so we could walk in. There was room for the three of us, since the van was made to carry a horse. We stepped onto clean straw heaped on the floor, and he closed the door behind us.

"Strip," he said to me, "and then bend over."

I handed my coat and shoes to Jonathan. The straw under my bare feet was disturbing. I bent at the waist, holding on to a horizontal bar in the front of the compartment. I could feel a greased dildo probing my asshole. I took a deep breath and Sir Harold shoved it all the way up, belting it into place with stout brown leather straps. And then I could feel a tickling against the backs of my knees and thighs. Hair. It was a long horse tail, attached to the end of the dildo. Sir Harold slapped my ass. "Up," he said.

He fit a set of narrow straps over my head, buckling it in back. One of the straps bisected my face, down the middle of my nose, and two more angled down from the top of my nose practically to the bottoms of my ears. Together, they held a hard plastic bit in place in my mouth, stretching it widely and making it impossible for me to speak.

"May I see her, sir?" Jonathan asked timidly. Sir Harold nodded and slapped my ass again, indicating, I realized, that I should turn around.

Jonathan stared raptly at me, as though he'd never seen me before. He stroked my breast softly and then rubbed me behind the ear as though I were an animal, to be communicated with in this way. It was unbearably humiliating, the bit making me mute, the tail making me less than human. I clenched my bare toes against the straw and looked at him miserably. He continued to stare at me, one hand on my ass under the tail, the other touching my face through the straps. I lowered my eyes, but he slapped my breast hard, and I knew that meant he wanted me to keep looking at him. They'd speak to me, I realized, as little as possible while I was a "custom pony." I raised my eyes, sighing and shuddering a bit.

"You're making her skittish," Sir Harold said and stroked my ass slowly with one of his big, meaty hands. Amazingly, his stroking did seem to calm me down. "Quiet now, quiet now, that's it," he crooned to me. They would speak to me, I corrected myself, but only like this, a kind of brief, phatic communication meant to elicit a physical rather than a verbal or cognitive response.

Sir Harold turned to Jonathan. "She's a nice bit of flesh, see, but high-strung, like you. It'll take some work, you know." He attached a set of reins to brass rings at the ends of the bit and tugged. The pain in my mouth was echoed by stabs of feeling in my cunt and breasts and waves of shame. This feeling was new, and very frightening. I turned in the direction of the tug, away from Jonathan and toward the front of the carrier. Sir Harold attached the reins to the bar that I'd been holding. Then he nodded in the direction of my hands, and I held the bar again. I figured I'd need to do this in order to keep my balance once we got going. He attached the rings on my cuffs to rings on the bar, on either side of the ring where the reins were attached. Jonathan stroked my ass one more time.

"In a week, you won't know her," Sir Harold assured Jonathan as they stepped out of the carrier and shut the door behind them. Would I know myself? I wondered.

The pickup truck's engine started. I held on tight. Pretty soon we were on the freeway, crossing the Bay Bridge. There was a little round window I could look out of at my side. At first I was frightened that people could look in at my bridled face, but passengers in cars didn't seem to see me—not even little kids, who were staring extra hard, trying to get a glimpse of the pony. Finally I decided, with some relief, that it was a one-way window. Probably it looked dark or like a mirror from the outside.

I didn't have a watch, of course, so I don't know how long we were on the freeway. Two hours, maybe? And the little window wasn't really angled to let me see the road signs. All I knew was that it was hot and sunny outside—I could tell by the bright sun through the window and the warm air coming through the vents in the carrier. From the little I could see, it looked very rural outside; we were somewhere in the Central Valley, I supposed. The ride became bumpy as we pulled onto a gravel road, and bumpier still after Sir Harold unhooked some gate and we went uphill for a few minutes on dirt and stones.

Finally we stopped. He came back into the carrier, wordlessly detached me, and led me out by the reins. I blinked in the brilliant sunlight, stepping onto a patch of grass. A young man in jeans, cowboy boots, and an Aerosmith T-shirt was holding a pair of sturdy, thick-soled laceup boots in his hands and grinning at me. He had dark skin and very white teeth, I could see as my eyes adjusted to the light, and he knelt to tie and buckle the boots onto my feet.

"Not bad, boss," he said. He was short and solid, the T-shirt stretched against a broad, hard chest and shoulders. "No experience, though. That's pretty clear. What's her name?"

"It's Carrie," Sir Harold said. "We'll put her next to that blond, curly-headed one. Hey, is she named Carrie, too?"

"Cathy, boss," the young man said, grinning again. He seemed easily amused. Maybe working all day with naked girls in bridles and tails had always been his dream job. The boots were tightly laced on my feet. They felt solid, making me want to stamp my feet. The young man gave my pubic hair a friendly little yank and then got to his feet. We were standing near a fenced-in ring of ground, maybe thirty yards in diameter, and he looped my reins over the fence.

Within the ring, maybe eight or ten girls, bridled and tailed like me, were going through various paces, supervised by a few guys in jeans with riding crops in their hands. The girls were all doing different things, so it was hard for me to get a fix on the general principles involved. One was jumping hurdles. A few others were practicing various gaits, walking, trotting, and a kind of slow run—a canter? Two were harnessed together, trotting in what looked to me like perfect precision. Another was goose-stepping. Yet another was marching, her knees very high. Unlike the rest of the girls, who wore boots like mine, she wore very high-heeled shoes. I winced as I watched her feet move over the uneven ground.

Just then I heard quick footsteps and a jingling sound. I turned in the direction of the sound and there it was, the whole deal, the finished product, coming down a path toward us from some rolling wooded hills. If they'd wanted me any more agitated than I was now, they couldn't have done better at that very moment than to show me this.

It was a cart, a small one-seater on two large wheels, designed a bit like a plow or a backwards wheelbarrow. There was a man sitting in it, holding reins and a whip, and, running quickly but carefully, lifting her knees elegantly in front of her, a harnessed and bridled girl. Her bridle looked like mine, and the man in the cart was holding the reins. I couldn't entirely make out the complicated arrangement of other straps that attached her harness to the cart, but I could see that her cuffed wrists were hooked to metal handles, which were like the handles of a wheelbarrow, and that this was where a lot of the pulling happened. It was, all in all, a simple but fiendish little contrivance, and it seemed to work well. I mean, they were going fast, and as they approached us, I could see that she was sweating and breathing hard, and that the man in the cart was smiling broadly.

They weren't slowing down as they approached us, and I figured they'd just go past. In fact, I could hear the crack of the whip as the man used it to speed the girl up. But just some twenty yards from us, he pulled hard on the reins, jerking her head back cruelly. "Whoa," he yelled, "whoa, Stephanie." She dug in her heels and stopped, almost on a dime, I thought, pulling up so close to us that I could see that her eyes were a violet blue.

The man jumped out of the cart, looping the reins over the fence not too far from me. I stared at Stephanie curiously. The bridle distorting her mouth and the dusty rivulets of sweat running down her face and body didn't stop her from being supernally beautiful. She had long black hair, and to keep it from getting tangled in all the straps, it was done in a thick braid, near the top of her head, coming out through the straps of the bridle. But tendrils and curls were escaping everywhere and you could see that when the braid was undone there'd be oceans of gorgeous black curls. They'd cascade almost to her perfect ass, crisscrossed with whip-marks and bisected by a tail like mine, and over her goblet-shaped breasts, which were heaving as she panted. Her peachy skin was flushed bright pink under the dust. I kept looking at her, transfixed, but she just looked straight ahead, consciously evening her breath, stretching and relaxing her muscles.

Aerosmith undid all the straps and buckles that attached her to the cart, and then began rubbing her down with a soft cloth. When she was dry, he stroked her ear a little, crooning gently to her, "Easy, easy, goo-ood girl," much as Sir Harold had done to me in the van. She seemed to need it a lot less than I had, though. Her breathing had quieted down and evened out, and she looked calm and serene—well, bored, actually. Aerosmith patted her breast—she looked off somewhere into the middle distance—and he sighed softly, took her reins, and led her down a path to some barnlike buildings, downhill from us. They disappeared into one of them.

Meanwhile, Sir Harold went to talk to the driver, a Mr. Finch, I gathered. Though Mr. Finch clearly had had the time of his life cracking the whip over Stephanie's bouncing ass, you could see that the experience wouldn't be complete for him if he couldn't find anything to complain about. Still, all he could come up with was a small squeak in one of the wheels and that he wished the weather were not quite so hot. Sir Harold nodded sympathetically, with the easy confidence of a tradesman who has utter faith in his product. He opened a small compartment at the back of the cart and pulled out an oilcan, oiling the offending wheel until the squeak was entirely gone, then putting the oilcan back.

The cart, I could see upon closer inspection, was no glorified wheelbarrow. Though I figured that its body was actually made of some kind of light fiberglass, it was covered with a molded wood veneer and painted a glossy black with red and gold detailing.

The spokes of the wheels were also gold, and the seat was soft dark red leather. There was a little brake apparatus over one of the wheels, I realized—otherwise it would have run Stephanie over when she'd stopped so short. It was skillfully and practically designed, but it looked like a tiny fantasy coach, reminding me of fairy tales.

Sir Harold was telling Mr. Finch that in the future, if he heard a squeak, he should use the oilcan himself. Each cart, not to speak of each pony, of course, he repeated a few times, got a thorough going-over between rides, but you never knew.

"It's a tough job," he sighed, with some relish, "old carts, new ponies, always something needing my attention. Like that one over there, by the fence, fresh and green and unbroken. Took her on as a special favor to her master, nice boy from the old days. She'll be all right but she'll take some work. You get to know the signals in my line of business. Nice body but likes to think too much. Not like that little Stephanie, who responds to the slightest tug, and you just lay the whip on for the pleasure of seeing the pretty marks."

Speaking of Stephanie made Mr. Finch remember that he'd also paid to be blown by her, and that she'd probably be cleaned up and groomed and ready for him in the stable by now. He shook hands with Sir Harold, and hurried down the path.

Sir Harold gave me a long look. It was the first time I'd been alone with him, and I realized that he frightened me intensely. He was onto me, I thought. He knew that, at least at first, I wouldn't be good at this, that I would need words, not strokes or slaps or tugs, to make me obey. He wouldn't tell me anything directly—nothing meaningful, anyhow—but he'd managed, through his little speech to Mr. Finch, to communicate all this to me. I returned his look solemnly, trying to communicate that I understood what

I'd have to work to overcome, and he nodded briefly, so I guess he was satisfied.

"Frank," he now yelled, to one of the guys in the ring, "take this new one, name's Carrie, down to the stable. Put her next to Cathy, feed her, and give her a nap. We'll start training her this afternoon."

Frank was tall, rawboned, freckled, quiet, and friendly. I guessed they'd all be friendly. He picked up my reins and slapped my ass. "Nice girl," he said briefly, "come on."

We walked down the path at a good clip and entered the barn-like building I'd seen Aerosmith lead Stephanie into earlier. It was a stable, divided into stalls on both sides of a center aisle, with straw heaped on the floor. It didn't look special in any way—I mean, I don't think it had been built for girls being treated like horses. I think it had, at one time, actually held horses. Maybe the only modification was that the door to each stall was just high enough so that it came up to your neck. And they must have cleaned it out with great care when they'd converted it. It didn't actually smell like a stable, but it did smell, a little—of straw, and of...of flesh, I guess. I counted seven stalls on each side.

We passed a stall where I could see Mr. Finch's shoulders and the back of his gray-blond head, and hear his moans. I could also see a chain attached to the stall's back wall, trailing down the wall and onto the ground. The chain was moving rhythmically, and I knew, even though I couldn't see her, that attached to its other end, in the straw on the floor of the stall, was Stephanie on her knees with Mr. Finch in her mouth. And I realized that part of me was glad she was having to blow this unpleasant guy—gorgeous, snooty, perfect little bitch. Dumb, Carrie, I thought. Before you're out of here, you'll probably have to do a lot worse. But I knew that I couldn't help what I felt.

Frank led me into a stall and quickly took off my tail and bridle, as well as my collar and cuffs, which I'd been wearing all morning, and which came from Jonathan's house. He hung the tail, with its straps and dildo, on a hook on the wall, and then took all the other hardware somewhere else. I wondered why he'd taken the bridle. Then he came back, took off my boots, slapped my ass again, and nodded to the door of the stable. I followed him out and he led me a little farther down the path to a kind of outhouse, a regular one, only rather large, with room for maybe a dozen people and no seats, just holes in the floor to squat over. It was quite clean for an outhouse, which is to say, just a few flies.

When I'd finished there, he led me back into my stall and put a loose chain collar around my neck, hooking it to a long chain attached to the wall at the back of the stall, like the one I'd seen in Stephanie's stall. Whistling as he did all these chores, he went out again and returned with a pan of food and a little trough of water, both of which he attached to the top of the door of the stall, so I could eat and drink standing up (and of course not using my hands), facing the stable's center aisle. The food was a kind of grain and vegetable mixture, tasting vaguely of oats, but formed into little pellets like breakfast cereal. Science Diet, I thought, specially balanced for girl ponies. The only pieces of the food that I actually recognized were the cubes of raw carrot and celery mixed in with the kibbles and bits. I hadn't realized how dehumanizing it would be to eat food that had been prepared entirely for its nutritional value. I didn't want to do it, but I was hungry and figured that I'd better. And when Frank came back holding a large, perfect green apple, it looked so appealing to me that I ate it out of his hand and, after he'd tossed away the core, licked his sticky fingers clean. He stroked my head to dry his hand, and then my face, and it frightened me that I was beginning to feel a kind of affection for him.

Then he came into the stall, stroked my ass, crooned to me that I was a good girl and needed some rest, and pointed to the pile of straw with some blankets on it. I crawled between the blankets and fell asleep.

When I woke up, it was a lot busier in there. There were lots of girls in the stalls. I guessed they'd given me an early lunch, because I was new, and I'd been asleep when the rest of them had come back. And now they—we—were all getting out again. The stable guys were busy bridling and harnessing.

Pretty soon one of them, whom I hadn't seen before, came in to get me ready.

"Back to work with you," he sang out, "up, up, thatta girl," as I stumbled to my feet and rubbed my eyes. He reattached my tail, first regreasing the dildo. Then he put a different bridle on me. It looked the same as the first, but the bit was cold, heavy metal. I guess the first one had been just for practice. He took off the chain collar and put a kind of harness arrangement around my torso. It buckled over my shoulders and ended in a new, stiff collar. There were also matching cuffs, which he hooked together behind my back, up a little above my waist, so they wouldn't be in the way of the tail. Then he put on my boots again, attached some reins to the bridle, and led me out of the stall.

As the business of the afternoon unfolded I figured out that there were four guys working fourteen girls in the stables. There was Frank, and Aerosmith, whose name was really Mike, and two others, Don and Phil. The four worked well together, yelling questions and answers to each other, sharing tasks. And they were fast. I mean, putting all the hardware on us was no loving B&D ritual; it was a job they were paid to do, like sweeping out the stable and greasing the wheels of the carts. It probably took Phil about as long to do up all the straps and buckles and laces on me as it has for me to describe him doing it. And this included a once-over, after he finished, a kind of general straightening and tightening of everything, until I felt almost corseted. Leading me out of the stall, he went along the center aisle, stall by stall, and gathered up a bunch of other girls' reins in his hand. So there were four of us that he was briskly leading down the path back to the ring, the midafternoon sun making everything look lovely and golden and pastoral.

Walking fast to keep up and trying to find a comfortable way to rest my tongue against the bit took a lot of my attention. So it took me a minute to notice that one of the other girls Phil was leading was gorgeous Stephanie, just sort of floating along, her tail bobbing. I tried to make eye contact with her, and when she clearly, if subtly, refused, I felt myself involuntarily rolling my eyes and sighing behind my bit. I doubt that I was audible, but my body language must have been expressive enough, because the girl on my other side bumped her hip against me, and when I looked at her, she nodded toward Stephanie and did a perfect matching eye-roll.

I would have smiled at her if the bit had let me, and I guess she could tell that. As we hurried along I got a chance to look at her. She had short, curly blond hair, a pointed chin and high cheekbones under the straps of her bridle, very firm conical breasts that her harness caused to jut way out, and great, lithe muscles under lovely, suntanned skin. Cathy, I guessed. And she looked familiar. Now where had I...well, the body remembers, even if the mind is overwhelmed by new rules and concepts. Involuntarily, I found my eyes moving to her thighs, searching for the marks. And yes, there they were, very light, almost but not quite healed but still unmistakable, those evenly spaced marks. I remembered her mistress from the dressage show, and Cathy's worshipful look. I was glad, though, that worshipful as she'd been there, she clearly had a sense of humor. Even if all we could do was roll our eyes at each other, I was glad she was here.

By this time we, and the groups of ponies led by the other guys, had all reached the ring. Sir Harold was there, supervising busily, and the guys were really hopping. Some of the ponies were being harnessed to carts—I noticed there was a two-seater, to be pulled by two ponies harnessed together, and even an elaborate little open coach, to be pulled by two pairs, one in front of the other. I would have been fascinated to watch the intricacies of the harnessing arrangements, as the nicely dressed folks waiting to drive were doing, but Frank led me and Cathy into the ring, with sharp tugs on our reins.

He led us to a corner where there was a pole, sort of a maypole arrangement with chains maybe ten feet long dangling from the top. A circular path had been placed into the ground around it. Looping our reins behind our backs, he attached a chain to each of our collars. Then he positioned us carefully at points in the circle around the pole, Cathy at twelve noon, me at three o'clock, both of our chains standing tautly out from the pole. Loudly but curtly he barked out, "Walk!"

And we did. I tried to copy Cathy exactly, her speed, her posture, and I was careful to keep the distance between us constant and the chain taut. You would think it would be a piece of cake, and I actually thought I was doing very well, but damned if Frank's riding crop didn't keep falling on my calves, or my ass or shoulders, almost every time I passed him. "Head up!" he'd shout, "Tits out! Knees higher!" and damned if he wasn't always right, too. Cathy's head would be held higher, I'd realize after the fact, her body more complexly and elegantly displayed than mine. Drooling behind my bit, I put everything into trying to get this together.

I must have improved somewhat, because we advanced to trotting and cantering (I guessed goose-stepping was part of the advanced course). And I felt I was really improving when, as the afternoon wore on, the times I didn't get hit started to outnumber the times I did, even though Frank was barking out his commands with great frequency, making us change gaits almost in midstep. I could relax a little, I realized, just enough to realize how painful and difficult this really was. The muscles in my legs ached, and my back and my belly, too, from holding myself up so perfectly straight as I circled around and around. And the accumulated bruises and welts from the riding crop began to hurt more and more. Dusty, salty sweat was dripping into my eyes, I was panting, and a little drool was running out of the corners of my mouth.

Finally we stopped, and Frank wiped the sweat off us while we cooled down. It had been hours, I realized, hours of painful, monotonous walk-trot-canter. The weather was still warm, but the sun was a lot lower in the sky than it had been when we'd started.

Sir Harold and our guy from this morning came over to where we were standing. The guy unhooked Cathy from the maypole and led her away, and Sir Harold said to Frank, "Let's see what you can do with her." Frank commanded me to trot, and I was off.

It was harder to do without Cathy in front of me, but my muscles seemed basically to remember the rhythm. Frank kept quiet, and let Sir Harold bark out corrections and lay his riding crop on me. He hit harder than Frank, of course, but even he didn't hit every time I went around, so I figured I was ahead of the game. And when I stopped, and he curtly told Frank to clean me up, adding, "You can have her if you want," I knew I hadn't disgraced myself or Frank (or Jonathan, I surprised myself by thinking).

Frank quietly led me back down to the stable. I saw that most of the other ponies had already been taken back and been cleaned up. The only ones left in the yard were some girl who was still being dried off, and Stephanie, whose hair Aerosmith was lovingly brushing. That hair, I thought, God, it must take hours of their time to wash out the dust and brush out the tangles. Still, Aerosmith looked like he was in heaven (it didn't look to me like this was just a job for him, and I wondered how he could stand it), and Stephanie, once again, looked like she wasn't here at all.

Frank took off all my hardware, putting it in a neat pile on the ground. Then he turned a spigot and aimed a hose of cold water at me. I gasped. I hadn't expected that. The water pressure was hard against my bruises, though nice against my sore muscles, as he thoroughly soaped me down from head to toe with a soft brush and then rinsed and dried me.

"Okay, okay," he sang softly to me, picking up all my straps and other assorted hardware, "back in your stall, just a little more work this afternoon and then you get a nice dinner." He slapped my ass and I hurried in, wanting to get both the work and the yucky dinner over with and just collapse in the straw.

He came into the stall with me, hung all the hardware neatly on its hooks, attached the chain collar, and then surprised me by kissing me on the mouth, a long, deep tongue kiss that made me moan and kiss him back. "Pretty mouth," he murmured, "so pretty without its bridle, oh yes..."

And then he surprised me some more by whispering in my ear, "And forget about this stupid horse thing. For the next little while you're a girl, not a damn pony."

Then he went over to the straw and lay back, leaning on his elbows, sticking a piece of hay between his teeth and jerking my chain to pull me along. He pushed my shoulders down to the floor so that I was on my knees, and lifted one of his feet. "Now, darlin'," he drawled, "you can use that pretty mouth to clean my boots."

Oh yuck. His old cowboy boots, leather and snakeskin, were covered with dust and dirt and pieces of grass and hay. I thought of licking Jonathan's meticulous shoes, of that first silly little humiliation when he made me lick the lipstick off. Welcome to the great outdoors, city girl.

It took a while—quite a while—to clean off those boots and my mouth really tasted awful when I'd finished. Frank gave me some water to drink, and then he undid his buckle and pulled off his belt.

"Now suck me good," he said softly. "You treat me as good as those boots, Carrie, or I will whale hell out of that little ass, and not with a riding crop, but with my belt, maybe with the buckle end."

If I was a girl, I figured, I could use my fingers to unzip his jeans and take out his cock, and I thought I'd test these new local rules a little. So I whispered softly, "May I use my hands to take out your cock, Frank? May I touch it with my hands?"

He grinned and cuffed me lightly. "Polite, aren't you? Well, yes, you may, darlin', if you hurry the hell up."

So I did. I unzipped him, fished around just a little until it practically jumped out of his pants, and sucked and sucked, while he grinned and moaned, his big hard hand on my neck.

After he came, rested for a while, and put his belt back on, he jerked the chain attached to my collar and whispered, "Pony time." And then we were back to the pony game, me standing quietly at the stall door and him whistling and patting me and crooning animal inanities at me as he got me some more healthy Science Diet for dinner. And as I crawled between the blankets on the straw, hoping my sore muscles would get rested enough overnight for whatever was in store tomorrow, I wondered just how many levels of mindfuck I'd have to deal with in this place.

And then, just as I was about to drift off to sleep, I noticed a really odd thing. A little piece of rubber hose, maybe two inches of it, was snaking its way through a knothole in the wall of my stall, the wall, I realized, that I shared with Cathy. Softly but unmistakably coming out of the hose was a whispering sound, "psssst" to get my attention.

I put my mouth to the hose and whispered, "Cathy?" and then put my ear to it.

"Yeah," she whispered back. "So, what do you think? What was Frank like?"

"A pervert," I answered. "He likes to talk to the ponies like they were girls."

She stifled a giggle. "I caught some of that. Sir Harold sure wouldn't like it if he knew."

"How'd you get the hose?" I asked.

"Yesterday, or the day before," she answered, "they had me crawling around the yard with a little saddle on, and I found it on the ground and palmed it, just in case I got a neighbor I wanted to talk to."

I felt like a new kid in summer camp who had just made a best friend. Life was looking up.

Cathy had been here for four days, and would be here another three before Madame, as she called her, picked her up to take her home.

"She's thinking of showing me at those dressage shows," she said, "so she sent me here to get some basic training. She may put in a ring, all that stuff, at her house. Hire a trainer, even."

"How do you feel about it?" I asked.

She surprised me then by a total transformation of her whispered voice. The bratty, giggly tone disappeared completely, and she answered simply, "I'm honored, of course. I just hope she'll be pleased when she sees what I've learned."

I didn't know what to say to that, so she continued, "And your master—he's the beautiful man with the gray hair, right?—why did he send you here?"

I explained, as best I could, about my training for the auction being interrupted by Jonathan's trip to Chicago. She knew about the auctions, but not much more than I did.

"But to have to leave your master. I'd die if it were me," she said. "How did you displease him, Carrie? Isn't your heart breaking?"

I was pondering how to answer all this when we heard footsteps. One of the guys was coming through, doing a bedcheck, I guess. I snuggled into my blanket and pretended to be asleep. And the next thing I remember is waking up the next morning in a pool of bright sunlight.

Feed, groom, harness. The routine really wasn't going to vary, I realized. My leg muscles were stiff, but not horribly so, and when the guy—it was Aerosmith this time—came to put on my bridle, boots, and all the rest of it, he skillfully rubbed my calves with some ointment out of a brown bottle, which seemed to help.

When they'd gotten us down to the ring, they harnessed me to a cart. This one, however, looked more like a wheelbarrow. It was clearly a practice cart, and might as well have had a sign on it that said "Student Driver." Still, I stood very straight as Don pulled the straps tight and attached the rings in my cuffs to the cart handles. Then he came up to me and silently showed me the whip he'd be using. It was long, braided, scary-looking, dark brown leather, and he looped it in his hand, stroking my breasts, my pubes, and my face through the bridle.

Finally, he climbed into the cart, pulled the reins, and yelled "Walk!" I started up and soon came to a fork in the road. It was easy to tell, though, by the sharp tug on the right rein that he wanted me to turn right, so I did, and we were off, soon trotting along what looked like a pretty hiking trail, up and down hills, through copses and over ridges. When he wanted me to change gaits, he'd yell that, but he'd also accompany it by a coded set of tugs and pulls on the reins. And after about half an hour, he stopped yelling, just tested me on my understanding of the tugs and pulls, and flicked the whip over me whenever I was slow to get a signal. It was difficult. I was scared I'd lose my footing, step into a hole, or turn my ankle on stones in the path, particularly as I ran down the steep downhill slopes.

And when I began to feel a little more confident about where to place my feet on the path and how to understand the signals, he started laying on the whip even harder. Because it wasn't enough to follow instructions, keep up a steady clip, and keep my balance. I had to look good, keep my head up, tits out, knees up, ass bobbing. Well, what did you think, I chided myself, that the folks who'll be driving you will be paying Sir Harold for a look at the pretty countryside? And I found myself flashing on mental images of racehorses, their snorts and the angles of their heads, and the fastidious ways they placed their hooves. I tried my damnedest to look good, and I began to feel a perverse pride in it all.

We were back on open, level ground now, heading, I guessed, back toward the ring. We turned a corner in the path, and I realized that we were heading straight for a low stone wall. I wasn't getting any instructions to slow down from Don—had he fallen asleep at the wheel? Hey, I might be perverse but I'm not crazy, I thought, and began to prepare for a halt, when all hell broke loose. The reins jerked my head back, the whip started raining down on my shoulders and ass, and Don started shouting insults; "Bad, bad, no! Bad pony! Stupid girl!"

I stopped running—the reins were certainly telling me to do that now—and he jumped out of the cart and ran up to me in a fury. "Did I tell you to slow down?" he yelled. "Did I tug the reins or yell to slow down? What the fuck made you think you could decide that? What the fuck made you think at all?"

Of course. The wall was supposed to be a test. And I'd flunked immediately. After the fact it seemed so simple. Of course they wouldn't let me go into the wall, and they did not fall asleep at the wheel around here. Don would have jerked me to a halt in plenty of time, I realized. I was stupid. And bad. I hung my head and wept in front of him.

He watched me for a while, then slapped my cheek lightly. "Head up," he said, but not unkindly. "We'll try it again."

He got back into the cart, reined me around, and we went back a few hundred yards along the path. And this time I just kept running toward the wall, proudly and trustingly, until at the very last minute he jerked my head back and I dug my heels in and stopped—stopped every bit as short as Stephanie had done the day before. And as we trotted back to the ring, which wasn't far from the stone wall, I was delighted by Don's murmurs of praise and encouragement, and almost ignored the thought that crept unbidden into my head just then: Sir Harold was right, Jonathan won't know me.

Don reported to Sir Harold that he thought I could pull paying customers now, giving him the specifics of the morning. Sir Harold looked almost convinced and said he'd think about it; Phil unharnessed me and took me back to the stable for grooming, food, and a nap. That afternoon, I got my first paying customer.

Given my luck, of course, it turned out to be a Muffy. I mean, not one of Jonathan's Muffies, just a specimen of the generic type. Which means, even though I think I did reasonably well, I got hit quite a lot. I think that there's something about me that gets to them, that I'm kind of a symbolic stand-in for themselves, for their fevered imaginings of how they'd do in my place.

But then, as Sir Harold said, I think way too much. I'll never be able to change that, but I realized that first afternoon that I was learning how to keep it at bay while I was pulling a cart. There was just so much physical data to have to deal with—the light and shade and colors whizzing by, the shape of the path under my feet, the complicated embrace of the bridle and tail and harness, the pleasure and desire of the driver, translated into tugs at the reins and slaps of the whip. Then there were the ache of my own muscles and bruises, the pounding of my feet and heart, the sharpness of my breath in my chest, and the burn of salty sweat dripping into my eyes. And the challenge, the ceaseless challenge to look good, proud, and upright through it all.

Well, wax poetic over it as I might, I didn't stop, once it was dark and quiet in the stable, gossiping and giggling with Cathy through the hose. It was a nice break from the pony game, a way to be myself. But not too much myself, or too deeply. Because I discovered that although Cathy liked nothing better than to talk endlessly about Madame, her elegance and her cruelty, I didn't want to talk about Jonathan. I was confused about what I felt about leaving him.

Cathy was cool. She didn't understand me, but she did understand that each slave was unique in what made him or her tick, and she stopped asking me things I clearly didn't want to answer. So we just used the evenings to compare notes on customers, on the stable guys—especially when, as bonuses for extra good work, Sir Harold let them use us—and of course on the other ponies. We pieced together the information that while most of us were temporary boarders, our masters and mistresses doubtless paying obscene sums to Sir Harold for our training, Sir Harold owned four girls himself. Those were the ones who could goose-step, or even, Cathy whispered to me in awe, negotiate the path through the woods in heels. I found this difficult to believe, but I watched them whenever I got a chance; Gillian, Cynthia, Anna, and Jenny. They were so astonishingly surefooted, so proud and gorgeous, that I thought maybe it could be true.

But our favorite topic of bitchy gossip was, naturally, Stephanie, nasty little good girl princess Stephanie. Because even Sir Harold's ponies didn't have her haughty manner, her way of doing everything perfectly but of not being here at all. It was as clear to Cathy as it was to me that Mike—Aerosmith as I still thought of him—was pathetically infatuated with her, and we didn't approve of that. All the rest of us had developed a rapport with the guys who worked for Sir Harold, an admiration for how good they were at their jobs, and a sympathetic acceptance of the idiosyncrasies (like Frank's girl perversion) that they each had. It was amazing how much you could express with a bit in your mouth, and how much people communicated to you. And I remembered, with a start of recognition, Kate Clarke's telling Jonathan that if I were hers, she'd put a bit and bridle on me. She'd been right, I thought, I had needed this training badly.

Stephanie, though—it was as though she didn't need this training, as though she were above it. Cathy and I were as nasty and bitchy as we could be, egging each other on to imagine humiliations for her, humiliations she never got, of course, because she was so prissy and perfect. If we'd been in summer camp, we would have shortsheeted her bed by now. Or dipped her hand in a bucket of water while she was sleeping to make her pee in her sleeping bag.

"What I would have liked to see," Cathy whispered one night, "was her pulling a plow." It was her last night here—Madame was coming for her tomorrow. She was so excited that she couldn't sleep, and I was so sad about her leaving that I couldn't, either. So we both were overtired and punchy, repeating all our old Stephanie jokes just for companionship. But this plow stuff was news to me.

"A plow?" I whispered. "They have a farm here?"

"Well," she answered, "when Madame drove me up here, on the road through the grounds, we passed a girl pulling a plow. They have a vegetable garden, I think, and they grow some flowers. Anyhow, the girl has gone home since then; she was all tired and muddy and everything, and, you know, kind of bent over. She looked terrible. Madame asked Sir Harold about it and he just sort of rumbled, 'Punishment.' And then he looked at me and added...'for a pony who didn't behave.'"

"Wow," I breathed, "it does sound terrible, it would be perfect for her."

And we were so taken with this image, both of us, that we didn't, it seems, even hear when Phil and Mike, both of them that night, came through for a bedcheck and shone a flashlight right at the rubber hose between my mouth and Cathy's ear.

"Well," Phil drawled, "will you look at this? Two little ponies talking on the telephone. Or pretending to talk, anyway, because everybody knows ponies can't talk. Why, that's so cute, Mike, I think we'll just have to show the boss. Get the fuck up, you two."

And while we scrambled to our feet, he and Mike gathered up all our hardware in their arms—boots, bridles, everything, and not forgetting our telephone. Then they each grabbed a riding crop and began hitting us hard, on the ass, driving us barefoot through the night, running up a path we'd never been on to Sir Harold's house.

It was an old-fashioned house on a hill, with a porch around it, plus gables and gingerbread and cupolas. There was a light burning in an upstairs window, so it wasn't long before Sir Harold came down to open the door, barefoot with bony, hairy ankles and wrapped in a voluminous maroon bathrobe with a big gold crest on the pocket. He nodded as Phil explained the situation and showed him the little bit of hose, which he had pocketed.

"Talking to each other," he murmured. "Shocking. Well, boys, we've got a busy night ahead of us. Get the two-seater out and harness these bad ponies to it. I'll be down in a few minutes."

Phil left to get the two-seater while Mike started getting us into our harnesses, bridles, tails, and boots. I was scared at the idea of a night ride—and of the fact that I doubted that this would be our only punishment—but I was even more afraid to look at Cathy. She was sobbing silently, huge tears coursing down her face, and I knew that she was thinking about Madame coming tomorrow: Sir Harold would doubtless tell her everything.

It couldn't have been more than five minutes before Mike returned with the two-seater cart and attached us to it snugly. Then Sir Harold floated down his front steps in shoes and socks but still in his bathrobe, carrying a large, menacing black whip. He shot us a fearsome look, climbed into the cart, and cracked the whip over us, pulling the reins to signal that we head out for the path over the ridge and through the woods, and at our fastest gallop.

And that's all that happened for the next hour. We ran and ran, faster and harder than I could have imagined, the whip cracking over us, both of us groaning and weeping and panting and feeling as if this would just go on forever. Once in a while one of us would slip—the path seemed different in the dark and sometimes in the thickest parts of the forest you couldn't even see the moon—and the other would have to drag her along until she got back into the rhythm. Once we both slipped, just about at the same time, and I thought dimly how lucky we were that we were going slightly uphill, so that the cart didn't just roll over us, because I didn't trust Sir Harold to use the brake. We staggered to our feet, the whip blows raining down on us, and started up again, and maybe ten minutes later, Sir Harold drove us back to the ring, where Frank, Mike, Don, and Phil were all sitting on the fence, waiting by the light of a Coleman lantern.

"I want them back at my house in an hour," Sir Harold said as Don and Phil jumped down to unharness us. "You boys can have 'em till then." And he hiked up the path to his house on the hill, his robe billowing behind him.

They took everything off of us except our tails and pushed us into the ring. Then, slapping our asses hard, Don said curtly, "Run!"

I couldn't see which direction Cathy was running in. I just started running, barefoot, in the direction the slap seemed to be telling me to go in. And I got about halfway across when I felt a rope around me, pulling me to the ground. I looked down at myself, puzzled to see a rough rope looped around my torso, and then I looked up, to see the other end of the rope in Frank's hand. Lassoed, my God, I didn't know these guys could do rodeo tricks. Which is what they did for about fifteen minutes, all of them taking cracks at roping us, pulling us down hard, reining us in.

Finally, they seemed to be tired of that one and it was Mike, I guess, who yelled at us, "Get down on your hands and knees, and look at us."

And when we did, in the center of the ring, he added, "You two look disgusting." It was true, too. We were a mess—filthy, sweaty, and wet with tears and drool.

The other guys nodded, and Phil added, "If we wanted to fuck you, we could wash you down. But that sounds a little too much like what we do on the job every day—the boss just throws in the fucking so's he can get away with the pitiful wages he pays us. And you know how damn hard we work. So, no, working's not what we have in mind. We were thinking, more like, of watching."

And then they were all very quiet, waiting to see what we'd do. And I looked at Cathy, and she looked at me, and bruised and miserable and exhausted and scared as we were, we had to smile a little. I mean, these really weren't bad guys and it really wasn't the world's worst punishment they'd cooked up for us.

"Uh, well, could we wash ourselves a little first?" I asked. "Or each other?"

"I guess," Frank said grudgingly, "but hurry up."

One of them threw us a rag, and we ran to a spigot near the gate of the ring. And we got a little of the worst sweat and crud off each other. I kissed Cathy softly on the mouth, and she stroked my breast a little, and then we came back, hand in hand, to the middle of the ring.

We just stood there, looking at each other and considering. I knew that the guys were starting to get restless but I figured we were entitled to think about this for a minute. Then Cathy took a step forward and pressed her front against mine. We were pretty much the same height and I loved how her breasts felt against me. I started to rub, started to paint designs on her with my own breasts, up and down and around. She was firm and smooth—sandstone, I thought at first, an Eskimo carving, but getting warmer and softer and more yielding every minute.

She pushed me down to my knees and I licked the shape of her concave belly, the ridges of her hipbones. I made huge circles with my tongue, stopping just short of her pubic hair, while my breasts ground into her thighs and my hands grasped her ass.

Finally, she couldn't stand being teased by my mouth any longer and pushed my head into her crotch. "Fuckin' A," I heard one of the guys mutter, and I realized that they'd gotten off the fence where they'd been sitting or lounging and were clustered around us. Good, I thought, maybe I'll teach them something. It wouldn't hurt things around here if they ate a little pussy now and again. I dug my tongue in and explored, tracing the shape of her labia, then settling in to suck. I heard her moan and felt her short, sharp orgasm. Fast, I thought. Shit, I paid too much attention to the guys and not enough to her. I looked up at her, expecting some mild disappointment, but was surprised by her intent look, her shining eyes. Like, I thought wildly, a vampire in the moonlight?

But no, this story does not make that wild genre switch, it just modulates, ever so slightly, as Cathy did, pushing me to the ground and lying down next to me. And kissing me deeply while her fingers opened my vulva and entered, and moved, and clenched, and moved some more, and...oh my God, I felt knuckles. My eyes flew open and I saw her green-brown eyes and wicked smile, and I remembered that I'd admired the muscles in her arms. Biceps, triceps—the girl was wasted on a pony farm, she should have been pitching in the World Series. Or so I thought, when she gave me a chance to think at all, just banging me, wide open and stuffed full, while also never so aware of the horsetail dildo up my ass, crowding things up even more. I came and came and it didn't seem as though she would ever stop; I realized that I was going to have to beg her to stop, which I didn't really want to do, but what a joke, me and I'm sure also the guys thinking that they were in for a show of some girlie lingerie sex, even if we were rolling around in the dirt, and getting this instead, and to hell with it, I'm not proud. Stop please! Cathy, beautiful Cathy, I beg you, thank you.

"Ohhhhh," I groaned, then pulled her down and kissed her.

And she whispered, "That was new for you, wasn't it? I'm glad it was me, then."

Then the guys were all over her. I was scared for a minute, not knowing whether they were going to gangbang her or what, but it turned out they were more interested in high-fiving her. And I couldn't imagine why she'd worry about Madame, who, it seemed to me, would be so horny after a week away from that genius arm that she wouldn't care less about a little length of hose. I mean, she might be cruel and elegant, but she probably wasn't stupid.

Still, it looked like our hour was up, and Don and Phil walked us up the hill to Sir Harold's, ringing the bell and waiting in the hall after he'd pushed us into a little office he had. He told us to get down on our knees in front of his desk, while he sat on the edge of it, swinging one leg. And then he took the little length of hose out of his pocket and just asked quietly, "Which one of you?"

And you know that he thought it was me anyway, and that I figured he might as well keep thinking it, because Cathy was looking scared of Madame again, and well, I didn't know what Jonathan would say or think about any of this, so I figured I'd risk it. That was how I finally ended up spending the rest of that strange night wrapped in a ragged blanket in a tumbledown little shack next to the vegetable garden, trying to get some sleep before I had to wake up the next morning to pull the plow.

It was actually dark when a rooster woke me up. I stretched and groaned. Everything hurt, especially my insides, and I wondered if Cathy had pulverized them beyond recognition. Cheap, I thought, at the price.

Because I was realizing that even as grubby, achy, and unsure of what the day would bring as I was, I was downright cheery. When you've been that massively fucked, I thought, life just doesn't look so bad. I looked at the filthy little hut I was lying in, the hairy, greasy rope looped around my neck and tied to a hook in the wall, the dirt under my fingernails and on just about every other inch of me, too, and I shook my head in disbelief that I could actually be feeling anywhere near good. And then I shrugged, turned over, and got another half-hour of deep, dreamless sleep.

When I woke up again, it was to some nasty kicks in the ribs, which I realized had probably been going on for some time. "Up, now, you lazy thing, get up now!" I heard. Right, okay, yeah, lazy thing, that's me, I thought groggily. Okay, how do you want me? I figured I'd try hands and knees, which would take less effort than any other position I could think of. And I guess that was right, or close enough, because the kicks stopped.

I looked up at a heavy, round-faced woman, dressed in overalls, work boots, and a floppy sunhat, holding a pan of what looked like garbage. Table scraps, I realized, as she put it in front of me. They were tastier, once you got over the weird feeling, than the Science Diet they'd been giving me in the stables. I nosed out a little slice of salami—pepperoni, actually—and thought, it could be worse, Carrie.

I was worried that I'd start to annoy the woman if I continued to be so cheerful. Hell, I was starting to annoy myself. But she really didn't seem interested in my mood. She gave me some water to lap, and then told me to stand up. But I couldn't, at least not all at once. My bruised muscles just didn't want to. They kept trying to fold back up, like cheap lawn furniture. The woman looked on stolidly, and when I could finally stand straight, she silently led me out of the hut by the rope, after having picked up my bridle, harness, and tail.

She put them on me (I guessed I'd have to go barefoot), and then she strapped the harness to the plow, which was just standing out there in the middle of a half-turned-up field. No stroking or crooning at me, that was for sure. And then she grabbed the reins and briskly began to lead me down the rows, occasionally swatting me with a thin stick she held in her other hand.

And that was that. We just kept going back and forth as the sun rose in the sky and sweat started pouring off me. It was hot and hard and boring. It was work. It didn't have the little gut-wrenching thrills of exposure and humiliation I had come to expect—I hadn't realized just how much I'd come to expect them. The woman hardly looked at me, and I had to admit that it was a hell of a lesson and a punishment, kind of a metahumiliation, being out there dirty, naked, exhausted, exposed, and—virtually—invisible. I remembered Jonathan, that first day in his study, asking me if I liked to be looked at. Had it really been so obvious?

From the field, I could see cars coming and going down to the stable area. Customers, of course, but it was also Sunday, and Cathy had told me that "Sunday to Sunday" was the customary term for a boarder. So Sir Harold had really done Jonathan, that nice boy, quite a favor by taking me on in the middle of the week and driving all the way down and picking me up, too. I wondered idly about just what had gone on in the old days as I watched a beautiful, expensive car drive up the road toward the gate. Briefly I caught Cathy's rapt, triangular face at the window and Madame behind the wheel. And then they were gone and the woman was swatting me to hurry me up. Now I was naked and invisible and lonely as well.

The field I was plowing was, of course, bare, being turned over for new crops. But there was a field opposite where they were growing vegetables and some flowers, and there was a greenhouse as well. You could walk down a path between the fields, and once a couple came that way to buy flowers from the greenhouse, the woman just leaving me to stand around while she helped them. The couple chattered happily as they walked away with their flowers, and it was so silent out there, except for an occasional car on the road and the slap of the woman's stick on my calves, that I could hear them even after the path curved away and I couldn't see them.

The voices faded eventually, and then I heard some new voices, new people coming my way. These voices were familiar. I heard Sir Harold's rumble first, though I couldn't quite make out his words. And then another, a woman's voice that was unmistakably familiar and melodious, the words quite clear as the speakers approached.

"I'll have to give her to the emir tonight. It's his last night and he's been drooling over her photographs. And he'll love the job you've done on her.... It's just that she's so unmarked-marked."

Then in a different tone, the voice said, "No, it's not your fault, darling. You were the good girl I've taught you to be, and Sir Harold just couldn't find enough reason to punish you. But we'll beat you when we get home, just to put some lovely marks on you."

And as they came into view, Sir Harold and Kate Clarke, with Stephanie between them, unbridled but harnessed to a little wicker cart, Stephanie said softly but joyously, "Yes, Kate."

Filthy and sweaty as I was, they seemed like creatures from a different world: Kate in a short, crisp, pale yellow sundress and wide straw hat; Stephanie, her eyes never leaving Kate, looking like an adoring child with her hair in two ponytails over her dazzling naked shoulders and breasts; Sir Harold decked out in a silly blue blazer. I looked down at my bare, dirty feet and I wanted to disappear into the earth.

I should have known, I thought. A slave as beautiful and perfect as Stephanie. I remembered Jonathan saying that Kate's standards were perfectionist, and now I knew what that meant. I felt that up until this moment I'd simply been pretending to play a game I didn't understand at all, one whose rules and parameters were written in a complicated and impersonal, perhaps a mathematical, language. I realized why Stephanie hadn't cared what went on here, except, of course, for learning to be a perfect pony. For Kate. All for Kate. I wondered if I'd ever be that kind of slave, worshipful and adoring and totally without irony. I wondered if I wanted to.

Kate Clarke was coming over to me, having sent Sir Harold and Stephanie to the greenhouse to get flowers. The woman left me in the half-plowed row as she hurried to help them. I watched Kate walk carefully through the plowed field, her bare feet in their perfect sandals somehow managing to stay clean. But she wouldn't touch me, I thought. I was too dirty, too abject for that. I wanted, more than anything, for her to touch me, any way she would deign to.

She was smiling at me, almost triumphantly, even as she looked at me with her hard, appraising stare. And then she amazed me by coming very close and softly stroking my breast.

Very quietly she said, "You are very much improved, Carrie. Even if you didn't steal the little hose—and I don't think you did—you needed this punishment. The world is a lot larger than Jonathan's precious little study, isn't it?"

I nodded, tears in my eyes, as waves of sensation rippled from my breast down to my knees. I didn't so much understand her meaning as feel it, glimpsing a kind of never-ending horizon of pain and challenge, as yet unimagined extremes of experience opening out for me if I were brave enough to try to encounter them. If they were what I really, really wanted...

And that was all. Sir Harold and Stephanie came back, Stephanie's wicker cart piled high with sweet peas and snapdragons, and Kate joined them on the path back to the stables. I just pulled for the rest of the day, numbly, barely noticing the little Mercedes leaving the ranch an hour or so later, mostly keeping my eyes on the hard, bright sky and the hawks circling in the distance.

The Party

N. Whallen

She said her prayers regularly, attended church every Sunday, and taught a Bible class that was a model of probity. So it was a constant source of amazement to Ingrid Jameson that she had enslaved herself to Bart Howells. She was a well-shaped blonde executive in her late twenties, and she had drifted into the relationship in gradual stages until one morning, in her own bed, in her own apartment, wearing her own flannel nightdress, she woke to the realization that there was another side to her existence.

She went through her daily, then weekly routine as she waited for her master's summons. He tended to be erratic in his attentions, partly because his business often kept him busy, partly, she knew, and her insides churned at the thought, because it was part of their relationship.

"Tonight at nine," he said abruptly when she answered the

phone in her office. She had been talking less than a minute before to Pastor Brunner, accepting an invitation to the Sisterhood brunch, and the contrast could not have been more glaring.

"Yes," she said meekly.

He lived in one of the anonymous high-rent towers of the city center. She opened the door with the key he had provided, then checked the mirror in the hallway. He often left her messages there, and he always insisted she be perfectly groomed before coming in to see him. She was dressed as usual. Brown knee-length skirt. Conservative off-white blouse held closed at her neck by an antique brooch. Her blonde hair was let down, in its natural color, and it curled slightly over her shoulders. Very little makeup: the pastor and her father, the latter away in the Midwest but still present in her mind, disapproved of heavy makeup. Plain pantyhose, medium-heeled shoes.

Her heart pounded faster as she walked into the apartment and peered into the large living room. Howells was not there, and she followed the rustle of his movements directly to the large master bedroom. He was dressing, busy tying a formal black tie over an immaculate shirt front. He whistled as he dressed, and when he saw her in the mirror, he gave her the boyish grin and quirk of an eyebrow that was part—a small part—of his attraction for her.

"With you in a minute," he said, then finished tying the knot with a flourish. He turned lazily and contemplated her, raking her from head to shoes, then back again. She quivered, and the hands she held clasped in front of her waist trembled.

"Take them off," he said mildly. She hastened to obey, and as she did so noted that he proceeded to reach for the chest, an elaborately carved and lacquered Chinese piece that held many surprises for her. She was naked by the time he had found what he wanted. He looked at her again, his face sealed. She stood there as she had been taught, arms behind her back, head held proudly up, eyes low, feet slightly apart. There was an itch in her pubic hairs, golden wires resting proudly at the base of her pale stomach. She was also conscious of the bobbing of her full breasts, the pale nipples hardening in the air.

Finally he nodded, then said, "On the dresser. Your clothes for the evening. Put them on."

She stepped over to the dresser, aware that he was examining her ass. The slight marks of their previous encounter had vanished: he was always careful not to mark her permanently. Her ass, she knew, was a work of art. He had told her so several times. He used it frequently, of course, and always remarked on its beauty. It was the sin of Sodom, and in the normal course of the day, if she ever thought of the subject, she trembled at the punishment for it.

On the dresser she found a pair of silken stockings. One was black, the other white, each with a design of swirling light worked into the ankle with tiny brilliants. There were two garters, both broad bands of lace, one black, the other red with a prominent red rose sewn on it. That, and a pair of silver stiletto-heeled pumps, was all. She bit her lip. She had to decide quickly. He hated waiting, and, more importantly, expected her to know without thought what he wanted. She smoothed the stockings on, black on the right leg, the black garter on the same leg. No punishment followed, so she quickly pulled the white stocking on the other leg, then the red garter, then bent to fasten the pumps around her ankles, conscious that he was standing by her. He held several objects in his hands, one of which clinked, and she shivered at the sound.

She rose to face him. He nodded in approval and placed whatever he carried on the bed. She did not look, but kept her face on his as she had been trained.

"The dressing room," he said.

Makeup articles were ready for her, without the need for instruction. She applied a dark blue eye shadow to her eyelids, with heavy eyeliner. The lipstick was a strong red and she followed her inclination and widened her mouth with broad strokes, outlining the red in a faint line of black. He nodded in satisfaction when he came in; then, reaching to a shelf, brought down one of the masks. This one was a full-face mask, that of a perfect, classic female face in repose. The mouth and eyes were cut away to expose her own beneath. He put the mask on, securing it with small silver chains, then with quick, neat motions built up her hair into an elaborate coiffure.

"Bend over," he said. "Grasp your knees."

She quailed at what was to come, but turned and presented her full moons to his critical appraisal. She felt him part her buttocks, then his fingers gently massaged her forbidden entrance. She used to beg him not to use her there, but now it sent a fearful anticipatory shiver through her frame. Something cool and slick was applied to the entrance, and she yielded to the stiff finger reaming her rectum. She braced for what was to come, trying to relax the muscles. Instead, he bade her stand up. She did so in surprise, without a word.

He nodded in satisfaction, then led her back to the bedroom. On the bed lay a magnificent black sable coat. She knew, even before touching it, that it must have cost a fortune. He smiled slightly. She reached for it automatically, drew on its lush soft weight. He turned her, and to her surprise and fright, headed for the exit.

The house he drove to was in one of the more expensive neighborhoods, screened by a high stone wall and a row of bushes. Several high-end cars were parked in the gravel driveway. He stopped the car, then handed her something that clinked. She knew the chains were to go around her ankles with one end around her waist. He inspected her when she was finished: silver fetters bound her ankles, joined by a foot-long chain. The chain ran through a loop at the other end of a chain that rose to encircle her waist. He closed a diamond- and stainless-steel studded collar around her neck. The inside was lined with velvet and felt soft to the touch. A large silver loop allowed him to hook on a silver-plated dog leash. He nodded in brief approval, then closed the fur coat again, and led her into the house.

The semi-dark hall had been divided into two by a table that served as a cloakroom. Ingrid almost gasped, but remembered to hold her breath in time. The cloakroom attendant was as nude as she, except that a large ivory-colored cock stood up before her, almost to the level of her full breasts. It was held on by red cords around her waist, and the veins were appliquéed in gold. Around her neck she wore a collar similar to Ingrid's own, but she wore no mask.

"The rules are simple," Howells said, yanking slightly on the chain to get her attention. "Slaves wear collars, masters don't. A slave unattached to a master must obey any master's command. If I let go of the leash, anyone can do anything to you. Masters uses nicknames. Mine is 'Vicomte.' You have none. You are merely Vicomte's slave."

She nodded dumbly in the gloom, and he turned and strode through the far door. She followed him into a large, high-beamed hall, which in other circumstances would have been the epitome of good taste. Now the recesses were lit by candles and dim lights. Fifty or sixty people were in the room, in large and small groups. Most were dressed in formal wear: long dresses or dinner jackets. Some, however, lacked even the basics. Howells led her through the crowd, his hand firmly on her leash. He exchanged greetings with people he knew. Some of them wore masks, none wore collars. The people who spoke were often accompanied by others who did not, and these, largely, wore collars.

He collected two drinks and handed her one. She looked at it doubtfully. Strong drink is a mocker, she recalled, but drank it all down obediently when commanded. Howells turned to face the room, and she perforce followed suit. Two men were eyeing her speculatively. She blushed under her mask. They looked her up and down, then approached Howells, who was peering in another direction.

"Sir?" The taller of the pair, wearing a black domino and evening dress, spoke. The other, broader shouldered, with the build of a football player, said nothing, merely eyed her crotch hungrily.

"Yes, sir?" Howells turned his attention to them. Ingrid quailed inside. Her nakedness embarrassed her, but there was also a greater fear there. Something was about to happen.

"Could we make use of your slave?"

Howells considered the request for a moment, while Ingrid's insides cringed at the blunt request. They were talking of her! She was being discussed like a slab of beef or the loan of a car! She wanted to yell in outrage, but instead remembered who and what she was, and lowered her eyes.

"Have you anything in exchange?" Howells asked pleasantly.

"I'm afraid not," the other replied. "For consideration, I thought..."

"I'm afraid not, sirs. No insult intended, but I don't know either of you. And I have something specific in mind. Will you pardon me?"

The two bowed and Howells bowed in return, then moved off through the crowd. "Look around you, but don't lag," he said.

She wanted to hide her face, to close her eyes to the sights, but obedient to his command, she looked. They wormed through a circle of people, with Howells looking at faces. Several people, slaves as well as masters, looked on at the scene that was being enacted before them. A man in an elaborate feather mask and collar was on all fours. Behind him stood a mistress in a matching mask, a lash in her hands. Around them stood six or seven women, their crotches exposed. The man was busily lapping at one crotch, and with each lick the masked woman struck him across the ass. Ingrid had time to hear the combined sound of the lash meeting flesh, the man's grunt of pain, and the pleasure of the subject at his tongue, before Howells moved on to another group. She had time to notice the tremendous erection that rose beneath the man's belly before the tableau was swallowed in the crowd.

They threaded through the party. Some people were dancing, and she was watching two masters entwined in an embrace, both naked and supported by fully clothed slaves, when they were accosted by another couple.

"Vicomte, how are you?"

"Ah, Blue and Silvertips. How nice," Howells responded brightly.

"I see you have a new one," Blue, the male said, looking Ingrid over with bright, dark eyes.

"Yes," Howells admitted.

"Have you thoroughly beaten her yet?" There was a suppressed eagerness in Silvertip's voice. Her lips were painted a garish green, as green as the streaks in her hair. Behind her trailed a young woman dressed in a black sheath from the top of her head to her waist. No features were visible, and her hands were imprisoned within the enveloping sheath.

"No, it wouldn't really do," Howells said, then proceeded to describe in specific and intimate detail what he had had Ingrid do since their relationship had matured.

"Would you care to swap?" Blue and Silvertips said together, each pulling on the chain they held. Blue's slave was a hefty black man, huge pectorals showing through a net shirt, his genitals bulging in a tiny sequined jockstrap.

"I'm afraid not. Perhaps later. I have something specific in mind."

The other two nodded in understanding.

"Have you two seen Big Bertha?"

"Well, Vicomte honey, no they ain't," a gravely voice came from behind them. It was redolent of the accents of Detroit, and Ingrid turned to see what she had expected. "But she is here nonetheless."

A large black woman stood before them. She wore a wide leather belt from which descended clanking chains, wooden and leather instruments, and bits of leather, feathers, and jeweled implements. Aside from that, she was stark naked. Massive heavy thighs sprouted from a heavy yet muscular belly. A thicket of close peppercorn ringlets grew at the juncture of her thighs. Between the legs, Ingrid could see heavy labia and a prominent clitoris peeking out. Her breasts were heavy and very large, slightly pendant but still firm, with large aureoles and prominent nipples. Masses of black hair fell in ringlets to her shoulders, framing a broad face with brilliant white teeth, wide lips, and deep laugh wrinkles.

"Bertha, my love." Howells bent to exchange a chaste kiss. "How have you been?" Then without changing his tone, "This is my new slave. Have her now?" He passed the end of the leash he was holding to the large dark woman.

Ingrid was too surprised to speak or protest. By the time she had recovered, her training had reasserted itself, and she was, in any case, in no condition to do much.

As she received the end of the leash, Bertha yanked at the chain and, with a swift and expert move, swept Ingrid's feet out from under her. Ingrid had enough time to hear, "trust a policewoman to know how to do it right," when her head was caught an inch from smashing, and lowered to the floor. Then the massive legs straddled her, and darkness descended as Bertha's long nether-lips were lowered to her face.

She opened her mouth to protest and found that Bertha used the expected opening to mash her vagina against the open lips. Ingrid's mouth filled with flesh and hair.

Above everything she was conscious of the smell and taste. Both were familiar, in that they were similar to her own. Howells had had her clean him several times after his pleasure in her own vagina. But Bertha's taste was stronger, earthier, and she was moving herself forwards and backwards, allowing Ingrid little time to pull in Bertha-scented air every time the large woman moved her ass forward.

A woman had never aroused her to such a degree. She had never imagined such a thing could be done, though she had heard the whispers. And the other woman's strong capable hands were doing things to her that only her master had done, but with the same result. Her body quivered with the exploration, her nipples so hard they were almost painful. And there was nothing in the scriptures, no guide, no "Thou shalt not" to show her the way. She let her body be her guide, jerking onto the exploring tongue like a trout on a hook. Then Bertha's strong hands found her own, and she found her wrists chained together with cuffs and a short length of chain that was clipped to her waist chain. Now she was truly helpless.

The kiss ended, and Bertha seated herself again on the blonde slave's face. Ingrid had the opportunity to see a circle of expectant faces, others having been added to those of her own master, his friends, and their slaves. She knew what was expected of her this time, and her tongue worked at the musky flesh that enveloped her face. Occasionally Bertha's moves brought her dusky anal opening into range of her tongue, and Ingrid instinctively knew that she was expected to service that opening, too. From time to time, the growing violence of Bertha's movements brought the surroundings into view. She could see the circle of expectant faces watching with interest as her lesson proceeded.

There was a change, as Bertha shifted her weight, and without preamble Ingrid found a long stiff object being rammed up her wet cunt. She dug her heels into the thick carpet in shock, waiting for the feel of male weight, and when that did not come, jerked her loins up to meet those of the man inside her. Bertha's fingers opened her lips wide, and the touch of the black woman's lips, as well as her throaty chuckle brought Ingrid the realization that it was one of the artificial male members Bertha wore at her waist that was being inserted, painfully but pleasurably, into her cunt. She forgot to lick for a moment in the joy of the feeling, and was brought back to her task by a sharp nip on her engorged clit. Obediently, she began licking enthusiastically again, and was rewarded some time later by Bertha's trembling and noisy climax. A flood of salty liquid bathed her tongue, dripping into the mask. Thankfully, she lapped at it, her tongue exhausted.

Bertha rose from the blonde form, grinning in appreciation at the spectators. She stood aside, then bent and wiped her favorite dildo on the white breast beneath her. The slave looked on in gratitude.

Blue, having completed a bargain with Howells for future

credit, placed himself between Ingrid's half-open legs. His cock, short but thick, sprouted from his tuxedo trousers almost to the level of the deep blue cummerbund he wore. He yanked the chain aside, forcing Ingrid's knees up, and threw himself roughly onto her. The chains dug into her flesh and she yowled softly as the cock penetrated her excited pussy. Blue rode her anxiously, biting at her nipples. He came explosively, grinding his pelvis into hers, the buttons on his fly boring into her flesh. He rose with a triumphant smile, and his companion's female slave immediately offered him her mouth to cleanse the gluey softening member. Another man threw himself on Ingrid's body, and she held back a scream as a wave of orgasm hit her with the first penetration. He, too, finished quickly, thanked Howells, and retreated into the throng. Several other anonymous men repeated the action until Ingrid could feel the rug under her soaked with their mixed liquids.

Howells stood over her, a smile on his loving face. He motioned to Blue's heavily muscled black slave. The latter, previously instructed it seemed, lay himself on the floor. Silvertips, her eyes glittering, stood on his hands, keeping them pinned to the ground.

Howells knelt by her side. "Get on him," he said tersely.

She pulled herself up painfully. Her stomach was churning in anticipation. Her nipples were painful. The orgasms she had felt earlier were mere signposts on the way to what she was hoping for. With her hands before her, she undid the supine slave's jockstrap. A massive black cock, its head a ruby red, rose majestically, lengthened and thickened on its own and seemed to stare balefully at her. Hampered by the chains, conscious that in her efforts she was displaying all parts of her person to the onlookers, she managed to straddle the man. She supported herself by digging her hands into the muscled dark brown stomach before her, then impaled herself on the waiting dusky column. It seemed to split her apart, and she knew that without the wetting of the other men's come, she would never have managed it. Breathing hard, struggling to keep her balance, she started shafting herself up and down on the monstrosity. Her movements quickened, and the face of the slave, which had been impassive at first, turned darker. Sweat appeared on his forehead.

Silvertips squatted, her feet still on the slave's hands. Her straddled stance brought her cunt to the slave's mouth, and an incredibly long and mobile tongue emerged and began laving her shaved lips. "You, too, bitch," Silvertips said. Ingrid complied, her soft chin rasped occasionally by the man's stubbled one, their tongues clashing and blending in the woman's dark, smooth slit.

Ingrid felt hands on her buttocks. She knew whose they were. Howells's cock pushed against her anus. The grease he had spread there was aided by the flood of gluey sperm that had dribbled down into Ingrid's crack. She relaxed, and with a quick thrust, Howells conquered her behind as he had done several times before, riding her to both their climaxes.

When her screaming and the power of her climaxes were done, Howells led her back to the cloakroom. As he passed, he was saluted respectfully by those who had seen the performance. He acknowledged the acclaim modestly and accepted, for later conclusion, several offers made by friends and acquaintances for Ingrid's person. She shivered in anticipation, pleasure, and dread. The parson's voice came back to her, the words about being willful, and she was glad they did not apply to her, who was only an instrument, but to her master.

She dared not dab at herself for fear of staining the magnificent coat. Understanding her difficulty, Howells placed a towel between her and the seat, hiking up the fur coat. When they walked into his place, he ignored her, merely walking into his study. She showered and dressed, deposited the party clothes where they had come from, and left his apartment. She never slept there overnight, and he had never been to her place. She wondered if he even knew where it was.

In her modest home on the tenth floor of a new condo, she undressed, brushed her teeth, put on her flannel nightgown, said her prayers, and went to bed.

Softly, Slowly

Carole Remy

sotto voce-Softly

It took me a week to get my life back on track. I got my car towed and tuned. I sent a card of thanks to Hank for rescuing me so kindly. I checked out the last twenty weeks of the biggest news magazine from the library and read diligently every night. I invested some of my nest egg in a new computer to replace the six-year-old relic I had struggled with for years. The hairdresser neatened up my hair, but I left it unpermed and gray. I took the brocade robe to the dry cleaner, who offered me three thousand dollars for it. I declined. I saw Danny and Erica almost every day.

I bought a load of healthy groceries, determined to continue eating as Bran and I had on the island. I even found the formula we had drunk in the local pharmacy as Bran had promised. I bought a box for nostalgia and cried all through the first glass. By the time I finished the box, my body felt energized. I resolved to fast with the liquid for a few days every month.

I even joined a health club. Though I still refused to do aerobics, I found I enjoyed the weights and the exercise bike, just as I had on the island. My only regret was that I couldn't swim; the water was too heavily chlorinated. Danny and Erica had both worked out for years and had tried to drag me along many times. They bought me an exercise outfit of cycling shorts and a giant T-shirt with a barbell across the breasts, an endorsement of my new regimen. The first time I wore it, I felt foolishly youthful. But no one else paid any attention to me, and I prized the clothes as a tangible symbol of Danny and Erica's support of my changed life.

I bought every CD I could find of Chopin's *Fantasie-Impromptu* and played them over and over for hours. Though no modern pianist matched Bran's fluid submersion in his friend's flawless melodies, I found I liked Arthur Rubinstein's interpretation best. The discipline of his immense technique supported the cascading fountain of notes. Like Bran's playing, the Rubinstein recording shaded Chopin's strict manuscript with the subtleties of the interpreter's emotions and spirit. I recorded the Rubinstein *Fantaisie* over and over on a tape and played it each night as I fell asleep.

I remembered Bran day and night, night and day. I mourned his absence from my life, but I couldn't really grieve. Our months together had been the time they were meant to be. As new daily activities claimed my attention, he remained with me in memory. His wry comments on modern life colored my thoughts like filtered glasses.

I found I viewed many objects and events now as symbolic, or mythic. The story of a celebrity convicted of assaulting his wife reminded me of Branwen's sad tale. The old stories repeated again and again and again through my consciousness, and I recognized finally their importance to my writing. As I relaxed into the flow of history, my sense of my own role as a writer changed. Instead of searching for a plot, I allowed one to find me, and the stories that elbowed through my mind resonated with truth. Characters were no longer the creations of my imagination; they simply were who they were, and I recorded them. My sense of invention dwindled and my powers of observation poked through the cracks. Though my work had no obvious commercial value, I felt I was on the verge of discovery at every moment. Writing excited me almost to ecstasy.

With the unleashing of my captive creativity, my physical needs resurfaced as well. The two aspects to my being were linked. I felt driven to pour out my thoughts on paper and equally driven to share my physical existence with my lover. Bran had promised that I would meet the man I would love, though I might not recognize him. I searched the face of every man I met, wondering if he was the one. The car mechanic, the grocer, the mailman quailed before the intensity of my searching glances. I realized that my own need might keep away the very man I sought, just as it had during the week of his absence from my dreams on the island. I tried to relax my scrutiny—to allow fate to find me—but I wasn't altogether successful.

The phone rang one day as I sat at my computer. I had an answering machine on the line, and I didn't bother to pick up. Several minutes later, the phone rang again. Though I still didn't get up, the ringing interrupted my thoughts. The third time it rang, I jumped from the computer, ready to blast whoever was on the other end of the line. By the time I got to the phone, I heard only a dial tone. I slammed the receiver into the cradle and returned to my work, determined to ignore any further annoyances.

The lack of ringing disrupted me now, as silence stretched through the house like an accusing finger. Shaking my head at my lack of concentration, I went to retrieve the calls. Though the phone had rung three times, I had only one message.

"Hello, Helen." The deep voice spoke hesitantly. I recognized both the tone and the hesitation immediately. It was Hank. My anger dissolved into his placid fluidity. Guilt snatched at me for missing my rescuer's call, or at least so I named the nameless emotion that called to me from his disembodied voice.

"Just wanted to see how you were doing," he continued. "You can reach me at 583-2647, if you want to."

He paused for a moment, and I heard his breathing.

"No need to bother, though, if you're busy," the tape continued, then ended with a click.

I picked up the phone and dialed immediately. How could I have been too busy to talk to Hank?

"Hello," he answered, and I sighed to hear his voice.

"Hi, Hank. It's Helen."

"Oh, hello," he drawled. "I guess you were home, then. I thought somehow maybe you were."

"I'm sorry I didn't answer the phone," I apologized. "I was writing."

"Geez, Helen." Hank's apology made mine sound fake. "I didn't mean to interrupt your writing. You didn't need to call me back right away."

"It's okay, Hank," I assured him. "It's great to hear your voice."

I realized as I spoke the words that they were true. I had missed Hank, though I'd known him only for a few hours.

"And I rang three times," Hank continued to apologize. "I hate talking onto a tape."

"Really, it's okay," I laughed. "How are you?"

"I'm fine, Helen. I always am." Somehow I believed Hank's words; he was a man who would always be fine —not a stoical fine, but a genuine liking-his-fate fine.

"That's good, Hank. I'm fine too." My words sounded inane as soon as I spoke them. I laughed. "Still babbling, but fine."

"How's your writing?" Hank asked after a short pause.

"Really good." It felt as though I spoke with my oldest friend. "I feel like I'm getting into the flow, if you know what I mean."

"I find that with the wood sometimes," Hank replied. "You find the grain and work with it, and the piece comes out the way it was meant to."

"Exactly," I agreed. "Listen—"

"Helen—" Hank spoke at the same time. After a few seconds' argument over who should go first, Hank convinced me to speak.

"I'd like to take you out to dinner sometime," I offered. "It would be great to see you again, and I'd like to do something to thank you for rescuing me."

"Your card was more thanks than I needed. Helen. Why don't you let me make you dinner?"

"That sounds wonderful!" I remembered his homemade bread and jam. "When would you like me to come?"

"How about tonight?"

"I'm going to my daughters' apartment tonight," I explained, then hurried on, so he wouldn't think I was declining the invitation altogether. "What about tomorrow?"

"Terrific!" The enthusiasm in his voice injected me like a hypodermic. "Well, I'll let you get back to your writing. What time would you like me to pick you up?"

"You don't need to pick me up, Hank." Though he seemed the soul of safety, still I wanted my car available if I needed to get away.

"Right." He seemed to sense and accept my caution. "Why don't you come around seven?"

"That sounds great," I agreed. "Can I bring anything?"

"Just yourself," Hank chuckled and I heard an elusive echo under the sound that sent a shiver of anticipation through me.

We hung up and I returned to my computer. My mind felt sharp and clear; the thread that had eluded me spun thin and fine beneath my fingers. I found the tale that needed to be told and the voice that wished to speak it. I worked the rest of the day outlining the story as it came to me, working feverishly as if in a dream, the need to order the next many months of my labor overcoming even the need for food.

I finished at last and stumbled into the kitchen. It was 6:30 P.M., and I was already late for Danny and Erica's dinner. I phoned and apologized. Danny laughed and accepted, though Erica was less forgiving of my lapse. The girls were used to my concentration when writing, though my lack of coordination with the outside world annoyed them occasionally. I took a five-minute shower to wake myself up, and hurried over.

I arrived to the aroma of meatballs and spaghetti sauce. My Sicilian university dorm-mate had given me the recipe years before, and my children loved to make it. Erica opened a bottle of red wine, and we drank a toast to my return. We feasted on pasta shells and sauce, cheese and garlic bread until no one could eat another bite.

As we ate in relative silence, I thought about the novel I had plotted that day. For years, I had never discussed my books with my children, until one day an eighteen-year-old Erica told me she had read my latest manuscript and thought it was pretty good. When I got over the shock of my daughter's reading erotica, I found her approval heartening. Thereafter, we discussed the ins and outs of my plots. At first Danny feigned disinterest, but two years ago, she, too, had begun to read my manuscripts and point out flaws in my reasoning.

After dinner, as we sat over coffee, I told Danny and Erica about the breakthrough in my writing, that my next story had found me. When they asked for details, I found I couldn't tell them. Neither girl understood my reluctance, for I had eagerly shared my other books as they emerged. This one felt too close to me, too fragile. I worried that it wouldn't withstand scrutiny, might crumple in upon itself if examined. The book felt fluid still, like a real life waiting to be born, and I couldn't circumscribe its existence with the rigidity of speech. Rather than face their continued questions, I changed the subject.

"I have a date tomorrow night," I dropped into a stunned silence.

"You have a date?" Danny asked. I might have said I'd seen a cat with three heads. "Not Dr.—"

"No!" I interrupted. The girls had despised my last lover, the English professor. They also knew that I'd sworn off men.

"Sort of a date," I amended.

"What do you mean, sort of?" Erica asked cautiously.

"He's making me dinner. It's pretty informal."

"Mom's got a daa-aate," Danny sang happily.

"You don't need to sound so surprised," I argued, pretending to be affronted. "You girls go on dates."

"But that's different!" Danny continued to tease me. "You're a Mom."

I thought back to my adventures on the island: Bran's whippings and my eventual acknowledgment of my own arousal, the Celtic gods and their different but equally inflaming stimulation. I hadn't felt like a Mom then; I had felt like myself. I still had a distance to go, to merge those two aspects of myself into a working whole.

"Life doesn't stop when you have children," I reminded my offspring, hoping they would do a better job than I had of maintaining their own selves in the midst of parenthood.

"So, tell us about him," Erica urged.

"I don't know much," I admitted. "He's a carpenter, and he lives by the ocean."

"That sounds good," Danny stated. "You love the ocean."

"Don't marry us off," I cautioned, laughing. I thought of my exciting phantom lover and continued, "Hank isn't my dream man."

"Where did you meet him?" Erica asked, a hint of concern and caution in her voice.

"On the beach," I answered truthfully enough.

"So how do you know he's safe?" she continued.

"He seems very kind and honest, Erica." I understood her concern, for I had felt it many times myself. "I'm taking my own car, so I won't be trapped if anything goes wrong."

"Give me his name and address and phone number," my stern eldest demanded.

"Erica!" Danny protested. "You sound just like Mom."

"She's right, Danny," I interceded. "I can't remember his last name, and I know what the house looks like, but I don't know the number. I have the phone number at home."

"Would you let me go out with a guy I knew so little about, Mom?" Erica's look told me the answer she expected.

"Probably not," I conceded. "But I'm forty-three years old, and—"

Danny interrupted me, infected with her sister's sternness. "As soon as you get to his house tomorrow night, we want you to phone and tell us his full name and address. Right, Erica?"

The two girls nodded and I agreed to their cautious measures, glad I had such loving protectors. I turned the subject then from myself to their concerns. Danny told me how her courses went; she had a strange professor of history, but the rest galloped along smoothly enough. Erica described her new job. She'd majored in journalism and had despaired of finding a real news job. A year before, she'd accepted a position as a gofer at the local press. She'd submitted unsolicited articles doggedly for a year and had been rewarded two weeks ago with a byline.

As I drove home, I thought about what I'd missed of my daughters' lives in the last eight months. I thought about how each of us had changed, and I thought about my writing. I had no idea whether my next novel would even be publishable, let alone great. The difference was that I didn't care; I would write it anyway.

When I got home that night, there was a message from Hank on the answering machine.

"I know you're at your daughters' for dinner. I just called to say good night, and I'm looking forward to seeing you tomorrow."

What a nice man.

rallentando-Slowly

I awoke the next morning, aching for Bran's touch on my shoulder. I wanted him to rouse me, and arouse me. I wanted to be whipped in the worst way—take that as you wish. My children's teasing had reminded me all too vividly how long it had been since I'd had a date. Since the professor, the rituals of courtship had seemed too much bother for the limited gains of occasional companionship and even more occasional intercourse. But the constant sexual stimulation of the last months had aroused my appetites to near-insatiability; the thought that tonight I would be having dinner with a very nice man drove me past endurance.

I decided to try to whip myself. I found a leather belt in the back of my closet. It was a long way from a whip, but it was roughly the right length and shape. No one could hear me in my solitary little house, so at least I would be spared that embarrassment. As I stripped myself naked, I imagined I was being forced to remove each piece as a masterly someone dangled a whip scarily before my eyes. Only the whipper didn't know that I really wanted—more than wanted—the lashing. My pretended hesitation aroused me, and I grew moist as I forced myself to walk naked through each room of my house. Because of the blooming shrubbery, no one could see inside, but still I felt exposed as I passed the undraped openings, and I loved it.

I walked at last into the bathroom and ran hot water and rosemary oil into the tub. Afterward, the whipper would force me into the water. I posed myself against the bathroom counter and paused for a moment to heighten the suspense, then flicked the leather belt across my bottom. Nothing. I hardly felt it, and the location wasn't right anyway. I tried to find a better position for my arm, higher, no lower, no... Nothing worked. I wondered how the ancient martyrs had managed to scourge themselves, because I certainly couldn't do it.

What a bust! My body felt tuned to concert pitch. My nipples throbbed, my vagina throbbed, I throbbed all over, but nothing was happening. I couldn't get any further without masturbating, and I wanted to save that for dessert. I wished then that I owned a dildo. For all my years of writing erotica, I had never bought one. I decided to improvise. I picked up a bottle of shampoo with a knobbed top, and dumped the last dregs of soap down the sink. I rinsed it carefully so no detergent would sting my tender skin. I swirled the knob, bottle attached, in a jar of petroleum jelly. My vagina oozed hot and wet in anticipation.

By then the bathtub was full, so I turned off the water. I lifted my leg onto the edge of the tub, pretending reluctance again. The steam from the waiting bath frothed around me. I tensed in nervous expectation as the hand with the shampoo bottle approached my lower door. I thrust the knob inside me with a swift, smooth motion. It felt like heaven against my tender inner labia, and I rubbed it in and almost out, over and over. My womb tightened, then relaxed again. The stimulation wasn't enough; the knob wasn't very big, and my vagina wanted larger and rougher pleasures.

I gave up. I threw the plastic bottle against the far wall of the bathroom, venting a smidgen of my frustration. I sank into the tub and eased my little finger over my aching clitoris. My finger couldn't press very hard and its gentle ministrations roused me to still greater tension and desire. At last I allowed my strongest, index finger to rub hard against my clitoris and bring me to climax. The waves in my body sent shocks through the bathwater, which sloshed onto the floor with my motion. I kept rubbing, hoping for an elusive second and stronger orgasm. I had never been very successful stimulating myself beyond the first release, and I didn't succeed any better now. Mildly satisfied, I climbed out of the tub and dried myself and the floor.

By the time I arrived at Hank's house promptly at 7:00, I had subdued my needs to a dull roaring. I didn't want to embarrass the shy man by pouncing on him as I walked in the door. He had never even touched me, except to help me into and out of his rowboat. He probably wasn't attracted to me, and I wasn't sure whether I was attracted to him or just desperate. Best let the evening proceed as it would.

Hank may have sensed a difference in my awareness of him, for he seemed changed himself. He was more self-assured than I remembered. When he helped me from my light wrap, his hands lingered at my shoulders for a second longer than necessary—not long enough to make me uncomfortable if I wasn't interested in him, but long enough to catch my attention if I was. The gesture was nicely done.

He looked good that night. His wavy blond hair had been recently cut and painstakingly combed into submission. He must have shaved shortly before I arrived, for his face looked silky smooth. He wore a dark cotton sweater with a plaid cotton shirt underneath. The brown brought out the warmth of his eyes, which I noticed were hazel. He was neither tall nor short, but definitely solid. He might have appeared overweight from a distance, but up close he was reassuringly muscular. His slacks molded slightly to large thighs and I wondered what he looked like walking away. Probably damn good.

I had bought a new raw silk dress for the occasion; silk was the only dressy fabric that didn't irritate my skin. The dress was a size ten, the smallest I'd bought in years. I had mentally thanked Bran from the fitting room. The cut was daring, in a middle-aged sort of way: sleeveless, with a scooped neck and large covered buttons down the front. I think Hank approved. Suddenly shy, I lowered my eyes from the warmth in his and walked briskly into the main room.

"Your house is even more comfortable than I remembered," I commented brightly.

"Thanks." Though my back was turned to Hank, I could hear the smile in his voice. He seemed to absorb my nerves into his large frame, and they couldn't escape out to reinfect me. I relaxed.

"I told my daughters I would phone them when I arrived," I explained. "I hope you don't mind."

"That's sweet," Hank commented.

"Do you think you could just say hello to them?" I asked apologetically. "They worry."

"I think that's great," Hank's hearty approval removed the last of my embarrassment. "The phone's right there."

Hank pointed toward a corner of the kitchen counter. When I dialed, he moved a few feet away to give me privacy.

"Erica?" I asked. "Put Danny on, too. Hank said he would say hello to you."

Erica snorted and I laughed into the mouthpiece. "Now, be nice."

I handed the receiver to Hank.

"Hello," his low voice murmured. I noticed then that his tone changed when he got on the telephone, deepening from a baritone to a bass. I could only imagine the other end of the conversation from his expression, which wasn't very expressive.

"Henry James." Someone had asked his name.

James, James, James. I committed the name to memory. Now they had asked his address.

"267 Bayview Crescent."

Hank smiled at me and shrugged.

"You'll have to ask your mother that," he said next. I couldn't imagine what the question had been and reached to take the phone from him to ask Erica and Danny what on earth they were saying.

" 'Bye," Hank preempted me and replaced the receiver on the cradle.

"What did they ask you?"

"You'll have to ask your daughters that," Hank replied maddeningly. "Would you like a glass of wine?"

"I'd love one." Maybe it would cool my curiosity. He poured us both a large glass and we moved to sit by the fire. The only sittable furnishings were an overstuffed sofa and a rocker. I sat on the sofa, wondering a bit nervously whether he would sit beside me. When he settled on the rocker, I felt a mixture of relief and disappointment. I took a sip of wine to cover my lack of ease.

"This is delicious!" I knew I sounded surprised, which was hardly a compliment, but the wine was really superb. "I bet you made it."

Hank smiled a lazy acknowledgment and lifted his glass toward me.

"Here's to a pleasant dinner, Helen."

I drank the simple toast and proposed my own.

"And friendship. Is it too early to drink to that?"

"Not at all," Hank assured me and leaned forward to click his glass against mine. We both drank deep.

"You said you make furniture," I broke the comfortable silence. Hank nodded. "How do you market it?"

"Well," he drawled, clearly reluctant. "I sell some of my designs to Halliwell's."

I raised my eyebrows, impressed. Halliwell's was the top-of-the-line furniture maker in town. I looked more closely at the rocker Hank sat in and recognized the curves.

"That's a James rocker!" I exclaimed. "I read an article about you in *The New Yorker.* They just put your rocker in the Smithsonian. They didn't say you lived here."

Hank shrugged his shoulders sheepishly. I had a hard time reconciling the quiet man in front of me with the renowned designer.

"You have a degree from the Harvard School of Design," I accused.

"Sorry," Hank apologized and we both laughed. I struggled to adjust my grossly mistaken first impressions. Clearly uncomfortable, Hank shifted the focus back to me.

"Tell me about your next book, Chantal."

As he intended, I was diverted by his use of my pseudonym, then remembered that I had blurted it out on the black sand beach. Still, I wasn't sure how to respond to his question. The passage of a day hadn't made me any more comfortable talking about my newly conceived novel. I gazed worried into Hank's kind eyes and decided to tell him the truth.

"I can't really talk about it yet," I apologized. "My daughters wanted to know what it was about last night, and I couldn't tell them either. I feel like I have to keep it inside me, hidden away until it appears on the page, or it will come out distorted."

"It's called privacy, Helen," Hank explained. "I'm sorry I intruded."

"That's okay." I smiled, pleased that he understood so easily. His openness made me want to reciprocate. "You asked me before about my books in general, and I wasn't very forthcoming. I don't mind talking about my work now, if you want to."

"I'd love to hear."

"I write erotica," I stated boldly, and waited, cringing inside, for his response.

"I know." Hank's answer was not what I expected. "I read one of your books once."

"And were never tempted to buy another, I bet," I added wryly.

"Not until last week," he admitted honestly. "I bought them all."

"Oh, dear," I joked. "They aren't very good. I'm afraid you wasted your money."

"Well," Hank spoke slowly, and I could see the impulse for honesty warring with the impulse to be kind. Honesty won, though he did manage to be gentle.

"They are"—he struggled for a word—"mechanical. The sentences are real smooth, but I didn't get a big emotional wallop from the stories."

"I like your words," I agreed earnestly. " 'A big emotional wallop.' That's what I want from the next book, a big emotional wallop."

"If you want it, you'll get it," Hank stated. His assurance was a tonic to my still-doubting soul, and I basked in the glow.

"How did you get the books so fast?" Two of my novels were out of print.

"I called your publisher, and he sent them by courier. One's a photocopy, but they found the rest in their warehouses."

I thought over his answer for a few minutes. He must have felt some stronger attraction than I did when he rescued me, to have gone to so much trouble and expense. I felt a little intimidated by the assurance and skill with which he pursued me—at least, the writer me. I took another sip of wine, and its warmth chased down my throat and into my stomach. I took another sip. It was exciting to be pursued, I decided. Especially by a man like Hank.

"I think dinner is about ready," Hank broke into my reverie.

We stood and moved to the dining table, which he had cleared of debris. A brace of candles stood in the center with a bouquet of wildflowers in a simple glass vase. Hank lit the candles, then seated me at the end of the table. I was glad to see that his place was set just around the corner from mine and not at the opposite end. First he brought a bowl of steaming soup and placed it before me. It smelled delicious.

"What kind is it?" I was eager to taste it.

"Leek. You'll like it. I made it myself."

I smiled at his self-confidence and dipped my spoon into the thick velvety green liquid.

"You're wrong, Hank," I teased him and was rewarded with a small frown. "I don't like your soup, I love it! This is delicious."

I don't think many people teased Hank—at least, not in recent years. He seemed not to know exactly how to take my comment. He settled at last on a self-conscious smile and I resolved to pull his leg more often. We enjoyed every spoonful of the soup in silence, and then I asked for more.

"Not tonight," Hank's refusal surprised me. "I have a container put aside for you to take home with you."

"You don't need—" I began to protest, then thought better of my words. The soup was really good. "Thanks."

Hank took the bowls to the sink and brought back a large metal pot.

"Rabbit," he announced proudly.

"Rabbit?" I asked skeptically. I had never eaten rabbit before.

"You'll like it," Hank repeated himself, smiling at his own little joke and I smiled, too.

He was right again. The rabbit was even more delicious than the soup. Hank had cooked it with the same dry red wine we drank and a mixture of herbs and spices and prunes. The rabbit tasted both finer and richer than chicken, and I was amazed to find prunes could taste so good. He plucked a bay leaf from his plate and licked it before placing it on the bone platter in the middle of the table.

"Would you like one?" he offered. I thought, Why not? and nodded.

"Be careful not to bite into it," he cautioned as he handed me the large leaf. I sucked the gravy from the rough surface, and my body was flooded with a rush of desire so hot it made me blink. Hank pulled the leaf from my unresisting fingers and placed it in the candle flame.

"Smell," he whispered and held the smoldering scent to my nose. The gesture seemed impossibly sensuous, and the aroma of burning bay aroused me to the point of faintness. I couldn't tell whether Hank was unaware of the effect the leaf had on me, or if he knew only too well and only pretended innocence to heighten my desire by prolonging the suspense. I would have followed—make that dragged—him to the bed that instant had he given me any hint of his own arousal.

Instead he returned to eating his rabbit, my only clue a small-but-persistent smile that wouldn't leave the corner of his mouth. I longed to tease that little smile with my tongue, until he felt as desperately aroused as I did. The hidden desire became a game; I determined to seem as casual as he did and to drive him as crazy as he was driving me. I placed a little bone of the rabbit tenderly in my mouth, drawing it in and out, until I had sucked every morsel of flesh and gravy from it. I fixed my eyes on Hank's and was rewarded when his strayed again and again to my eager lips.

"Time for dessert." After several minutes of my sucking rabbit bones and Hank pretending not to notice, his voice sounded a bit drier. Good.

"Great!" I smiled. The game both cooled and fanned the fire in me. The fun calmed my most immediate need, and the tension stoked the deeper ache. I placed my hand casually by my place mat, where Hank's fingers could brush it as he placed the dessert plate in front of me, if he wished. His knuckles grazed mine and added another glowing ember to the fire. This was a really good game, and he was an expert player.

When I came back to a sense of the room, Hank sat opposite me, his mild eyes belying his inner pleasure. I knew he knew what was going on; he had lit the kindling with the bay leaf.

"Do you like your pie?" he asked me a moment later. I had taken a bite without registering even what kind it was and had no idea how to reply.

"It's delicious!" I resolved to taste the next bite. The mouthful proved me truthful; the pie was delicious. I tasted apple, but couldn't sort out the other flavors. "What's in it?"

"Apples from the yard." I nodded that I had guessed as much. "And passionberries."

I choked. Score one for Hank. I had never heard of passionberries, but I doubted he had made them up. If that was what he said was in the pie, then that was what I ate.

"It's really good," I managed to squeeze out around the lump in my throat. We ate the pie in meaningful silence. I was thinking about the night ahead, and I would have bet any amount of money that Hank was, too.

il canto marcato-He Sings

I ate the pie slowly, savoring the hot spicy sweetness in my mouth and prolonging the suspense. I was powerfully attracted to Hank. I had hoped to meet the man of my dreams right away, and I wasn't at all sure Hank was that man. Still he was a wonderful human being and the chemistry between us was electrifying. But I had always had a love/hate thing with first times—the suspense was incredibly arousing, the outcome often disappointing.

Hank sat watching me, amused as I dawdled over the last bites of my pie. He had finished several minutes earlier. My game of arousal over the rabbit bones seemed embarrassing in hindsight. Now that the real event approached, every anxiety resurfaced. This time Hank, the patient chef, did nothing to calm my nervousness, but left me to stew. Finally he took pity and spoke.

"Would you like to walk along the beach with our coffee?"

I jumped at the invitation. Hank helped me into my jacket.

Again his hands lingered on my shoulders that extra second. His touch calmed me instantly, and reawakened my desire. Clutching hot mugs, we walked down the short stretch of grass toward the black water. The Pacific lived up to its name that night, the water so still we could almost see our reflections. We walked down the pier to the end and stood sipping in silence as the smallest of waves lapped gently against the pylons. After a few minutes, I felt chilly and instinctively moved closer to Hank's side. He put his arm around my shoulder. His solid warmth was as comfortable as an old afghan.

When Hank set his mug on the railing, he pulled me close so that my body followed the movement of his. Then he shifted me in his embrace and held me with both arms. I lifted my head for his kiss, wondering whether his lips would be soft or rough, whether he would touch my lips gently or demand the sweet release of immediate passion. He looked deep into my eyes and perhaps read the lingering questions there, for he turned my head sideways into his chest with his hand and stroked my hair as he held me in a warm embrace.

"Nothing is written in stone, Helen," he murmured in my ear. "We don't need to do anything you aren't ready for."

"My body is ready, Hank." I turned my face to look up into his and smiled ruefully. "Boy, is it ready."

"But your mind isn't sure?" he asked.

I shook my head, then changed my mind. I might never be sure as long as I dangled the hope of meeting my one true lover like a carrot before my eyes. Hank was a warm and solid reality in my arms, not a man to be banished for desire of a phantom. I pulled my arms from beneath his and reach up to cup his face. A hand on each cheek, I pulled his mouth down to meet mine.

"Hank's lips," I breathed into his mouth, "meet Helen's lips."

I pressed my mouth softly against his and the touch awakened every dream, every ember, every fountain of moisture inside me. His lips were both soft and rough, gentle and insistent in perfect balance. Mine parted eagerly, inviting his tongue to explore my first hot moist cavity. Our two organs tangled playfully in greeting, then settled into a soothing, seeking rhythm. My hands moved from his cheeks to the back of his head and twined in his springy curls as the kiss deepened. Hank groaned deep in his throat and pressed me back into the railing and I felt the pulsing of his erection against my abdomen. I pressed against him, my empty womb aching to be filled by the so-near hardness, and he ground his hips into mine until the pressure brought me almost to orgasm.

"Can we go back inside?" I gasped, pulling my lips from his.

"Unbutton your dress," he ordered, brushing aside my request. He meant to have me here, as we stood against the railing of the pier, surrounded by the ocean. I had never made love out of doors, and the vulnerability of our situation made me pause in fear. Hank parted my jacket, then reached his hands down and began to unbutton my dress from the bottom up. I stood caressing his hair, neither helping nor hindering his work. When he reached my waist, he stopped unbuttoning and moved his hand to grasp the top of my panties and pantyhose. He pulled down, and I wriggled to ease the tight fabric past my hips. He abandoned my left leg at knee height and lifted my right to free it completely. The chill ocean breeze skimmed the bare skin of my exposed thigh.

He moved his hands to his zipper, but I brushed his fingers aside and slid the metal pins slowly apart. I reached inside and pulled out his organ and massaged its substantial length and girth. He sighed beneath my hand and pulled a condom from his pocket.

"Were you a Boy Scout?" I asked in a shaky whisper. He shook his head and I took the condom and peeled off the wrapper. I held it up to the light of the moon to determine which way it unwound, mildly annoyed by the interruption, but thankful for Hank's caution. Thank goodness one of us still had a brain. I rolled the thin latex down the length of his penis, smoothing and stroking as I worked. The movement further aroused us both, and Hank tucked a probing finger into the moisture of my vagina. His finger roused my womb to frenzy and I couldn't wait any longer to feel him inside me. I lifted my right leg and he grasped the knee and held it firm in his hand. He slid his finger from my cunt and I guided his penis toward me. He bent his knees slightly to adjust our heights, then lifted upward as he entered me.

His penis slid inside my empty dripping cave and filled it with light and warmth and pressure. I recognized that pressure with an awestruck delight and burst into ecstatic tears. He pulled back, and I hurried to reassure him.

"It's all right, Hank," I sobbed and held his hips into mine. "It's all right."

When he kissed me, I abandoned myself wholly into his embrace. All fear, all hesitation fled, and I ground my hips against his and drove my tongue frantically into his hot mouth and clutched at his organ with the powerful muscles of my own. As I strove to caress his penis inside me, my own efforts pushed me up and over the first peak of orgasm. The involuntary spasms sped through me, tighter than I could achieve by will, and Hank moaned deep in his throat beneath my kiss.

"Come!" I tore my mouth from his to whisper urgently. "Come now. I'm ready."

"Not yet," he panted. He lifted my knee higher and his penis hammered farther inside me, again and again, until I screamed my release a second time. As my body relaxed, he shifted me hard against the railing and held it tight in his hand, and thrust into me and withdrew, and thrust and withdrew. I was caught between the hard wooden railing and his insistent organ. The restraint loosed the last remnants of my control and I came over and over in deep inexorable pounding waves. I fell through the no-longer-there railing and into the boiling ocean and beneath the waves, and we became part of the sea, my demanding lover and I.

My absorption was so complete, I knew Hank had climaxed only by the eventual slackening of his organ inside me. He withdrew and we groaned in unison, then laughed together weakly.

"Hank," I began, trying to find words.

"Shh!" Hank quieted me and pulled me to rest against his chest. He rocked me gently as we stood, and I absorbed the tranquillity of the sea and of my real and phantom lover like a balm into my soul.

"I love you, Helen," Hank's words were an inevitable benediction. I fought neither their sense nor their timing.

"I love you too, Hank," I whispered back, knowing it was true. We stood thus beneath the rising moon, two boats finally at rest in their own harbor. Then Hank bent and picked up my right shoe and placed it in my hand. He lifted me into his arms without visible effort and I felt supported as I hadn't since early childhood. He carried me back to the house in silence, the other shoe and pantyhose and panties dangling from my bobbing left leg.

"My sweet witch," he murmured in my ear as we crossed the threshold. He placed me on the sofa and I relaxed into the cushions with a contented flop. Hank disappeared into the back of the house and reappeared in a moment with an armload of fluffy blankets and comforters. He laid them out in a thick cushion before the fireplace, then built up the fire to a crackling heap of flaming logs. The setting complete, he sat in the rocking chair and gazed contentedly at my totally relaxed posture.

"Don't tell me you've had enough already, Helen," he teased me.

"I'm insatiable," I tossed back at him, the hot wetness returning to my vagina to confirm my words. "What about you?"

"Men take longer to recover, my dear," he reminded me and I felt contrite. He had satisfied me beyond human expectation only moments earlier, and I didn't want to pressure him. His next words banished my doubts. "Why don't you strip for me? Maybe that will do it."

Ha! He was still as eager as I was. I stood and flicked my shoe in his direction with my foot. Then I rolled the last section of pantyhose and panties down my left calf and flicked them, too. As I walked toward him, I swayed my hips so that the front of my dress, still unbuttoned to the waist, flapped open. When I stood in front of him, I reached down and unzipped his pants. I grasped his bulging organ and squeezed hard, once, twice, three times, then let go and stood again.

"You don't need a strip show, Hank," I drawled. "You're as horny and hard as a bull already."

"But I like it," he argued simply, so I obliged. I had never stripped for a man before and had only watched strippers in brief flashes on television. Had I thought of what I looked like, I would have felt foolish; but the hot approval in Hank's eyes banished all self-consciousness. I had almost nothing left to remove—only the dress—so I made the most of each button. I unhooked the top fastening slowly and flapped the fabric back and forth. The second button offered more scope, for when I slid the fabric, it revealed a glimpse of aching rigid nipple. Only one button remained and I glanced mock-shyly at Hank from beneath my eyelashes. He grinned like a lovesick monkey. I slid the casing from around the button and flipped the fabric open once, then clutched the ends together tightly and turned my back. I let the dress slide down my body and stood naked, but still facing away.

"Turn around!" he commanded and the hint of authority and sternness in his voice thrilled me.

"Or what?" I egged him on.

"Or I'll whip you."

I almost fainted.

I hadn't begun to think how I would explain my love of whipping to Hank. As my phantom lover, he had stroked me in daydreams, and in his unsteady strokes I'd felt the virginity of his effort. I'd never paused to wonder whether he, too, had been aroused by the experience. Now that I'd met Hank in reality, the action seemed foreign to his gentle nature. I had much yet to learn.

"Go to the hutch and open the top left drawer." His command interrupted my thoughts. I walked past the dining table, careful always to keep my back to him, and opened the drawer. Inside was a shiny black case. I lifted it out and placed it on the table. Hank's presence at my back startled me. He whispered in my ear.

"Open it."

I pretended to hesitate; Hank waited me out. My curiosity was no match for his patience, and I lifted the lid. Inside lay a shiny new black whip. Each tip had been carefully flame-hardened.

"Lean over and hold onto the back of the chair."

I obeyed him, all nervous expectation, and hot juice flowed into and through my vagina like a tap. I stood waiting, and waiting, until the anticipation was a thin metal taste in my mouth.

"I can't reach you from this angle," Hank's laughing comment broke the spell. I fought not to laugh with him—to preserve what was left of the mood—and walked slowly to pose, ass poked provokingly outward, behind another chair that offered him more space. His first stroke landed before I had recovered from the surprise of the interruption and sent me farther along the path to climax for my unpreparedness. Hank had been practicing. His strokes landed with a steady rhythm that drove my already-aroused body to an endorphin-assisted orgasm within brief minutes. I thought he would stop then, for I screamed out my release and pleasure, but the next stroke landed before the echo of my scream died.

I settled into the rhythm of the whipping, the white heat of the lash falling with even regularity. I began to pant as I built toward a higher peak. Suddenly the strokes broke their rhythm, and I groaned in frustration. A harder lash choked off my groan and brought me back to the edge. Then a pause, and I slid backward until the next stroke sent me back up toward the peak. Stop and start, up and down, Hank rode my frustration like an unbroken pony. I panted and moaned and finally screamed for release. He stroked me three times, hard, without a pause for even a breath and I came in a crashing symphony of climactic orgasm. Still the strokes continued, gently now and in rhythm with my spasms, until the last quaver was wrung from my satiated womb.

I collapsed against the back of the chair, exhausted. I dimly heard Hank breathing hard by my side. I turned my head to see his grin as he stood panting, the whip dangling from his fingertips.

"You're incredible!" I gasped. He shook his head.

"You're the one who's incredible, Helen."

"So we're both incredible," I agreed with a shaky laugh.

"Come lie down," he offered. We walked side by side to the mound of cushions and I lay gratefully on the soft heap, while Hank threw another log on the fire then stripped off his clothes. His performance was low key but no less arousing than mine had been. I grew excited again watching him.

"You're ready now," I commented, reverting to our earlier conversation. His erection stood sturdy and hard, nestled into the curly black hair of his groin.

"Nothing like a good strip show to get a guy aroused," he teased.

"My strip show was a feeble prelude to your whipping, Hank," I protested.

"Nothing you do is ever feeble, my dear," he complimented, then lay down beside me. We lay on our sides in silence, not touching, absorbing each other's bodies with our eyes. When Hank ran his hand along the length of my side from shoulder to knee, his fingers felt as silky as an extension of his gaze. His hand caressed my skin like that of a blind man, learning as it skimmed. He rolled me onto my back and explored me as thoroughly as Columbus ever explored our eastern coast— even more, for he left no smallest hill or hollow untouched. Each inch of my skin came alive beneath his fingers and I closed my eyes in blissful relaxation.

When his hand lifted my leg and placed it bent and raised alongside me, my labia burbled an eager welcome. A single finger lightly flicked my swollen clitoris, and I gasped as the shock swam upstream through my body. My nipples hardened to pebbles of desire and my lips parted in invitation. His mouth settled its hot wetness against the hot dryness of my right nipple. As his tongue pulled the essence from the marrow of my breast, his finger descended again across my clitoris and flicked it into aching alertness. The dual stimulation continued until I heaved and moaned beneath his touch. His mouth shifted from breast to breast, and his finger from clitoris to vaginal door, each with maddening irregularity and more than compensating dexterity. I rose again and again almost to the peak of desire, but each time he sensed my ultimate arousal and pulled me back.

At last I could wait no longer and pleaded for him to enter me. He rose and I begged him not to leave; then he returned with a box of condoms. I was in no condition to put the safe on this time, so he unrolled it down his penis himself in one smooth motion. Then he turned me onto my back and pulled up my hips to a squat. I moaned in fear and excitement as he rubbed his penis up and down the crack in my rear, pushing hard against the yielding skin. He entered me with a swift thrust, not into my anus but in my vagina, filling it with his rockhard red-hot shaft. The different position put new pressure in unexpected directions, and I groaned in delight. He rode me swiftly and I came within seconds, then again, and again—and then I felt him grow to the final hardness. His explosion matched mine as we pounded together toward home.

When he swiftly withdrew, I cried in alarm for I wanted to hold his warmth inside me. I heard a sizzle and smelled the faint odor of burning latex as the safe melted on the fire. The ripping of another condom wrapper confirmed my suspicion that our intercourse was not yet over. Hank held me firmly with my ass in the air and began to push his penis gently, slowly, calmly, but insistently against my back door. I groaned, half in protest, half in exhaustion, half in anticipation of mixed pain and arousal. Still he pressed, and I could feel that his penis had deflated slightly in the aftermath of climax, and I understood his intention.

I relaxed the muscles of my anus, panting hard. One ungentle thrust of his penis pushed the condom-greased shaft through my portal and wrenched a moan from my throat. He showed me no pity and held my hips in a vise as he pressed inside in one long, smooth stroke. We rested together then, both breathing heavily, but only for a moment. He soon began to stroke his swelling penis up and down inside me, and the pressure filled my backside and womb and pressed against my stomach. He was already larger than the Oriental man had been at climax, and still his penis grew with each stroke. I moaned softly in protest and he laid his chest weightless along my back and wrapped one long arm around my hips to hold me steady.

His other hand found my hungry vagina. He placed two fingers inside, and pressed and wriggled against the other massive hardness at my rear. The dual pressure sent me on a solo journey beyond the horizon. I came in an orgasm so strong I would have collapsed had Hank not held me firm. When his fingers found my clitoris, I lost all reason and sense and I could no longer describe what I felt. I left reality and drifted again in the realm of fantasy with my phantom lover. We traveled to the moon and stars and down into the bowels of the earth. I was both full and empty, filled with satisfaction, emptied of care.

Our mutual and final scream of release returned me to a vague sense of the room and my companion. I felt him withdraw and felt the emptiness of my vacant cavity with an aching, swiftly passing echo of hunger. We collapsed to one side, his fingers still inside me, savoring the lingering pulses that lapped the walls of my vagina. We panted in unison. Slowly our breath calmed, and we fell asleep.

The Movie House

Sara Adamson

From the garishly lit lobby of a theater in lower Manhattan, a steady stream of adults spilled onto the sidewalk outside and the streets beyond. It was a chilly evening, mid-winter, and the crowd evidenced a curious mixture of well-worn leather jackets, sensible down parkas, and elegant fur coats. People gathered in small groups around the posters displayed under the marquee, and there was a strong buzz of conversation all along the block.

"Disgusting," intoned a matron, husband tightly in tow. She was looking at one of the scenes from the film, a single moment's image of a woman in a tightly laced Victorian corset, bound helplessly inside a doorway, her breasts displayed, her mouth filled with what appeared to be a ball on a strap. The woman's husband only nodded in agreement as he meekly followed her toward the street.

Four people looked after the couple and laughed. They too

studied the series of photos from the film. "What about you, Guy,?" one of the two men said, pointing at another picture. "Did you think it was disgusting?"

"Oh, absolutely! So disgusting, I can't wait to get home." Guy slipped an arm around his wife. "I can think of a few more disgusting things as well...shouldn't we get going?" Allison giggled nervously, and nodded her head toward the movie poster hanging nearby.

"I think we'd better go before Guy gets any strange ideas," she said, rubbing one hand across his back. "He might begin to think of himself as one of those leather-master types."

"Okay...your place or ours? We went out to you last time." William slipped an arm around his own wife and glanced down at her. "Shall we try our house for a change?"

"Yes," she replied, softly. "It's closer."

"Whoa, I hear that!" Guy smiled and winked. "In this case, your wish is my command, Terri. I can see that movie is having the same effect on you as it has on me. Let's not waste it!" He began to walk steadily toward the nearby parking garage where they had left his car. The other couple followed after one more lingering glance at the posters and promotional photos.

"It wasn't a movie, it was a film, an *art* film," Jen explained for the tenth time. "You're not supposed to take it literally!"

"Oh really? Then what does that mean?" Lisa, Jen's lover, pointed at an excerpt from a review, blown up to seven-inch-high letters on one of the framed posters. It read, "The most explicit exploration of the dark side of sexuality ever filmed!"

"Explicit doesn't mean allegorical," Lisa said pointedly. "And it was still full of patriarchal violence against women. The degradation! The humiliation! How would you like it if you were made to wear a dog collar and crawl around like that woman was?"

Jen sighed, pulling her lover away from the theater. "Lisa, you're making a scene."

"Damn right! This is just typical of you...you drag me to some trendy movie, and then expect me to wallow in the obvious manipulation on the screen and thank you for the experience. This was terrible... what about the scene with that, that, *dildo!*"

"Lisa." Jen ground her teeth together, trying to keep calm. Why did every fight have to become a production number? "Lisa, there were plenty of scenes where men got treated like that too, remember?"

Lisa tossed her blonde hair in an angry turn away from the theater, and shrugged her lover's arm from hers. "Yes, but it was clear that they wanted it."

"That's a double standard...Lisa, Lisa, wait!" Jen ran to catch up with her.

"Oh God, that was soooo gross!" A dark-haired woman in a stylish jacket too light for the weather mimed one of the scenes from the film with an expression of exaggerated glee on her face. Her friends, a group of six women all of an age and dressed somewhat alike, shrieked with laughter. Their shoes and dress suggested that they had gone out after work on this Friday night.

"No, wait, what about the scene where the red-haired woman dances on the guy wearing those spiked heels! Like, I couldn't even walk in those, let alone dance on someone in them!" More laughter.

"Come on, the best part was that orgy..."

"That wasn't an orgy, it was a gang bang!"

"Yeah!"

"No! It was an orgy, you could tell."

"Oh, maybe *you* can tell, Gina!" The young women erupted in laughter and fell into good-natured ribbing as they began their walk toward the nearest subway station. They were loud and friendly, as only a group of women out on the town can be.

"I liked the part with all the rubber stuff."

"No way!"

"Oh, you *would*, Margaret."

"Well, at least I didn't, you know, moan out loud during the scene with the feathers."

"I did not!"

"Did too! The whole row could hear you!"

"I liked the part with the maid."

"Oh, god, Rox, how could you?"

"Yeah, that was so silly."

"Like, that guy looked sooo stuuupid!"

"If some guy pulled that on me, I'd just barf!"

"Hey, look girls…there's someone who can't wait 'til they get home."

Their attention all turned toward a couple, the man pressing the woman against a nearby building, pushing her skirt up her leg while he passionately kissed her. The woman's arms were locked tightly around his neck.

"Oh, God, I mean, can't they hold it?"

"I think she is holding it!"

The young women laughed together and began to head for home.

"That was a hot movie."

"Yeah."

Mike and David left the theater lobby and stopped by the promotional display. They scanned the reviews posted up and read out loud.

"'Perverse'!" David snickered. "Yeah, it was certainly perverse."

"But it was also 'Powerfully erotic', like it says here," Mike looked at the color photos of some of the more notorious scenes. "There wasn't much gay stuff in it."

"Well, we knew that. Besides, you know where to go to look at boys in leather..."

They said it at the same time, "The Shaft," and laughed together.

Looking at the crowd and the shortage of taxis, Mike said, "Care to walk across town? We can get home in about twenty minutes."

"I'm not in the mood to go home yet." David stuffed his hands in his pockets and looked carefully at the ground. "But let's walk. I need to talk to you."

"About the movie?" Mike's voice was low and seductive. David looked back up at his lover's eyes and nodded.

"Yeah, me too. Let's take that walk."

They too, passed the couple making out alongside the building, but they were too interested in each other to notice.

"Well, so that was the movie everyone's talking about." Marsha pulled her coat tighter around herself, keeping a watchful eye out for purse-snatchers.

"It was...different."

"Ha! You can say that again." She took her husband's arm as they walked out under the marquee. "Do you remember where you parked the car?"

Bob looked back at her patiently. "Sure...down that way a few blocks. Do you want to wait here, and I'll pick you up?"

"No, no, let's just walk. After all that sitting, I need the exercise."

"Odd mix of people in this crowd, wasn't it?"

"Well, it is the hottest art movie playing right now. I guess it's all the desire to be trendy...I mean, we wouldn't have come if Steve and Brenda hadn't been pushing us for so long."

"Well, it wasn't so bad. Just...weird."

"Yes, it was certainly weird."

They walked in silence for a moment, hearing snatches of conversation and the shrill laughter of a group of women who seemed to be comparing favorite parts of the film. As they passed the couple who were making out against the neighboring building, Marsha gripped her husband's arm tighter. She waited until they were out of earshot and said, "I think it's terrible what some people think they can do in public. Couldn't they have waited?"

Bob nodded, thinking of their warm bedroom at home, and he bent down to gently kiss her cheek. "I can hardly wait."

It worked. Marsha relaxed on his arm and pressed closer to him. "And I want you, honey. Let's get home."

They walked a little bit faster.

Mark pulled Thea's skirt up higher, so that it almost bunched around her waist. It was only his knee pressed into the hot wedge between her legs that kept her pussy shielded from the passers-by. From time to time, he whispered overheard comments into her ear, telling her how many people were seeing them, and what they thought of her. "You're a slut, you know...displayed like a cheap 42nd Street whore, and all these people know it."

She moaned and squirmed under him and gripped him tighter. "Do it, do it now! Let's just do it in front of everyone, please!"

He slipped a hand between them, sliding it along her wetness, teasing, pulling on her hairs and making her arch against him.

"You'd like it if I fucked you now, wouldn't you? You'd love my big dick slapping into you right out here on the street, with everyone watching. Tell me, say it right."

"I want you...I want you to fuck me, oh God, please..." Thea pushed her hips forward into him. She shuddered in erotic anticipation, reaching for him, holding his hand between her thighs. Suddenly, he laughed, and pulled away from her, his hand glistening with her juices. Casually, he wiped it across her face, and then raised that same hand to hail a cab, leaving her to smooth her skirt back down across her thighs, allowing a few people a glimpse of her bare pussy.

As the two of them got into the cab, no one, including them, could believe that they had just met, barely two hours ago.

As the crowd thinned and the marquee lights dimmed and went out, the cashier noted once again how the people leaving this particular film always seemed to be in a hurry to get home.

The ride on the Long Island Expressway was a little more silent than usual, but there was no real discomfort between them. Bob kept glancing at Marsha with loving concern. It was rare enough for them to get out of the house together, and the decision to see that particular film had been a difficult one. But then, there wasn't much of a choice, really. Everything else seemed designed for teenagers—big budget, violent, loud movies without the burden of a plot.

Not that this one had any real plot, he thought, as he guided the sedan further east. Just a lot of different scenes of people doing things to each other. He remembered how silence kept sweeping through the theater, as though the audience couldn't exactly keep up a pretense of being nonchalant about the action on the screen. The film certainly deserved the X rating it almost got! But the company had decided to release it without a rating, and people were flocking to see it, compelled by the hauntingly mysterious advertising posters and the outrageous word-of-mouth reports.

Which was how he and Marsha heard about it. Steve, one of his co-workers, had gone to see it with his girlfriend, Brenda. The following day, he had taken Bob aside in the men's room and told him what a great night the two of them had after seeing this film.

"It was sick," Steve had said, leaning against the wall. "But some of the scenes were so hot, I swear I was as stiff a board. Brenda was so wet, we couldn't wait to get home. I'm warning you...some of the scenes aren't for everyone, you know? But I guarantee, you'll see it, take Marsha home, and fuck her brains out."

Bob smiled as he signaled for his exit. He liked any excuse to fuck Marsha's brains out. Even as she sat beside him in the passenger seat, her eyes softly closed, he loved the way her face looked, the way she breathed, the lift of her breasts. She felt him glancing at her and opened her eyes, smiling. When he saw that smile, he felt the beginnings of a swelling behind his fly and grinned.

"I know what you're thinking," Marsha noted. "Don't take too long with the sitter. I'll be waiting for you in bed."

"I love the way you read my mind, sweetie," Bob said.

Home was a two-story brick house with a huge, sprawling lawn. Bob pulled into the driveway and waited for Marsha to go inside and pay the sitter. The high-school student came bouncing out, after what Bob knew was a night watching MTV, eating the chips they always stocked for her, and chatting with her boyfriends. He drove her home, politely chatting. She used to linger a little while with him, stalling perhaps, or flirting, but he never gave her encouragement. He heard from other men about their affairs with various young women. College and high school students, tutors and baby-sitters, au pairs and even a swimming coach. But he was never tempted to try something like that.

He had a girlfriend at home, waiting for him.

So he bade her a good night, avoiding her questions about how they liked the movie, and broke all the speed laws heading back home.

By the time Bob had turned back into the driveway, Marsha had already checked on the kids, turned the thermostat down, and gone around the house making sure everything was all right. Mark, their first-born, was asleep in a tangle of blankets, toys scattered all over his floor. At eight years old, he was just becoming interesting to her. She could see his father in him, and a little of herself, and she liked to watch him work things out for himself.

Then there was Cathy, restless until her thumb found its way back into her mouth. At five, she was a real cutie, with her mother's curly blonde hair and her father's laughing disposition. "You're going to break some hearts some day," Marsha whispered as she worked her daughter's thumb out of her mouth. "If your teeth grow in straight."

She heard the sound of the front door opening and closing and smiled as she headed toward the master bedroom. She folded down the bedcovers and turned down the lights, casually killing time until Bob came upstairs.

He paused in the doorway, a deliciously lustful glint in his eye, teasing her until she laughed. "Ready for me?" he asked, already unbuttoning his shirt.

"More than ready." She reached out to him and they hugged warmly. He took the bottom edge of her sweater in both hands and slowly pulled it up, over her head, and kissed her bare throat. While his tongue danced on her neck and around her ear, she purred and pushed his shirt back over his shoulders.

"You're so hot, baby," he murmured, pulling her tightly to him. "I want to sweep you off your feet and fuck you silly."

"Mmmm. If movies like that make you feel like this, we should go out more often." She cupped his hardness with one soft hand as he wrapped one hand in her hair to kiss her firmly. When the kiss finally broke, they were both flushed with sexual warmth, and they moved together toward the bed.

"Did you like the movie?" he asked, pushing her gently back and unfastening her skirt. "I couldn't tell." He eased the skirt over her hips when she raised them off the bed, pulling her pantyhose down at the same time. He leaned over her to plant a kiss on her navel, and then slid his tongue down to the ridge above her pubic mound, making her shiver in delight.

"I...I thought some of it was hot," Marsha said finally, as he tossed her clothing aside, leaving her lying back against the bedspread in her panties. "You liked it."

"Yes." He stretched out next to her and reached for her nipples with one hand, propping himself up with the other. He caressed one softly, watching and feeling it become erect under his fingers. "I liked a lot of it. But I like you more."

She gasped as he pinched her nipple, and let a moan escape, and then rolled to face him, reaching again for the bulge in his pants. He suddenly grinned and moved out of her reach. She looked at him in surprise.

"I think you liked it more than you're saying," he whispered. "Tell me."

"You tease," she said. Then, she leaned up on one elbow and looked at him squarely. "Do you really want to know?" He nodded. "I liked the part where that woman in the miniskirt was all tied up and the man with the mask...you know." Suddenly, she found herself blushing. But Bob seemed to find that as arousing as anything else that evening, so she moved closer to him again. "What did you like?"

He avoided answering her for a moment. "You liked it when that woman was tied up and raped, huh?"

"She wasn't raped! She enjoyed it. And it was so good...you could tell." Marsha blushed again, both at the memory and the quick feeling of wetness between her legs as she spoke about it. "Come on, what did you like?"

"I liked that part too," Bob admitted. "But I also liked the spanking scene."

"Which one?" Marsha asked warily.

He smiled. "All of them. All I could think of was how it would feel to lie under you while you rode me, and feel my burning ass against the bed."

"What?" Marsha sat up in surprise. "*You* want to be...spanked?"

He sat up too. "Well, if I'm going to tie you to the bed, you should do something for me too," he said, seriously.

She smiled through her amazement. "Would you really tie me up? Do you think we should?" Marsha asked, looking around the room. "It's so...kinky. I don't know...they seemed to have a lot of, well, stuff, in that movie. Paddles and things...and honey, what if I hurt you? What if you don't like it? What if the kids..."

"Listen." Bob took her hands in his and looked into her eyes. "You would never hurt me." He kissed her again, slow and lovingly. "And," he said, when they broke the kiss, "I bet we can find anything we need right here. I say we do it. If the kids didn't wake up the night we rented that *Kama Sutra* tape and tried some of those positions, they won't wake up now." She giggled at the memory of that night, the pillows on the floor and the "love lotion" everywhere else. Then, she looked at him again and nodded.

"Good. Let's see...I'll go find stuff to use on you, and you find stuff for me. I'll meet you back here in...ten minutes?"

"In ten minutes." Marsha got up and threw her robe on, and purposefully left the room. Bob chuckled, thought for a moment, and then slipped a sweatshirt on.

Marsha found herself in the kitchen, standing in her bare feet and looking at the utensil rack. Once, when she had been small, her mother had used a wooden spoon on her behind—for what crime, she couldn't remember. She never struck her own children, but she did have a full rack of things her mother would have probably loved to use. She took one wide spatula down and swatted it against her hand. Instantly, she yelped. It stung! She would have to be careful...she took two more, and then went back upstairs, suddenly inspired.

Bob slipped out to the garage, where he spent a few minutes uncovering the items in storage for spring. Coiled neatly in a net bag was about fifty feet of soft but strong clothesline. He sprinted back to the house, turned off the kitchen light that Marsha had left on, and then softly walked upstairs. She wasn't in their bedroom...he briefly wondered where she could be, and then stashed the clothesline under the bed. Waiting for her, he dug into one of her drawers and took out a silk scarf he had given her while they were still dating. It smelled of her, of her perfume. He tucked it under one pillow, and then stripped off the sweatshirt and his shoes.

Marsha was tip-toeing through her son's room, looking for a bright red box she had noticed earlier. When she found it, she opened it silently, and felt around inside for what she was seeking.

One scene in the film had depicted a caning. Marsha remembered flinching as she watched little lines form on reddened skin, and while she was standing in the kitchen, she had been wondering if the handle of a wooden spoon would work like that. It seemed too hard, to thick and brittle. The cane in the movie had been whipper-thin, and so supple it could be bent into a circle. Then, she suddenly had a flash…there was something in the house like that…the wand from little Mark's magic set.

She pulled it out with a flourish and quietly left the room. Her last visit was to the hall closet where she stored the summer items. There, in a box with a pile of white plastic balls, were two matching ping-pong paddles. She took one.

If he wants a spanking, she thought, good-naturedly, *I'll give him a spanking he'll never forget!* As she headed back to their bedroom, she had a moment of doubt. Could she really do this? Hit her husband on his bare butt, hurt him and make marks on him? Would he really like it as much as the handsome actor did in the film?

A sudden wetness between her thighs gave her the answer. Whatever Bob felt when it actually happened, she was turned on by the very thought. Even if it didn't work, she would end up tied to the bed with his big cock slamming into her welcoming pussy. She took a deep breath and walked into their room, holding her handful of improvised implements.

She was surprised to find him already there, his bare chest quietly rising and falling in the deep rhythm that signaled a strong but quiet turn-on. He was standing by their bed, still wearing his dark slacks, his feet bare. He immediately noticed her burden and came forward to help her.

"No." She stopped him on an inspiration. "Just stand there, exactly like that. And remember, this was your idea."

Bob grinned and stood still, watching his wife empty her armload of objects onto the bed. Carefully she separated them and laid them out next to each other, arranging them in what she felt was an order of severity. As she did this, she glanced around the room, trying to figure out what Bob had brought. To her dismay, there seemed to be nothing different about the room.

What is he planning to use, his ties? She frowned slightly, more than a little annoyed. Couldn't he think of anything?

When she glanced at him again, he was still grinning, and she realized that her disappointment at his seeming lack of preparation could be used in the game they were about to play. Not returning his smile, she stood straight and asked, quietly, "Do you expect to take your spanking over those pants?"

Bob noticed the swift change in mood, and stammered. "Uh, well, I guess not. Do you want me to take them off?"

"No." Marsha got another inspiration. She sat primly at the edge of the bed and straightened her robe over her thighs. "I want you to drop them to your knees and drape yourself across my lap." She half expected him to balk; this wasn't exactly what had happened in the movie, and she didn't think it was what he had bargained for, but her fleeting doubt was banished in an instant. Behind the dark material of his trousers, Bob showed her proof that he found what she was doing exactly right. As he moved to her side and ran the zipper down, his cock was hard and curved against his stomach, trapped by his clean jockeys. He started to run a finger around the waistband of those too, but she stopped him again.

"Just the pants," she said, a surprising hoarseness in her voice. She loved the sight of him, erect yet contained, and wanted to keep him that way for just a little while longer. Without showing any disappointment, he did as she told him and pushed his pants down around his knees. Then, a little awkwardly, he bent forward over her lap, and shifted his body until he found a position he could stay in. She felt his manhood tight against her thighs, and was glad that her knees were close together. If they weren't, she would have actually dripped on the floor.

Marsha took a deep breath and examined her husband's ass, and the backs of his thighs. She ran her hand lightly across his cloth-covered ass and he shivered against her, a delightful sensation. She tickled the hairs curled on his lags, and ran her fingers across his taut muscles. He wasn't the college athlete she had married, but he was a strong man, in good shape. Having him across her lap, and in her power, was a thrill.

"Are you ready?" she asked, her voice a little more assured.

"Yes. God, yes!" Bob's voice sounded strained, and it wasn't just the position. Marsha immediately knew that he was feeling the same emotional charges that were wracking her, and in response, she raised her hand and slapped it once against his ass.

The thin cotton muffled the sound, but the sensation was amazing! Bob jerked under her hand, and ground his still-hard cock against her legs. The slight sound he made was like a sigh. Marsha raised her hand again and struck the other cheek, and Bob's reaction was the same. *This is easy*, she thought, delighting in the game. She began to spank him regularly, first one cheek and then the other, until he began to squirm.

Bob was trying not to lose control. The details of making up his mind to ask, asking, and then planning for this had kept him too busy to really think about how it was going to feel. It was wonderful! His hot dick was pressing against Marsha's lap, feeling ready to spurt every time she whacked him. The position he was in raised his ass up, and tightened his balls against his body, causing sweet torment with every move. And Marsha was enjoying it! He could tell by the way she aimed her swats and kept pausing to run her fingers across his ass. Pretty soon, he wouldn't be able to hold back! He tried to think about other things, tried holding his breath, counting, thinking about work. Nothing was working.

Then Marsha stopped. He relaxed his body for a moment and panted.

"That's hard work," Marsha commented, shaking her hand out. "Maybe we'd better switch tactics." She reached for the line of household objects on the bed and picked up the wooden spoon. Aiming carefully, she brought it down sharply at the very center of his ass.

He yelped in shock and jumped. That thing hurt! Marsha also reacted to his reaction, by pulling back, thinking she had gone too far and had really harmed him. "Oh," she started to say, feeling bad, "did I..."

"I'm all right," Bob said. "It just surprised me." That was true...the sensation was already fading away. "Go on...please." Impulsively, he bent further and kissed her calf.

Marsha hastily rubbed her husband's butt where the spoon had hit him and smiled as she felt his lips against her leg. Then she abandoned the spoon and picked up the ping-pong paddle, judging it to be too wide to cause such a sharp pain. She was right. The first smack with the paddle made Bob nestle firmly back into her lap and fairly purr with satisfaction. She used it for a while, liking the feel of the broad paddle against his ass, liking the way it pushed his cheeks forward, and loving the feel of him rubbing his cock against her again.

She stopped long enough to hook her fingers into the waistband of his shorts and pull them down to his thighs. His ass was slightly reddened by her attentions. She couldn't resist running her fingers across the redness, and he shivered again when she did that. Joyfully, she laughed, and used the flat of her hand again, spanking him with enthusiasm.

When her hand was sore again, and he showed no sign of wanting to stop, she used one of her spatulas, making small, rapidly reddening marks all over his butt until she sensed that it was too harsh for him. She switched back to her hand for as long as she could stand it and then picked up the magic wand. For effect, she swished it back in forth in the air above him.

"Are you ready for this?" she asked.

Bob felt ready for a a repeat of the invasion of Normandy. He felt he could lead it, too. His butt seemed to be afire, an all-through warmth that had alternately wilted and strengthened his prick until he could barely stand the sensation. It was almost free now, the head poking out of the pushed-down waistband, and nestled against the flesh of his wife's thigh, where her robe had been pushed aside. He lifted his ass a little more, and knowing what he was doing, Marsha parted her legs, allowing his cock to edge neatly between them. It sprang free of the confines of the shorts, and Bob gasped as he felt the heated moisture that had been trapped inside Marsha's tight delta. If nothing else, her arousal made him even more eager to shoot his load, but he wanted to do that inside her, while she was tied down. That image almost pushed him over the edge! But he didn't want to stop. He remembered the caning scene too, and he wanted to feel that wand.

"Keep going," he whispered, bracing himself.

Marsha raised her hand and brought the wand sharply against Bob's upturned butt. The black plastic whistled as it flew and left an immediate white line behind it when she pulled it away. Bob's body jerked against her, and his breath expelled in a gasp, but he found the strength to say, "Yes, do it, keep going!," fearing she would stop. Made bold by his plea, and excited by the sensation of his manhood trapped between her thighs, she did as he told her and left another white line, and then another. These lines rapidly turned red as they added up, and before long, his entire ass was a crosshatching of red and white lines. He squirmed and wiggled against her, biting the inside of his lip, trying desperately not to come! But he had to, his balls were full, and the strain of holding back was unbearable.

"Oh, Jesus, oh God...Marsha, I'm gonna come, you sweet bitch, you're making me..." He gasped and then felt the explosion build.

Marsha heard him and dropped the wand in her excitement. Not knowing what to do, she tightened her thighs around him and hit the underside of his ass with her bare hand.

That did it! Bob came like a roaring freight train, bucking against her lap, and holding onto her leg. His come spurted out of him, hot and thick, splattering her legs...he had never looked at his cock when he was coming, at least not from this position. The tension on it, trapped between her satiny thighs, was too much...out of breath and slightly out of his mind, he could only whimper and stretch against her.

She understood immediately and opened her legs again. The scent of her own arousal was overwhelming. Bob just relaxed and allowed his body to roll off her lap, hissing when his ass touched the bare floor.

Marsha giggled at the sight of him. "I guess you liked it," she said, softly, leaning down to flick his jism off her calf. "But now what?"

"Now what?" Bob repeated. "Now, I get to do things to you." He pointed at her solemnly, and she giggled again.

"It's going to take a little time," she said mischievously. "Since you couldn't wait..."

Bob pushed himself up and ended up on his knees in front of her. "Fucking isn't the only thing I have in mind for you, sweetie." Suddenly, he pushed her back onto the bed and grasped her right hand as she fell. She struggled a little, more out of confusion than fear, and her struggles allowed him to get that hand under her body, at the small of her back, where he held unto it with his left hand. Then, firmly shoving her thighs apart, he ripped the front of her soaking panties down, bent into her and took a long, loving taste of her.

Marsha's breath exploded from her in a moan that almost seemed loud enough to wake the kids. Bob thrust his tongue deeply inside her, washing her inner lips with broad strokes, lathering the sides and the sensitive top, where her pleasure nub was prominent and awaiting attention. She moaned and squirmed, his firm hand holding her down more in her imagination than in reality. But she arched her back and pretended that he was holding her down all the same, and when his lips and teeth finally found her aching center, she was totally unprepared for the thrust into ultimate pleasure. Her hips moved against her will, and a spurt of new wetness met her husband's tongue as she thrashed and came into him mouth.

It was a sudden, swift, and harsh orgasm, and as she found herself on its wave, she also found herself crying out to her husband, over and over again, as though his name made it better for her, took her over the top. "Oh, Bob, Bob, do it baby, do it!" And as her pleasure peaked and her body shook in the tremors of passion, Bob pulled himself up onto the bed, dragging something with him. He left his crumpled trousers on the floor. Before she knew it, heavy rope was looped around one wrist. Too weak to move, she let him drag her other wrist out and up, and smiling, he tied them together.

"You...you *cheat*..." she managed to say, as he pulled his knots tight. "You got me when I was too weak to fight."

"That's the idea. Come on, my lady love, up to the head of the bed. I'm not finished with you yet." With that, he proceeded to tie her wrists to the wooden headboard. Then he pushed a pillow under her ass and, running the rope under the bed, tied her ankles spread apart. Casually, he untied her robe and spread the sides, letting them fall. Pushed up by the pillow, her loins were on display, partially hidden only by her wet and crumpled panties.

He reached over to her and pulled those panties back up, and she emitted a sad groan. "You kept mine on for quite some time," he explained, smoothing the cloth over her. "Now, it's my turn." She moaned in anticipation and tried to arch her back even more to get pleasure from the touch of his fingers. But he pulled them away, and thrust one hand under the remaining pillow at the head of the bed. When he pulled out the scarf, she trembled.

"This one is for your eyes." Awkwardly, he managed to blindfold her, tying the knot by her ear. Then, he pulled a chair near the bed and sat to look at her.

He had been honestly shocked at the enthusiasm she displayed while she was spanking him...and the feeling he got when he sat down was a reminder of that! But he had never really taken the opportunity to really look at her, like this, her body bare and on display, waiting for him. He loved the gentle swell of her full breasts, the roundness of her thighs and the way the dark golden hair now hidden under those soaked panties curled upwards toward her belly. She was every bit as beautiful as she was when they first began to go out together. He sat still, admiring her, and remembering the feel of her hand against his bare ass, until he felt a stirring that signaled he was getting close to full recovery, and then he slowly moved toward the bed. Without warning, he reached out and pinched her nipples.

Marsha bit back a scream. She had been lying there, loving the wait, loving the feeling of him still in the room, watching her. But at the same time, she was itching for his touch, wanting to beg for his cock. She had kept silent because she couldn't decide what to do! The sudden sharp feeling in her nipples scared her and excited her at the same time. She moaned her appreciation as Bob gently kneaded them, bringing them to little twin erections. She felt his body settle near her on the bed, and gasped as he leaned over her and took one nipple and then the other into his mouth, to suck and nibble on. Then he began to run his tongue against the sides of her breasts, under her collarbone, and around to her shoulders. Wherever he left this trail of wetness, she shivered. He worked his way across her face, nibbling on her earlobes, kissing her lips and the curve of her cheeks until her moans began to intensify with urgency. He brought his body far up on the bed and planted his knees on either side of her chest, his cock now hanging inches over her gasping mouth.

"I want you," she declared, writhing in ecstasy. "Stop teasing me!"

"I'll tease you as long as I want to," he replied, settling into position. "Maybe all night."

"Damn you! Please, Bob, please..." She shuddered as he reached behind his back and pinched her right nipple with one hand. His hand brushed his still hot ass cheek, and his cock stiffened immediately, almost drawing him down to ease into her mouth. But still he held himself back.

"Please what?" he said, balancing over her. "Tell me what you want...and make it dirty."

"Let me suck your beautiful cock," Marsha moaned instantly, shocked at how easily the words came to her. "Let me have it in my mouth, let me taste you, let me please you, oh God, Bob, please..."

"Whatever you say." Bob lowered his waiting cock into his wife's open mouth and she immediately wrapped her wet lips around him, engulfing him in hot, soft pleasure. He gasped as she drew him in, swallowing him to the root in one delicious slurp. Ecstasy flooded his nerves and almost made him cry out. He gently began to slide his cock past those tight lips, back and forth, back and forth, rocking, holding himself up by grasping the headboard.

"Oh, yeah, that's it, baby, take it all...so nice!" He groaned in delight at her eager mouth and throat work, the way she pulled and caressed him, and the way she followed his movements as though she were afraid he would take this treat away from her.

"That's good, sweetie, so good, I love your mouth on me like that...I might let you do this all night, wouldn't you like that?" Bob was also getting off on the sheer power of the situation; having Marsha helpless under him, yet so hot for him she was taking him in like a pro! She gasped and he drew his cock back for a moment.

"Yes! Yes, give it back, I'll take it all night, I'll make you feel so good! Oh, Bob, this is so hot! Please, and Bob...make it hard! Fuck my mouth, make me feel it!"

He cut her off by thrusting his impossibly hard cock straight into her mouth, no gentleness here, only hard, fast face-fucking! He couldn't take it anymore, both Marsha's overwhelming erotic response, and her willingness to take even more from him. He shoved his cock neatly to the back of her throat and felt the contraction around the head that meant that she had gagged. He eased back slightly, to let her breathe, but then shoved his way back. She made muffled, shared sounds of pleasure as he plundered her throat in a way he never had before. Could this be her gentle but imaginative lover, her partner and the father of her children? She gulped him deep into her mouth and lavished all the attention she could on that relentless piece of flesh that battered and so wonderfully filled her. Finally, he pulled back all the way and drew his cock from her lips, glistening with her spit.

"No, no, give it back!" Marsha pleaded, bending her head up, seeking it. "Don't stop, please..."

"I told you I'd do what I want, right?" Bob asked, moving down the bed. "Well, now I want to fuck you. Any complaints?"

Marsha only moaned, and he reached out to grasp the waistband of her panties and tugged at it until they tore off, exposing her delicate but soaking-wet mound. She gasped in surprise. Her pussy was displayed before him, splayed wide open, glistening with her moisture. He gently touched the soft hair and began to tease her again, making small circles with the edge of his finger.

"Oh...yes...right there!" Marsha pulled and strained against her bonds, amazed at the intensity of every touch. "I want...I want you to fuck me! Come on, Bob, give it to me! I'm so hot...so ready!"

"Oh...you want this?" Bob slid down the bed and lowered himself to her, and then edged just the head of his throbbing penis into her. She gave a sharp, high-pitched squeal of pleasure and he felt her close around him, spasming in pleasure. He pressed his thumb against the engorged nub poking out from behind its protective hood, and forcefully, skillfully, brought her to levels of pleasure she had never even imagined before. She thrashed against the bed, her hips churning, and when she had spent all that energy he thrust his cock into her as far as it could go.

If she'd had the breath, she would've screamed. Instead, she gasped and tightened around him, and as he began to fuck her in earnest, she brought her hips even higher, to meet each thrust. He was unstoppable, hard and eager, and he soon forgot that he had already come not so long ago. Her furious passion drove him, harder, faster, deeper, and she met him with a loving acceptance that brought him immediately to the brink. There would be no trying to hold back now.

"I love you, sweetie," he gasped, driving into her, the taste of her on his lips, the feel of her spanking still burning his ass. She groaned even as she nodded and began to convulse in yet another pinnacle of pleasure. The feeling of her tightening and kneading his manhood was just what he needed. With one final push, he emptied himself into her, shooting with a raw strength that left him gasping, stretched out over her body.

It was at least ten minutes before either one remembered the ropes. And as they finally curled up, wrapped in each other's arms, they both realized that the kids had blissfully slept through the whole thing.

Helga's Pleasure

Don Winslow

I climbed on the bed to sit beside the elongated ovals of Helga's sleek upturned bottom. My hands longed to explore the sinuous lines of that streamlined body. I reached down to place a hand on her left foot, touching her lightly on the ankle. The stockinged toes curled with pleasure when I drew a fingertip along the curve of the instep and ran it up over the knob of her heel and on up the back of taut-muscled calf, relishing the slick, smooth feel of the warm nylon-sheathed leg. I followed the sleek curve up to the hollow behind the knee and up the back of a gently tapering thigh.

Helga hummed with contentment, wriggling her hips and opening her legs invitingly as I traced a long flowing line right up to the wide band of elastic at the top of her stocking. Following the circular ridge of that stocking top, I delighted in the sensual feeling of her silky leg as my fingertips dipped between her loosely parted thighs.

Helga's low hum grew to an urgent mewing as my fingertips sampled the silken band of flesh along her inner thigh. Then I traveled a few inches higher, and my questing fingers explored the soft purse of her pussylips. I pressed along her love-cove, feeling my way along the rubbery, slick lips, testing her wetness and getting a soft shuddering moan of pleasure from the blonde, before I ran my teasing finger up to the perineum and then drew it along the center crease of her lovely derriere. She twitched in a simmering excitement she could barely control.

And now I spent a few leisurely moments delighting in the warm, satiny feel of Helga's splendid ass. I affectionately fondled those twin heavenly mounds, so neatly symmetrical, so caressingly soft, yet so deeply resilient. I couldn't resist cupping my hand and whacking her ass. Helga jerked and kicked up her heels in shocked reflex. But I calmed her by laying my flattened hand on the small of her back and moving it in a slow caress up the sweeping slopes to clutch a single rubbery orb and squeeze it reassuringly. And so I played with Helga's superb bottom, feeling her up, mauling, kneading those twin mounds to my heart's content, while the girl herself squirmed in rising sensual heat, writhing in animal passion on the silken sheets.

With a reluctant sigh, I finally gave up this idle pastime, determined to get on with the main pursuit. For this I would have to turn my playmate over on her back. I leaned down to bring my lips close to her ear, and muttered that it was time to get started. Helga rolled over immediately and her eyes flew open. She looked up at me, blue eyes shining with excitement. Without being told, she raised her arms up over her head as if in surrender—for she knew exactly what I had in mind—and the very thought sent a surge of wild excitement through her. Sitting beside her at the top of the bed, I lifted a proffered wrist and carefully strapped a leather cuff in place. These were thick, wide leather straps, lined with padded silk so the cuffs would not chafe sensitive skin. A slip lock allowed the strap to be buckled in place snugly, but not too tight; a D-ring sewn into each cuff provided a convenient anchoring point for restraints to be attached. For this purpose I used elastic strapping, running it to the ring set in the corner post, tightening it so that her supple arm was pulled taut. I especially prefer the strapping, rather than cords or chains, since it is strong enough to hold the arm outstretched, yet allows a bit of slack should the girl thrash about. I knew from experience that Helga was wont to do this once caught in the throes of an all-consuming orgasm.

As I banded her other wrist, I looked down at her to find Helga's big blue eyes on me, watching me with interest. She said not a word, but I knew she was powerfully aroused, for Helga, usually a strongly independent girl, found the helplessness of restraints to be an incredible turn-on. She had once confided in me that it made her wet just thinking about it. Again, I secured her wrist to the corner post and took up the slack, stretching her extended arm so that both arms were now raised at an angle over her head. I paused to admire the neat symmetry of the V and the way the silken strands of her pale blonde hair had fanned out on the sheet between her outstretched limbs.

With Helga's eyes following my every movement, I came around the bed to stand at the foot, with the second set of straps in my hands. She lay with her legs loosely parted. When she saw what I wanted, she obligingly parted them more for me. I sat on the corner of the bed and studied her pretty foot. Then I ran a hand down over it to clasp her ankle and pulled the slack leg farther toward the corner of the bed. Although I was burning with impatience, I forced myself to take my time, carefully banding her left ankle, and then her right, attaching the restraints and tightening them so that her long legs were extended to the corners of the bed, her thighs held well parted, her blonde pussy gaping, open, vulnerable.

Spread-eagled and totally naked but for the high collar encircling her throat and the black leather straps banding wrists and ankles, the statuesque blonde was a mouth-watering sight. A surge of lust ran through me, and my cock throbbed with a vibrant ache of desire.

Every fiber of her passionate body was pulled taut by the restraints. The sinews of her arms and legs took much of the strain, tightening her sleek torso and stretching her tits into two elongated, slightly flattened swells; the bottom ridge of her ribcage was dimly visible under the tightly stretched skin, and below that a slight hollow had been formed as her belly was pulled between the points of her prominent hipbones. My eyes were drawn to the splay of pale silvery pussyfur that marked the mounded pubis, the little fleshy pad that sat there so invitingly that I had a powerful urge to slip my fingers between her outstretched legs and palm her mons, pleasuring her till she cried out for mercy. The thought made my cock jump with excitement.

I looked up to check on Helga and found that my adorable playmate had raised her head to look down at me through hooded eyes. She held me with those captivating eyes, and as I returned her even gaze, I saw her tongue peek out to quickly rim her lips in an anxious flicker.

Now I got up to sit beside her on the bed. As I reached out to touch her cheek, she turned to kiss my hand, nuzzling my palm and extending her tongue to lick my fingers lavishly. I rubbed my fingers over her lips and then traced the lines of her face, the curve of her soft cheek, and on down her chin to her throat, pausing there to finger the supple leather of the high collar. I continued my explorations across the ridge of her collarbone, around the shoulder and along the sensitive flesh of the underside to sample the soft underarm with its trace of blonde stubble, while Helga's shoulders jerked from the light tickle of my teasing fingertips and she uttered a barely suppressed whimper of delight.

Now I followed the route down her sleek side, admiring the gentle sweep of curving flesh that tapered down and then swept back up to the flaring cradle of her hips. Helga's hips twitched in her growing agitation as I drew lazy circles on the side. I went on, tracing the curve up and over an angular hipbone to circle her navel, pressing on the dimple before I started that single finger up the narrow path between her distended breasts.

The tense blonde closed her eyes, and I saw her throat muscles working as she swallowed, once, twice. Then her lips fell open in a long, shivering hiss of breath while my fingers splayed out to ride up the slopes of her taut breasts. I passed my hand lightly over both breasts and then pressed my finger on the fleshy nub of her left nipple, embedded in the soft pink crinkled flesh of her thickened aureole. I worried the nipple a bit, indenting it, tugging on the pliant flesh, rolling the little nubbin between thumb and forefinger, while Helga whimpered with tortured pleasure, arching up and uttering tiny urgent moans through tightly drawn lips.

I watched the sensitive tips swelling with passion, the coronas of her aureoles expanding, nipples stiffening with excitement as I played with her boobs—first one, then the other. I looked up at her face as she stirred. Her breathing was ragged, coming through slightly parted moistened lips; nipples tense and excited; pinkish aureoles in full blossom. She twisted and rolled her head helplessly from side to side, arching up with eyes clenched shut, locked in her inner world of rising waves of pleasure.

I edged closer to her, and my upstanding prick brushed against her naked hip. A wild electric thrill ran through me, causing me to jerk my hips back even as I leaned over her. Primed and ready, I knew the slightest touch might well send me off, spewing wads of sperm to splatter that writhing naked body. And I didn't want that...not just yet, anyway.

And so I drew my loins back as I slid my hand down her belly to cover her furry mons protectively. Helga let out a long sigh of satisfaction when I cupped her sex and held her lightly, curling my fingers into her superheated crotch.

She was burning with excitement, squirming and twisting uncontrollably as I palmed her mons, rubbing deeply while the passion-crazed girl cried out with urgent whimpers that soon became mumbled pleas. She made a high-pitched keening sound as she strained back, raising her hips as much as her bonds would allow, thrusting her sex against my palm while the tendons of her thighs went rigid, the muscles tightening as she strained upward.

Her cries increased in pitch and intensity till, with a sharp yelp, she tensed and a tiny spasm rippled through her stiffened body. Then a long low moan slid out from between her lips and her body went limp. Sagging in her bonds, Helga closed her eyes to savor the delicious afterglow of the tiny climax that overtook her. I watched her lying there, her face flushed, brow sheened with sweat, her slack limbs outstretched, her breasts rising and falling in great swells—and I touched myself because I couldn't help it.

I grabbed my prick and pulled once or twice, reassuring my needy cock of the satisfaction soon to come. Then I scrambled down to the foot of the bed to release her ankles. Helga stirred languidly, scissoring her freed legs on the silk. Still groggy, she raised her head and shoulders to look down at me through half-lidded eyes where I knelt on the bed. I lifted up her slack legs, ran my hands up the backs of those stockinged columns, and forced them apart to fully expose her wet, gaping pussy.

Half-crazed with lust, I fell on her, plunging my painfully swollen cock into the warm sanctuary of her slick spasming cunt. I luxuriated in the delicious feel as my prick slid easily up the silken walls of her enfolding womanhood. Immediately the blonde beauty wrapped her exquisite limbs around my hips, welcoming me joyfully, embracing me with a fiery urgency.

Her strong thighs tightened, and the thrill of those delicious columns clamping my naked loins drove me wild, sending my passions skyrocketing, while the lusty blonde spurred me with urgent pleas whispered in my ear. At first our fucking was wildly erratic, but I somehow managed to slow down and we became more rhythmic, even and smooth. She was thumping my butt with her heels and meeting each plunge with her own bounding pelvic thrust. In this way we rode to new heights, my hips pumping furiously, her loins bouncing and gyrating, her lips babbling incoherently.

I could feel the tension rising in her body before the first convulsive shudder racked her thin frame, sending me careering over the edge at the same time. I surrendered to the inevitable and came with a violent tremor, crushing my groin against her furry mons, flooding her innards with my sperm in deep rutting thrusts, holding myself there buried to the hilt while a spasm of pure lust tore through me and obliterated all in a single flash of blinding pleasure.

The Parlor

N. T. Morley

It was a rainy New Year's Day when Kathryn entered bondage.

The limo driver was there in front of her apartment at the appointed time. He helped Kathryn with her bags and offered no more than a few polite words. As the car moved across the Golden Gate Bridge, Kathryn relaxed into the plush seats of the limousine. She was a little surprised to note that the upholstery felt like fur, though she was fairly sure it was fake. The limousine moved smoothly through the many curves of Highway 1.

Kathryn felt somewhat nervous, not quite confident in the decision she had made. She watched the scenery go by, vaguely afraid of the afternoon.

It was an hour's drive north of the city. Kathryn found her mind wandering over thoughts of the man and woman who had made the offer.

John and Sarah. Kathryn still found it hard to think of them that way; they were more accurately "the man" and "the woman." Kathryn knew that John and Sarah weren't their real names; the couple had told her so. They were maintaining an odd air of mystery, and Kathryn imagined that might be dangerous. But if it weren't dangerous, she wouldn't be here.

There, in the diner near the bookstore, they had made that bizarre proposition, and Kathryn had agreed to think about it. She had most certainly thought about it.

How could they have known? The words that the woman had used had lingered in Kathryn's mind, had worked their way through her body, had sent her home early from work with a feigned headache. Kathryn had hardly been able to keep still while she rode home on the bus. The press of human bodies, of sweat and rain, had only augmented the sound of the woman's words in Kathryn's head. Her breath had been shallow, her legs weak. She had barely made it up the stairs to her studio apartment.

Kathryn's tights had come off in seconds, and she had flung herself across the futon with her ass in the air and her tight skirt pulled up to her waist. That was the position that made her come the quickest, and Kathryn had been desperate for release.

That had been the story for several days as Kathryn had thought about the offer. She was a wreck. The possibilities consumed her. She couldn't take the sight of the woman out of her mind. She couldn't see straight. She could only visualize the woman's ruby lips forming the words: "We want you to be our slave."

That was all she needed to hear.

Despite her fascination and enthusiasm, Kathryn wasn't quite sure why she was doing it. The money, of course. But that wasn't really it. Kathryn had accepted the couple's proposition because it was something she wished to do. She never dreamed it would be possible, and therefore she had never considered that she would do it if asked. But here she was.

The limousine worked its way into the turnaround and stopped before the large door. Kathryn was astonished at the size of the house, with its iron grates and its carved stone statues. She should have assumed that a couple with the money to make her such an offer would have this kind of house, but it still seemed like a daydream to her.

A man in a blue uniform appeared outside the car, opening the door for Kathryn. She stepped out, and the man closed the door behind her.

The man said, "Pleasure to have you visit, ma'am. I'll take care of your bags and see that they're placed in your quarters. Please come this way." Kathryn felt a little strange abandoning her army-surplus backpack and her duffel bag in the trunk of the limousine, but she figured they would be all right. Kathryn followed the man to the front door of the enormous house.

He opened the door and indicated that she should go inside. There, she was met by a man in a much finer uniform, something more like a tuxedo. He did not introduce himself, but hung Kathryn's black overcoat in a closet and led Kathryn into a parlor off of the mansion's entryway.

"Please accept the welcome of the master and mistress," said the butler. "If you will be so kind as to wait here, they will be with you momentarily."

The butler closed the parlor door behind him. Kathryn looked around in awe. Several walls of the parlor were hung with tapestries and paintings, and those that weren't had shelves of leather-bound books. Kathryn wanted to see what books they were, but she was afraid to go near them for fear of smudging one. The parlor was furnished with velvet couches that looked brand-new but were styled as if they were a hundred years old. The velvets were rich: reds and blues and purples. Kathryn was afraid to sit down at first.

Finally, she forced herself to sit on one of the velvet couches. She was afraid she would damage it, but she managed to relax a little. She leaned back into the couch and found that it was incredibly comfortable. She had to tug down her tight black skirt, for she had worn a very short one, as the woman had requested. In addition, Kathryn had worn her death-rock boots: knee-high, buckled, with pointed toes. They were her favorite boots, and she hoped they looked acceptable. Kathryn had worn her slinkiest top, a black lace number that laced across the front and showed her matching bra. Her curly hair was beautiful, lustrous, and coal black; it hung well past her shoulders and was still wet from the rain.

Kathryn's mind wandered over the things the woman had said to her. They were things that Kathryn had fantasized about hearing for years. How could the woman have known in such detail what Kathryn's fantasies were? With such vivid imagery, Kathryn found her thighs tingling and her breath coming short. Her face began to turn red and she wondered how long her new employers might keep her waiting.

Relaxing into the plush velvet couch, she closed her eyes for a moment, and strange visions overwhelmed her; visions of what the man and the woman wished to do to her. John and Sarah. It seemed impossible to think of them as people who had names. They were going to do unspeakable things to her.

Kathryn's imagination warmed her, and before long she had dropped into a delectable half-slumber. She thought about the money she would receive at the end of her tenure in John and Sarah's house. She would be free. She could do anything she wanted.

But in the meantime, she would be their prisoner, their captive.

Kathryn was lost in a dream of warm, pulsing sex when the woman appeared before her.

"Kathryn," said the woman. "I didn't mean to wake you. You must be exhausted after your long journey!"

"Not...not too bad," Kathryn managed to mumble. In the warmth of the parlor and the depths of her nap, she had become sweaty. Kathryn got up as the woman sat down on the couch.

"Don't be ridiculous," said the woman, taking Kathryn's hands. "Sit down beside me. There's no need to be formal."

Kathryn obeyed, relaxing into the velvet couch again. The woman did not release her hands, and Kathryn found that she did not mind the ice-cold fingers holding hers.

"I'm so glad you're here," said the woman. "I was afraid you wouldn't show up. John was much more confident. He said he knew you'd be here."

Kathryn nodded, still feeling sleepy. She stifled a small yawn. The woman laughed and bent forward to kiss her on the cheek.

Kathryn was startled at the feel of the woman's wet lips on her cheek. She didn't respond at first, not until Sarah snuggled closer and placed her lips on Kathryn's.

The woman's lips were soft and supple. Her tongue slipped into Kathryn's mouth and Kathryn felt her body tensing. Her daydream had become reality. Kathryn felt desire building like heat in her crotch, and she knew that her panties were growing wet.

When the woman pulled back, she smiled at Kathryn.

"Now, a few things to talk about. You accepted our terms, and you signed the contract. The medical care and birth control will, of course, be covered by us. We'll have to arrange for what we discussed—you know, the piercing and branding."

Kathryn nodded sheepishly as a guilty tingle of pleasure went through her body. She still wasn't entirely sure about that part; it turned her on incredibly, but it seemed so strange. Well, they were paying for her. Kathryn was willing to try anything.

"But that will come later—after you've gotten used to us."

Kathryn spoke softly (she was shy and reserved). "It will be done professionally? By someone who knows what they're doing?"

The woman laughed. "Heavens, yes! Only the best for our...little girl." She giggled and bent forward to kiss Kathryn again. This time Kathryn responded, letting her tongue laze gently along the woman's lower lip.

When the woman pulled back, she looked Kathryn in the eye.

"Well, I don't mind telling you, I want to get started. I want to see how things work out, and I'm very eager to...see you."

Kathryn felt her breath coming quicker as the woman slid away from her just a bit. The woman's eyes roved over Kathryn's body.

"Why don't you take off your clothes," said the woman.

Kathryn quivered, her chest feeling tight. She had never received a request like that—certainly not one so direct. She had known it would come, but did it have to be so soon?

Of course it did. She had agreed, and she knew it was time. She would obey the woman's request.

Only it wasn't a request, and Kathryn knew that. It was an order. It was not to be disobeyed.

Sitting on the edge of the couch, Kathryn bent over and slowly unbuckled the twenty buckles on each of her knee-high boots. The woman sat on the edge of the couch, patiently watching her as she did this. Kathryn slid off her boots and placed them upright on the floor beside the couch.

Kathryn got off of the couch and stood before the woman. She felt a wave of panic but managed to quell it.

She reached up and unlaced her top, slowly opening it to reveal her black bra. Kathryn had never stripped for another woman, and she had never seen a woman with Sarah's hungry, devouring gaze.

Kathryn slipped off her shirt and looked around for a place to set it.

"Oh, Kathryn, how foolish of me." The woman clapped her hands twice, loudly, and called out, "Rogerio!"

The butler appeared in the doorway. Kathryn held the shirt over her breasts, shocked. Rogerio paid her no attention, however.

"Yes, Mistress?"

The woman noticed Kathryn's discomfort and laughed. "Rogerio is my servant. He knows everything that goes on here, and you won't be modest in front of him. It would be most awkward if you were! Please, continue undressing. And hand your clothes to Rogerio."

The woman's words were friendly and encouraging. But Kathryn knew that this was not a request, either. She handed her shirt to Rogerio and continued to take her clothes off.

Kathryn slipped out of the tight black skirt and the stockings. She handed each to Rogerio, acutely aware that both he and the woman were watching her. Nervously, Kathryn fumbled with the front-catch of her bra. She breathed hard, unable to work the catch. She realized that the catch had stuck, and looked down, trying to unfasten it.

"Rogerio, the lady seems to be having some trouble with her bra. Could you please undo it for her?"

Kathryn hardly knew what was happening, but she dropped her hands to her sides as Rogerio, with her skirt and stockings and shirt slung over his arm, stepped up to her and deftly unfastened her bra.

"Th-thank you," said Kathryn. She slipped the bra off, exposing her breasts with their hard pink nipples, and handed the bra to Rogerio.

Next, Kathryn slipped out of her panties and handed them to Rogerio, too. She knew that the panties were moist with the desire she had felt when the woman had kissed her.

The woman spoke to Rogerio: "Now see that the clothes are laundered—especially those panties!" She giggled a little and winked at Kathryn. "Take the clothes and the boots and place them in safe storage for Kathryn's departure. She won't be needing them before then."

"Very good, Mistress."

Rogerio took Kathryn's boots and clothes, and left the parlor. He closed the door behind him.

Kathryn felt acutely isolated and exposed, alone with Sarah in this parlor. The woman's gaze burned over her naked body, and Kathryn stood, allowing the woman to inspect the body she now owned. The woman leaned back on the couch, kicking off her shoes and lifting her feet onto the pillows. She reclined, looking at Kathryn hungrily.

"Come closer," said the woman. "Stand in front of the couch."

Kathryn obeyed, her skin tingling with anticipation. The woman's hand moved slowly up to Kathryn's breast. The fingers enclosed it, gently caressing the flesh. The woman pinched Kathryn's nipple gently and found that it was hard.

"It's not cold in here," Sarah said, and smiled deviously.

Somehow Kathryn found that comment embarrassing. That embarrassment brought a warm heat to her cunt as the woman's fingertips gently massaged her breasts. Kathryn found it difficult to stand, but she was afraid to sit on the couch: that would put her naked body up against the woman's. Kathryn felt dizzy.

"You seem uncomfortable. Would you like to kneel?"

A bolt of fear and desire went through Kathryn's nude body. She nodded. "Yes."

"Go ahead."

Kathryn got slowly to her knees, leaning against the edge of the couch. The woman's arm snaked out and her fingertips slid into Kathryn's damp, lustrous black hair. She felt submissive, possessed, helpless. The feelings churned together and Kathryn was afraid she might pass out.

"I think we'll sit here together for the afternoon," said the woman. "I'll have Rogerio build a fire and bring our lunch in here. Are you hungry?"

Kathryn shook her head vigorously. If she ate now she wouldn't be able to keep the food down!

The woman leaned back in the soft couch. She used her free hand to unbutton her silk blouse. Kathryn saw that she wasn't wearing a bra.

The woman's fingers tightened on the back of Kathryn's head. Kathryn caught her breath in her throat.

"First, though, we have a few things to attend to." The woman laughed as she pulled Kathryn's head down to her breast. "I want you to start by calling me 'Mistress.'"

Kathryn was a little surprised, but she really had expected this. Her face was pressed against Sarah's bare breast, the smooth flesh caressing her cheek. Kathryn's lips were very close to the pink nipple; she took a deep breath, trying to summon up the reserve to say the words Sarah wanted to hear.

"Say it, Kathryn. Just a whisper is enough. Acknowledge me as your mistress."

"Mistress," whispered Kathryn. The heat in the parlor was almost unbearable, and there was a sheen of sweat over Sarah's breast. The unfamiliar scent of Sarah's body wafted over her and she breathed deeply.

Sarah rubbed the back of Kathryn's head soothingly. She sighed pleasantly and guided Kathryn's mouth over her nipple.

"Not yet," said Sarah firmly when Kathryn moved to embrace the firm pink bud with her lips. "Don't touch it yet. First you must acknowledge that I own you. I know you signed the contract, but that doesn't mean a thing, not in reality. I want you to tell me that I own you."

Kathryn swayed gently, seduced by the warmth of the room. Sarah's body was so soft against her. Kathryn's eyes fluttered closed. She felt hypnotized, overwhelmed.

She said in a drunken, mumbling whisper, "You own me."

"You will address me as 'Mistress,'" Sarah told Kathryn very gently.

"You own me, Mistress." The heat and desire made Kathryn feel as if she were on some exotic drug that took away her will and her ability to think.

"That's very good. I own your body. Say it, Kathryn. Just a whisper is enough."

"You own my body, Mistress."

"And I own your mind."

"You own my mind, Mistress." Under the influence of the warm, seductive arms around her, and the erotic smell in her nostrils, Kathryn almost believed it.

"Oh, Kathryn, you're so submissive. I wish it were true. I wish I did own your mind. But no, no, it's not true. Not yet. I will own your mind, but it's going to take a long time. Tell me you'll be willing to work at it."

Kathryn hesitated, her lips hovering very close to Sarah's nipple. Kathryn had never made love with a woman before. She was overwhelmed with curiosity and desire, and Sarah's arms felt so good around her....

Sarah's voice grew stern. "Tell me you'll work at it, Kathryn. Tell me you'll work hard to give me possession of your mind."

Kathryn finally answered, almost in a moan, "I'll work hard, Mistress. I'll work hard so that you can own my mind."

Sarah sighed, smiled, and arched her back, bringing her nipple up to Kathryn's mouth. "You can make love to me now, Kathryn. You can pleasure me."

Kathryn's lips closed over Sarah's hard nipple. Her tongue snaked out and she began to lick, the salty tang of sweat filling her mouth. Kathryn breathed deeply, caressing Sarah's nipple with her tongue and lips. Sarah's hand lazed through Kathryn's luscious curly hair, and she guided Kathryn's head so that her mouth moved over to the other nipple. Kathryn set upon that one with equal hunger, and her desire began to rise. Sarah took hold of Kathryn's wrists and pushed her hands onto her breasts. Kathryn curved her fingertips around the mistress's breasts, as she had indicated, and began gently to stroke the flesh of Sarah's tits. Sarah had much smaller breasts than Kathryn or most of Kathryn's friends whom she had seen naked. The mistress's breasts were firm and taut, just barely large enough to play with. Kathryn's own breasts were so sensitive, she thought most other women didn't like them to be played with so much. But Sarah was enjoying it very much, to judge from the soft moans that were escaping her slightly parted lips.

Kathryn's many fantasies washed over her as she worshipped her mistress's breasts.

Kathryn had fantasized many, many times about making love to a woman, usually in submission to her or her husband or master. She had pleasured this fantasy-woman in every way possible. It was both a sexual attraction to women and a desire to satisfy a gentle but stern mistress. This mistress inevitably had large breasts; wide, rolling hips; strong, smooth thighs; strong hands; and very long, straight black hair flecked with silver. Kathryn herself was smaller and rounder, with larger breasts and more slender hips than her fantasized ideal mistress—and much shorter. Her hair, like that of the imaginary mistress, was black, though Kathryn's was curly and not straight. Sarah was rather thin, had small breasts (though very large nipples) and slender hips, and her hair was a lush golden blonde, not black, with not a hint of gray. Even so, Kathryn's ideal fantasy seemed to be cradling her head and moaning softly on the couch as Kathryn worked hard to pleasure her. Sarah seemed closer to Kathryn's ideal of feminine beauty than any other woman had ever been, if only because Kathryn was kneeling before her naked, charged with satisfying her bodily needs.

Kathryn's teeth came together softly and she bit the mistress's nipple hungrily. Suddenly she panicked, afraid she might have offended the mistress. But Sarah let out a low moan of pleasure and smiled down at Kathryn lasciviously. "I like that," she said to Kathryn. "I like it when you use your teeth. Bite my nipples— hard."

Kathryn worked her teeth together and hungrily bit at the mistress's nipples, raking her upper teeth over the soft flesh. Kathryn loved to bite—none of her male lovers, except a couple, had really liked to be bitten. But Sarah was begging Kathryn to bite her hard—and on her nipple, a very sensitive spot.

"Harder," breathed Sarah, demanding.

Kathryn bit harder, restraining herself, afraid of hurting Sarah.

Sarah moaned loudly, "Bite my tit harder! Harder!"

Kathryn bit as hard as she dared, afraid she would damage Sarah's tender flesh. But Sarah let out a low groan of ecstasy and gently pulled Kathryn away from her nipple.

Sarah bent forward, still reclining on the couch, and gripped Kathryn's hair gently. She pulled Kathryn's head back, and Kathryn gasped in surprise. But Sarah only wanted to look into Kathryn's eyes, and then to kiss her, hard, scraping her teeth across Kathryn's lower lip. Sarah's tongue plunged violently into Kathryn's mouth, and Kathryn caught her breath against a sudden wave of desire that almost made her collapse.

"I hope you know it's tit for tat," said Sarah. She grinned evilly, a soft, cruel laugh going through her. "So to speak." Her gentleness was gone in a flash; her nurturing exploded into sudden angry passion. Her smile disappeared and she glanced over Kathryn's large breasts as if sizing them up. Her eyes burned with the fire of a cruel mistress, and Kathryn was overwhelmed with fear. Then Sarah smiled mischievously, her thick red lips slightly parted, her full tongue inviting, hungry. Kathryn's fear gave way to a rush of desire, churning up inside her belly, making her slip deeper into the warm, hungry sense of dreamlike abandon.

The furnace must have been turned up, as the parlor only seemed to have gotten warmer. Kathryn could feel a thin film of sweat covering her body, and the warmth fogged her brain. She felt as if she'd been drinking red wine. Kathryn surrendered into Sarah's strong embrace as Sarah kissed her again, softer this time. The insane gleam of cruelty and control seemed to be gone from her eye. Sarah pulled Kathryn gently against her, cradling Kathryn's head and stroking the soft coal-colored hair.

"Help me get this skirt off," said Sarah.

Kathryn felt a momentary wave of panic, knowing she was expected to go down on Sarah. She felt terrified of that possibility—actually slipping her tongue inside Sarah's cunt, doing something she had fantasized about so many times but never actually done. But Kathryn knew she couldn't turn back now, not with her desire raging so high in her body. Her cunt felt ready to explode. She was tingling all over, and she knew that Sarah expected satisfaction. Kathryn gave herself over and began to help Sarah slip out of the skirt.

When the skirt was a rumpled heap on the floor, Sarah guided Kathryn's hands to the sides of her panties. Her fingers quivering, Kathryn obediently took hold of the panties and slipped them off of Sarah. Sarah now reclined naked on the plush, red velvet couch, and her body was really quite impressive. Sarah's firm breasts looked even more complemented by the muscular slope of her shoulders and chest, and the silky sweep of the golden hair across her neck. Kathryn hesitated, looking over Sarah's body in awe.

"You've never done it before, have you?"

Kathryn's face went red, her head spinning and her cheeks hot. She was unable to answer. Kathryn shook her head reluctantly, feeling like an embarrassed schoolgirl who's been shown up as a Goody two-shoes.

"Never?"

Kathryn shook her head again.

With her head fogged and her lust raging, Kathryn knew she couldn't lie to her mistress. She had wanted to do it so many times, and had been asked by her best friend, Sharon, once, for nothing serious, just to play around and see what it was like. But she had chickened out after the first tongue-kiss, when Sharon's thumbs had paused over Kathryn's nipples. Kathryn hadn't been fingered, hadn't done anything more than that first, furtive kiss in Sharon's bedroom. Kathryn was a virgin with girls, and she felt ashamed and helpless.

Sarah's fingertips caressed Kathryn's face. Kathryn could feel Sarah's sharp fingernails grazing her jaw.

"A sweet little virgin," said the mistress. "You don't know how that turns me on. I'm going to enjoy breaking you in, little virgin. I know you'll be a natural."

Sarah peered forward, studying Kathryn's face. "You've gone to bed with men, though. Haven't you?"

Kathryn nodded.

"How many?"

It took Kathryn a few seconds to answer sheepishly; "Twelve." She felt like something of a slut, having gone to bed with so many men. It seemed like more than most of her girlfriends, even though she was counting David, whom she had only sucked off (she hardly knew him) and Arthur and Frank, whom she'd only slept with once. She didn't count Mike, who had been a good friend of Steve's, for that time when the three of them had fooled around on her bed and Mike and Kathryn had fucked with Steve watching. She didn't know why she didn't count that. She just didn't.

"Twelve. You're something of a slut, for your young age."

Kathryn felt a wave of shame and arousal going through her. The mistress was calling her a slut. She felt vaguely ashamed of her sexual history, and hearing Sarah berate her for it made her give in to Sarah's control.

Sarah smiled, caressing Kathryn's lips with her thumb. "You're still a virgin, though, as far as women go. That makes you something very special. I get wet just thinking about virgins. I'm pleased to know that you're one."

Sarah turned slightly and reclined more completely on the couch, so that she could slide one leg up along the back of the couch. The other leg Sarah lifted gracefully and slipped over Kathryn's shoulder, so that Kathryn knelt between her mistress's very wide open legs. Sarah indicated that Kathryn should move slightly, so that she was perfectly centered and ready to please.

Kathryn felt terrified. She knelt here, ready to service her mistress with her mouth. She knew the mistress would be very demanding, and she had never even tasted a cunt before. She tried to breathe deeply, feeling as though she would pass out.

Sarah slipped her fingers into Kathryn's thick hair again, guiding her head down. But Sarah didn't press Kathryn's mouth into her cunt; instead, she lay Kathryn's head most gently across her lap, just above her cunt. Kathryn could feel Sarah's wiry blonde pubic hair against her chin and smell the sharp tang of sex rising from Sarah's cunt. The smell was overwhelming and Kathryn felt her desire rising further, her fear dissolving into a lust for the mistress's cunt. But Sarah just relaxed into the couch, stroking Kathryn's hair and face and the back of her neck. Sarah sighed, enjoying her total dominion over Kathryn, knowing how frightened the girl was.

Sarah reached behind the couch and pressed a buzzer. Kathryn started to sit up, startled, as Rogerio entered the room. Sarah gently but oh-so-firmly pulled Kathryn's head back into her lap.

"Yes, Mistress?"

"Rogerio, would you please stoke the fire? I'd like it a little warmer in here for the occasion." Sarah laughed softly. "I think a fire would be very romantic on the occasion of this young girl's defloration, don't you?"

Kathryn's eyes went wide. She felt ashamed and exposed here in front of Rogerio, with her head in Sarah's lap, so close to her cunt! And now Sarah was discussing her virginity with women as a topic of casual conversation. Kathryn's face turned red—not with anger, but with shame and humiliation. She couldn't pull away, though. Sarah's hand gripped her hair very tightly, making sure that Kathryn couldn't move. And Kathryn felt very strongly that she couldn't disobey Sarah. Even when she was humiliated like this.

"Yes, certainly," said Rogerio. "I didn't realize the girl was a virgin or I would have thought of it. I apologize."

"Well, she's only a virgin with women," said Sarah. "She's most experienced with men. As a matter of fact, I think she's something of a slut."

Hearing that word again brought a tremble to Kathryn's body. She felt more exposed than ever, ridiculed in front of Rogerio. What's more, the way that Sarah was holding her, Kathryn leaned forward so that her crotch was, no doubt, plainly visible to Rogerio. She couldn't see if he was looking at her, but she felt that his eyes were covering her, roving over her body and her naked cunt.

Rogerio laughed lightly as he worked on the fire. "I could tell from the way she walked."

Kathryn's face flushed deeper red. She felt hot and dizzy. But she knew from the familiar tingling in her belly and her cunt that she was getting wet. Being discussed like an object was turning her on. Could Rogerio really tell that she was a slut by the way she walked? Kathryn was horrified to think that he had known, but she felt her embarrassment giving way to a hopeless surrender. What did it matter, now that she had come here? She was kneeling before Sarah while Sarah discussed Kathryn's sexual history with the butler and prepared to introduce Kathryn to sex with women. What difference did it make? Kathryn felt herself slipping into her vague, dreamy state, giving up control to Sarah and even Rogerio.

It took Rogerio some time to finish with the fire. As he did, Sarah caressed her face and hair and shoulders. Kathryn began to feel very protected, giving up her shame over what Sarah and Rogerio had talked about. She was almost falling asleep, enveloped in Sarah's arms and kneeling against her. The thick carpet felt so good on her knees; she felt very natural like this, kneeling to her mistress.

When Rogerio finally got the fire going, Kathryn could feel the heat against her exposed ass and thighs. She was already sweating from the cozy warmth of the parlor, but the added heat just lured her deeper into a relaxed, pliable state.

Sarah thanked Rogerio and he left. The fire grew hotter, overwhelming Kathryn with its warm caress.

"Oh, Kathryn. You're so perfect for me. John is going to be so pleased. I can't wait to share you with him. Mmmmm...won't that be delicious?"

Kathryn whispered softly; "Yes, Mistress." She was seduced. She couldn't deny Sarah anything.

"It's time for you to use your mouth on me," said Sarah. "You're going to have a lot to learn."

"I know, Mistress. I'll try..."

Sarah snuggled deeper into the couch, spreading her legs wider. She eased Kathryn's head down, guiding Kathryn to her cunt.

Her eyes closed and her lips parted, Kathryn let Sarah guide and control her. Kathryn felt the thick, fleshy cunt against her face, and she began to lick gently. The taste filled her mouth and Kathryn slurped hungrily. She hadn't expected a cunt to taste so strong, but it wasn't bad at all. In fact, she felt herself getting more and more turned on as she began to worship the mistress's cunt.

Kathryn tried to imagine what she would want if she were the mistress. Kathryn liked being penetrated, but her clitoris was incredibly sensitive. She began to work on the mistress's clit, flicking it gently back and forth with the tip of her tongue. Kathryn felt a rush of relief and satisfaction as Sarah let out a long, low moan of pleasure.

"You *are* a natural. You were born to eat pussy."

Sarah caressed Kathryn's face as Kathryn flicked her clitoris back and forth, then up and down, again and again. She tried sucking on it gently—very gently.

"Don't suck," Sarah growled. "Don't suck on my clitoris until I tell you to. I only like that after I've come a couple of times. And don't use your hands. Keep them behind you until I ask for them." Sarah's manner had turned cruel and domineering in a second, all because Kathryn had done something wrong in eating her out.

Kathryn quickly returned to flickering her tongue over the clit, and obediently put her hands behind her. This made it hard for her to lean forward and service the mistress, but Sarah supported Kathryn with one strong hand on her shoulder and one hand on the back of her head, twined into her hair. Kathryn was afraid that she had made Sarah angry by sucking on her clitoris. She felt ashamed and embarrassed again, as if she had failed her mistress. A flush of desire went through her, the desire to make her mistress come. Kathryn tried harder to satisfy Sarah by licking, listening very carefully to the sounds her mistress made.

Sarah began to moan softly again. Kathryn's jaw relaxed as she realized that Sarah was enjoying herself. Kathryn kept working on the clitoris, not daring to stop. She kept her arms behind her, not touching anything. She was completely helpless and engulfed by Sarah's cunt. But Sarah was moaning contentedly. Still kneeling, Kathryn lowered her ass to touch her heels, sitting more comfortably.

Sarah was harsh again, only for a moment, with a tender kind of cruelty that sounded like the firm instruction of a schoolteacher: "Keep your ass in the air. Don't sit—kneel. And you're not doing it right. Lick around the lips, too, the inner lips. But not too much. Keep going on the clit. And keep your ass in the air—and your arms back, out of the way."

Kathryn obeyed, afraid of Sarah's anger. It was hard to get her ass in the air, and she had to spread her legs to do it. Kathryn went to work on the mistress's inner lips, just as she'd been instructed, and her mouth was overwhelmed by the sharp taste as she licked around the inner lips and the entrance to Sarah's cunt. Sarah was very wet, and her thick cuntjuices were mingling with Kathryn's saliva and dribbling over Kathryn's chin. Kathryn was terrified that it would get on the expensive velvet couch, but she didn't dare pause, and to open her eyes would break her concentration. Kathryn kept working diligently, moving back to Sarah's clit and servicing it as Sarah whimpered and moaned and made stern demands.

"Use your lips, too. But...uh...only between tongue strokes. God, that's good. Come on, use your lips, Kathryn. On the clit—but don't suck! Oh, yes. Oh, that's good. Now your tongue! Right... right there...oh, yes..."

Kathryn submitted to the instructions, giving her mouth over to Sarah's pleasure. Kathryn could feel her own cunt wet with desire, but in order to keep her face in Sarah's crotch without using her hands, she had to keep her legs spread and her knees wide apart. She could feel the fluids from her cunt dribbling gently down her thigh, drop by drop, one drop every minute or so. The warmth of the fire heated her exposed cunt and made her feel even more violated, even more open and receptive. Kathryn knew if she could just rub her thighs together for half a minute she would come like an avalanche. But she didn't dare move her thighs together, for she would lose her balance and have to put her ass against her heels, and that would make Sarah mad. Kathryn desperately wanted to follow all orders.

"Right there...keep going on the clit! Forget about the lips, just stay on the clit!" Sarah was frenzied, and Kathryn knew she was going to come. Desperately Kathryn worked on Sarah's clitoris, keeping her tongue going even though it was exhausted and she felt ready to pass out. Sarah was right on the edge, but she didn't come right away. Kathryn kept going, servicing her mistress, her head spinning as she waited for Sarah to come. But it seemed to take forever, and Kathryn forgot who and where she was as she gave herself over to pleasing Sarah, the woman who owned her, the possessor of this cunt that was being tongued endlessly....

Finally, Sarah let out a scream of "Oh, God!" and wrapped her thighs tightly around Kathryn's face, pulling her between them and forcing her mouth against her cunt. Kathryn could feel the spasms of Sarah's cunt, pulsing against her lips. She kept licking until Sarah spread her legs again and pulled Kathryn away, gasping for air. Kathryn breathed deep, her eyes shut tight and her lungs aching. Her tongue seemed swollen and raw, and her head was fuzzy with the heat and her own need. She had never needed to come this badly. Men didn't take so long—whenever Kathryn gave head, she knew it was only a few minutes before her mouth was full and she could get off. But the mistress had kept Kathryn kneeling, her cunt throbbing and aching, for what seemed like an eternity. Kathryn felt like she would explode.

Sarah slowly sat up on the couch, caressing Kathryn's face. She guided Kathryn around, turning her until she sat on the floor with the back of her head between Sarah's spread legs. Sarah bent over Kathryn and pulled her head back so they could kiss.

Kathryn was panting, and her pale flesh had turned bright red. She was slick with sweat from her feet to her cunt to her breasts. Her thighs were wet with her own juices.

Sarah's tongue tasted incredible, making Kathryn's whole naked body quiver. Sarah invaded Kathryn's mouth with her strong tongue, diving in deep, licking at the thick cunt fluid that filled Kathryn's mouth. Kathryn's thighs settled together and she began to rub them together slowly, bringing her pleasure higher. She would come in another ten seconds.

Sarah pulled her tongue out of Kathryn's mouth and said, very harshly, "Stop that! Spread your legs. All the way!"

Kathryn hesitated for a second, and Sarah repeated the command. Kathryn was right on the brink of orgasm, about to come in thundering spasms. She would prefer just to come, rather than having Sarah play with her and bring her off. But she was so afraid of displeasing Sarah, and she managed to spread her legs, opening them wide so that her cunt was exposed.

Sarah smiled. "You're lucky I caught you before it happened," she said. "You're right on the edge, aren't you?"

"Yes," whimpered Kathryn.

Sarah's face became hard and her eyes fiery. "What?"

"Yes, Mistress," Kathryn choked, her whole body aching with need. She could feel the impending orgasm in her throat, her breasts, her arms, her legs—she was consumed with the need for release.

"You're dying to come, aren't you?"

"Yes, Mistress," moaned Kathryn. "Please! Oh, please!" Kathryn had to fight to keep herself from putting her hands in her crotch and bringing herself off right away. But she managed to keep her legs spread and her arms at her sides, though she found her hands gripping the mistress's feet tightly. Oh God, thought Kathryn, why doesn't she let me get it over with, I need it so bad....

"Let's get one thing straight," Sarah told Kathryn, very firmly. "You do not come when you want to come. You belong to me. Body and soul. You will orgasm when I instruct you to have an orgasm."

Kathryn's eyes were wide, childlike, staring up into the mistress's hard face, desperately begging for relief.

"You don't make yourself come. I own your orgasm, and you aren't allowed to take it from me. There are severe penalties for stealing from the mistress, you little slut."

Kathryn moaned, insane with desire. "Please, Mistress..."

"If I ever catch you masturbating in my house, Kathryn, you will be very, very sorry. If you wish to have an orgasm you must petition me for permission! Do you understand?"

"Please, Mistress..." Kathryn was sobbing, squirming in her mistress's arms, but she managed to keep her legs apart. Her orgasm didn't seem to diminish, but kept throbbing in her legs, denied, very close but never happening.

"Do you understand?" Sarah was her angry self, the ice queen, demanding submission from Kathryn.

Kathryn nodded, her desperation fogging her vision. "Yes, Mistress. I understand."

"Do you promise never to have an orgasm without my express permission? Not by yourself, or with anyone else?"

"Yes, yes, Mistress, I do. Now please, please may I have an orgasm? Please...?"

Sarah smiled. "If it pleases me, I'll let you come from time to time...do you like to have your breasts played with?"

Kathryn did, but now was not the time—to be tormented like this was almost more than she could stand, and certainly more than she had expected. She felt as if the blood in her head had flowed into her cunt, which was throbbing with the volume of it all. She felt dizzy and weak as the mistress's hand slowly traveled down her body toward her breasts, and she realized with horror that the mistress was going to play with her, to torment her further, before she was allowed to come.

"No...please, Mistress...have mercy...make me come...."

Kathryn's hands crept up to her thighs, and Sarah noticed

them. Kathryn had been about to touch herself, unable to control her desire.

"Stop that!" the mistress said, angry. She took hold of Kathryn's wrists and placed them on the floor as Kathryn whimpered in frustration and fear. Sarah reached over and buzzed Rogerio, who appeared in an instant.

"Handcuffs," Sarah spat out before Rogerio could say a word. "This little slut can't control her hands."

Kathryn thought she would explode. One of her strongest fantasies of her imaginary mistress was that this woman would handcuff Kathryn and torment her cunt to orgasm. Just the thought of handcuffs was enough to make Kathryn's hands creep involuntarily toward her cunt again, and Sarah took Kathryn's wrist firmly as Kathryn's hand slid between her legs.

"Stop that, you little bitch. You're going to be punished for that later."

Rogerio appeared with the handcuffs. The mistress had Kathryn's wrists and before Kathryn knew what was happening, she was handcuffed with her arms pulled painfully back and her wrists behind her. She was helpless in Sarah's cruel embrace.

"Thank you, Rogerio." The butler was gone, and it was just Kathryn and Sarah, locked in their struggle over Kathryn's desire.

Kathryn's orgasm would have diminished now, if it wasn't for the damn handcuffs. They were such a fetish for Kathryn, such a fantasy, that she was pushed even closer to orgasm—but her legs were spread, and she couldn't make herself come unless she could close them. Or unless the mistress would touch her.

Sarah smiled, looking into Kathryn's reddened face. Kathryn's lips were slightly parted, and Sarah kissed her softly. Kathryn bit hungrily back, sliding her tongue into Sarah's mouth, hoping that if she begged the mistress, she would be allowed to climax....

"Please...," whimpered Kathryn.

Sarah's smile broadened as her hand slipped down to Kathryn's breast. "Now then, I was saying...do you like to have your breasts played with?"

Kathryn moaned in agony. She did like to have her breasts played with; in fact, she could almost come from having her nipples pinched and stroked. Almost. If she could rub her legs together she could get off that way, or if she was being fucked at the same time. But Kathryn knew that was hopeless.

"Don't make me bind your legs, too," Sarah exclaimed. "If I have to do that, your punishment's going to be something horrible!"

Kathryn managed to keep her legs spread. Sarah's fingertips curved around Kathryn's breasts, and Kathryn could feel the mistress's strong fingers pinching the nipples, hard.

"Please...Mistress..."

Sarah began to toy with Kathryn's nipples, using both hands at once, leaning over so she could kiss Kathryn deeply as she worked on her breasts. Surges of pleasure exploded through Kathryn's naked body, but nothing drove her over the edge. She moaned and begged as Sarah played with her tits, but nothing would make Sarah bring her off. Instead Sarah just kept stroking the large, firm breasts, chuckling softly, kissing Kathryn, stroking her throat from time to time or caressing her lips. The nipple stimulation was keeping Kathryn right on the edge of orgasm, and the feel of the handcuffs made her delirious with climactic need.

"Please...Mistress..."

"You have very large breasts," the mistress said casually. "They really are quite impressive. You like to have them touched, don't you?"

Kathryn managed to nod, helpless.

"You like it when men suck them...when they're fucking you?"

Kathryn almost broke into tears as the mistress tormented her breasts. Sarah continued to pinch and play with the nipples as she spoke conversationally.

"You're very proud of them, aren't you? You like to wear clothes that show off your bust?"

Kathryn nodded, and a tear ran down the side of her face. Oh, God, she wished she could come; she needed to come; she wished the mistress would touch her clit, or stop touching her at all. She couldn't stand it anymore....

"A girl like you should be," whispered Sarah. "They're very beautiful. And they're so sensitive...."

Sarah bent forward, pushing Kathryn's head back. Kathryn let out a desperate "Oh, God, no...no..." as Sarah's mouth descended on her breast. The feel of Sarah's tongue drawing circles around the nipple was more than Kathryn could bear.

"Oh, God...please, please don't do that," she begged. It felt so good...she couldn't have imagined it would ever feel so good to have her breasts tongued.

Sarah pushed Kathryn onto the couch faceup, making her keep her legs spread wide. The feel of the soft velvet against her ass was almost enough to drive Kathryn over the edge and make her come. Sarah hovered over Kathryn, careful not to touch Kathryn's crotch, and her mouth closed tightly around Kathryn's nipple.

"Oh, God...oh, God, Mistress..."

Sarah lifted her mouth off of Kathryn's left nipple, smiling broadly. Her fingers crept up to Kathryn's right breast, covering it, preparing to pinch the nipple hard. Sarah breathed warmly over Kathryn's breast.

"Oh, God...oh, God...please, Mistress, please please please may I have an orgasm?"

Sarah laughed lightly, her tongue snaking out.

"No, you may not," she said cheerfully.

Her lips closed over Kathryn's nipple as her hand went to work on the other breast. Kathryn let out a desperate, hateful "ohhhh Goddddd—" as her mistress began to work on her. Sarah had been prepared for Kathryn's momentary indiscretion, and, using her own knees, she wedged Kathryn's knees quite firmly apart on the couch. Kathryn was not permitted to close her legs, for Sarah knew that would mean an orgasm in seconds.

Kathryn moaned in frustrated fear and anger, her whole body ready to explode. Sarah's mouth and hand worked her tits and Kathryn kept trying to force her legs closed, but Sarah wouldn't permit it. Finally Sarah buzzed Rogerio again, breathing hard, never once letting her mouth off of Kathryn's nipple.

"Yes, Mistress?"

"Leg cuffs," said the mistress harshly, angrily. "And you're going to have to help me with her, I think."

Kathryn was barely aware of the exchange, intent only on reaching her long-denied orgasm.

"And bring me a dildo. Any size!"

The sound of the word almost made Kathryn do it right there, without her cunt being touched at all. She was going to be fucked. She had never used a dildo, herself, but she had heard girlfriends talk about how good they were. She was going to find out. And it was going to make her come....

Kathryn only dimly felt Rogerio and Mistress Sarah cuffing her legs and fastening them wide apart on the couch. She realized that the couch must have been fitted with eyebolts, for her legs were now wide apart, with one over the back of the couch and one cuffed to the leg. With her wrists cuffed behind her, Kathryn was totally helpless.

But Sarah had the dildo. She was going to make Kathryn come.

Kathryn moaned in desire. "Please...oh, yes please, Mistress, use it on me...."

The dildo was flesh-colored and large, and Kathryn knew it would bring her off fast. She lay there, thankful for Sarah's torture and waiting to be fucked.

Sarah laughed heartily, sliding her nude body against Kathryn's. Kathryn's head spun as she felt the base of the dildo against her thigh, cupped in Sarah's hand. Then Sarah fitted the head of the dildo into her own cunt and pushed it in, settling down against Kathryn so that she could fuck herself as she lay on top of her naked slave.

Kathryn moaned in horror. Sarah was going to bring herself off again as she tortured Kathryn. The dildo was for Sarah, not Kathryn.

Sarah began working the dildo in and out, whimpering. Her mouth descended onto Kathryn's breasts, as did her free hand. Kathryn had been primed and ready to receive her satisfaction, and now, with the feel of Sarah's mouth and hand against her breasts, she lost any sense of power whatsoever. She wasn't going to come. But she couldn't stop herself from tottering on the brink, there, spread on the couch, as her mistress used the dildo on herself. Sarah had known that Kathryn would only get hotter and hotter as she felt her mistress humping on top of her, sliding the dildo in. Kathryn let out a forlorn, desperate wail of agony as Sarah sucked and tongued harder at Kathryn's defenseless breasts, using her fingers to grope and rub the flesh and pinch the nipples. Meanwhile, Sarah's hips pumped back and forth, plunging the dildo in and out so that Kathryn could feel every thrust.

"Please...oh, God please Mistress, please let me come...."

Sarah laughed as she tormented Kathryn's tits. The nipples

were hard and bright red from the long torture, which made them look that much more delectable to Sarah. She pounded the dildo into her own cunt as she took incredible pleasure in depriving Kathryn's.

Kathryn was oblivious to almost everything except the feel of her mistress's hands and mouth on her nipples and the overwhelming ache in her own cunt. But she could tell from the way that Sarah was working her tits that the mistress was about to have her second orgasm. Kathryn moaned in desperation, begging again and again to be allowed to come. Sarah laughed, choking back her own orgasm, barely able to speak. She moved her lips up close to Kathryn's ear as Kathryn begged her, "Please Mistress, may I have my orgasm? Please?"

"No, Kathryn, you may not."

And with that, Sarah molded her lips to Kathryn's nipple and used both hands to frig the dildo in and out of her own cunt. She bit Kathryn's hard nipple, chewing on it and pulling it out painfully as Kathryn felt shudders going through her mistress's nude body. Sarah was screaming, moaning, panting in orgasm, torturing Kathryn's breasts the whole while. Finally, Sarah's pumping ground to a halt and she lay on top of Kathryn, laughing. Sarah's tongue lazed in slow circles around Kathryn's nipple, the torment lessened to a dull pain throughout Kathryn's body. Her wrists and ankles ached from the tight bonds, and her nipples were sore from the tonguing and pinching, though they still tingled with unbearable pleasure. Kathryn's head throbbed with what would be called "blue balls" if she were a man. She had forgotten who she was. She knew only that she served this mistress who was cruelly denying her orgasm, and that she would do anything to be allowed to come. She heard the buzzer, faintly, and she heard Sarah talking to Rogerio.

"She needs to do some more work. She thinks too much of herself. She'll service you now. And hold off for as long as you can, Rogerio."

"Certainly, Mistress."

"Kathryn," said the Mistress. "Do you understand? You're to use your mouth on Rogerio. You've done that before?"

Kathryn nodded fervently, desperate to serve her mistress, even if it meant sucking off this man she didn't even know. She had agreed to that in the contract, though she hadn't really believed it would happen—she would service any person John and Sarah told her to. In her current state, she had no shame and no will of her own. She would do whatever it took to please Rogerio.

"You'll do it well," Sarah said. "And you won't come while you do it, either. See to that, Rogerio."

"I'll have to get a few things to do it properly, Mistress."

"Then do so, by all means. We want this done properly. Give me a cigarette first."

Rogerio lit a cigarette for the mistress and handed it to her. "Now go get what you need. Before she cools down. I can't keep her going forever, you know."

"Yes, Mistress."

Sarah curled up on top of Kathryn, careful not to let any part of her body touch Kathryn's cunt. The slave was like a keg of dynamite waiting to go off. Sarah drew deeply on the cigarette and sighed.

"You're really quite a willful slave," said the mistress as she smoked. "But I'll forgive you a few things because you came so close to orgasm just by going down on me. That's a real change, and something of a thrill. Most girls your age have to be trained to have easy orgasms. With you it's the other way around. You're going to require a lot of stern treatment to be controlled. Your punishments will be very strict. If I let you come once, just once when you want it and I don't, you'll want to do it every time. I'm starting early so we don't waste time later."

Sarah placed the end of the cigarette to Kathryn's lips. Kathryn had quit smoking months ago, but she had never wanted a cigarette so bad. She drew in at the mistress's command and felt the delicious smoke go through her. Sarah gave her three more drags and then left her wanting a whole cigarette almost as bad as she wanted an orgasm.

Rogerio appeared behind Sarah. Kathryn knew the time had come.

Sarah lifted herself off of Kathryn's naked, vulnerable body. Kathryn felt Rogerio's strong arms circling around her, and his strong male scent seemed to filter through her. Rogerio lifted Kathryn's shoulders up so he could unfasten the handcuffs from behind her back.

Kathryn would have thrust her hands into her crotch and tried to bring herself off as soon as her hands were free, but Rogerio was too quick and strong. He held onto her firmly, and before Kathryn knew what he was doing, she felt soft leather restraints being padlocked around her wrists. She realized that the restraints were attached to a thick wooden dowel three feet long. Her arms were forced to be spread.

Kathryn moaned in desperate need, her orgasm still throbbing in her cunt, yet cruelly denied. She had had so many fantasies of being bound, even tied to bars like this one or placed in stocks, but to be denied release like this was more agony than she had ever dreamed she could endure. But she knew she would have to service Rogerio, whatever that would mean, and maybe then the mistress would allow her to come.

Rogerio deftly unfastened Kathryn's legs, wedging them open

as he pulled her onto the ground. He forced the bar down and instructed her to put her knees over it. The whole time, Rogerio kept Kathryn in a firm grip that prevented her from closing her legs. Kathryn obeyed him, aroused by the smell of his sweat and the firm, male grasp. She would serve him as she had served her mistress, and as she had served so many in her fantasies—and as she had agreed to do in the contract. She wondered desperately if she was going to suck his cock. That would be what he wanted, she supposed, but she had assumed he was going to fuck her. But if Rogerio put his cock inside her, even just one thrust, Kathryn knew she would come. The thought of that was overwhelmingly delicious to her. If she did suck his cock, assuming she was made to kneel, Kathryn was sure she could rub her thighs together enough to bring herself off.

Kathryn realized that Rogerio had placed her ankles in restraints, and Kathryn moaned with horror as he wrestled her legs painfully far apart and fastened Kathryn's ankles to the outside of the bar. Outside her hands, so that her legs were kept spread wide. He worked Kathryn to a kneeling position—she was forced to kneel with her arms hanging rigid and her wrists fastened just beside her ankles.

Kathryn was trapped.

She was cuffed in this kneeling position, her hands immobilized, her legs spread. She wasn't even able to lower her cunt to the ground and rub it against the carpet to get off. She could almost reach...but not quite!

Kathryn moaned in surrender. She was not going to be allowed to come. She was being taught a lesson, she supposed.

But her body still needed the orgasm, and her lust was all-consuming.

Rogerio stepped back, surveying his handiwork. Sarah reclined in a big velvet chair, nude, smoking another cigarette and looking on disapprovingly.

"She really is a little slut," said the mistress. "She can't even control her need to come."

"If I may be allowed to urge patience, Mistress. That will come with time."

"Perhaps. Until then, she'll require constant vigilance."

"I humbly offer to provide it."

"We'll see," said the mistress. "For now, get to work on her. She's going to cool off before long."

"I humbly offer that there's little chance of that, Mistress."

Sarah laughed.

Kathryn turned to see Rogerio undressing. His body was big and muscled and she saw, as he opened his pants, that his cock was very large. But what shocked Kathryn was that it was totally soft. Rogerio must have had incredible control—that, or he was just doing a job, and Kathryn was nothing more than a trainee.

Rogerio saw Kathryn looking him over, but he didn't react. He was truly a gorgeous man, though Kathryn was so hot she would have found anyone gorgeous.

Rogerio picked Kathryn up with his hands under her arms, and his cock brushed against her shoulders. Rogerio dragged Kathryn over in front of a big black easy chair, placing her in her imposed kneeling position on the floor. Then Rogerio seated himself in the chair, placed his hand on Kathryn's head, and guided her down to his crotch.

Kathryn had always loved giving head. She had surrendered to the knowledge that she would not be allowed an orgasm, but her body still pounded with the heat and blood of sexual need. Almost without knowing what she was doing, completely surrendered to Rogerio's will and that of her mistress, she lowered her mouth on his soft cock and began to run her tongue over it. She was overwhelmed with pleasure and satisfaction as she felt the cock growing in her mouth. She kept licking, all over it, slathering her saliva over the sensitive head. Rogerio's cock swelled and the head grew thick inside her mouth; she swirled her tongue around it and lowered herself onto the cock.

She felt the thick length of flesh pressing against her tongue, the head at the very top of her throat. Kathryn wanted to deep-throat him, but she needed him harder, first. She almost felt as though she was going down on a favorite boyfriend, a man she loved to please. But Rogerio was Sarah's butler, her servant, and Kathryn was a slave to both of them. Knowing this only made her desire worse.

Kathryn gave herself over fully and took Rogerio's cock down into her throat.

She was very proud of the way she gave head; she loved doing it so much. She forced Rogerio's cock back down into her throat, pumping it in and out. She let it slip out of her mouth and caressed the head with her lips. She rubbed the saliva-slick head of his cock across her cheek. Kathryn felt ashamed that she was enjoying this so much when she didn't even know this man. But it was the most erotic thing she had ever done. Kathryn's cunt still ached for release, and she needed her orgasm badly. But she was totally engrossed in pleasing this man, in sucking his cock, in doing everything she could to please him.

Kathryn licked down the shaft to Rogerio's balls, taking each one gently into her mouth. Then she moved back up to the head, slowly, caressing every inch of the shaft with her lips and tongue, and slipped his cock back into her mouth. She could taste his precome. She sucked it off and swallowed it, remembering the delicious taste. She hadn't given head since her last boyfriend,

Carl, dumped her. She loved it, and she poured her desire into it, trying to blot out the pounding needs of her own cunt.

She let his cock slip out again and rubbed it over her face, aroused by the feel and the smell. She bit the shaft gently, squirming against the cuffs and the wooden bar, wishing she could curve her hand around the cock and rub it against her tongue rapidly. But she was restrained, and she had to rely on her mouth alone. She started wondering what Rogerio's come tasted like. She was sure it was delicious. She hungrily smeared his precome over her cheeks and into her beautiful black hair, mingling it with her sticky saliva, then licked her way up to his cockhead and slid it back into her mouth.

She took it all the way down, this time, deep-throating it until her lips were pressed around the base of his cock. Still Rogerio did not make a sound. Kathryn kept working on it, pumping his cock in and out of her mouth, submitting wholly to him. She used her tongue and her lips and her throat, worshipping his cock. Rogerio sat impassively, his face a mask.

"Is she doing it right?"

"She's not bad. She's really enjoying herself."

"She's a little slut."

Rogerio chuckled. "Only sluts really love to suck cock."

That made Kathryn go at it with a newfound fervor, working Rogerio's cock in and out of her mouth more quickly. She could feel her cunt, wet, hovering a few inches above the wooden bar. She desperately sucked at Rogerio's cock, fantasizing about the taste of his come, wanting him to release himself in her mouth.

Kathryn realized with horror that Sarah had told him to hold off for as long as he could.

Kathryn wasn't even going to be allowed this release right away. She wouldn't taste Rogerio's come until she had exhausted herself.

She knew if she gave up trying, it would take even longer. Kathryn always wished that her boyfriends would hold out longer while she was giving head—but she knew that Rogerio would hold out until she was worn out and gasping.

Just knowing that, Kathryn wanted to suck him off even more.

She plunged his shaft down her throat, feeling the head thick and hot inside her. She moved up and began sucking around the head, hungrily tonguing the sensitive underside. She worked it in and out, wishing she could use her hands to satisfy him, wishing she could jerk him off into her mouth. That always worked. But she had to rely on her lips and tongue, and she kept thrusting his cock into her, hungrily swallowing it over and over again.

Rogerio did not make a sound. He reclined in the chair and let Kathryn work on him. He must have been enjoying it, since he was still hard. But he didn't even grunt.

"Mistress, if I could be allowed to smoke a cigarette?"

Kathryn looked up in horror, letting Rogerio's cock slide out of her mouth. She was offended, insulted, horrified that she was boring him so. Sarah's harsh voice cut through her surprise.

"No one told you to stop sucking his cock, did they, you little slut?"

Kathryn paused, on the verge of tears. She looked over at Sarah, whose rage grew on her face. Kathryn lowered her head and started going down on Rogerio again.

Sarah spoke angrily. "Fucking willful little slut. She thinks she can decide what to do. She thinks she owns her own body. We've got our work cut out for us if John is going to bother wasting his time with this slut."

She handed Rogerio the pack of cigarettes and a clean ashtray from the coffee table. Rogerio set the ashtray on the arm of the chair. He lit a cigarette and smoked it absently, flicking the ashes into the ashtray. Occasionally a few ashes settled into Kathryn's hair.

Kathryn kept working on him, overwhelmed with shame. She was sure she wasn't pleasing him, that her blowjob wasn't good enough. She felt tears dribbling down her cheeks and onto Rogerio's cock, and she tasted their salt as she drank his prick into her mouth again.

"Mistress, I think she's lost interest," said Rogerio.

Sarah's voice was angry and threatening. "Is that true, Kathryn, you little slut? Think you've given enough head for now? You want to give up?"

Kathryn let the cock slip out of her mouth, hiding her tears behind the thick veil of her hair. "No, Mistress."

"Then ask me for permission."

Kathryn choked back a sob. But her body was still aching in desire, and she did want to feel Rogerio come in her mouth. She wanted to taste him.

Forcing down her shame, she said, "Please, Mistress, may I be allowed to continue sucking Rogerio's cock?"

"I don't care," said Sarah. "Keep it going."

Kathryn returned to sucking his cock. She did it with renewed fervor, desperately wanting to make him come. She used all her tricks, trying to satisfy him as he calmly ignored her and smoked another several cigarettes. Her jaw and tongue ached. Her head was spinning with the smell and feel of his cock, and her whole body seemed filled with the sharp taste of his precome. She knew he had to come eventually, and she wanted it to be in her mouth. But Kathryn was delirious with exhaustion.

"Mistress," said Rogerio calmly. "I think she's almost ready to go upstairs."

"Very well. Then go ahead and ask me."

"Please, Mistress, may I be allowed to orgasm in the slave's mouth?"

"Kathryn?"

Kathryn hesitated a second, but she let Rogerio's cock slide out just long enough to say hoarsely, "Please, Mistress, may I be allowed to receive Rogerio's climax in my mouth?"

"Only if you promise to submit later, willingly, to punishment for trying to orgasm without permission."

Kathryn didn't know how to respond to that. She said, "Yes, Mistress."

"Very well, then. I give permission to both of you."

Kathryn began to take down Rogerio's cock, hungrily servicing it. She moaned softly as she felt the first pulses coming. Then she tasted his spurt, felt his warm fluid filling her mouth. She swallowed gratefully and continued to suck him until she was sure he'd finished. Then she let her head rest in his lap.

Kathryn saw the sunlight slanting through the windows and realized that the day had passed while she was here in the parlor. The parlor was almost pitch black. She couldn't believe it had been the whole day that she had worked on these two—or they on her, depending on which way you looked at it. She felt exhausted and just wanted to sleep. But her orgasm, still necessary, wouldn't let her sleep, even though she felt warm and very comfortable with her head in Rogerio's lap and her cheek against his soft cock.

A few moments of silence passed. Then Sarah said, "You know if you release her for a moment, just to move her upstairs, she'll try to orgasm."

Kathryn was still on the brink of orgasm, more or less, but she knew it would take several minutes for her to come. Just the same, if they released her, she knew she probably couldn't help herself.

"Quite right, Mistress. Even if I keep her wrists bound behind her, she can rub her thighs together as she walks. She'll have her orgasm for sure, and that would require more punishment than we could possibly give her."

"The current arrangement won't allow her to move, and she would be awkward to carry." Sarah stood over Kathryn, considering the problem.

"A stretcher?"

"I think that's the only way. See to it, Rogerio. She'll be taken upstairs and secured to the bed, in the proper position. Make sure her clitoris can't have any contact— she comes very easily."

Rogerio eased Kathryn's head out of his lap. Sarah took his place, and as Rogerio began to dress, Sarah smiled down at Kathryn.

"You'll rest soon, my dear. But for now, you've more work to do. Don't worry; you know I have less self-control than Rogerio." Sarah spread her legs, pulling Kathryn forward in between them.

After Rogerio left for the stretcher, Kathryn remained on her knees before the mistress. She obediently serviced the mistress's cunt again, sucking on the clitoris since Sarah had told her that's what she liked after a few orgasms. Sarah did appreciate the attention paid to her clit, and ordered Kathryn on to a new frenzy of cunt-eating. When Sarah was very close to orgasm, but holding off just to make Kathryn work harder, the mistress started moaning insults, telling Kathryn what a worthless whore she was. Kathryn heard the insults (she had always liked dirty talk during sex, though it sometimes embarrassed her), but what she answered to were the angry demands for more urgent services. Sarah threatened and cajoled, egging Kathryn on. Kathryn, desperately hoping that if she served the mistress properly she would be allowed to come, did her best to please.

The taste of Sarah's cunt was sharp and delicious after the subtle bitterness of Rogerio's semen, and Kathryn found that even though she was bound and submissive, she was enjoying herself more than ever. Now that she had satisfied the mistress twice, Kathryn knew she could do it a third time, and she wanted very badly for Sarah to come. Kathryn didn't know what was coming over her, but she was drowning in desire for Sarah's delectable cunt.

Sarah's hips rocked in time with Kathryn's tongue. The moans grew louder and the insults and demands grew vaguer and softer. Sarah began to play with her own nipples, pinching them eagerly.

Finally the mistress orgasmed, clasping her thighs around Kathryn's face so that Kathryn felt as if she was going to suffocate. The sound of the mistress moaning in release heightened the desire coursing through Kathryn's body; also, Kathryn imagined that now that she had satisfied Sarah, perhaps she could come herself. She had no choice but to remain on her knees, bound to the wooden post, and Kathryn's face remained in the mistress's delicious cunt. Kathryn breathed as deeply as she could, acutely aware of her own need pounding in her cunt.

Rogerio didn't come back for what seemed like a long time. As the two women waited, Sarah stroked Kathryn's hair soothingly and smoked a cigarette, giving Kathryn a drag every now and then. Sarah talked casually; she told Kathryn that the bar she was cuffed to was called a "spreader bar." It was for very disobedient slaves who needed to be restrained completely, and Sarah suspected Kathryn would be wearing one quite a lot.

In some strange way, Kathryn was soothed by Sarah's gentle but contemptuous talk. She felt enveloped, warmly cared for, protected. With her face in Sarah's lap and her body supported by Sarah's knees, her nude form being caressed by the fire, Kathryn fell into an erotic half-sleep while Sarah caressed her head.

† † †

Kathryn awoke to a more urgent pounding in her crotch. She couldn't recall who she was for a moment, or where she was, only that she needed release—sexual release. It was very dark, and she seemed enveloped in warmth. She could smell the moist, musky heat of Sarah's cunt very close to her face. She could still taste it in her mouth. Kathryn would have slipped her hand between her legs to masturbate, but she was restrained.

Kathryn felt Rogerio's strong arms around her, and it all came back to her in a delicious but terrifying flash. Kathryn looked around with her sleepy eyes and was conscious of the fact that there were two more men there as well. The winter sky had gone to black outside the windows, and the parlor had no lamps. Only the light from the dying fire illuminated the forms that controlled Kathryn. She relaxed into Rogerio's arms as he lifted her out of the mistress's lap and unfastened the cuffs that held her wrists to the wooden post. Leaving the cuffs on Kathryn's wrists, Rogerio released them from the post so that Kathryn's legs were still spread wide by the yard-long piece of wood. So exhausted was Kathryn that as her arms came free she didn't even think of reaching for her inflamed sex to try to get off; the agony in her clitoris and cunt had dwindled to an ache, and her arms were weak from being held in one position. But Rogerio was prudent, and insistent. He kept very firm hold of her wrists, ensuring that she could not get free as one of the other men took hold of the wooden bar and lifted her lower half into the air.

Kathryn was set on a wide board and her wrists were padlocked over her head, wide apart. Her ankles were similarly fastened to the board, the spreader bar still attached. She was spread-eagled, unable to move or protest. Freed thus from all responsibility, Kathryn suddenly felt very safe.

Sarah appeared above Kathryn, kneeling on the carpet, still

nude. Her hand traveled up the inside of Kathryn's thigh. Kathryn shivered at the touch, and Sarah's hand moved into her crotch.

"She's still on the edge, I hope, isn't she?" Sarah began to stroke Kathryn's throbbing clit, and an excruciating bolt of delicious agony went through Kathryn.

"Oh, God," she moaned through drowsy fog, heat building up in her still-wet cunt. "Keep doing that!"

The hand disappeared from her cunt and Kathryn felt a sudden slap on her face. She gasped, drawn out of her pleasant semi-slumber in a rush. Her face and breasts seemed to flush hot with shame.

"I believe the correct statement is 'Please, Mistress, please keep doing that.'"

Sarah's hand slipped to Kathryn's cunt again, and her fingers deftly began stroking Kathryn's thick, swollen lips and hard clit.

Kathryn said breathlessly, through a fog of near-orgasm; "Please, Mistress, please keep doing that."

Sarah smiled vaguely as her hand caressed Kathryn. Kathryn began to moan, louder, begging the mistress to keep stroking her. She couldn't believe how good that felt. She was going to come soon. The mistress was a genius, and knew all about her cunt....

Sarah changed what she was doing slightly, and Kathryn felt her orgasm slip away. But she was still riding the crest, very close to it. It grew stronger as Sarah began to play with Kathryn's nipples. Kathryn moaned and whimpered, thrashing about against her bonds, on the torturous brink of orgasm once again. Sarah removed her hands.

"Oh, God, Mistress," groaned Kathryn in agony. "Please, Mistress, don't stop doing that...."

Sarah ignored Kathryn, and bent forward, letting her mouth close around Kathryn's nipple. Kathryn choked back a sob of frustration as pleasure flowed into her, her orgasm slipping just out of reach. Sarah worked both nipples, one with her mouth, one with her hand, just as she'd done before. Kathryn was kept in moaning, panting frustration on the stretcher.

Finally, when she knew she had tortured Kathryn to the brink of madness, Sarah kissed her very deeply, passionately. Kathryn returned the kiss with hunger and desperation.

With a nod from the mistress, the two faceless men, who had been watching the whole time, lifted the stretcher and Kathryn up into the air and bore her out of the parlor.

Kathryn moaned softly, looking up into the dark, seeking the faces of the two men. But the whole mansion seemed to be dark, and Kathryn couldn't see anything. She didn't know how the two men could walk in the dark.

Kathryn was carried very, very gently up three flights of stairs and down a long corridor. Her thoughts wandered over the taste of Sarah's cunt and Rogerio's cock, over how her jaw ached and how much she needed to come and to pee. She didn't feel the least bit hungry, though. Deep in her mind, she thought without humor that she had, after all, been eating all day.

She was still very warm, though, and she was so exhausted that she started to drop off to sleep despite the aching need in her body.

The room she was brought to was in near-total darkness. Kathryn was dimly aware of being untied, lifted off of the stretcher, and laid facedown on an incredibly soft bed. A single candle flared into life. The bed felt comfortable and seductive, begging her to fall into a dreamless sleep. She couldn't be sure if it really was velvet underneath her, against her breasts, against her thighs and face, but it felt like the most expensive, luxurious velvet in the world. Strong hands continued their work on her body, and she felt someone touching her cunt very gently, but firmly. The agonized pleasure raged through her again, and she was aware that she was still on the edge of orgasm. Kathryn's whole naked body twitched and jerked and she moaned, softly, helplessly. The hand disappeared from her cunt and Kathryn felt her arms being stretched out. The cuffs were still on her wrists and ankles, and she was tied in those four places to the posts of the bed. Kathryn was spread-eagled, facedown, and once again she could not bring her thighs together.

An arm around her waist lifted her hips well off of the bed, and several silk pillows were placed underneath her belly. This lifted her crotch several inches above the bedspread, and shattered even the vague hope that she might be able to rub against the bed and bring herself some pleasure. Another silk pillow was placed under her head, and Kathryn found that, in fact, she was quite comfortable. She felt well cared for, knowing that these strong hands could control her. Her full bladder and the incredible itch in her cunt that demanded satisfaction was almost bearable in this delicious, warm cocoon.

Across the room, as Kathryn was placed in position, was Sarah. Kathryn heard her laughing. Then Sarah told her, "My little slave, you now have permission to have your orgasm. But only one."

Kathryn barely heard it. What good was Sarah's permission if she couldn't move? Sarah left the room, closing the door behind her, as the men checked Kathryn's bonds, making sure she was totally immobilized and secure. Then they blew out the candle. One of the men's hands slid gently over Kathryn's ass and down the inside of her thigh, and the feel made Kathryn's flesh feel electric, her cunt open and ready. The hand disappeared and Kathryn's hunger flowed through her.

It took her several minutes to realize that the men had gone away. She had been left alone on this bed, bound so that she couldn't move or touch herself. Just knowing that made her fantasies flare, and Kathryn's body began to ache with desire anew.

She was tied so that her cunt was very exposed. That made it worse, made her hornier, knowing that anyone who came along could do anything they wanted to her. Who would come along, though? She was locked in the bedroom, alone.

Kathryn drifted into sleep again, unaware of anything but her need. Her dreams were of violent intercourse, of men with huge cocks fucking her. But Kathryn couldn't come, and she had never been so jealous of men, who could have wet dreams. Kathryn was sure she would have had one.

The smells overwhelmed her as she slept: the smell of her own body and of the perfumed silk pillows with their sandalwood-musk scent, and most of all the smell of Sarah's cunt, permeating her memory.

Kathryn awoke hot in pitch blackness, sheened faintly with sweat. Her bladder was painfully full. She whimpered and groaned, once again unsure where she was. She looked around, half expecting to see her apartment in the Mission, and the view of the park from her window. But she could see nothing, and when she tried to move and couldn't, the hunger came flooding back to her.

Kathryn let her eyes flutter open a few times, then held them open, desperately wanting to be awake and to think. The day dribbled back to her in the faintest memories. The room was almost pitch black, lit only by the moonless night outside, and it wasn't until several minutes had passed that Kathryn became aware of the smooth pair of feminine thighs so close to the edge of the bed.

Kathryn gasped, a little surprised that Sarah had returned.

Kathryn had expected to be left alone until morning, forced to suffer with her aching desire. She was exhausted, and not really ready to take part in any further playing, but she had given over control of her life to Sarah (and John), and she was willing to keep going if Sarah requested it. Kathryn had enjoyed eating Sarah out, even if the whole scene was a little heavy for her, and she would do it again if given the chance. In fact, she could do it now, here on this soft velvet bedspread.

Kathryn felt a soft touch on the back of her head, stroking her hair. The smell of the sandalwood and musk were in her nostrils, but she caught the delicious odor of Sarah's cunt, very close to her.

Sarah lowered herself to her knees, leaning forward against the bed. Kathryn parted her lips as Sarah began to kiss her. The kiss was more tender than before, and the lips seemed full and soft. Kathryn's eyes gazed into the dark and then fluttered closed as the delicious sensation of the woman's kiss overwhelmed her. Sarah slipped her tongue into Kathryn's mouth, and it felt different than before: gentle, more teasing, less insistent. Kathryn felt her desire rising as Sarah slipped her hand more fully into her hair and lifted Kathryn's head just enough to give her a fuller, deeper kiss.

Kathryn moaned softly, hungry for Sarah's tongue. The tenderness in the kiss was incredible—so unlike Sarah's previous kisses. Kathryn surrendered to Sarah's mouth and tongue and felt her nipples hardening against the velvet and silk. She breathed deeply and could smell a spicy, sexy perfume. Kathryn sighed as Sarah pulled away from her.

Sarah moved to the side of the bed, her hand running down Kathryn's naked form. Kathryn could feel the strong hand on her ass, stroking her flesh, gently slipping into the cleft and parting her cheeks. The fingertips traveled down the inside of her thigh, up and down, very gently, and Kathryn became acutely aware of the fact that she still had not had an orgasm after the torturous teasing of the day. Sarah's fingertips strayed very close to Kathryn's cunt, but didn't quite touch. The fingers then moved back up Kathryn's side as Sarah climbed onto the bed and lay down on top of Kathryn.

The legs spread their way around Kathryn's ass, and the soft bush of pubic hair rubbed against the swell of Kathryn's cheeks. Sarah's breasts settled against Kathryn's back and she was astonished at how large they felt. They had seemed smaller in the parlor. The supple tongue slid up Kathryn's shoulder, toward her ear, and Sarah's hand worked its way between their two bodies so she could pinch and knead the flesh of Kathryn's cheeks. Kathryn sighed contentedly, as Sarah's hand worked her flesh and then moved around, under her belly, to touch her breasts. Kathryn moaned as Sarah began to pinch her nipples. The tongue slithered into Kathryn's ear, teasing and tickling her, and Kathryn felt Sarah nibbling at the lobe flirtatiously. Sarah's breasts, with their very hard nipples, moved slightly and invitingly against Kathryn's back. Then Sarah, with her free hand, pulled Kathryn's long hair up sensuously, bunching it on top of her head. The other hand continued to work on Kathryn's nipples, pinching and stroking them, teasing them into full erection. Kathryn's whimper escaped her lips in a hungry, desperate plea. She had been prepared to service the woman's cunt again, but not to be teased in such a delicious way.

Then Sarah's teeth descended on the back of Kathryn's neck, and a shudder went through the girl's naked body. Kathryn let out an uncontrolled moan, overcome by a shivering sensation as Sarah began to gnaw and suck at the back of her neck, at the center, between her shoulders. It was a teasing, tingling sensation, and Kathryn's whole body responded. Sarah continued to stroke Kathryn's breasts as the pressure of her teeth increased. Kathryn snuggled deeper into the soft silk and velvet, and Sarah's fingers pinched her nipple harder.

"Oh, God, Mistress, yes, that's so good.... Thank you, thank you...."

Kathryn heard a laugh, a soft, tinkling sound. Kathryn's eyes opened and she tried to twist, to look. It didn't sound like Sarah. The smell was different, she realized. Kathryn panicked as it came to her that the woman who was making love to her wasn't Sarah.

The breasts were indeed heavier, and larger, and the woman's hips were broader. Kathryn's head spun as it struck her in full force that she was responding, submitting, to a woman she had never seen and couldn't see.

"Who are you?" she asked, her voice hoarse.

The woman's mouth traveled from the back of her neck to Kathryn's ear. The tongue darted out and teased Kathryn a little as the woman whispered soothingly: "Shhhhh...don't say a word, or I'll have to gag you, you little slut." The words were said in such a caressing, gentle manner that Kathryn almost didn't realize that she was being called a slut. Instead, she let her head fall to the pillow as the woman lifted her hair more insistently and dug her teeth into the soft flesh of Kathryn's shoulder and neck.

Kathryn let out a groan, unable to keep herself from responding. She surrendered to the woman's hands and mouth as the woman worked on her breasts. Kathryn thought she was going to explode. Her whole body tingled with desire. She could feel from the weight of the woman's body that she was large-breasted and that her hips were wide and powerful, though she wasn't very heavy. And her hands were very strong.

The woman's hand released Kathryn's hair, but Kathryn didn't move her head to stop the gnawing at the back of her neck. Instead,

Kathryn relaxed into the bed as the hands descended on her, one on her breasts, the other wedging itself between her legs.

The woman's fingers moved into Kathryn's cunt, and Kathryn felt herself being penetrated. The sensations were incredible, and the woman didn't have long fingernails like Sarah. Two fingers went into her while the thumb flicked her clitoris. Kathryn was about to come.

The woman seemed to sense it, and her hand slid back to caress Kathryn's ass. Kathryn whimpered in frustration, but her arousal was so heightened that she wanted to be teased further. The woman kept manipulating Kathryn's breasts, stroking them, pinching the nipples, as she got to her knees over Kathryn.

Kathryn felt the woman's large breasts rubbing against the back of her head. The woman checked Kathryn's bonds, making sure they were very secure. Then she lifted herself off of Kathryn, standing beside the bed.

Kathryn lay there, trussed, afraid that the woman was going to leave her. Kathryn had never been touched like that, on the back of the neck, and she wanted more. She needed more. She heard herself moaning softly.

Kathryn heard a door opening and closing and a lock turning. She heard footsteps—heavier than the woman's. She heard the wet sound of a kiss, but no words.

"Who's there?" Kathryn whispered softly.

The woman's lips were against her ear. "Remember what I told you?" the woman asked sternly. Kathryn felt her lips being parted by the woman's fingers, and she obediently opened her mouth. Something was pushed in, and before Kathryn knew it, she had been gagged. It was some sort of a padded ball, the size of a large egg, and it tasted of fresh leather. Straps fastened it around the back of her head, and the woman buckled it quickly.

Kathryn whimpered and tried to speak, but found that she couldn't. Being immobilized that much further served to take her deeper into her dreamland. Kathryn submitted to her fate and to the will of the woman she couldn't see.

The woman's hand was on her ass again. Kathryn felt it stroking, prodding, coming close to her cunt. She heard the wet sound of kisses again. The woman had brought her someone new. Kathryn felt the woman's hand sliding into her crotch, two fingers, parting her cuntlips, which were swollen with lust. Kathryn shivered at the touch.

There was a weight on the bed. She felt someone behind her with strong, thick legs and hairy knees planted in between hers. It was a man. Kathryn was going to be fucked.

She relaxed into the bed, her head spinning with mixed thoughts and feelings. She could do nothing, though, but surrender to the will of her owners. She relaxed and moaned softly behind the gag.

The woman tugged Kathryn's netherlips slightly farther apart, and the man's hands came to rest on the cheeks of Kathryn's ass. With her other hand, the woman guided the man's cock up to the entrance to Kathryn's cunthole. The head felt very thick.

The hands slid skillfully around, taking possession of Kathryn's hips and holding her body in position. The cockhead began to penetrate her.

Her cunt was on fire from the woman's caresses, and Kathryn groaned, very loud and uncontrolled, behind the leather gag as she felt the thick head spreading her open and entering her cunt. Waves of pressure throbbed into her as she surrendered to the thick shaft. Her cunt was filled, and the man's hips settled up against her ass.

Kathryn could feel the woman's fingertips curved around the base of the man's cock, brushing Kathryn's cunt and thighs, feeling him enter Kathryn. She could tell that the woman was kissing the man, and that Kathryn was like a gift from her to him—or him to her. Once again, Kathryn was barely an object, and this made her feel better about surrendering to the pleasure and enjoying anonymous sex like this. In fact, it allowed her to give up responsibility and fade deliciously into the sensations of her naked body.

The man began to fuck her, slowly, sensuously, inserting his cock with cruel tenderness as he kissed the woman. The woman's hand traveled over Kathryn's back, feeling the way it arched when the man thrust into Kathryn's wetness. Then the hand returned to the cock, feeling its shaft, slick with Kathryn's juices, pumping into the vulnerable, willing body. The woman tousled Kathryn's hair and reached around to stroke her face with the hand that smelled, deliciously, like Kathryn's own cunt. Kathryn hardly realized it until she could feel her lips, around the leather gag, being stroked by the woman's deft fingertips, which coated Kathryn's sensitive lips with slick juices. The man began to fuck Kathryn with greater urgency as the woman climbed onto the bed again. She lay with her nude body fully against Kathryn's side, and her mouth descended once again on the back of Kathryn's neck.

Kathryn bit against the gag as the woman's teeth began to scrape and gnaw at the back of her neck. She had never known what an erogenous zone that was for her, but now she was completely controlled by the feel of the woman nibbling at her back there. And as the man's cock thrust inside her and his rough, possessing hands encircled her hips, Kathryn knew the man and the woman were going to make her come.

Sarah had given Kathryn permission to orgasm, so there was nothing to be done. She was going to receive release at long last, and before the man satisfied himself inside her.

Kathryn moaned, mouth still filled by the leather gag. She was going to be brought off. She was going to climax.

The woman's hands worked their way around Kathryn's body and took hold of her breasts, one each. Kathryn felt her nipples being played with, sending shivers into her body as the pounding in her cunt grew more insistent. The man had not made a sound, but his hips were moving faster, his cock hammering into Kathryn like a piston, more quickly, deeper, harder. The woman fell completely on top of Kathryn as the man took firmer hold of her hips. The woman's breasts pushed against Kathryn's back, and her hands pinched Kathryn's nipples as her mouth bit at Kathryn's shoulders and neck. Then Kathryn felt the tongue sliding into her ear, and she wished she wasn't wearing the gag so that she could scream in ecstasy.

There was a grunt from behind her, and Kathryn felt the man fucking her harder. Kathryn was right on the edge.

The woman reached down, releasing one of Kathryn's breasts. She slid her hand down Kathryn's body and Kathryn almost passed out as she realized what the woman was doing.

The fingertips pressed against Kathryn's clitoris, and she soared over the edge. Her groans were only partially muffled by the leather gag as the orgasm exploded through her body. Her entire nude form bucked and jerked, and she felt she was passing into some sort of drug high. A terrible ache went through her pelvis, the bunched-up arousal of a full day of sex without satisfaction. She relished the sensations, every muscle in her body going taut and then slackening as the man continued to fuck her harder than ever. The penetration felt more delicious now that she had come, and Kathryn gave herself over to it, aware that the man was going to climax inside her at any moment.

Finally, the man pulled out, and Kathryn felt the woman bending down, taking the man's cock into her mouth. The two of them leaned heavily on Kathryn's body, and Kathryn could feel the woman's head bobbing back and forth, sucking the man off, and heard his faint groans of pleasure as he orgasmed in her mouth.

The man's weight disappeared quickly, leaving only the woman on top of Kathryn. Kathryn's bladder was still full, and this had intensified her orgasm, adding to the pain of its intensity. The woman spread her legs and straddled Kathryn's ass as she reached up and began working at Kathryn's cuffs.

Kathryn heard the jingling of keys and felt her wrists coming free. The woman then unfastened Kathryn's ankles, and lastly, unbuckled the gag.

Kathryn was so stiff and exhausted that she could hardly move. The woman helped Kathryn to turn over, facing up. The woman's thumb parted Kathryn's lips, and they began to kiss.

The woman's mouth was still filled with the man's come. Kathryn felt a brief wave of revulsion, followed by acceptance, and she swallowed what she could as the woman kissed her deeply. The woman's body slid on top of Kathryn's, and Kathryn's face slipped between the woman's breasts. Guided by the woman's strong hands, Kathryn took one nipple into her mouth, only to gasp as she realized that there was a ring piercing it. Kathryn certainly knew all about piercing—it was all the rage on the Haight, and Sarah was going to pay for her to be pierced—but she hadn't expected to find this mystery woman's nipples pierced. The woman insistently pressed Kathryn's head up, and Kathryn obediently began suckling at the woman's pierced nipple, toying with the small metallic ring.

The woman moved up until she straddled Kathryn's face. Lowering herself onto Kathryn, she parted her own cuntlips with her fingers and pressed herself down on Kathryn's face.

Kathryn obediently began to eat the woman's pussy. She was shocked to feel that the woman's labia had two rings on each side, similar to the piercings in the nipples. At first Kathryn was somewhat repulsed and frightened of hurting the woman, but she became even more turned on as she traced the outline of the thick rings in the woman's cunt, then moved up to toy with the thick, hardened clit. She gave herself over to the darkness and began eating the woman's pussy with relish.

The woman tasted very different than Sarah—much sharper, more pungent, less salty. Kathryn found herself hungrily comparing the feelings of the two women's cunts. Meanwhile, the woman was moaning on top of Kathryn, rocking her hips back and forth. Kathryn's hands moved up to cup the woman's ass.

Kathryn moaned "Oh, God" as the woman lifted her body and repositioned herself so that she and Kathryn were in a "69" position, and the woman settled her mouth eagerly onto Kathryn's cunt.

In the thrall of after-orgasm, Kathryn's body quivered in pleasure—almost too much pleasure—as the woman started to lick her. After the long buildup and intense, mind-shattering orgasm, Kathryn's cunt was too sensitive, and the mouth manipulating it caused her an almost painful torture—too much stimulation at once. The woman settled on Kathryn's clit, seeming to know that the clit was what would cause Kathryn the most agony. Submitting to the darkness, though, meant that Kathryn couldn't stop the woman, couldn't make a noise, could hardly breathe—she could only suffer with this divine, overstimulating torment, aware of every tiny movement the woman's tongue made against Kathryn's clit, every second of pleasure/pain that the woman was forcing upon her. Kathryn let the unpleasant feelings flow through her body, trying to control herself so that she wouldn't lose the rhythm of her own tongue on the woman's cunt. Gripping the woman's magnificent naked ass, Kathryn thrust her tongue with urgency, working the clit and desperately wanting her to come.

The woman laughed, feeling Kathryn squirm. "Pleasure soon becomes pain, and the other way around. Isn't that right, little slut?"

With that, she dove onto Kathryn's cunt with hunger, working the clit as Kathryn strove to make her come. Kathryn let out a desperate, mournful groan as the woman tormented her. Worse, the woman parted Kathryn's cuntlips with her fingers and lifted her clit hood, exposing enough of the tender flesh underneath to make Kathryn scream in overstimulated agony. With her other hand the woman reached up and began to pinch Kathryn's nipples again, toying with them, making the torture worse. Kathryn let out another shriek and groan, afraid to beg the woman to stop after the treatment she'd received so far.

"Shhhhhhh..." The woman breathed warmly on Kathryn's aching cunt. "Be quiet, or I'll have to gag you again. I'd hate to do that. Keep your mouth working."

Kathryn tried to ignore the suffering in her sensitive clit and nipples, and worked toward the woman's orgasm, praying that she had less self-control than Rogerio or Sarah. She tongued the woman's clitoris in as perfect a rhythm as she could, trying to match the rhythm she had used on Sarah and the rhythm she herself used when masturbating. It was no use. The woman was deliberately holding off so that she could heighten her own pleasure by torturing Kathryn.

"You know how it turns me on," she said with a sigh into Kathryn's crotch, "feeling you squirm like that. If you beg me maybe I'll have an orgasm."

"Please...God, please, please come, will you? Please allow me to make you climax...."

Kathryn's back arched and her whole body twitched as the

woman's mouth descended on her cunt again, and the stimulation on her nipples increased. She began to lick the woman again, desperately trying to bring her off. Kathryn realized that it was working, that the woman's tongue on her exposed clit was getting less insistent, less powerful. The woman began to moan.

"That's more like it," she said, her hips coming down to press her cunt and clit to Kathryn's working mouth. Kathryn kept it up, and finally the woman slid two fingers into Kathryn's cunt while she worked Kathryn's clit with her thumb, causing Kathryn's body to go rigid and her breath to come short as the woman climaxed on top of her. The woman came very quickly, and her moans were very, very loud.

The woman lifted herself off of Kathryn, releasing her. Kathryn whispered a thank you, the exhaustion flooding through her. The woman curled up next to Kathryn, turning her onto the side so that she could snuggle against Kathryn's back as if they were two nested spoons. The woman's hand rested on Kathryn's breast, but she did not play with it. The hand was just a warm, protecting presence there.

The woman's breath slid warmly over Kathryn's ear as the two of them faded into sleep.

The last thing Kathryn remembered was the woman whispering to her, "It's a long time till dawn, little slave...."

Then oblivion took Kathryn even more completely than Rogerio or Sarah or the woman had taken her.

When Kathryn awoke again in the middle of the night, the woman was gone and she had been slipped under the covers. The sheets were a delightful, soft satin, and somehow a very soft, silky nightgown and a pair of panties—neither of them belonged to her—had been put on her body. Her bladder felt about to explode.

Kathryn stood in the darkness and felt around, very slowly, lost in stupor, for the door to the bathroom. She finally found it, but could not find the light switch. She managed to sit on the toilet, and though it was very painful to pee, the sensation awakened her more. She thought about the woman's cruel treatment of her cunt. Kathryn still ached, but she was more turned on than she had ever been before in the middle of the night.

She returned to bed in darkness, getting under the covers even though the room was incredibly warm. The nightgown was cut low and very thin, and felt deliciously sensuous against her body. Kathryn drifted languorously into a vague fantasy of her old boyfriend Steve. With her customary quickness, Kathryn took the panties aside and brought herself off with her hand, facedown among the soft sheets, and fell asleep again; her dreams turned to matters of surreal confusion and warm, protected, womblike spaces.

Presented in Leather

Claire Willows

I. a white form in the night

Who does not know Beaulieu-sur-Mer? Those who know it now, who have not visited that ravishing winter resort with its sumptuous villas set among palm trees, olive trees, and clusters of exotic red hibiscus flowers, may truly be pitied. Just seeing the manicured foliage surrounding the estates convinces even the superficial observer that there is class distinction among flowers as there is among peoples.

The evening that concerns our story a sultry April night the moon had disappeared behind the pines on Mt. Pacanaglia, which dominates Beaulieu and Villefranche, leaving the bay plunged into thickening night. Some automobiles were parked along the beach, and two boats were anchored on the water, while fishermen's barks everywhere balanced themselves against the soft waves of the sea. For some hours, a cable had been anchoring a yacht visible only, against the blackness of the night, because of its mast lights.

Two noises alone troubled the universal silence: the sound of the waters lapping against the boats, and the monotonous croaking of frogs. But a third noise was presently heard, produced by two oars striking the water in cadence. In a few moments, a woman enveloped in a long cloak jumped ashore.

The two men in the bark rose. One of them lifted a long white-covered bundle, bound around with thick rope and stepped over on the beach with this heavy load, while his companion balanced the boat against the water's edge.

"Be careful not to let her fall," cautioned the woman in a low voice. "Oh, she is stirring—I might have known she would! She is beginning to struggle, that nasty thing!"

"Well, it doesn't matter," responded the man.

Mounting the steps giving access to the highway, they scrutinized the night's opaque shadows anxiously.

"I see nothing," said the man.

"The machine should be there," answered the woman. "Miss Bennett distinctly promised it would be."

The man whistled softly, but there was no response. Swearing beneath his breath, the mysterious stranger deposited his burden along a low wall bordering the highway. Then he straightened up and commenced whistling again. This time a responsive whistle in the same tune came back. It appeared to have its source about one hundred yards away.

"Come!" said the woman. "I knew that an automobile would be waiting for us."

They walked toward the spot from whence the whistling came and presently perceived an automobile standing against the wall of an estate. A chauffeur stepped before them slowly.

"I this Miss Bennett's car?" asked the woman.

"It is, Madam," the chauffeur responded.

"Open the door."

The man who had been carrying the long bundle lifted it carefully from his shoulder as he approached the car and deposited it on the wide seat of the limousine, and he and the woman made themselves comfortable on the jump seats.

As the chauffeur closed the door, he heard inarticulate groans coming from the bundle and even saw it move, despite the black night. Nevertheless, he asked no questions. He started the motor and pulled away noiselessly.

No machine passed them on the road, although at this hour, usually, some of the visitors to the gaming tables at Monte Carlo are to be found en route to their homes. A few minutes later, the car swung around at the extremity of that curious quarter of Beaulieu known as Little Africa and stopped before a half-open wrought-iron gate.

A woman swung it open, permitting the car to enter the graveled inclined road which led to a grand villa constructed on a base of those enormous red rocks of which Cap Roux is constituted.

Before the entrance hung two powerful electric lamps, illuminating the white facade of the house brilliantly. On the left column at the base was lettered neatly in gold:

VILLA CLOSE

The woman who had opened the gate followed the car in. She reached the first steps of the house as the chauffeur opened the door of the limousine. The woman passenger stepped out of the machine, nodded, and asked:

"Miss Bennett?"

"Yes. Lady Price?"

"I am..."

"You have...the young person?"

"Here."

The woman pointed to the white bundle the man was lugging.

"Oh! Indeed! She is troublesome?"

"Oh, very! You will have a lot of trouble with her, you know."

Miss Bennett smiled strangely—a little harshly—revealing a wolflike expression.

"No!" she said. "We are well-equipped here and fully capable of calming these turbulent natures. Will you come in, please?"

The two visitors, with the man still pulling the burdensome load which twisted like a huge white snake under his arm, entered a spacious room decorated in yellow and furnished with a number of armchairs and restful divans.

Miss Bennett rang a bell: a door opened at once and two young women appeared, dressed in nurse's uniforms. "Take that into the Special Waiting Room," she said.

The nurses nodded understandingly and picked the bundle up without any apparent effort.

"What is this Special Waiting Room, Miss Bennett?" asked Lady Price.

"That is the room where we put all newcomers who seem too restless or nervous."

"And why in this room rather than in any other?"

"Because it is entirely padded, and..."

She stopped, glanced at the man, and then turned back to Lady Price.

"Oh, I beg your pardon," Lady Price said quickly. "I have actually forgotten to present Sir Arthur Ryan, an intimate friend. Miss Bennett, Arthur, Directress of Villa Close school, who is going to take charge of—"

"All right!" said the man. "My respects, Miss Bennett."

"You may talk, Miss Bennett," Lady Price resumed. "You were saying that the Special Waiting Room is padded, and that—"

"And that we can completely strip those who are rebellious and leave them there as long as we like for observation."

"Why strip them completely?"

"Because every person, man or woman, boy or girl, deprived of all clothes, has a clearer sense of helplessness; and you can do with that one as you will."

"Oh! I understand!" said Lady Price. "Have you prepared the contract?"

"Yes. Please step into my office." It was a large room, furnished severely with desk and chairs of black wood. On the desk lay two sheets of paper completely covered with typing. Lady Price read them, signed her name, and motioned to Sir Arthur, who pulled from his pocket a large wallet from which he extracted a batch of notes that he deposited on the desk.

"Thank you," said Miss Bennett, after having counted them. "Now, then, I shall mail you a report once a week to the addresses you will send me."

"That's fine," said Lady Price. "And unless there are some unforeseen events, you will keep her two years."

"Two years. After which we will renew this contract if need be."

"Perfect! Will you please show us out?"

The car deposited the two travelers at the steps of the dock. The little boat was waiting. The figures merged into the blackness of the night.

II. a troubling adventure

Six months after the mysterious events we have just related, a fashionably dressed young man, with the air of a rich sportsman, followed the road from Beaulieu to Monaco. It was noon, and he strolled along dreamily, puffing on a cigarette, his eyes on the road ahead. He had reached the section called Little Africa when he was startled by a noise. He distinctly heard the muffled voice of a woman!

"Sir! Stop! Look here!"

He looked around. To his right was the street and the rails of the tramway running from Nice to Monte Carlo, and a little wall surmounted by a grille, with a garden beyond. In the garden, no one. To his left, and very close to him, was a white wall with no opening but a single door, closed tightly, on which was painted: VILLA CLOSE ANNEX. He was greatly astonished, for he saw no one anywhere, and he was wondering if it could be a trick of his imagination, or if he were suffering from hallucinations, when once again he heard the same voice:

"Here! Look over here!"

More mystified than ever, he looked down toward his feet and perceived, across a grille of a tiny window not more than the width of two hands, the ravishing face of a blonde girl of a pure Anglo-Saxon type; her eyes of a profound blue, though shadowed by an indescribable anguish.

He looked down at the dusty road, made conspicuous by the rays of the sun. An automobile rushed past, leaving a cloud of dust behind it. He let it pass and bent down.

"Miss? Whom have I the honor…"

"I shall soon tell you, sir. I am urgently in need of help—can I rely on you? I have been watching you pass by at this same hour for three days…."

Her shaken voice had a definite American accent. She was trembling with fright.

"I am the aviator, Sistero, Miss. Perhaps you have heard of me?"

She blushed faintly, and her voice became excited.

"Oh! Yes, really! I have read about you! I am so happy! You are a brave man. I couldn't hope to find a better person than yourself!"

"But you, Miss?... Who are you?"

"I am an American, but a pensionnaire of...of the Villa Close, sir. But...I repeat...can I have absolute confidence in you?"

"I give you my word of honor that no person shall know whatever you may wish to confide in me, Miss."

"I am sure of it...but I am so confused now. I had prepared a diary—a sort of journal—and I should like to give it to you...but I wrote it without reflection and, really, I feel miserable when I think of a man reading it."

"Miss, you can be—"

"I know, but I keep thinking now of all the things my indignation made me write. I've told all. Oh! How could I write such things down! I daresay, sir, there are passages in it...I don't know what to call it...sometimes improper..."

"I understand very well, Miss, but you have nothing to fear, and I shall be as silent as the tomb. Confide your journal to me. But I should also like to know in what way I could be useful. Would you like me to bring this matter to the attention of the American consul?"

"Oh! That wouldn't do any good. I would only be taken out of here and put somewhere else. Here is my diary, sir. Read it and take whatever decision seems to you the best, but do not forget that I am begging for help."

Still leaning over the rail, Sistero searched the marvelous face of the blonde across the little grille.

"And if I get you out of here?" he stammered, trembling at his own audacity.

The marvelous beauty of the strange girl added to the mysterious quality of the conversation, and he divined that he was about to participate in an adventure of the greatest daring, involving a young lady from the best society.

A lively color spread over the young girl's cheeks. "How can you get me out of this place?" she asked. "I am so perplexed, I don't know how you could get into the Villa Close."

"Oh, well, but...what about here?"

"Oh!" she said reprovingly, believing that he was jesting.

"I am serious, Miss. Tonight, could you get near this grille again?"

"I do not know...I shall try, but then what?"

"I shall come with my mechanic. We will pick some of the stones away, and you can pass through. Afterward, I shall lead you to a yacht belonging to one of my best friends, and tomorrow we will fly away to some quiet spot on the Italian Riviera. Is that clear?"

"I shall like to shake your hand," she answered. "It's understood, then. But how sorry I am that I revealed my indignation and wrote everything down so—oh, how should I say it?—as frankly as I did. So much the worse, but perhaps you'll forgive me, won't you?"

"Oh! How can you doubt it? I had better go along now; someone may come. What hour would you prefer that we attempt your escape?"

"Midnight. Everybody is asleep here then."

"Good. At midnight. Good-bye, Miss."

He hastened away, after taking one fond look at the girl who was already beginning to trouble the depths of his soul. He clutched the mass of written sheets she had delivered to him, burning with impatience to dig into them for the solution of her mysterious predicament.

III. the manuscript

Jean Sistero was thirty-one years old, possessed of a modest inheritance bequeathed to him without any restrictions. He devoted himself almost exclusively to his particular hobby, aviation. Thanks to his courage and composure, he had quickly become one of the most world-renowned aviators. At this particular time, he was piloting a hydroplane that could be seen each day resting on the blue waters between Beaulieu and Monaco, or else somewhere between Menton and San Remo. For the present, he was occupying a large apartment at the Brighton Palace Hotel, from the window of which he could see his gigantic seabird balancing near the beach.

Abandoning his earlier project to visit one of his friends, he returned to the hotel, threw himself into an armchair, and plunged right into the variety of sheets of irregular size which constituted the manuscript. These sheets were covered with fine writing, crowded, nervous, sometimes almost illegible. It was evident that the lines had been written under the influence of intense emotion. He started reading, surprised at feeling his heart thump a sensation he was a stranger to, even in the many battles he had waged against hostile air currents.

We shall spare the reader a further analysis of the variety of sentiments he experienced through the long reading of the manuscript and shall content ourselves by proceeding forthwith to the "Journal" in which Flora Price had certainly, in spite of herself, unwittingly revealed a strange charm and sensuality to which Sistero was definitely not insensible. It was a series of separate pieces, curious and strange pictures painted in rapid strokes, complaints, considerations, and reflections. Most of the pages were written in pencil; only a few in ink.

There were crudely formed sentences, mixed tenses and awkwardly expressed thoughts; but, on the other hand, some of the episodes were reported more vividly and written better than the average author might have done. Naturally, that was made possible chiefly by the fact that she experienced the events related, while the professional author could only imagine them. Then, also, the very unevenness in the style of her writing was the best proof of her honesty, and gave the most convincing evidence of the true nature of her present life.

Sistero read:

I write these pages for two reasons: the first is that I wish to find some relief for my distress and anguish; the second, I hope to be able to throw this someday to some passerby who may be able to help me. A mad hope, I think, for I am well guarded! But still I hope.

I must first of all present myself: Flora Price, of Chicago. I am nineteen years old, an orphan, and until recently I lived with my aunt, who has been exceedingly wicked to me. A man—an unscrupulous adventurer—won her confidence. I do not know what they are up to together, but since he arrived on the scene, she has become more and more cruel toward me. I suspect that they want to rid themselves of me, as well as capture my small inheritance, and if they could have disposed of me surely and simply, they would not have hesitated.

Three months ago we left for Europe on board a yacht which

my aunt purchased. It was the *Kadidja*, a very pretty and comfortable boat. What a beautiful voyage that might have been if I did not have my aunt and this man for company! (I can name no names in this diary. I can only confide them verbally to the person who will help me out of here. At least, that is my present idea.)

No sooner were we aboard than my aunt thrust me into a narrow cabin, very badly situated down below. I had to take my meals all alone. I had no complaint about that because her society and that of her friend were odious to me. I passed the long hours reading and dreaming, and little by little I became attracted to the gentleness and sweet disposition of a little mulattress about eighteen years old, the maid charged to look after my tiny room. I could not converse with the vulgar sailors whose features were absolutely repugnant to me, I believe that my aunt and her friend had especially chosen them for their brutality, it was then quite natural that I should become attached to this young girl whose name was Dora, and who was my only companion. But my aunt kept a stern eye on her. She sent for the girl and forbade her to exchange henceforth any unnecessary word with me, and to confine herself strictly to the services it was her duty to perform. My surprise was very great when I saw the change in Dora's attitude, and I was deeply perplexed at the reason therefor. I had to question her at great length before I was finally able to learn that the sudden change was due to the express order she had received from my aunt. My indignation was so intense that I complained vigorously about this cruel and vexatious interdiction. My aunt contented herself with a shrug of her shoulders and a grim smile. Not a single word of explanation did she advance.

This one-sided conversation took place one morning, but in the course of the same afternoon, one of my aunt's two maids came looking for me. Both of those maids were powerfully built girls, ugly and ill-tempered. I detested them both, and I made no effort to conceal my intense dislike. Their names were Jenny and Elise.

When I arrived in the little rear salon, I found my aunt, her friend, Dora, and Elise present. Dora's face was red and wet with tears. Jenny closed the door behind me carefully and placed herself near my side. I was in a state of deep anguish.

"Flora," said my aunt, "I have forbidden this girl to address any words to you except those absolutely necessary in the course of her work. She has deliberately disobeyed me and has repeated to you the confidential orders I gave her. As to you, you have not only demonstrated defiance to my will, but have also attempted to reproach me. I certainly do not intend to tolerate such acts here. Dora is a young servant who deserves to be chastised severely. I have ordered you brought here so you may witness the infliction of her chastisement. Elise, prepare Dora!"

I trembled in all my limbs, but it was with indignation rather than with fear.

"Oh!" I cried. "You cannot do anything like that before me! That is shameful! I forbid you to—"

I had no opportunity to continue. On a signal from my aunt, Jenny seized both my arms and pulled them behind me. Before I could make the least movement to prevent it, my wrists were tied and secured to a chair on which Jenny forced me. And as I cried out with all my strength, she gagged me. Then I witnessed the first of a many, many spectacles to come in which I had to play a role of humiliation and suffering.

Elise ordered Dora to kneel on the chair where she was sitting, and the poor girl obeyed, while clasping her hands and begging for pity. The maid pulled her hands behind and tied the wrists together above the loins, after which she pulled a long cord tightly around her legs, thus preventing Dora from changing position.

I tried to disengage my hands, but the cords which held them were much too solid. I only succeeded in bruising my wrists and arms. The gag silenced me effectively. I understood that I had no choice but to resign myself to my aunt's will. I looked at her and her friend. They did not seem to be at all disturbed or angry. My aunt's lips were pressed tightly together, and her eyes seemed half-closed. But I could still see the wickedness in them. Meanwhile, her companion was swaying back and forth in a rocking chair, his hands closed over his stomach, a sanctimonious expression on his face.

Elise stepped behind Dora, picked up the girl's skirts and pinned them to her shoulders, and then she pulled her bloomers down to her calves.

Why do I go into all these details? Because I want to demonstrate to the person who reads these lines what sort of people I have had to deal with, how strangely cynical they all are, and how urgent it is that someone come to my aid. And when I recall these facts and those which followed, I become beside myself with indignation and abandon all discretion. I had resolved to conceal certain names—now I shall write them. Lady Eleanor Price, my aunt; Sir Arthur Ryan, her friend; and Miss Bennett, the Directress of Villa Close.

I was saying that Elise prepared the clothes of the unfortunate girl, who doubtless must have been aware of certain dire consequences to let herself be handled that way without putting up a desperate battle, as anyone should have expected. Nevertheless, her intense shame was clearly visible; despite her fright and anguish, her face was as red as if it had been slapped continually and violently. I also had the strangest feeling, very difficult to compare unless possibly to shame, when I saw Dora's body right before my eyes—a beautifully formed body, the most shocking portions of which they were exposing for the purpose of beating cruelly.

"Elise," said my aunt, "take hold of this good strap beside me and lash Dora's bottom. Be firm and severe, and pay no attention to the guilty girl's supplications or tears; let her have thirty-six hard lashes with all your strength. That will be sufficient, I think, Arthur?"

"I think so," he replied.

Elise took hold of the strap and placed herself at the left of Dora who was already groaning in anticipation of what was ahead. I remember that at this moment I was praying for a great storm to arise suddenly and shake the boat so hard that my aunt's project could not be executed. But the sea was perfectly calm, so Elise had as much freedom for her movements as though she had been on terra firma. Although Dora was kneeling on the chair, bound so that she could not make a single movement to evade the whipping, Elise considered it her duty to grip her firmly by the waist. Thus she could not possibly miss a single blow.

"Jenny, count the lashes!" demanded my aunt. And Jenny counted.

Elise whipped slowly and with all her strength. Each blow left a red trace on Dora's skin, which was practically white. Only her face seemed to have the color of light amber. Dozens of purple stripes soon blended to form an ardently red surface.

A thousand different sentiments traversed my brain. Indignation, fury, horror, and also, I humbly admit, a strange curiosity! In spite of everything, I could not stop looking at Dora's body, on which the stinging lashes of the strap fell, or at the convulsive shivers between each blow. Jenny's hands rested heavily on my shoulders. The maid's voice resounded in my ears, and it was harsh, dry, passionately severe.

"Thirty!... Thirty-one!... Thirty-two!..."

At last the number thirty-six was pronounced, at the same time that the final and formidable lash fell across the swollen posterior of Dora, from whom there issued a strident cry of agony. The punishment had been duly inflicted. For a moment, the executioner remained in contemplation of the young mulattress, who was still gasping from the effects of the whipping.

Then Lady Price spoke.

"That was very good, Elise. I thank you. Now release Dora and straighten her clothes."

The maid obeyed, and soon my little servant was on her feet, her face in her trembling hands, her shoulders shaken by her sobs, her body bent forward as though she lacked the strength to stand erect.

"Will you remember after this that you must obey me implicitly? Will you remember that you will be terribly chastised for any disobedience? On your knees before me and ask my pardon!"

Lady Price stood up very straight, her hands behind her back in a proud attitude of domination and with a fearsomely menacing expression toward poor Dora who shivered at her feet. The young girl let her hands down, disclosing a face saturated in tears, as red as if it had itself been whipped, while she stammered through her sobs:

"Pardon, Mistress!..."

"Kiss my feet!" my aunt growled.

Dora prostrated herself and pressed her shivering lips on the tip of Lady Price's elegant little shoe.

"Get up," my aunt commanded, "and never forget what happened to you today!"

IV. my first whipping

Dora had scarcely left the little salon than my aunt advanced toward me. Her eyes sparkled; her nostrils throbbed; her white lips trembled with anger.

"Take her gag off, Jenny," she ordered.

The servant obeyed, but not without pulling strands of hair on my neck. Tears of rage ran down my cheeks.

I uttered a great sigh of relief and cried out: "Shame on you for doing such things as that! I can no longer remain with you! And this girl—this girl who has been so brutal to me—I shall make a complaint!"

My protest was interrupted by the sobs which were convulsing my body. My aunt leaned over on me so close that her breath burned my face.

"This girl has done well, and she will do more presently — everything that I shall command her to do!"

I shrieked a vigorous "Oh!" of indignation, but I could not pronounce another word because two vicious slaps almost stunned me.

"You dare to argue with me?" my aunt cried. "I am going to teach you to keep quiet! Would you like a whipping?"

In a veritable crisis of nerves, I made a violent effort to break my bonds, but I only succeeded in hurting myself more. I fell back on my chair, exhausted.

"This young person is very nervous, my dear friend, and you know that the best remedy for this sort of sickness is a good chastisement, don't you?"

I made a movement toward Sir Arthur Ryan, who needed only to pronounce such words to set me beside myself. If I had been free in my movements, I believe I should have bounded on him with the force and fury of a tiger....

A third blow struck my cheek.

"Are you going to keep quiet?" I heard my aunt say as she shook me furiously by the shoulders. "Indeed, I am a fool! You are right, my dear friend, we must give her a whipping. That will do her more good than anything else in the world!"

"Me! Whip me? Oh! Don't touch me! Don't touch me! Oh! Help! Someone help me! Horrors! Oh! How awful!..."

I cried and twisted like one possessed, but what could I do against these four demons? I do not remember how, but suddenly I found myself kneeling on the same chair on which Dora had been whipped. Cords were being run around my knees and waist, while my wrists, tied together, were being pulled forward over the rear slat of the chair.

Jenny stood before me, holding both my ears; she pulled so hard on them that I thought she would tear them off. Right behind me I felt hands I was sure were Elise's; they were reaching under my dress, along my hips, and searching apparently for the elastic of my drawers. Oh! the horrible and humiliating contact of those fingers running up and down my flesh through the thin fabric of my dress! What shame I experienced at the slow and soft gliding of her hands, prolonged for her own pleasure, I am certain, until I suddenly sensed that she had that whole part of my body bare!... All of this passed as though in a dream—a nightmare, rather—and I suffered a thousand deaths in my modesty and pride. When I felt the sensation of fresh air on my skin I was profoundly depressed because I divined that I was indeed in a state ready for the whipping....

Then I lost all control of my self-respect. I reacted in the identical manner that a child would. I cried and begged for mercy. But behind me I heard the ironic laughter of Sir Arthur Ryan, then his voice again.

"What did I tell you, my dear? Nothing like it for calming such a violent nature! If I were in your place, I should do this always, the more so because it is certainly amusing to see her in this position!"

I contracted my muscles in a silly endeavor to shrink my person while I sobbed still louder.

"Oh! pity! pity! Aunt! Aunt, dear! Do not expose me like this to such humiliations! Oh, have pity on me!"

"No pity!" she declared. "Elise is going to whip you as you deserve, and to prove to you the personal interest I take in your chastisement, I am going to begin by giving you with my own hand a good smacking, such as they give to the commonest little brats!... Here! Here! Here! You can twist your bottom as much as you like! I know just how good a whipping you should get!"

Indeed, she slapped me so forcibly and with such expertise as to inflict simultaneously and the same time a smarting as painful physically as it was humiliating. She struck me about twenty times, and then stepped back to Sir Arthur's side, saying:

"Take the strap, Elise, and you, Jenny, count aloud to thirty-six! Give her a good whipping that she will remember for some time, the dear child!"

This cruel irony wounded me as much as all the rest, but I had not the leisure to reflect very long, for Elise took up her work with the same vigor she had exhibited for Dora's punishment. How can I describe what I felt then? How can I paint the torments of Hell to which I was prey during the minutes my punishment endured! Later I kept asking myself how it was I had not died. I have had many experiences since then, enough to know that one does not die of that, but how in the process shame and suffering are so intimately mixed that they attain, I believe, their maximum possible intensity. I cried, I shrieked, I threatened, I implored;

in vain, to be sure. I received my thirty-six lashes with the strap, and when Jenny untied me, I collapsed.

My aunt ordered the two maids to take me to my room and put me to bed, make me drink a glass of sherry, and then to keep a steady eye on me. The order was executed carefully, and presently I fell into a sort of sleep, disturbed by fantastic dreams of female devils whipping, with the full force of their arms, the naked flesh of the loveliest of the damned....

Two hours later, more or less, I awoke and began to cry. However, I dressed myself and put on a pair of jersey silk panties which clung very tightly to my hips. I do not know why I selected these especially, except that I thought perhaps they would be more difficult to manage in the event of another emergency. Finally, I started to go out for some fresh air, but I noticed that the door of my cabin was locked. Several holes had been drilled in it, and at these holes I heard certain little noises where Elise or Jenny, my aunt's cruel servants, must be watching me. In spite of the fear I had of a new humiliation, I could not resist the temptation to speak to them.

"Open up!" I cried. "I want to go on deck! Take care! If you keep me locked up in here, you will pay dearly for it!"

Elise's mocking laughter was the only response—it was she who was watching me! A wave of anger overcame me, and I began to kick the door, making so much commotion that the noise drew my aunt and Sir Arthur Ryan. I heard her sharp angry voice:

"What is this noise? Is that Flora? Is she mad? Open the door!..."

Mad? Yes, I must have been, for I imagined, foolishly enough, that my energy would be rewarded! Exhibiting a great deal of anger would give me some satisfaction.

Ah! What a mistake! Scarcely was the door opened than my aunt rushed on me like a Fury, grabbed my hair, and slapped my face hard slaps at least a dozen times while Sir Arthur, who carried his customary cane, struck me vigorously across my legs. I fought desperately, succeeding in freeing myself, and in heedless, insane disregard of the consequences, I rushed toward the rail of the yacht. My pride rebelling against all the odious treatment to which I was being submitted, I was fully determined to jump overboard. Alas! That act of despair proved fatal to me. A deckhand, standing nearby, pounced on me and clutched my skirt before I was able to put my desperate project into execution. He dragged me toward my aunt who had turned as white as a sheet.

"What were you trying to do, you miserable girl?" she muttered. Her strength seemed to abandon her.

"I was going to kill myself!" I cried. " I prefer death to remaining with you."

"Arthur! Oh! dear friend!" she groaned. "What a monster she is! What can we do with her?"

The big man answered, "To begin with, I am persuaded that she has not been whipped sufficiently. If one beating does not suffice, a second must be given, and if that still does not work, there must be a third! Don't spare the rod! You know that, my dear! Afterward, when we reach our destination we shall consider the matter further!"

"Then you think that a new whipping..."

"I certainly do!"

"Let us go back to our suite."

"No! In public! That will have much more effect, you know!"

"In public! But where?"

"Here, on the deck! Before everybody!"

I made a new effort to escape them, but I confess I wasn't going to try to jump overboard again, for I lacked the courage this time.

In any event, Elise and Jenny threw themselves upon me and held me powerless; in spite of my desperate cries and kicking, they conducted me to the foremast and tied me quickly to the wooden post. I thought that my last day had come when I felt Elise pulling back my skirts and pinning them to my shoulders. I was going to be whipped again, and this time under the open sky, and in the presence of the whole crew whose jeering eyes burnt into me, as they gathered without a trace of pity to watch the spectacle!

"She has put very tight pants on, Madam," said Elise, who struggled desperately in her attempt to pull the elastic over my hips. "Shall I pull them all the way down?"

"That's not necessary," Lady Price answered harshly. "These pants fit tightly and will not interfere at all with the parts to be chastised."

"Pity! Oh! Mercy!... Kill me instead!" I implored, succumbing to the prospect of this unspeakable humiliation.

Jenny returned from the rear of the deck, where she had gone to look for a strap.

"This strap is too soft," Sir Arthur said. "Don't forget that she is wearing pants! They're just like a shield! Jenny! Take that rope over there and make a cat-o'-nine-tails for Elise. That's the proper thing to use."

"But that's going to tear her skin!" my aunt said.

"Oh, no, not at all! That's going to warm up her bottom a little—nothing else. Twelve lashes only, Elise, twelve lashes. And don't draw any blood, eh? Not on account of her bottom—Flora deserves to be scorched alive—but not to break her skin!"

"Oh, monster! monster!" I shrieked, above the vulgar roars of the crowd.

"Come on, Elise, proceed with her punishment and show her no pity!" snapped my aunt.

And the horrible girl swung that awful whip against my tender body. So painful were these lashes that several times I felt myself on the verge of fainting. My heart ceased to beat; my head seemed to burst; my eyes saw nothing but red. Everything was swimming around me! At last this awful torture ceased, but something still more terrible was about to follow. On my aunt's orders I had to remain lashed to the mast—two mortal hours—skirts pinned up, exposing to the full view of everyone who passed the deck—and God knows they all passed by—that part of my body that had been lashed so pitilessly.

Kathi's First Time

Grant Antrews

She couldn't delay any longer. Inside, in truth, she knew that she had to get this over with. However terrible it might be, it promised closure and peace, and she would exert herself to accomplish those things. She stood before the dark wooden door, gasping, her head threatening to blur and overload. A deep breath. She raised her right hand, turned her knuckles toward the wood, and knocked again—three clear, individual times.

"Come in." She turned the knob with great care, quietly, and pushed the door open. The room inside was dim, foreboding. She breathed deep again, and took a small step into the darkness. Carefully, tentatively, as her eyes grew accustomed to the colorless chamber, she moved inside.

"Close the door behind you." Heavy drapes obscured the windows. Four candles flickered to her left, three more straight ahead, and another trio to her right. They were scented, and the room had a perfumed heaviness, or closeness. It was a large room, fairly open, but with ponderous dark equipment shapes looming. Carpeted and silent, intimidating.

Kathi glanced nervously about at the wooden trestle straight ahead and the canopy of heavy wooden beams like a latticework across the ceiling and walls. At the massive wooden X-frame on the far wall, the leather straps dangling loosely, awaiting a victim. She might be that victim. And the low, upholstered bench to her left, the rings and fittings for bondage ropes and leather restraints.

He said nothing. She couldn't find him at first. He was in a huge leather executive's swivel chair with the back toward her. She closed the door, the darkness seeming to envelop her, and when he heard the latch fall home he turned in the chair to face her.

"Good evening, Kathryn." He spoke softly, but his voice, or perhaps it was his tone, terrified her. Strictly business. This was the moment. Silence screamed throughout the room, and she had to speak, say something. Anything!

"Good evening, Sir." It had come out all right.

"And what can I do for you, my dear?" She was trembling, sweating profusely under her arms. The scented candles were intoxicating, too syrupy, but a nice touch.

"I'm here for...my, uhh, my appointment." And then, "Sir!"

"You're to be punished?" Had he missed her fault?

"If you require that, Sir." Willingness.

"We'll see." His eyes devastated her. Her knees shook.

"Yes, Sir." She was flustered, losing her composure. She needed to pee. She wished she weren't there, that she could be anyplace else, that she might awaken from this nightmare.

"You'll be disciplined, Kathryn. Disciplined. If you misbehave, then you'll be punished. Do you understand the difference? It's critical that you understand."

"I think so, Sir." She wasn't sure. Of anything!

"Good. Get undressed then."

His eyes seemed to drill holes in her, to melt her. He was dressed in a black leather vest and golden corduroy trousers. His forearms were wrapped in black leather gauntlets to match the vest, and his upper arms bulged with muscles that frightened her. He seemed calm, which upset Kathi more. She struggled to make her fingers work the buttons on her dress. Her eyes were swimming, threatening to overflow. She wanted to run, to go home. This was insane, foolish. She didn't want to be hurt! The front of her bodice was gaping open now, and she shrugged the dress off her shoulders and down, and stepped out of the skirt. Oh, God, she had to pee! She lifted the crisp white uniform dress and folded it over her arm.

"Put it on the bench to your left." Her fingers were leaden, cold. God, he must be getting an eyeful of her breasts in her pretty new bra! She saw his smirk; he was enjoying the show. She pushed the half-slip down off her hips, blushing furiously, her skin cold and goose-bumped. She tried to half turn away from him, so he might only see the silhouette of her.

"Don't turn away! The slave does not turn her back on her Master. She stands proudly for him, and offers herself, and hopes her actions are pleasing lest she be beaten. Focus, Kathryn. Think about where you are, why you're here. That's the kind of misbehavior that will earn you punishment strokes." She stood before him in her bra, panty hose, shoes, and panties. She knelt, unlaced her shoes, then rose and pried her feet out of them in a most ungainly fashion, hopping on one foot and then the other. She could hardly breathe, and the turmoil inside her was the more uncomfortable because it contrasted so with his calm, unmoving presence. Another quick glance his way, and Kathi began to peel away her clinging hose. She was awkward again, dancing on one foot and then the other to free her toes from the retentive nylons. She blushed, took the shrunken mist of hose to her other clothes, and stood before her Master in only bra and panties.

"Undress, Kathryn! You've earned two punishment strokes for delaying!" She couldn't breathe. Her hands went behind her, timidly, and failed, twice, to release the hooks. Then she got them, and the tension on the bra released, and she had only to shrug to be rid of it. But he was studying her and waiting to ogle her breasts, and no man had seen her naked in almost three years. "Kathryn!" She took away her brassiere, exposed her teats to this man, this stranger. And in that moment she found something inside. Resolve? Courage? She had chosen the panties carefully from the many choices at Victoria's Secret. She knew she looked great in them, all shiny and sleek upon her hips. And now she hooked her fingers in the waistband, and gave him a saucy little bump-'n'-grind flourish as she bared herself. She turned, folded them neatly, stooped to pick up her bra, and placed them carefully atop her other clothing. What now? She felt empowered, bold. She strutted back toward him and stood proudly in front of his chair. Jeez, she had to pee! His eyes devoured her. Kathi felt the blood rushing to her sex, inflating the membranes and tissues there. She felt herself increasingly moist, and her nipples expanding, ballooning in the cool air. He waited until her confidence wavered, until he saw her lower lip quiver, and then he abruptly rose out of his chair. He stood, so close his vest touched her breasts, and she almost stepped back, but he shrugged past her.

"Take one step forward, Kathryn. Spread your feet a little more, bend forward at the waist and place your palms flat upon the cushion of the chair. I want your bottom to jut for me, woman. To invite discipline. You want to strut? Offer your ass to me, Kathryn!" She bent, feeling terribly exposed. "Have you ever been spanked by a man?" he asked.

"No, Sir." Her whisper trembled. Her breasts hung like fruit, and oh! she needed to use a bathroom.

"Ever had a man up your ass?"

"No!" She was disgusted at his crudity, but before the thought could even form, his palm exploded against her bottomcheek like a pistol shot. It hurt, stung, and startled her, and she pulled her right hand up off the chair toward her steaming...but quickly remembered herself and lurched forward all akimbo to resume her position.

"Breaking position. Two more. Total of four, young lady. I wouldn't advise you to continue these little lapses. Are you supposed to work tomorrow?"

She heard a vivid tearing sound behind her, then recognized the sound of a latex glove being stretched over his hand. She whimpered. "Yes, Sir."

"Then you'd better pay attention." She was embarrassed, spread for him, her tits hanging like fruits on a vine, her bottom, and probably her sex, exposed to him. "Ever had clamps on your nipples?"

"Yes, Sir." A whisper.

"Who put them on you?"

"I did, Sir."

"Your mother's?"

"Yes, Sir." He came alongside her on the left, knelt. His rubber-gloved hand took her breast and caressed it, then stroked her teat as if she were a cow, and gathered its bulk just behind the areola to make the nipple stand out. "This will hurt, Kathryn. Tell me when you're ready."

She squirmed a little, needing to empty her bladder. "I'm ready, Sir...aaaahhHH!" Her right knee bent a little, but she held position. The clamp was awful, biting, fiery, cutting into her tender flesh. Tears rushed to her eyes. He stood, moved to her other side.

"Say please, Kathryn." The hurt on her left breast was soaking in now, becoming unbearable, agony incarnate. Could she ask him to double it? To inflict this upon her other sensitive nipple?

"Please, Sir." Through clenched teeth, against all reason, and he gripped her as he had before, brought her to full flower and snapped the clip into place, and it was worse than the other, far worse, and she shuddered and flinched, damn him, and her eyes overflowed, but she held her position.

"Ass up, Kathryn. Bow your back. That's a good girl." She was miserable, embarrassed, in pain. His hand came up behind her, clad in taut latex, and smeared Vaseline around and—Oh, God no!—into her anus! A finger, plunging into her, scouring her, hurting and then slipping out with an audible suction, leaving her craving something to plug her. She thought she might... CRACK! The left buttock this time, and she flinched and writhed, oh, how it stung, but he didn't assign punishment strokes so she thought she had done okay. He came up beside her on the right, peeled away the gloves, stroked her.

"Good girl. Grit your teeth now." He removed the clamp from her nipple and the hurt rushed in like a wind-driven forest fire into dry brush, and she almost cried out. He moved to her left, touched her, unclamped her, and watched her fight against the raw hurt. "Good girl." He leaned underneath her, ran his finger up between her womanly folds, withdrew it. "You're sexually stimulated, Kathryn." A statement of fact.

"Yes, Sir." She was crimson in her shame.

"Nice fragrance. I noticed it on your pad before, in the kitchen. You keep yourself clean." She felt herself swelling there and soaking. He moved against her shoulder. "Stand up." She did, and he sat down in his luxurious chair. "I want you to show me your sex, Kathryn. Use your fingers, spread back the lips, thrust it out to me and show me your clit, the depths of you. Pry it and tug it, invite me in. Be nasty, Kathryn. Tempt me. Sell yourself to me. Try to swallow me up in it." Degrading. She had expected this, but still it wouldn't be easy to overcome the years of training, the cultural baggage. Why did she need to do something so tawdry? A tear trickled from her eye and bumped down her cheek, and she brushed it away and moved toward him, quivering with apprehension. She moved close, jutted her knees to the sides kind of bowlegged, and threw her pelvis forward and her shoulders back. She put her hands there, cautiously, and opened herself to the Master, and she knew she was swollen and fragrant and wet. A second tear escaped her and cascaded down her cheek.

He stroked his beard thoughtfully. "Dear little Kathryn," he whispered, "I'm not sure you understand this. I am your Master, girl. You are a submissive in session. There are rules, strict codes of behavior. I don't think you're trying, Kathryn. I don't believe your heart is in it." She arched forward, bent her back precariously, spread her womanhood as far as it could possibly stretch. "Do you know what you did wrong?" His voice had become gentle, fatherly.

Her breasts were upright, pointed toward the ceiling. Her position was so strained it was difficult to speak. "No, Sir."

"When I give an order, slave, your only thought must be to obey. No other consideration, least of all a personal consideration, should ever come before my order. Your comfort is of no concern, girl. None! If a tear falls down from your eye, you do not wipe it away before complying with my command. You obey immediately and without any thought of your discomforts. Do you understand?"

"Yes, Sir. I'm sorry."

"Sorry! What is this? Do you think your being sorry wipes the slate clean? Don't be a child, Kathryn. A child doesn't have breasts like yours, or slime all in the hair on her sex. You put your own pleasure before mine. You will be disciplined. When you view your bottom tomorrow, then you can be sorry. Tonight you can only be obedient, or be punished. Nothing else. Your vagina is foaming, girl. Soaking. Now turn around and show me your anus." She turned, now bending forward instead of back. "Bring your hands back, Kathryn. Grip your buttocks and spread them wide for me, so I can see right up into you. That's it. Good girl." And now he touched her. She sucked a horrified breath, even rose up onto the balls of her feet, but she didn't break position, and this time he didn't impale her. "Do you see the door to your right, girl?"

"Yes, Sir."

"It's a bathroom. When I give the command, you are to rush into that room. Alongside the commode you'll find a cheap aluminum cooking pan, the kind you buy in the supermarket and use once, then throw away. You'll recognize it. You'll fetch it, Kathryn, and bring it to me, and place it at my feet. Do you understand?" His hand roamed over her now, up the inside of her thigh and across her buttock, down the sensitive divide and across the other. "You've already earned eight punishment strokes, Kathryn. You're very soft here, and they're going to hurt you terribly. Don't disappoint me, girl. Go now!"

She sprinted, her breasts and backside shaking and bobbling obscenely, her hair flying. She rushed, collided with the door and tore it open, saw the corrugated aluminum baking pan alongside the porcelain commode and grabbed it and reversed herself. She ran across the room toward him, frantic to please him, her wonderful body rippling and jiggling, and he smiled broadly as she placed the burden before his boots. She stood then, her eyes wide and questioning, resuming her original stance. Her pubic bush was directly in front of him, blatantly exposed.

"Squat over it, Kathryn, and empty your bladder." She was appalled, shocked. What kind of pervert... "Three strokes for any drop that falls upon my carpet. Begin." His eyes sucked life from her, frightened her.

"I, uhh, I..."

"I did not give permission to speak. Obey, woman." His tone left no question. "It's time, Kathryn. You want to question me, but I am not the question here. You came tonight, you have arrived at this moment because it's something you have to do." She knew he was right, and as he spoke she began to lower herself over the horrible pan. "You must conquer yourself, Kathryn. The questions are all about you. How will you do it? What's going to happen is inevitable now. You cannot avoid it, but you can receive it in many differing ways. You will win skirmishes tonight, or battles. And the next time you'll accomplish more, and if you persist, one evening you'll win the war. The war against yourself, Kathryn. You'll be free, because you'll discover the courage within yourself to defy the rules, to defy what others may think. You'll answer only to your dominant, and in giving so much you will gain so much, so very much more. The gift is meaningless unless you assign it worth, Kathryn. Only you know the value of your self. Spread your legs, dear. I want to see it flow out of you." She was teetering, perched precariously. "Piss for me, Kathryn." Her left hand steadied her against the carpeted floor. Her right now moved to her core, and she spread herself wide and raised her eyes to him.

"Permission to begin, Sir?" It was a tiny, questioning whisper, but he recognized its implications.

"Permission, slave. Nicely done. Empty yourself."

And now, as badly as she needed to relieve herself, it wouldn't come! She wanted to, but there were invisible barriers in her head, so she closed her eyes and imagined Niagara Falls, and slowly, ever so slowly, she felt muscles in her loins relax. She dared to look up at the Master, and he was sitting quietly, relaxed, smiling, watching her.

"Relax," he said. "It's a natural thing, just relax and let it come. You'll feel better, and so will I. I don't want you across my knee in your present condition, girl. Three spanks and you'll lose control and soak me, and I don't want to be wet by you." He said it lightly, almost laughing, and it made sense, and then his fingers touched her cheek. Gently, carefully, to reassure her. Kathi looked up toward his eyes and he nodded slightly, and she felt herself unwinding. She settled lower over the precarious target, and dared to breathe, and it started. A timid stream at first, and then her need overcame her modesty and it rushed from her, and she heard the humiliating sound of it and smelled the acrid stench, and color suffused her face even as her entire abdomen shrunk back to size and felt oh, so much better. It gushed from her, a huge uncontrollable flood, and she prayed he wouldn't interrupt her, and he didn't. The pan was almost an upturned bell, and the metallic sound it gave off filled the room, but now her stream was losing its immediacy, and the deep cargo in the trough was absorbing its impact, and it was quieting. She was scarlet with shame, hiding her eyes, but also carefully holding her labia open and her knees spread to please him.

"You know, Kathryn, I find that people who make the appointment and come up the front steps and ring the doorbell, well, they'll go through with it. You won't fail now. You're here because you need to be here." Her flow dwindled and died. She had to decide what to do. She looked around, but there was no paper, and so she dried herself with her finger and shook it carefully over the steaming pan. What a foul thing to require of a woman! She wished she could cry, but her ducts had dried up. She had little left to give.

"Is that all, Kathryn?"

"Yes, Sir." She could hardly hear her own tiny squeak and hoped he wouldn't be angry.

"You may stand. Carefully, don't spill it. Someday I hope you'll come here and squat over a clear glass bowl and do the other job for me. When you're ready, call for an appointment. If I ask you to go to the X-frame, Kathryn, do you know what I mean?"

"Yes, Sir." Whispered very timidly.

"You'll be fastened facing the room, fully on display. Take your position."

She scampered, feeling the unfamiliar sensations of her nude body in motion. The giant wooden beams were set into the wall, dark and foreboding. She tried to approximate the spread-eagled position they demanded, stretching herself, feeling horribly vulnerable and exposed. Her sex throbbed and seemed to dance upon the air. He watched her squirm against the timbers, then bent and picked up the pan of her urine and put it onto the bench beside her clothing. He turned, approached her, and began to tighten the myriad straps that would incapacitate her limbs. He was businesslike and firm; the restraints would not allow her even a hint of freedom, but still his fingers seemed to respect her flesh, and even to caress her sometimes. He fastened her left arm, then the right, four straps each from the shoulder to the wrist. There was a waist belt, and he hauled it tight, like a corset, she thought. Her legs were spread, but he forced them even farther apart and began by buckling the fetters at her ankles. She was completely helpless now, and he seemed to toy with her as he fastened straps at her knee and across her outflung thigh, and then the other leg in the very same way. She was exposed, horribly displayed to him, and he slipped his hands all up into her gaping, soaking sex before he rose, tearing an anguished groan from her. She hadn't been touched by a man in so long, and she knew her juices were spreading onto her thighs.

He stood, went to a dark wooden box and took out some implements. She watched him with attention beyond any she had ever experienced, and yet she nearly rebelled when he put the leather bulb of a gag to her lips. He convinced her with just his body language, as if he were becoming disappointed, and she opened her teeth and felt the thick leather pouch fill her mouth. He buckled the strap behind her head; she couldn't defend herself. He rolled something tiny between his thumb and forefinger and put foam rubber plugs into her ears that would expand and obviate her hearing. She saw the heavy black scarf and knew it was a blindfold, and she shook her head and tried to protest, but he calmly left her. She quieted, but he returned and matter-of-factly took her right breast onto his left palm, and applied the clamp again. She fought, helpless in her bonds, and he laughed at her struggles and clamped the vicious teeth over her other rubbery nipple, and while she was writhing in unimaginable pain he threw the black scarf over her eyes and knotted it beside her left ear, and she was alone in utter darkness and pain. Utterly alone.

She waited. Ten minutes, or maybe half an hour. She couldn't move, her muscles knotted, the gnawing clamps threatened to devour her breasts.Suddenly she felt his fingers at her right tit, the clamp came off, and a huge red wave of pain tore through her. She was insane, it subsided, and then she felt the clamp snap down upon her sensitive flesh again. He repeated the process at the other nipple, cleverly waiting as the blood rushed painfully in, clamping her again to chase it away and replace it with a vivid scarlet shrieking hell of unimaginable pain. She hung, suffering, rolling her head from side to side insanely because it was the only expression allowed her, because the discomfort was so vivid and devouring she had to react some way, any way, or fall victim to it altogether.

The clamps were removed and refitted; the agony renewed. She shrieked into the gag, her body utterly rigid in its bonds. She quieted slightly, searched inside herself for composure. A finger insinuated itself into her sex! She wrenched at the straps, it stroked her intimately, she screamed. She quieted again, tried to ride the probe, to extract the pleasure. Another hand squeezed in to cup her buttock, to insulate her flesh from the hard timber but also to make her turn slightly sideways against her restraints, and the strain was uncomfortable, and the hand squirmed tighter, and a fingertip touched her anus! Just the slightest touch, but she exploded again, and then the hands withdrew and her clamps were released, and the pain washed over her once again. It dimmed, finally, and the hand came back to her vulva, and the clamps weren't reinstalled onto her nipples. She rode the finger, eager to suck satisfaction off it, but when her loins became rhythmic it pulled away. He was kissing her tender nipples now, mouthing them, sucking, pinching between her lips, tonguing the vital excited buds until she thought she would lose her mind, and then he returned to her clitoris and drove her crazier, crazier than hell! He took her to the very precipice of her sensual endurance, through the *O* and *R* and *G* and *A*, across the *S* to the very fiendish perimeter of...

But then he left her, a million-megavolt nerve ending shrieking for that one last stroke to tip her over. He left her to hang, to relax, to cry, to wish. He left her for what seemed eternity, then ripped off the blindfold and strutted before her with the riding crop. The instant her eyes adjusted to the light and she recognized the instrument, he flicked it and let it bite her at the inside of her pinioned thigh, just at the most sensitive place on her entire anatomy, and she was insane for a moment. She recovered, slobbering over the pouch of the gag, sweaty and tiring, desperate, and he flicked the other thigh and sent her off into that place again. When she recovered, he flicked her, sharp stinging little crackling fiendish slaps as precise as surgery, and she watched his wrist with incredible fascination and it barely, barely moved. She howled, the crop stinging her like a hornet's fury, just scant inches from the dripping trough so opened for pleasure, and then he turned the crop and put the knob of the handle against her clitoris and stroked her. He removed the earplugs, then the gag.

"Do you deserve pleasure, Kathryn?"

"No, Master." She was nearly delirious. He withdrew, whipped her left nipple seven terrible times, until she screamed.

"It's Sir, foolish girl."

"I'm sorry." She hung, her skeleton out of commission. He punished her other nipple wickedly.

"You're sorry what?"

"Sir! Sir! I'm sorry, Sir! Please don't, no more! No more!" He caressed her, putting his whole hand up under her now, and he was incredibly gentle and kind. She softened again, began to ride him toward her ultimate goal.

He paused, then turned and walked away; he opened the door and left the room. She hung in her bonds, alone, and wept.

† † †

In a few minutes the young woman, Marion, slipped quietly into the room. She tidied up a bit, then approached Kathi and pushed a sweaty hank of hair back from the pitiful girl's forehead. "How ya doin'?" She whispered, like a co-conspirator.

"Okay."

"You've really impressed him. I think he had tears in his eyes." She knelt and began to release the straps at Kathi's ankles.

"Why? Is it all right if you do that?" The girl's hair was a brilliant golden cascade across her shoulders and down her back. Kathi felt the straps loosen, one by one, and wondered if she could stand. She was tired, drained.

The girl touched her inner thigh. "Oh, he really worked you, didn't he? I don't know why he's in this mood. He just barked at me as he rushed past me. As soon as I get you free, you can use the bathroom. Freshen up. I brought some sorbet to freshen your mouth. Mine always gets dry. He wants you in your bra, panties, and half-slip, waiting in front of his chair. You can kneel, he'll like that. Clasp your hands behind your back and keep your eyes lowered." The final straps came loose from Kathi's wrists, and she sagged against the girl for a moment until she caught her balance. Kathi moved awkwardly into the bathroom while the girl, Marion, prepared the studio to her Master's instructions.

Kathi soaked a washcloth in cool water and sponged herself. The mirror showed angry maroon marks on her inner thighs, but she wasn't injured. She rinsed the cloth and wiped her loins, washing away her abundant juices. She pushed her hair into place, wiped her eyes and blew her nose, then emerged into the torture chamber. There was a heavy sweet scent of cinnamon-apple incense on the air, and a Suzanne Ciani CD on the stereo created a comfortable, languid atmosphere. Kathi sat, nude and exhausted, and ate the creamy peach sorbet, letting it refresh her. She was both reluctant and eager, uncomfortable in her altogether but oddly relaxed in this place. Marion placed a large wooden hairbrush onto the round table alongside the Master's chair, then extended her hand to take the empty glass dish from Kathi.

"It's time, isn't it?" Kathi asked.

The girl whispered, "I'm sorry, but yes it is," and touched her cheek lightly. "You'll be fine," she whispered before turning and going out of the room.

Kathi felt lethargic, but she rose and slipped into the specified underclothes. She looked around anxiously, then knelt on the thick Oriental carpet in front of his chair and clasped her hands behind her back. She was alone again, waiting, and she wondered if there would be more. The intensity of the crop slapping into her sensitive thighs had taken her to the very edge of her endurance, but she was recovered. With eyes closed she imagined him, and she secretly thrilled at the thought of him. He was so big, so strong, but with a crazy boyish intellectual look, just something totally unique and very, very exciting. His hair and beard were statements, of course. He was an individual, an outdoor man. His eyes balanced the physique. There was incredible kindness in his eyes, even as he had whipped her. It was crazy, but true! He exuded caring, but not without a price. And that was only sensible, wasn't it? That he would ask something of her, even as he gave her pleasure? She thought about his hand up under her crotch, about the games his fingertips played and the sensations they stirred, and his eyes as they measured her reactions. She needed a man! All the masturbation in the world couldn't replace ten seconds of a real man's loving touch....

He entered, came immediately to his chair. "How are you doing?" he asked tenderly.

"Okay!" She nodded her head just slightly, avoiding looking

toward him. It was purely Kathi Lawton, cheerful and optimistic. She meant it. Despite the humiliations or the pain, she was doing just fine. Fascinated, stimulated, traveling in a foreign land as exotic and mysterious as Marrakesh or Siam. Her mind had vacationed, or maybe the word was vacated, escaping from the concerns of mothering and her job.

"Have you ever been spanked by a man?" She cringed. It wasn't over!

"No, Sir." She kept her eyes lowered.

"Not even when you were a little girl, Kathryn?"

"No, Sir." She wanted to look at him, to see his handsome features as he looked down upon her, discussing spankings and creating this busy tingling in her feminine parts. But she held position, kept her eyes locked onto the toes of his boots as they extended from under his trousers.

"You look very lovely, Kathryn. Very sweet and feminine. But you're a naughty lady, aren't you? You came here tonight because you recognize something inside yourself, and it screams to be dealt with. I'm going to spank your bare bottom, Kathryn. When I give the command, you're going to stand alongside my right leg and lift your slip and take your precious panties down to your knees. You're going to put yourself right across my lap, with your bottom the very highest and most prominent part of you. Then I'm going to take up the wooden hairbrush, and I'm going to smack your pretty snow-white ass until it's fire-engine red, until I'm satisfied that you know what it is for a lady to be truly spanked by a man. Do you remember your safe word, girl?"

"Overload, Sir." She was beginning to feel chills of fear creeping over her skin, and goose bumps prickling, and her breathing becoming strained. The cinnamon scent tugged at her mind, and the simple New Age melody seemed to carry her along on a path of adventure and challenge. She withdrew into herself and felt a calm, a tranquility that was almost religious. She was not afraid of the pain, only of failing.

"Then position yourself." She clamored up, still ungainly. Alongside his knee, she realized that she might appear too eager, that she must maintain her dignity. She slowed her movements, even put the fingers of her right hand to her décolletage and breathed in an enormous deep breath, like a Victorian grande dame near to swooning. She half-curtseyed, brought up the lower edge of her slip, then hesitated for an instant. Cold, hard dread chilled her. He would take the strumpet out of her in just a few moments. She caught the waistband of the beautiful panty on both index fingers, resolved herself, and slipped it down to her knees. This had to be done. She tried to be graceful and ladylike as she lay down over his knees, but there was no tasteful way to accept that position. When she was properly in place, the hot pink blush of shame had stained her face and ears.

He touched her, spread her cheeks and teased her, running his fingertip around and around about half an inch outside the round pucker of her anus. She shivered, and her hips tried to accompany the finger. She was aroused by it, and she groaned with desire.

She felt him move ever so slightly, but she wasn't sure if he had reached for the instrument. "I'll begin when you request it, Kathryn." She was nearly bursting! He wriggled slightly under her, lifting her weight effortlessly. Her toes came up off the floor, dangled in midair. Ohh, this was a shameful, uncomfortable position!

"I'm at...your...pleasure, Sir."

"Yes, you are. Your ass is exquisite, girl. Ask me to spank it."

"Please, uhh, spank me, Sir."

"What part of you, Kathryn? Stop delaying!"

"Please spank my...bottom, Sir."

"Your ass, Kathryn?"

"Yes, Sir!" Her breath came so hard in this position.

"Say it!" Damn him!

"My ass, Sir!" His palm caressed her lightly, roaming over her creamy bottom mounds like a child's breath, and she was embarrassed because her bottom contracted slightly from the stimulation.

"Focus, Kathryn. I'm going to apply six hard swats to your pretty ass, just to wake you. Then, if you know what's good for you, you'll obey, and ask me to spank your ass, hard!" CRACK! It exploded suddenly, shockingly hard, at the very crest of her right buttock. She lurched wildly, completely startled by the awful sting of it, but before she could escape he struck the other cheek, and again! Then again to the right buttock, and the left, and the right, and she was just beginning to wail a miserable mad howl when he stopped. "Ask me, Kathryn." She was frantic, electric in a cocoon of scorching pain. "Ask me!" There was threat in his tone, and she clawed at reality, struggling to recall what he wanted her to say before he struck her again.

"Please, Sir! My...ass, Sir!"

"What about it, Kathryn?"

"Spank it, my ass, Sir!" An awful stinging heat was beginning to glow up under the skin.

"Don't forget your manners, girl. You're in no position to be discourteous."

"Please, Sir!" WHACK! WHACK-WHACK, CRACK! SMACK! Even as the flat hardwood hairbrush paddle continued to explode upon her buttock like a machine-gun burst, the pain welled up in such incredible waves that she cried out, but he did not pause. The left hillock now, THWACK! SMACK! WHACK-WHACK! CRACK!

Fiendish pain, hot and stinging beyond any expectations, and as she reeled and everything was eclipsed by the sore sensations blazing over the skin of her rump. The Master continued mercilessly. Again and again he struck. She howled, and her hands tried to rush back to protect her, but he caught and pinioned them and just spanked her the harder! Her pristine flesh had turned blotchy as vivid crimson imprints began to overlay and stain her something closer to purple than maroon, and her cries melted together into one long, continuous, pitiful wail of misery and pain. She tried to lurch away involuntarily, but he controlled her. She was helpless, and still the hardwood cracked down upon her quivering flesh.

He paused. "Stand up! Face away from me, panties at your knees and your slip gathered high at your waist so it drapes your pretty red bottom like a frame, and if you allow those elegant underpants to fall you won't sit comfortably for a week!" She scampered, smarting terribly. He had noticed her special panties! "Spread your knees, Kathryn! Show me your sex, your darling little anus. Bend forward slightly, girl! Be vulgar, please me, or by God you'll sit carefully tomorrow!" She tried. He let her stand a moment, as the smarting hurt overwhelmed her.

"Normally this would be the end of your session, Kathryn. You've done well, very well. Still, you're inexperienced and willful, and you've made mistakes. You know the seriousness of the games I play here. Mistakes can hurt people, Kathryn, and so you must learn a lesson tonight. And then, although it is your first experience of this sort, I counted six times that you spoke without addressing me as Sir. You caught yourself once and tried to fix it, but you were obviously more attentive to your own needs than to showing me the proper, and very simple, respect I requested. Your bottom is red and swollen, Kathryn, but there are the punishment strokes before I excuse you. Will you take them willingly?"

He reached out and caressed her steaming backside, low and deep within the cleavage there.

Her voice was raspy, and she flinched as his thumb pushed upon the rigid elasticity of her rear opening. "If I, AHH!...must, Sir." She was breathless, dreading any more stimulation of her pulsing, pain-bloated bottoms.

"Yes or no, Kathryn?"

She paused a moment, then whispered, "Yes, Sir. May I ask you to be merciful, Sir? I'm terribly sore already."

"I can see your condition clearly, Kathryn. You've earned more, but yes, I will be merciful. You'll have twelve strokes, four each from the hardwood paddle, the leather strap, and the rattan cane."

He rose from his chair, allowed his hand to sweep over her tender buttock and down and under her! She stiffened, and he worked his fingers skillfully until her core was molten and verging upon release. She stood hunched forward, boldly offering herself to his knuckles and fingertips. She rode his fist shamelessly, wantonly, crimson with shame but unable to control the hot yearning in her loins. The incense assaulted her, and the sound of the piano swept cautiously over her like a warm cloak. She moaned, whispered something plaintive but unintelligible. He took his hand away and she groaned pitifully, even bending one knee, flinching. He pinched her earlobe now, and kept her bent as he led her to the bench. Marion had removed her clothing and the precarious pan of urine. She had sat upon the bench when she ate the sorbet, but now it looked frightening and harsh.

It was low and ominous, narrow but sturdy, of dark-stained hardwood with thick leather restraining straps and gleaming silver buckles. A simple structure, basically just a heavy wooden bench except for the huge, obvious mound growing up from its center. A sloping reverse V, it flared out to a length of about two feet, growing in width even as its height fell away toward the lower end of the platform. He led her close, then released her ear. "The hump goes under the pubic mound, Kathryn. It lifts the hips and separates the thighs. At its crest there is a removable portion. Look at these." He held two wooden squares for her to see. The first was carved to a wicked peak, a narrow spine that would, she realized, be excruciating under a woman's mons veneris. The second was flatter, but it featured a myriad of tiny metal points like tacks upraised. She imagined them penetrating her, the effort one must expend to lift up away from them, and the inevitable result when the whip landed upon the buttocks. As if he read her thoughts, he put the two blocks aside. "This one is just a smooth pedestal," he said, patting the crest of the strange mound atop the bench. "Punishment strokes are always applied to naked flesh, Kathryn. Please bare yourself now and stretch out here." He pushed a limp strap away. She felt queasy and weak, but she removed her underclothes for the second time that night and approached the bench. He showed her how to straddle the mound and put her knees up along its sides, then lie forward over the hump. She felt the thing cleaving her, wedging in between her knees, lifting and presenting her rear obscenely for punishment. She whimpered, and he had to drag her wrists to the waiting restraints. She was stretched far forward now, head and shoulders lowered, and he went back to fasten her knees and ankles. Her feet were at the same height as her head, but her hips were raised about sixteen inches and separated even more. Her bottom, she realized, was perfectly but terribly exposed for the infliction of pain. He moved away, came alongside her and showed her the first instrument.

"The wooden paddle, Kathryn. Perhaps you've seen a sorority hazing at college? No? The paddle is a simple tool, really. It tends to crush the flesh, to create hurt all the way through the meat of the buttocks. You'll have four applications, I'm afraid. I'll do two from this side, then go across to the other to spread the fire evenly. I'll begin when you request it, Kathryn."

She was paralyzed, tired, and afraid. She searched herself, pulled the finest threads of courage from the depths of her heart. "May I ask the name of that song, Sir?"

He was startled by the request. It was a special song to him, haunting and adventuresome, the definition of the word "composition." A melody about being composed, about triumph over chaos. He liked to play it at moments like this, in the background. How profound that she would relate to it, that she would find it so important that she must ask about it at this moment. No other person, in all the years, had ever questioned the music! He went to the stereo, studied the CD's jacket. He knew the title, but it had to be pronounced correctly for this woman. "It's called 'Sailing To Byzantium' by Suzanne Ciani." He clicked two buttons on the stereo controls. "It will repeat for a few minutes if you like it."

"Thank you, it's beautiful. And now, may I be paddled please, Sir?" Just like that. He took up the implement, stood over her, and marveled at the symmetry of her contours, the smooth complexion of her skin even upon her ass. Whhhop! It painted her with a wide and awful patch of burning hurt, full across the seat of her and about four inches wide. She wrenched against her fastenings, hollered an agonized "Ooooa! Oh, my! Please, Sir!" Whuuuack! Worse than the first, parallel but lower, on the fatty undercurve of her, and she erupted in frenzied, helpless discomfort. He moved quietly to the other side, touched the paddle's blade across her as if measuring, then raised it slowly and WHOMP! Repeated immediately, WHACK!, and she was insane, her assmeat so fevered and full of hurt that she felt the blood pulsing through the narrowest capillaries.

He came around to her left again and crouched beside her. She was subsiding, but still rigid and shaking with the effects of the punishment. Her eyes were swollen, closed but bulging, and her hair was tousled and unruly. She was frantic, rigid, and he touched her reassuringly as he whispered encouragements.

"You're too stiff, Kathryn. The hard paddle contacts hardened muscle and breaks it, but at great cost. You must learn to relax, girl. To accept that this is part of your reality, a necessity. In some secret corner of your mind you find reinforcement in this, and courage. You must learn to access that place, Kathryn, and to swim in it while the punishments are falling over your body. It will protect you, and magnify the accomplishment a thousand times for you. Search now, lovely lady. Search deep. The next will be the leather strap, and you'll notice the difference immediately. The strap conforms, and wraps itself over the hills as it dives deep into the valleys. The strap, Kathryn."

She whined, raised her head far back and emitted a strangled sound through gritted teeth. Her eyes were clamped tightly shut. The tip of the strap had curled far down into the cleavage of her buttocks to lick fiendishly at her puckered, sensitive anus. He saw drool upon her chin and wiped it away, and he kissed her forehead. "The other side, Kathryn. Invite it to wash you. To cleanse you." The first stroke came low, where the buttock and thigh met, and the tip kissed close to her right labium majora. She cried out, a choked burst of raw anguish. The second came over a bit higher, cracking home at the very perimeter of her rear rosebud. Her reaction shook the bench against the floor. Again, he knelt close. She was perspiring, gasping for breath. "Only four more, Kathryn."

"May I ask a favor, Sir?" Her lips seemed to sneer as she forced out the words.

"Ask." He thought she would request to be spared the remainder, and he was prepared to grant her wish.

"Would you turn up the music, Sir?"

"Of course." He did not make it uncomfortably loud, but he knew she could distinguish it clearly. He brushed back her hair. "How are you doing? Do you remember your safe word?" He spoke very softly and thrilled at the touch of her as he wiped tears from her cheek.

"I can't describe it, Sir." She forced the words between her clamped teeth. "It is somewhere between hell and Byzantium. I may be insane. It's so intense, Sir." Her breathing was labored, ragged.

"You want to finish, then?"

"No, but it has to be done. Sir! Oh, forgive me, Sir!" She was desperate.

"Just this time, Kathryn. The rattan cane. Present yourself."

She emerged from the shower feeling refreshed. Her bottom was frightfully sore, and she had seen the terrible weals in the mirror. She should be appalled, but in some way she was proud of them. Not that she would show them to anyone, of course, but she could feel the swelling and the striated flesh, and she knew she had comported herself proudly. The room was still dimly lit by candles and sweetly fragrant with the scent of apples. Her nipples ached. She needed to get home, to masturbate while all the sensations were still reverberating throughout her.

He was in his chair, slouched listlessly, sipping brandy from a huge snifter. He had replaced the crisp white shirt under his leather vest. That's odd, she thought. He must have unbuttoned the vest and shed it, shrugged into the shirt, buttoned it, and tucked the tails into the waistband of his cords, adjusted his belt, then slipped back into the vest and buttoned it. An elaborate ritual, and one which must seem worthwhile to him. In a way, she was reassured. He had re-covered his arms, as if the physical acts, the disciplines and punishments— she certainly understood the difference now!—were over. She considered kneeling between his legs, offering to suck him in thanks for his attentions that evening, but she couldn't think of words that would be tasteful. She didn't want him to think less of her. Instead, she knelt at his foot and kissed his boot. "Thank you, Sir." He brought her to her feet, encouraged her to get dressed. She dropped the towel and turned her derriere to him. "I'm sorry, Sir."

"Sorry?" His eyebrows arched, and he struggled to be more upright in the chair. She noticed that he had allowed the music to move on into another song. "Why are you sorry?"

"I think I disappointed you. I wasn't ready for it to hurt so ferociously. I lost control of myself. I'm sorry, Sir."

"Come here, Kathryn, and stand before me." It was said in a curious way, without threat but with no room for discussion. She was naked, her expensive lace-trimmed panties in her left hand. She stood solemnly, hands clasped behind her, eyes lowered. Surely he wouldn't punish her again? "Look at me," he whispered. He was incredibly sexy in the soft candle glow, powerful and self-assured in his favorite chair. The white shirt was effective now, somehow dignified. Formal. She was nude, at his mercy. She felt excitement heating her pelvis again, her sap running. He placed the globe of brandy onto the table and straightened his back, then leaned forward toward her and put his left elbow to his knee. His face took on a look of concentration as if he was studying her, and she had to look away.

"I pride myself on my ability to communicate, Kathryn, but at this moment I'm sadly lacking. I am the head of the English department at the university, I have published books, spoken in front of ten thousand crowded lecture halls. Tonight I am speechless." His eyes seemed almost to plead with her, and the room became very shrunken and intimate. She had to listen carefully to hear his whispers as he continued. "You came directly from work, so I know you haven't eaten. I'm famished. I've asked Marion to put out something, even if it's just leftovers. I want you to join me, it won't be anything special. The truth is, I don't want you to leave. I'm not sure what I'm feeling, Kathryn, or how to describe it to you." He leaned closer, his eyes imploring her.

"I think I should be going. I have to pick up my daughter and go to work tomorrow. You know how it is." She was vividly aware of her breasts, which were rigid and sensitive, stretching toward this man as if seeking attention.

"But you think you have disappointed me! I need you to stay a few minutes, to talk with me outside of this room. You have not disappointed me tonight, Kathryn. If you leave abruptly, you will. Please. You have to eat, just something quick. Please." He knelt then, so close she had to take a step back. "Please," he said, and then he bent and kissed her bare toes. "Please, I beg you."

She giggled, but only a little. "Okay, but get up. I'm the slave, remember?"

He rose and took her into his arms. He smelled wonderful, of some rich and very manly cologne, and Kathi found herself yielding to him. She was naked, but she embraced him and gloried in the feel of his arms around her. She was tucked under his chin, tight to his chest. "I've never done anything like this before," he whispered. "From the very first phone call, I thought you were special somehow. I can't explain it, but now... I've never had a first session like this. I'm sorry, I was too demanding, but you seemed to understand so much, to accept, and then to challenge me to go beyond. You have to tell me what you felt, what you're feeling now." His huge hands roamed her back, avoiding her wounded bottoms.

Suddenly, he pulled back from her. "You're probably cold. Get dressed, I'll see how Marion's doing and be right back." He looked at her, his eyes misting, then dragged her close to him again for a moment, released her, and kissed her cheek all in one quick but awkward moment. He was like a teenager stealing his first kiss, she thought, and she smiled as he closed the door behind him.

She was showered, dressed, and had dared to mist cologne behind her ears. He came for her, accompanied her down the stairs. She asked the time, and was shocked to hear that it was going on ten o'clock. "I really should be going," she said.

"Please don't. You need to eat, Kathryn." He was being stern again, a typical man demanding his way, albeit politely.

"On one condition." The moment she said it she realized that it was terribly out of place here. His eyebrows arched, then his face slowly melted into a wide grin. She had been warned, but in the gentlest manner imaginable.

"And what might that condition be, madam?" Exaggerated emphasis upon the words, and in his gestures, made him seem to be kidding her. He could not, she realized, ignore her impertinence. And at the same time, he wouldn't punish her. He wanted her to share a few moments with him. Did he know how much she longed to do just that? How she hoped he would embrace her again?

"That you call me Kathi." She winked at him. It was the equivalent of a jailbreak, she thought.

"If you wish, but in the room upstairs you will always be Kathryn." He winked back at her, and her body gushed sexual juices. He would not relinquish the upper hand.

"You're absolutely radiant," he added. "Tell me your thoughts."

She thought for a moment, both to swallow and to sort her thoughts from her emotions. "I've never been so aware of my physical being, of its limits, and maybe its possibilities. I was going to say my sense of touch was magnified a thousand times, but maybe every sense was heightened."

"A wonderful observation, actually!" He swallowed from his beer again. "People often use the words 'sexual' and 'sensual' interchangeably, but they're really quite different. This is sensual play. It's scent and sound and texture, soft breeze over naked genitalia, stimuli to excite the various facets of the mind. The body is only one receptor, isn't it?" He was aroused, the college lecturer playing to his audience.

"Some of my receptors are only maroon and purple, but I think they're going to be black and blue by morning!"

"I have never disciplined a woman who accepted it the way you did tonight, and it was your first time! But there is so much more. Will you come back?"

"I don't know." She realized that she would have to consider this carefully, that her very acceptance of it could be threatening. As if to reinforce that thought, she changed position upon the caned chair seat and felt the raw hurt across her bottom so sharply that she released a startled "Ahh!"

He smiled. "I think you do know, Kathi. It's good that you digest this meal before you eat another, but I think you recognize your hunger." His voice changed slightly then. "I want you to come back. But also, I want to pursue what I'm feeling tonight. What I tried to say before. May I call you? See you? Maybe Saturday night?"

She studied her plate. "Only if I can say no if it gets too intense." Her eyes rose to challenge him, or to open doors to him. "I think I understand what you're trying to say, Horace. Maybe I feel it, too. It has been an overwhelming night, I'm not sure what I'm feeling or thinking just now. My life is very hectic, and I have huge responsibilities. I dared to be irresponsible for a few moments tonight, and it was exciting, and you were wonderful. Yes, I find you very exciting, and I won't tell anyone, but I think you're a very gentle, kind man. But I'm not sure I have room in my life for a man." Her eyes were suddenly misty, and she stopped.

"Then you'll accept my calls?"

She heard the hope in his voice. She nodded, raised her eyes to him. "Yeah." She felt her face relax into a broad smile.

"The movies and books try to make it seem noble to lose at love, don't they? But in reality it's just pain, and it makes it difficult to try again. It doesn't build character so much as barriers." He drained his beer mug.

"Are you divorced?" She dared.

"Widowed. Cancer. She was twenty-seven. Nine years ago."

"I'm sorry." She thought he had spoken in fragments because the pain was too much, even for him. And she felt a kinship. He had asked about her divorce one night on the phone. She had told him guarded bits of it, but hadn't thought to ask if he had ever experienced anything so devastating. She was sorry for that omission, as well as for his loss.

"We go on, don't we? Death, divorce, disappointment. 'The web of our life is of a mingled yarn, good and ill together.' Life. You can't let it get in the way of living, can you?"

"Was that Shakespeare?"

"Yes, from *All's Well That Ends Well.* Do you know Shakespeare?"

"No, not at all."

"His work is a foundation upon which people build huge mansions of pretense and bullshit, pardon my French. If he lived today he would have a late-night talk show and be compared to Johnny Carson. Personally, I prefer Carson." She glanced at the clock over the kitchen sink. "I've really got to be going," she said.

"I've had a wonderful evening. Thank you." They pushed back from the table, rose to their feet.

"Come here," he said. His great arms were open, and she hurried to him. He enfolded her in a magnificent big bear hug, and then he released her, only to bend and sweep her up again. Their lips met and she responded as she hadn't dared to respond in years. She surrendered to his kiss, to all that she had experienced that evening. Enormous waves of emotion flowed between them, waves crashed upon their individual shores, storms raged and answers came up out of the dark depths. They had experienced some wild animal comforts from each other, and in sharing those indefinable truths they each had accomplished something, and it was enough: it was everything. Finally, it had to end. "Call me when you get home, so I'll know you're safe?" he whispered. She promised. "And, Kathi…" She had her coat on, the door open. "I'm sorry if I hurt you."

"You didn't. I think you healed me." It was snowing, a treacherous night, but Kathi Lawton had no trouble driving. Her thoughts were skis, and she was racing an Alpine downhill. Exhilaration made her alert to any hint of a problem, but at this moment she was excited and happy beyond her dearest expectations.